Imogen Parker is the author of *More Innocent Times*, *These Foolish Things*, *The Men in Her Life*, *What Became of Us* and *Perfect Day*. She lives on the south coast with her husband and son.

PERFECT DAY

Imogen Parker

BLACK SWAN

PERFECT DAY
A BLACK SWAN BOOK : 0 552 99938 5

First publication in Great Britain

PRINTING HISTORY
Black Swan edition published 2002

3 5 7 9 10 8 6 4

Set in 11/13pt Melior by
Kestrel Data, Exeter, Devon.

Black Swan Books are published by Transworld Publishers,
61–63 Uxbridge Road, London W5 5SA,
a division of The Random House Group Ltd,
in Australia by Random House Australia (Pty) Ltd,
20 Alfred Street, Milsons Point, Sydney, NSW 2061, Australia,
in New Zealand by Random House New Zealand Ltd,
18 Poland Road, Glenfield, Auckland 10, New Zealand
and in South Africa by Random House (Pty) Ltd,
Endulini, 5a Jubilee Road, Parktown 2193, South Africa.

Printed and bound in Great Britain by
Cox & Wyman Ltd, Reading, Berkshire.

For Connor

Acknowledgements

Thank you, Jo Goldsworthy, for your enthusiasm and friendship from the beginning. Thank you, Mark Lucas, for your insight and charm. Thank you, everyone at Transworld, for your energy and commitment.

One

In the end, this is a love story.

The first thing Alexander says to Kate is 'American Hot'.

The first thing he notices is her fingernails. She's standing behind him, taking his order, and as he turns his head, his eyes are level with her hands. The nails are small and round. Each is painted with a different sparkly shade. They are the fingernails of a child secretly sampling exotic little pots of paint on a mother's dressing table.

'Anything to start?' she asks him.

Six or seven little plastic butterflies hold dark hair away from her face. Her skin is white in the blue neon light of the sign on the window. There is a slight gleam of sweat on her forehead. She waits for him to say something, and when he doesn't, she wipes the back of her hand across her face, inadvertently dislodging two of the plastic butterflies which ping ungracefully to the floor.

'Oh bugger.' She bends to retrieve them.

Her hair is so close to his face that he can smell that she has washed it this morning in coconut shampoo.

'A green salad?' He feels he has to offer something in exchange for her trouble.

Later, he will wonder whether he would always

have remembered the fleeting encounter if he had not chanced upon her again. Would his memory have retained those fingernails, or the suntan-lotion smell of her hair, or would it have discarded the information as rapidly as the details of his colleagues' choice of pizza and the number of times he refills his glass with the house red attempting to numb out the prickly restlessness that has been bothering him all morning?

There is an end of term feeling at the school even though it's only midday Thursday. The students have just finished their exams and a bunch of them are celebrating outside the pub across the road. All the teachers are seated at a large round table in the usual pizzeria. The get-together is in honour of Mel and Joe, a recent couple, who are leaving tonight for jobs on a remote Indonesian island.

Alexander watches their faces, elated with love, cheap Chianti and the prospect of travel. His hand slips inside his jacket and touches his own brand new passport there. The postman delivered it just as he was leaving home this morning. On the train in, Alexander tore open the envelope, took it out and stared at the pristine pages with a creeping feeling of misery.

The smart middle-aged woman who always sits opposite him seemed to sense his distress and leaned forward conspiratorially.

'They're not as nice as the old blue ones, are they? There was something special about travelling with a British passport, wasn't there?'

He gave her a wan smile, unwilling to explain that it was not the imperial indigo leather he was missing, but the multicoloured jumble of visas and entry stamps. His old passport was his diary, each stamp conjuring a memory of the smell of a foreign airport or the exhilaration of a new beginning.

*　　　*　　　*

He sees that his pizza has arrived without him noticing. He looks round, but whoever brought it has disappeared behind the stainless steel shelving unit with its glass bowls of chopped mushroom, green pepper and onion. Everyone else at the big round table is eating. He picks up a knife and cuts his disc of pizza into eight wedges, then pulls a section away, holding it carefully just above his mouth to catch the elastic drips of mozzarella. The tomato sauce beneath the skin of cheese is hotter than he expects. It scorches the roof of his mouth and a soft blister begins to form. He takes a gulp of wine and a kind of mouldy blackberryness mingles with the taste of his own flesh. The pizza is now just a combination of wetness, crunch and moments of chilli heat.

Vivienne, the assistant director of studies, scrapes back her chair and proposes a toast to Mel and Joe.

'. . . and we're all envious, but we wish you a safe journey. Have a fantastic time!'

'Bon voyage!'

A couple of people clap. Malcolm calls out, in his actor's voice, 'Speech!'

Then there's a moment of almost-embarrassed silence while everyone makes up their mind what they're going to do next.

The teachers who have not been drinking each put a £10 note on the table and go back to the school to sort out their files and write their reports. The drinkers order more wine, and coffee.

Alexander's tongue worries at loose skin in the top of his mouth. He spoons soothing white foam from the top of a cappuccino.

'Are you coming?' Mel says to him.

'Why not?' he says, as if he has been involved in the decision to move on.

As he steps out of the restaurant onto the pavement,

the brightness of the afternoon is a surprise. He has no idea what time it is. He follows Mel and the others down several streets he does not recognize. Even though he has worked in this part of London for several years, the only streets he is familiar with are those he uses every day that lead from the tube station to the school and from the school to the sandwich shop.

The pub has a cellar bar with a jukebox. They occupy a table in a low-ceilinged brick alcove with hard wooden benches like pews. Malcolm puts a glass of lager in front of him. Alexander rests his head against the wall. He hears Vivienne say as she raises her pint glass,

'Here's to escape . . .'

He dreams that he is walking along a great white curve of sand. There are palm trees back up the beach and a wind blowing in off the sea which is cooling one side of his face. There's someone walking along next to him. For some reason he cannot turn his head to see who it is. She says, 'It's so like you expect a paradise island to be, you can't believe it's real, can you?'

He hears the echo of a laugh that slips away as he wakes up.

Mel and Joe are slow-dancing near the jukebox to Roy Orbison's 'In Dreams'. Mel is looking over Joe's shoulder at Alexander. Alexander smiles at her, and wonders whether any of them have noticed his brief lapse into sleep. She stares back at him with the meaningful look she has sometimes given him since they snogged each other a little too long, a little too passionately, in the passage leading to the pizzeria toilets at the Christmas party.

The following day they had lunch together at an

Italian café, a turkey special on a flat white plate spilling over with pale gravy.

'What happened,' she said looking just over his shoulder, 'didn't mean anything, did it?' Then she attempted to spear a Brussels sprout casually, as if his answer didn't matter to her at all. The sprout slid off the plate onto the Formica table top.

'No,' he replied, trying to dredge some charm from his dull hungover brain, 'I mean, I think you're lovely, but . . .'

'I know,' she cut off the sentence he was never going to finish anyway, the effort of trying to smile making her eyes fill.

'Well, at least I won't spend all of Christmas hoping you'll call!'

Soon after New Year, she hooked up with Joe. But Alexander still catches her looking at him sometimes, and he can't decide whether her eyes are saying 'I still want you,' or 'Look what you've missed.'

Vivienne sees that Alexander is awake.

'Welcome to the land of the living,' she says; 'you must be exhausted.'

'Wine at lunch.' Alexander stretches, unwilling to be drawn.

Vivienne likes to be the confessor of problems which she then will keep on returning to, giving both the problem and herself a status they never previously enjoyed. He knows that she means well, but he finds her way of being friendly depressing.

'My round?' Alexander asks, looking at the empties.

'We're just leaving,' Vivienne says, taking Malcolm's arm. As she pulls on her jacket, she leans down to Alexander's ear and whispers, 'He's going to give Werner the big heave-ho tonight and I'm going along for moral support.'

Which leaves Alexander with Mel and Joe. He does not want to stay, but he does not feel like going home. He looks at his bare wrist. When he is teaching he takes his watch off and puts it on the desk, and today he forgot to put it on again.

In the mirror above the cracked white sink in the Gents, he sees that one cheek is stippled with the imprint of the brick wall, his eyes are slightly blood-shot and his hair is a little damp from the sweat of an afternoon sleep. His mouth tastes yeasty and sore. He ought to go home.

The cellar is crowded now.

Alexander orders soda and lime and stands at the bar. The bartender has ambitions to be a cocktail waiter and makes a performance of being busy. A pint glass is thrown from one hand to the other, cordial is poured through a chrome spout from a great height. Alexander stares past him, ignoring him as he would a child who is showing off. Then suddenly the smoke and the noise are too much for him. He pushes upstairs through the tide of office workers coming in the other direction. Outside, he breathes deeply. It is still bright and sunny. He realizes he has not said goodbye to Mel and Joe, but he cannot face going back in.

He walks away from the pub quickly, determinedly not looking back, as if he has committed some petty crime there. The street he is on is quiet but as it meets Oxford Street the roar of city noise blasts him again, and subsides as he crosses into the relative tranquillity of Soho Square. His shoulders relax. He looks again at his bare wrist. He feels very thirsty.

He's drawn into the bar by the football match on the television. The old man behind the chrome counter hands him a tall glass of water and sets about making the espresso he asks for. Out go the old grounds with a sharp tap, in twists the dry coffee, and whoosh goes the steam. It's an extraordinarily labour-intensive process for such a tiny amount of thick, dark coffee. As the little white cup is placed before him Alexander looks up at the young woman who has come in just after him and settled herself a few barstools down.

'Hi, Marco,' she says to the bartender.

She gives a quick sideways smile to Alexander acknowledging his presence. There are only the three of them in the bar.

There's something familiar about her. Black hair cut short like a boy's at the back with a long fringe flopping over her dark eyes. She's wearing a pink T-shirt that looks as if it's been washed a lot, black trousers that are a bit short and big clompy black boots.

He inclines his head in a tacit question. She shrugs. Then she says in a strong Northern accent, 'You're not a film star, are you?'

'No,' he says, cautiously.

'I said hello to Tom Cruise the other day. He was coming out of this club in Greek Street and I thought I knew him, you know, like he was a friend, or something? He probably gets it all the time. He smiled at me – you know how his eyes go crinkly and then there's that flash of really white teeth? – and then I realized and I said, "Oh sorry!" He ducked into this car that was waiting for him. And I spent the rest of the afternoon, telling people, "When I met Tom Cruise earlier . . .", you know?'

He smiles. He thinks it's her way of saying that she thinks his face is familiar too.

'. . . when I *was speaking* to Tom Cruise earlier,' she says, repeating the joke, 'you know?'

'You like Tom Cruise, do you?'

15

Alexander doesn't know what else to say.

'I do fancy him,' she tells him, giving his question due consideration, 'but I couldn't put up with all that Scientology stuff, you know? Not that we'll ever meet again anyway,' she adds quickly, in case he should think she's taking her crush too seriously.

On the television above the bar, a goal is scored. It's an Italian game and the commentator goes wild.

The young woman laughs, then claps her hand over her mouth, as if she's made too much noise. Alexander stares at her fingernails, each painted a different sparkly shade.

'You're the waitress,' he says.

'Yes? Oh, right!' She recognizes him now. 'Did you enjoy your pizza? Four Seasons, was it?'

'American Hot,' he says, wondering why it should bother him even for half a second that she doesn't remember what he ordered.

'Who's playing?' he asks the bartender.

'Lazio v. Roma.'

'Local derby, then.'

'You know Roma?' The bartender's old eyes shine a little brighter.

'I lived in Italy for a while.'

'You like Italy?'

'I love Italy.' Alexander turns and looks directly at the young woman. 'Very good pizza,' he says.

He's touched to see that she blushes; alarmed to discover that he's flirting.

'You've been to Italy, have you?' she says.

'A while back.'

'What's it like?'

His eyes travel round the gleaming chrome bar, the football flags on the walls, the sunshine in the street outside where other customers are sitting at pavement tables. 'It's a lot like this,' he says.

16

'I've only been abroad once,' she says. 'Coach trip to Lourdes with my nan. I'm from Lancashire.'

'I never would have guessed.'

She looks momentarily surprised, then sees that he's teasing.

'I've lived abroad most of my life,' he volunteers, 'for work.'

'What do you do, then?'

'I teach English as a foreign language.'

'So what are you doing in London?'

'Good question,' he says.

When he trained to be an English teacher, it was a means to an end. He wanted to travel. It was a way of paying his way. He's never had any vocation for teaching. The most enthusiastic description he could make of his career would be that it isn't bad, as jobs go. Now that he's back in England, there's no reason to be doing it except that it's what he does. It's poorly paid, but it's not an unpleasant job. The prospect of continuing like this for ever is unimaginable but he's never given much thought to changing his situation. Sometimes he feels he's just doing it until something happens.

The bartender puts a cappuccino in front of the woman. The chocolate powder on the top is swirled into a heart shape. As he turns away he winks at Alexander.

'*Bella*, Katy, no?'

The woman gives Alexander a kind of exasperated smile, indulging the old man.

'Katy?' Alexander hears himself saying.

'Kate,' she corrects him.

'Alexander,' he says, and holds out his hand.

'How do you do, Alexander?' She mocks the length of his name.

'How do you do?' he says. 'Do you come here often?'

He puts on an exaggerated, formal voice to show that he knows it's a cliché.

'Every morning. Couldn't get through the day without one of Marco's cappuccinos, could I?'

The bartender smiles. He's frothing up a metal jug of milk, pretending not to be listening.

They're sitting side by side with two barstools separating them. The knowledge of each other's names is an intimacy they don't know how to handle yet. They both look straight ahead, she at the brightly coloured matchstick packets of sugar in a bowl by the corner of the Gaggia machine, he at the television.

'What brings you to London?' he asks, without taking his eyes off the screen, as if the question arises naturally from the progress of the game.

'I want to see the world,' she says quite seriously.

'Whereabouts in Lancashire are you from?' As if he knew one end of Lancashire from another. He swivels round on his barstool to face her.

'Bolton.'

'Bolton Wanderers,' says the bartender.

She raises her straight dark eyebrows and Alexander grins at her. The conversation is theirs now, but it's still fragile. They don't want the old man barging in any more.

'Where are you planning to go?' Alexander asks.

'Bali,' she says as if it's the most exotic location she can think of, 'or Thailand. But everyone goes to Thailand now . . .'

'Everyone goes to Bali,' he tells her.

'Where would you go, then?' she asks.

'Where?' he repeats.

'In the whole world?'

He likes the childlike wonder in her voice.

'There are still some places in the Philippines,' he says.

18

'Do you think you could write down the names for me?' she asks.

'Sure,' he replies.

Neither of them makes any move to produce pen or paper.

'What's the time?' he asks her.

'Half-past six,' she says.

'I left my watch at work,' he explains.

'Can anyone teach English abroad?' she suddenly asks him.

'There's a qualification you need to get a job in a school. It doesn't take long.'

'Do you need A levels or something?'

'I don't know,' he says quickly, not wanting to offend her. He hadn't imagined that she might not have A levels. She sees through his attempt to be polite.

'I was good at English at school,' she says, defensively. 'I got an A in my GCSE. And Art.'

'Well done!' he says and cringes because he sounds just like a teacher.

'Well, then,' she says, tipping up her cup and drinking the remains of her coffee.

He knows that if he doesn't say something now she will slip off her barstool and leave the bar and he knows that he does not want that to happen and there isn't time to think about why.

'Look, are you doing anything? I mean, if you wanted we could talk about it . . . maybe . . . dinner . . .'

The more words he adds to the nonsensical sentence, the lamer it sounds, as if he is trying to pick her up. Which, he supposes, is what he is doing. Sort of. Maybe it's the coincidence of her dreams of a palm-fringed beach with his, or maybe it's the after-effect of drinking at lunchtime that makes him feel as if he's not quite responsible for his actions.

'I see enough food all day,' she says. 'Have you noticed how disgusting people are when they eat? I don't mean you,' she adds quickly as he instinctively touches the corner of his mouth. 'And they don't cut up their salad and they're trying to shove in this great bit of iceberg lettuce and talk at the same time.' She imitates, and he watches her, fascinated to know where this is leading.

'It's a test of how much you love someone,' she says, categorically, 'if they're a messy eater and you still can sit across a table from them. Sorry,' she says, for talking too much. Her accent makes the word 'sorreh'.

He doesn't know whether this is her way of saying that she's not interested in having dinner with him.

'Another test,' he says, wanting to keep the conversation going, 'is whether you can stand to be with them when they're speaking a foreign language.'

'Yeah?' Now she looks at him as if he's crazy. Then she says, 'I'm going for a walk. D'you want to come?'

'OK.' He quickly picks up his espresso cup and tips it into his mouth as if there is still liquid inside it.

In the street, she walks briskly, slightly ahead of him, dodging pavement tables, not looking around. He watches her slight but determined body weaving through the passers-by.

'Where are we going?' he calls.

He was born and brought up in London but he cannot remember ever going for a walk in London. They lived in Kentish Town, he and his mother, and when they went into town it was to do something, like see a play or an exhibition. Later, when he and his friends were teenagers they hung around the pubs of Camden, or roamed about on skateboards in scrubby playgrounds where there were tyres for swings and disused turquoise paddling pools spotted with brown puddles of rainwater. The centre of town was for tourists.

At Charing Cross Road, Kate looks back, misses him for a second, then sees him, and her face goes from grumpy to pleased, like a child getting the lollipop she wants at the checkout in Marks and Spencer.

'Let's go through the piazza. See if there's a band.'

He's content to be led.

They walk through a cloud of caramel-flavoured air around the vendor of sugared nuts, past a near-naked man painted grey, sitting in the pose of Rodin's *Thinker*, down the back of the newly refurbished Opera House.

His mother used to bring him here. He was always the youngest person in the auditorium and he has never been able to dissociate opera from the fidgety tiredness that comes from sitting still for long periods. He remembers struggling to understand what it was about the murky spectacle on stage that kept the adults around him so rapt, and inventing counting games to make the time pass. Sometimes, in the stifling heat of the amphitheatre, his mother would fan him with a red programme and whisper a translation of an aria. At the interval as they stood in line for cardboard tubs of ice-cream, she would try to explain the story. He remembers the pain in her eyes when he asked once, 'How much longer is it going to go on?'

There's a string quartet playing in the basement level of the piazza. Kate leans over the rails and when they finish the piece, she claps hard.

'I'm going to ask them what that one's called,' she says, as if it's a pop song.

'It's called "Air on a G string",' Alexander tells her.

'Go on!' She looks at him as if he's having her on, then runs down the steps and asks the black guy on cello. He looks up from sorting his music and smiles at her. She makes people smile. Alexander notices how faces going in the other direction lift as she passes. She bounds back up the steps.

'You were right,' she says, in astonishment, when she returns.

'It's the name of one of the strings on the cello,' he explains.

'I know that,' she says impatiently, heading off across the cobbles.

'Where are we going now?' he calls after her.

'The river.' She turns and smiles at him. He likes her quickness to take offence, and to forgive.

He looks at his bare wrist again and wonders what he is doing roaming the streets of London with a woman he does not even know.

The Thames is at full tide. In the evening light, the bulging expanse of water is breathtaking. He looks upriver into the mellowing sunshine. The London Eye revolves slowly like the giant paddle of a surreal steamer.

'This way is my favourite big view,' says Kate. They lean on the railings, side by side, sharing it.

'Do you have a favourite little view?'

'Blue sky through pink cherry blossom,' she replies immediately, unaware that he is teasing her. 'You have to narrow your eyes and try to forget what you're looking at,' she demonstrates, 'and then the blue is so blue, and the pink is so pink it's amazing, like if you were painting it, you'd never put those colours together, because you wouldn't believe that nature had such bright colours.'

'You'd think nature was more subtle.'

Out of habit, he is an English teacher introducing more complex vocabulary into the conversation.

'I've never thought of dividing views into big and small before,' he says quickly, hoping she didn't notice.

'It's just my way of having two favourites,' she says, and starts to walk on. 'I'm like that. Always want more than I'm allowed. My mum says to me, why can't you be satisfied with what you've got, you'd be a lot happier . . .'

'My mother was just the opposite,' he says: 'she always wanted me to want more.'

She turns her face to look at him.

'That's the difference between us,' she says. 'I'm working class and you're middle class.'

She starts walking again.

His inclination is to protest, which would anyway only prove her point, but he finds it odd that she's chosen that to single out, he thinks, as if it were the only factor that distinguishes them. To him there is nothing obvious they have in common, except that they are there, together, on a busy road bridge, shouting to make themselves heard above the traffic.

'Where are we going?' he asks, quickening his step to catch her up. The pavement on the bridge is wide. There's no danger of bumping into each other if they walk side by side here.

'I haven't walked that bit yet.' She waves towards Bankside.

'Me neither,' he says.

'Never?'

'No.'

'I want to walk every inch of the river before I leave,' she says.

'When are you leaving?'

'When I get the money together. How much d'you think I'll need?'

'A thousand?' he ventures, not really knowing

23

whether she's asking his opinion, or whether it's some kind of test.

'Oh! It'll be a year at least, then,' she says. It's the first time he's seen her face look sad, almost panicked.

'Maybe not that much. I really don't know . . .' he tries to retract.

'If I live on five pounds a day, I can usually save twenty pounds a week.'

'Five pounds a day?'

'I get a meal at work.'

'Five pounds a day doesn't go very far.'

'You find ways. Let's go down these steps,' she says, as they reach the other side of the bridge. 'Now listen!' She pauses at the bottom.

'What?'

'Nothing,' she says. 'No traffic noise down here. The water soaks it up.'

He wonders whether he would have noticed the relative stillness without her pointing it out.

'Have you ever been in there?' she asks, pointing at the grey concrete façade of the National Theatre.

'Yes,' says Alexander.

'Me too!' she says, as if it's another remarkable thing they have in common. 'There was a bloke playing jazz piano, and there's a balcony where you can look at the view. Nobody minds if you're not seeing a play. I used to want to be an actress, when I was young . . .'

There's a slightly wistful tone that makes him say, 'You're still young.'

'How old am I? If you're wrong, you can buy me a drink.'

She stands still for a moment and makes a face he takes to be her idea of sophisticated.

'Twenty-one.'

He calculates that it's a safe number. If she's eighteen, she'll want to look older. If she's thirty, she'll want to look younger. As he looks at her properly for the first time, he has no idea how old she is. Her body and clothes are a runaway teenager's, but her eyes have seen more of life. Blue eyes, very dark blue, he notices, then looks away as if he's been caught staring.

'Wrong!'

She wants him to guess again.

'I give up,' he says.

'I'm twenty-four. People always think I'm younger. Your turn,' she says.

He imitates her pouting pose.

'Thirty-five,' she says.

'Correct.'

'No?' Her face lights with triumph.

'Actually, thirty-six,' he says, 'but only last week.'

'I would have said thirty, except that you're getting a bit of grey at the sides,' she says, as if that will make him feel better.

'Thanks for pointing it out.'

'Happy Birthday for last week, anyway. What does that make you – Aries?'

'I think so. What are you?' he asks, out of politeness.

'Aquarius. The only definite thing you can say about Aquarians is that they don't become astrologers,' she says.

'Why's that?'

'Because their stars are always crap,' she says, 'and if you were an astrologer you wouldn't write crap stars for yourself, would you?'

She's off again looking across the river, pointing things out to him.

'Look at all those churches peeping over the top of the buildings,' she says. 'Look at this duck. The river's so high, he's frightened to go in. Go on, Mr Duck, you'll float, you daft bird!'

Alexander looks at the duck who's standing on the embankment wall shivering.

'Look at this!' Kate scampers over to a row of little shops called Gabriel's Wharf. The wall behind has been painted to look like a pastel market square. 'Gorgeous, this, isn't it?' she says.

He thinks it's a kitsch tourist trap, but he doesn't say so.

He watches her longingly gazing into windows filled with beads and rings and mirrors with sparkly mosaic frames.

'Like treasure,' she says.

The word unravels the knot of memory that has been tugged tight ever since he found himself following her out of the bar into the bustling sunshine of Soho.

When he was a child he had an imaginary friend who appeared in his dreams and led him on adventures. He remembers exactly the excitement of following him through the gap in the hedge at the bottom of their tiny patch of garden, along the overgrown path down the back where the dustbins lived, through the used car lot, and down the warren of terraced streets towards the swishy long grass of Parliament Hill Fields. In search of treasure.

The memory seems so clear now, he's slightly shaken by it, as if what he is doing now was foretold long ago.

'What?' Kate asks him.

'What?' he repeats, inanely.

'You look as if you've seen a ghost,' she says.

Beside the river, where the Jubilee Walk ends and the pavement narrows, a man and a woman are kissing on a bench in the softening light, drinking each other, oblivious to anyone else in the world.

The waterfront path winds its way between converted warehouses and wharfs. Beneath the arches of

Blackfriars Bridge a saxophonist is playing 'Moon River'. The melancholy notes sing that the day is ending, the adventure almost over. Soon Alexander will wake up, his imaginary friend will be gone.

In front of the Tate Modern Kate looks back at him to check he's still there, misses her footing on the slippery gravel and crashes down onto her left knee.

Alexander crouches down beside her.

'Sorry,' he says, feeling guilty that she was looking at him and not at her feet.

'It's not your fault,' she says.

Her left hand is grazed. She brushes the dust off, then turns her leg over cautiously. Her trousers are torn and there's gravel embedded in the bloody wound of her knee.

'Yuk,' she says.

'Can you walk?'

'Course I can.'

She takes his hand and he pulls her to her feet.

'We'd better get this washed,' he says, looking round, as if a first aid post will suddenly manifest itself on the lawn.

He holds out his arm and she half hops along beside him. He feels her energy in the grip on his arm and he can tell that she's in some pain but determined not to cry. Instinctively, he drops a kiss on the top of her head. She looks up at him.

'I'm sure there's a hospital near here,' he says briskly, trying to divert the sudden frightening and overwhelming sensation of attraction.

'I don't need a hospital. I just need cleaning up.'

There seems to be nobody around. The Globe theatre has closed for the night. A last crocodile of Japanese teenagers is piling onto a coach. The other buildings around are offices. The air temperature has dropped a degree or two.

'Look,' says Kate: 'the water is so high, it looks like the City is floating.'

Across the river a couple of gold weather vanes atop church steeples glint with the last rays of evening sunshine, but the buildings are lifeless grey. It does look like a massive island, almost sinister, and it is eerily quiet apart from the slop of water beside them. It feels as if they are alone in a deserted city.

And then, around the next building, they find themselves in the hubbub of the forecourt of a busy pub. The noise and laughter of after-work drinkers and the smell of cigarettes and beer are as welcome as an oasis in the desert. Kate looks up at him.

'London's like that,' she says.

'Like what?'

'One minute you're all alone, then you turn a corner and it's so noisy, you can't even hear yourself think.'

They shift apart.

'Sit there.' Alexander points to a wooden table with benches on either side.

At the bar he asks for a bottle of still mineral water but they've run out. He returns to the table with a little green bottle of Perrier, then takes a tissue from the pocket of his jacket, holds her leg out horizontally by the ankle, rolls her trouser leg carefully up over her knee and inspects the wound, as if a long enough look at it will give him a clue as to what to do. He pours some water on it. It fizzes over the surface of her skin and drips onto the ground.

'How does that feel?'

'Stings,' she says, biting her lip.

He soaks a tissue in the water and dabs tentatively at the periphery of the wound. The blood and some of the gravel come away easily, making it look a lot better, but there are still some bits embedded.

'What you need is a nice bath,' he says. 'Come on, I'll get you home.'

She looks at his outstretched hand but does not take it.

'Aren't I even going to get that drink you owe me, suffering as I do?' Her accent has taken on a mournful Irish lilt.

He knows that he should say no because whereas an hour before going for a walk with her meant just going for a walk with her, now, having a drink with her seems to mean more than just having a drink with her.

'Owe you?' he stalls.

'In fact you owe me two.'

'How do you work that out?' he asks.

'I guessed your age, you didn't guess mine. And my knee hurts . . .' she adds, seeing that he's giving in.

At the bar he buys an orange juice for her and another Perrier for himself. The Perrier is a compromise. He will have a drink with her, but not a real drink. He will have no excuse not to go after one, or two, if she insists on holding him to their bet. The bargain seems to quell the slight nausea of guilt in the pit of his stomach.

She drinks from the neck of the bottle and they look out over the river. The pub lights come on, making the sky seem darker. She looks at the graze on her left palm then bends the fingers over to inspect her nails. He's about to say that her nails were the first thing he noticed about her, but he stops himself. He can't think of a way of saying it that won't sound too intimate.

'Were you a waitress in Bolton?' he asks finally.

'No, I worked in a shop. On the tills,' she adds hurriedly as if he understands what that means in supermarket hierarchy. 'They offered me promotion to assistant manager of produce, but you couldn't be so flexible with your hours. Anyway,' she adds, 'I want to live a bit before I start getting into a company pension scheme, don't I? And my sister had a place I could stay . . .'

'Your sister's here too?'

'Yes. Both us girls left and all four boys still live at home. What made you come back to England, anyway?'

'My mother was ill,' he says, 'and then she died. I had to sort out her stuff. I'm an only child.'

'I'm sorry,' she says.

'Thanks,' he says, not knowing whether her sympathy is for the loss of his mother or the absence of family. He takes a breath, then exhales, like a sigh. He knows that he should say more, but the moment passes.

'How long ago?' she asks.

'Nearly four years.' He decides he really doesn't want to talk about it. 'How long have you been in London?' he asks.

'Nearly four weeks,' she says.

Their eyes keep meeting, speaking to each other without speaking, then looking away when one of them says something.

'I was up at Tower Bridge the other day,' Kate says quietly, as if it's a secret she doesn't want anyone else to hear. 'There was this cruise ship moored on the other side, all glittery with lights. I thought about stowing away on it.'

'Why don't you get yourself a job on one?' Alexander suggests.

'I'd still be a waitress then, wouldn't I? I want to experience things. Write about them . . .'

'You want to write a travel book?'

'No. A novel. You have to have seen things to write a book, don't you?'

'Isn't it more to do with the way you write than the location?'

'No-one wants to read a book about a checkout girl, do they?'

'If you wrote it, they might,' he says.

'Yeah?'

She beams at him, her transparent delight paying him back tenfold for the compliment.

'Come on,' he says, looking away, 'let's get you home.'

'OK.'

She limps after him in an ironic reversal of their progress earlier. He wants to help her but he dares not touch her now. They pick their way over cobblestones that look as if they have just been laid. The area is in the process of being turned into a historical theme park and Kate is its first satisfied customer.

'Oh look, this was a dungeon,' she exclaims delightedly.

A museum of wine has opened in one of the old warehouses.

'Vinopolis,' Kate reads. 'D'you think that's Roman?'

The steps up to London Bridge have a notice saying that this is the place where Nancy was killed in *Oliver Twist*. Alexander is surprised that they have not painted on her blood to make it more authentic. Back on the bridge, he feels as if he's been delivered back to his life.

He hails a cab.

'I'll get a bus,' Kate tells him.

'No, you won't. I'll pay,' he says. 'Now, where to?'

She says the name of a street in Soho then sits back and tries to put her seatbelt on. From the way she watches everything out of the window, he thinks it might be the first time she's travelled in a London taxi.

31

'Where do you live, then?' she asks him as they stop at lights on Cambridge Circus.

'In Kent,' he says.

'Oh. That's a long way,' she says, leaving the sentence open for him to fill in more information.

'Not really,' he says, unwilling to give it.

The cab drops them at the end of her street.

She walks down an alleyway he wouldn't have noticed and stops at a door with several bells.

'Well, this is it, then,' she says. 'D'you want to come up for a coffee?'

'Is this where you live?'

All his assumptions about her flip over, as his eyes scan the names on the bells. Model Mandy, Big Susie, Betty Bonds, Joy.

'It's not what you think,' she says. 'Well, it is. It's my sister's place. I just sleep here. She doesn't use it much now. Mostly she stays with her boyfriend in Romford.'

'Which one is your sister?' He points to the bells.

'Joy. As in stick. As in ride. Her real name's Marie. Sorry,' she says, 'it was a bit of a shock to me when I arrived. She told us she was a supermodel.'

She says it so seriously it makes him laugh, and then she's laughing too, and before he knows it, he's walking up the stairs to the top floor behind her.

He tells himself it's just curiosity. He's never been inside a brothel before. In Tokyo his flat was in Shinjuku. He liked the seediness of the area, but never sampled any of the experiences on offer there, except once when he was with a group of teachers who'd been drinking all Friday evening and dared each other to go to a peep-show. When the two prostitutes who were supposed to be engaging in lesbian sex for the entertainment of men saw that there was a woman with them, they started shouting abuse. Afterwards nobody could work out how they knew unless there were two-way mirrors or hidden cameras, which had made them feel even more sordid.

Inside, he's half expecting a tunnel of love with pink marabou or fake leopardskin or even leather, but it's more like a shabby bedsit with a worn patterned carpet and a smell of air-freshener that doesn't quite mask the underlying notes of cooking and damp.

Joy's bedsit is on the top floor. It has four different locks. The room is L shaped. There's a battered black leather sofa as you walk in with nothing in front of it, like a waiting room. In the far corner there's a double bed tented with lengths of shiny, silky material in magenta, orange and purple. The room is painted very dark blue. Including the windows.

'Look at this!'

Kate flicks the light off. He's momentarily nervous. What is she going to do to him? And then he sees dozens of fluorescent stars glowing on the ceiling.

'They're always falling off,' Kate says, switching the light back on.

He follows her round the corner of the room, staying as far away from the bed as he can. As she swishes back a black curtain, he draws his breath in, anticipating some sort of bondage gear, but there's just a pink bath that is so out of place it doesn't look plumbed in, and next to it, a cooker and a fridge.

'Everything but the kitchen sink,' Kate says, matter-of-factly. 'She got Des to take it out and put the bath in instead. We've got a plastic bowl for the washing up,' she says, in case he was thinking that they took it into the bath with them. 'Coffee?'

'Er, I won't, thanks,' he says.

Kate turns on the bath taps.

He knows that it's time for him to go, but it is so strange, so completely unexpected to find himself in such a room, he finds it difficult to make the move. It's like that bit of a dream when you're beginning to wake up but you don't want to leave, and you try to will yourself back to sleep.

'Did your sister decorate it herself?' He hears himself sounding like a guest making polite conversation at a vicarage tea party.

On the bedside table there's a glass bonbon jar filled with brightly coloured wrapped sweets. Without really thinking about it, his hand goes into the jar. They're not sweets, they're condoms. He looks at the flat strawberry-coloured packet in his hand and drops it quickly back, hoping that Kate hasn't noticed.

'God, this is the worst gum I've ever chewed,' Kate says.

'What?'

'That's what Marie says.'

She nods at the jar.

'Oh. Right.'

'What do you think this is, then?'

Kate's fingering the shiny tenting.

'Silk?' he suggests.

'Lining material from gents' suits,' says Kate triumphantly, as if she's caught him out again. 'She got it cheap from somewhere in Whitechapel. She saw them doing the same sort of thing on *Changing Rooms*, you know, romantic, a touch of the *Arabian Nights* about it. The carpet spoils it . . .'

He notices for the first time the dusty Axminster in an ugly pattern of red and brown.

'. . . but you can't have stripped boards in a place like this,' Kate tells him knowledgeably, 'you'd hear everything. Sit down.'

There's a choice of a hard wooden chair that has clothes piled on top of it, or the bed. He perches on the chair.

'How did your sister get into this line of business?' he asks, waving a hand around.

'She's always had men after her. She had a load of photos done and came to London. She got a part in a movie, you know the sort I mean. It went from there, I suppose. She's a table dancer now,' Kate informs him.

She bends to test the temperature of the water in the bath. A gap between the edge of the T-shirt and the top of her pants reveals the base of her spine and the two slight hollows just above her buttocks.

He wants to touch her there.

She kicks off her shoes, pulls down her trousers, wincing as the material catches her wounded knee, and then before he's had time to think about leaving, she steps into the bath with T-shirt and knickers still on, sits down and smiles at him as if to say: you didn't think I was really going to take my clothes off in front of you!

A few wisps of her blood thread up through the water.

Her panties become transparent, showing her little triangle of black pubic hair. The bottom of her T-shirt goes loose. He's more aroused than if she had stripped. He feels his erection pressing against the zip of his trousers.

'I must go,' he says quietly.

He bends over the bath and touches her lips with his. For half a second there is a slight, soft adhesion. Her breath tastes orangey, his nostrils breathe in the coconut smell of her.

'Thanks for the walk.'

He turns to leave, not able to look at her again.

'I enjoyed talking to you,' he says at the door.

'Me too,' she says, then bends her knees and slides the top half of her body, including her head, right under the water.

*   *   *

The front door slams behind Alexander. He looks at his non-existent watch again.

A woman with short peroxide white hair is walking up the alleyway. She stops in front of him. She has a key in her hand. It takes him a moment to realize he is standing in her way.

'Did you leave something inside?' she asks in the same accent as Kate's.

He looks at her. She has Kate's face, but rounder, some would think prettier, but her eyes have no expression. It's Kate's face when the dream turns into a nightmare.

'No,' he says.

'It's just gone nine,' she tells him.

'Right. Thanks.'

'The night's still young,' she says. Her lifeless eyes glimmer with invitation.

'I'm going home,' he says, and hurries down the alleyway, not looking back.

Two

It's silent under the water. Kate stays down as long as she can, and when she bursts up for air, she hears the door to the flat being opened. She knows that it can't be him coming back in, but she allows herself a moment's hope. The touch of his lips is still on hers. She shuts her eyes and sinks down into the water again. Her breasts feel weightless.

She wonders if it's the same for him. Is his heart now beating in his dick like hers is beating in her crotch? Have his nipples gone all hard? Is he imagining what it would be like to be inside her? The muscles in her pelvic floor contract involuntarily. She sits up quickly, pressing her thighs together. A wave slops up to the top of the bath and back over her chest.

'Kate?' her sister calls from the door.

'Yes.'

'What are you doing in the bath with your clothes on?'

'I felt like it.'

Marie puts down her handbag and flops onto the bed.

'I've had it,' she says. 'They want me back at seven in the morning. Seven!'

'Who's in at seven?' Kate asks, not really interested.

'Men who go to work,' Marie says, 'that's who. Men with money to pay to see my bits in the morning.'

'It's disgusting,' says Kate, sinking back under the water.

'You sound like Mam.'

'Mam would die,' says Kate.

Marie leans forward and gets a cigarette from her bag.

'Is it more disgusting, d'you think?' she asks, matter-of-factly, 'table dancing? I feel terrible about getting them all worked up and then sending them away, you know . . .'

She still talks as if she's a teenage cock-tease deciding how far to let a bloke's hand slip down her jeans. They used to have whispered conversations in their room at night about how far they would go. Marie was always prepared to go further, and she is two years younger.

'At seven in the morning they won't go home and bother their wives,' Kate says.

'That's a point,' says Marie, pulling on her cigarette. 'Their secretaries'll get it instead.' She shrieks with laughter.

'I'm making as much money' – she empties notes out of her handbag, then unzips her jeans and non-chalantly pulls out a roll of new twenties she's stuffed down the front of her thong – 'and you don't have to talk to them. You soon get a sense of what they like. You should try it.'

'No, thanks.'

'You'd be out of here sooner if you did,' Marie argues, zipping up again.

'I'll find somewhere else if you don't want me.'

'It's not that,' says Marie, with the little offended look that comes readily to her face. 'I'm saving to go to college,' she says, as if to defend her work.

'To do what?' Kate asks. It's the first she's heard of it.

'Interior design.'

'What happened to opening a bar in Ibiza?'

'Yeah. What have you done to your knee?' Marie suddenly shrieks.

'I fell over.'

'Where?'

'Outside Tate Modern.'

'Tate Modern?' Marie thinks she's unbelievably pretentious. 'What were you doing there?'

'Mind your own business.'

Kate sees that she's given herself away by trying to hide something of no importance, and then makes it worse by saying, 'I didn't think you were coming back tonight.'

'Got other plans?' Marie's on to her immediately.

'No.'

'Liar!'

Kate stands up in the bath and peels off her knickers and T-shirt. Marie hands her a towel. One of the few rules of the house is that you dry yourself before you get out of the bath. Otherwise the carpet starts to smell like an old flannel.

'I met this bloke,' Kate says. She might as well tell Marie because she's bound to wheedle it out of her if they're going to spend the evening together, which it looks like they are.

'Yeah?'

'Not like that,' says Kate.

Marie's only half listening as she takes a small mirror off the wall and puts it on the bed beside her. She extracts a little plastic bag from her handbag then chops three lines of coke on the silver surface, rolls one of the crisp £20 tips she has earned today, and snorts up a line.

Kate thinks it's the paraphernalia of the process that Marie likes. As she sniffs and brushes her nose with her finger, she has exactly the same satisfied look on her face that she used to have after giving herself a manicure as a teenager. Marie loved all the emery boards and buffers, orange sticks and cuticle cream. Her half of the dressing table in their room at home was covered with her beauty equipment lined up in rows. Eye shadows, lipsticks, brushes of every size. Kate's had a pile of library books all open at different places.

'Want some?' Marie asks, dipping her head down for the second line.

'No, thanks.'

She always asks, as if it's something that Kate does too, and Kate always says no, colluding in the pretence, because she knows it wouldn't be any use arguing with her. It'd only make her try something worse, just to prove she could handle it. Marie's like that.

Quickly Marie does the other two lines, dabs the pad of her thumb around the edges of the mirror, licks it, and replaces the mirror on its hook.

'So, is it just you and me tonight?' she asks.

Kate pulls a small suitcase from under the bed. She opens it and takes out fresh knickers, a white T-shirt and a short black skirt.

'You want a plaster for that knee,' says Marie, sagely.

'Got one?'

'No.'

'Where's Des?' Kate asks.

'Driving a load of prawns from Scotland to Barcelona.'

'Go on!'

Des is a long-distance lorry driver Marie met when she was working in a service station.

'What d'you mean?' Marie's eyes narrow.

'Well, it's coals to Newcastle, isn't it, prawns to the land of paella?'

'The lying bastard!'

Marie smiles affectionately. Kate's never pretended to try to understand what makes her sister and her boyfriend tick. But they seem happy and, oddly, trusting.

'You look like a schoolgirl in that skirt with that knee,' says Marie; then, as if the two thoughts are inextricably connected, 'Who's this bloke then?'

'Just a bloke I served, and then he was in Marco's later. We got talking.'

'Talking,' repeats Marie.

'He's lived abroad. He gave me some tips.'

'Tips?'

'On where to go,' says Kate impatiently.

'What's he look like?'

'What's it matter?' She doesn't want to talk about him now. Marie turns everything sordid.

'Not exactly drop dead gorgeous, then?'

'He is.'

'Really?'

'He's so good looking that you kind of feel you know him. Like a film star. D'you know what I'm talking about?'

'No . . .'

'He's tall, and a bit stoopy, you know . . .'

'Stoopy?'

Kate imitates the slightly awkward way that Alexander stands. 'Kind of sad,' she says. 'No, not sad, more troubled.'

'I'm mad with jealousy now,' says Marie sarcastically.

'Oh, he wouldn't be your type at all. Too serious,' she adds quickly.

'What's he doing with you, then?'

'He's not doing anything with me. I just met him, that's all. Then I hurt my knee and he brought me back here in a taxi. He's kind.'

'Gay?'

Kate hasn't thought of that possibility. The soft kiss he gave her is still on her lips. A current of sex shoots from her chest to her vagina.

'I don't think so,' she says.

'Married?'

She hasn't thought of that either. He didn't look married. She tries to picture his hands. She's sure there wasn't a ring. What does it matter? She's never going to see him again.

'What's it matter? I'm never going to see him again anyway,' she says to her sister. The dark blue room seems suddenly oppressive.

Marie looks in the mirror again, snatches a tissue from the box by the bed, twists it, licks it and wipes away a trace of lipstick that has bled at the corner of her mouth; then she smooths her skin-tight jeans over her thighs languorously, looking pleased with herself.

'Come on,' she says, 'let's go for a drink.'

Marie drinks vodka and Red Bull. Kate drinks orange juice. Kate remembers her father coming home from the pub, the smell of beer and cigarettes blowing through the door with him, and the sweet odour of his sweat as he kissed them both goodnight. Kate doesn't like the taste of alcohol.

'You can't really taste it with Red Bull, though,' Marie tells her. She always wants Kate to share in her sins. 'It'd pick you up a bit,' she says.

'I'm not down,' Kate says.

'You're thinking about that bloke.'

'I'm not.'

'Did you snog him?' Marie wants to know.

'He kissed me,' Kate says tentatively.

'I did that once,' says Marie.

'What?'

'Snogged a stranger. On a train. We were sitting opposite each other, you know, and we kept looking, then looking away. Then you know . . .' Marie smiles to herself at the memory '. . . the looks turned to smiles, and, when the people in our bit got out, we snogged . . .'

'And . . . ?'

Kate wants to hear the end of the story.

'It was great.'

'But what happened?'

'He got off. I thought about him a bit that night, you know, and the next day . . .'

'But you never saw him again?'

'No. Didn't even remember till just now.'

'Oh.' Kate can't help feeling disappointed.

'You're allowed to fancy someone, you know,' Marie tells her. 'It's normal.' She finishes off her lurid drink and spots someone she knows drinking on the other side of the pub. 'Back in a mo,' she says.

The pub's clientele is mostly gay men. It's where Marie comes on a night off. There's little chance of being propositioned. Kate watches her sister flirting exaggeratedly with a grey-haired man in his fifties wearing a lilac polo shirt and his much younger boy-friend who's wearing a vest and a leather collar with studs around his neck. In London, Kate sometimes sees Marie as other people must see her. Her eyes look huger and bluer than they used to at home because of her cropped hair and the drugs she takes, and her plum-painted mouth is always open, laughing or talking. Marie's not the sort of person who can walk along the street just listening to her personal stereo: she has to sing along with it. She's petite, but she's what people call larger than life, and she's got a beautiful singing voice. Perhaps one day, someone will discover her.

The streets of Soho are like extensions to the theatres dotted around. People act like they're on stage here. At home, they'd call it showing off. Kate expected London to be more serious and monumental. It still takes her breath away when she turns a corner and sees a view, like Trafalgar Square or St Paul's Cathedral, that is so familiar it's unreal. But the rest of it is a never-ending series of urban villages. She likes the fact that you can walk all day and not get to the end of it. She never feels lost exactly, but she has never felt so alone. You need a big personality like Marie to be part of it. Des says she's turbo-charged.

Kate could sit on her own in a pub for hours and nobody would say a word to her. She's had a coffee in Marco's bar every day since she arrived. On the first day, Marie arranged to meet her there because it was easy to find. She had some explaining to do before Kate saw her room. Kate sat there for two hours waiting and Marco was friendly, but until this afternoon she's never had a conversation with anyone else.

Alexander.

She didn't really notice him in the restaurant until he smiled. When his face is normal, he looks like he could make someone unhappy. When he smiles, the air around him sparkles. She has an image of him as he followed his crowd out of the restaurant. He's looking at the sky, enjoying the feeling of sun on his face after the dry chill of the air-conditioning, the heaviness of his jacket hunching his shoulders. He's with the others, but not with them, somehow. The battered flying jacket with pockets so full they droop makes him look like a teacher.

But she didn't know that he was a teacher then. She wonders if her brain's created the image to fit the facts.

Marie's on her way back. She shimmies through the

men, unable not to draw attention to herself even amongst a crowd of uninterested guys.

'Listen to this,' she says, squeezing her bottom onto Kate's seat. 'Have you ever had a pigeon on your right shoulder?'

She points to Kate's right shoulder.

'No,' says Kate, warily. It's bound to be something crude.

'Have you ever had a parrot on your left shoulder?'

'No.'

Marie points to her mouth.

'I bet you've had a cockatoo in there!'

'Gross!'

Marie's delighted with herself.

'There's this club they can get us in,' she says.

'I want an early night,' Kate says.

'Oh.' Marie's face twists with indecision. Will she try to bully Kate into going with her, or not? 'You're right,' she says, finally, 'I'm going to be dancing at seven. What do I want to spend the whole night dancing for too?'

Kate's surprised, but pleased too, specially when Marie links her as they're walking back. Sometimes London makes Kate feel as if she's floating about in a whirl of sensation. The friendly press of a sister's arm grounds her.

'Des wants me to move in with him,' Marie remarks, as she puts her key in the lock.

The sisterly, companiable feeling vanishes. Marie's clearly been working up to telling Kate that she'll have to find somewhere else to live. She feels momentarily betrayed, then ashamed of herself. It's a significant step for Marie to settle down with Des. She should welcome it.

'I don't like the idea of giving up my freedom,' Marie says, slumping down on the leather sofa, 'but I'll have more money.'

'And you'll be with Des,' Kate says. 'Is it a nice house?'

She pictures them in a little modern place with Marie up a ladder, singing along with Jennifer Lopez on Capital as she slops lime green paint on the ceiling, or lilac or some other bright colour she's seen on *Changing Rooms*.

'Listen to you!' Marie suddenly snaps. 'Why should I settle down? You're not.'

'I don't want you to settle down,' Kate protests.

'Yes you do.'

'Only because I'm frightened for you sometimes,' Kate says carefully.

'Why don't we go round the world together, then? I've got enough money for both of us . . .'

Kate has never suspected that Marie wanted to share her dream with her. She wonders why it hasn't occurred to her. It's typical of Marie. Now she understands the generosity of her sister's invitation to London.

Go for it, Kate. Stay at my place.

'You'd do more things with me along,' Marie presses on, capitalizing on Kate's surprise. 'What's to lose? If I give this place up, you'll have to go back home anyway. You'll never survive and save, working in a pizza restaurant.' She blows out a smoke ring contemptuously.

With typical impatience, she's moved from suggestion to blackmail in less than a minute.

'I can't go with you,' Kate tells her. 'It'd be great with you, but different,' she says, trying to soften the refusal.

'You won't change, you know,' Marie taunts her, 'you'll still be who you are even if you're in Timbuk-bloody-too.'

'I don't want to change,' Kate says carefully, 'I just want to see something different.'

'Well, I'm moving in with Des, then,' says Marie, defeatedly.

'Up to you.'

'D'you want a coffee?' Marie's as quick to forgive as to threaten.

'No thanks, it'll keep me awake,' says Kate, feeling suddenly enormously affectionate towards her sister.

She takes her skirt off and climbs into the bed. Marie's scrupulously clean about changing the sheets each time she brings a client back, but the bed still smells of sex and her current perfume.

Marie fidgets about the flat rearranging things and smoking. Kate sits up and folds herself over the side of the bed to reach her suitcase. She yanks it out, opens the catches and pulls out her notebook. The cover is navy blue leatherette and there is a strap with a lock. Kate has the tiny key in her purse along with a St Christopher medal she was given as a First Communion present.

Marie watches Kate as she starts to write.

'Still got that book?'

'Yes.'

Marie gave it to her on her eighteenth birthday. Kate suspected she'd nicked it from W.H. Smith.

'I bought that for you.'

'It's the best present I ever had.'

'Really?' Marie's face lights up. 'Let's have a look.'

Kate happily hands it over, knowing that Marie hasn't the patience to decipher her tiny writing.

'I met this bloke, but I didn't bonk him,' Marie pretends to read.

'Give it back!' Kate laughs.

Marie tosses it at her.

With a stranger, you can be who you want to be . . . Kate writes.

Marie draws back the covers and lies down next to her.

'D'you mind if I have the light out?'

'Go ahead.'

Kate closes her notebook, locks it and swings down to put it back in her suitcase.

There's a light-pull above the bed. The room is dark apart from the pink, green and orange fluorescent stars and the tip of Marie's cigarette.

Kate wishes she'd had a chance to write everything she wanted. Sleep will make her more distant from him. In the morning she may have forgotten what it felt like when he kissed her.

'Do you ever make bargains with God?' she asks Marie quietly in the darkness.

'What do you mean?'

'You know, promises in return for favours . . .'

'Oh, you mean, like, I promise I'll give up smoking if I'm not pregnant . . . that sort of thing?'

'Yeah . . . well, sort of . . .'

'All the time,' says Marie. 'Why?'

'Doesn't matter.'

There's a moment's silence then Marie says in a singsong voice, 'Dear God, if I can have this stoopy film star bloke, I promise to go to Mass every day for the rest of my life . . .'

'Be quiet,' Kate scolds, but she's giggling.

Please God, give me one day with him, and I'll go back home.

The thought flies through Kate's head before she can stop it. She doesn't think it counts unless you say it out loud.

'If I could just have a day with him . . .' she says.

'You'd promise what?' Marie wants to know.

'Do you think going to Mass would be enough?'

'For a whole day with the man of your dreams?

48

Doubt it,' says Marie, giving the hypothetical nego-
tiation serious consideration. 'Anyway, a day wouldn't
be enough. You don't want just a day, really. You're
only saying it because you think that in a day he
would see how wonderful you were . . . and then
it would be up to him, not God . . .'

'Don't be stupid!'

But Marie's analysis is uncannily close to what Kate
was thinking.

Marie starts to murmur the Lou Reed song, 'Perfect
Day'.

'Stop it!' Kate says.

But Marie just gets louder.

'. . . drink champagne in the park . . .' she trills in a
Lesley Garrett crescendo.

'It's not champagne anyway, it's sangria,' Kate interrupts.

'What's sangria when it's at home?' Marie wants to
know.

'Cocktail or something.'

'It's about heroin, that song,' says Marie.

'No . . . ?'

'Everyone knows that,' Marie says, contemptuously.
She takes one last drag of her cigarette, stubs it out,
fidgets around a bit in the darkness, settling down for
the night.

'No relationship lasts a day,' she says, authori-
tatively. 'It's five minutes to five hours after you've
fucked, depending on how well he's been brought
up . . .'

Then there's a long silence.

'. . . or it's destined to be longer. A month . . . a
lifetime . . .'

'As if,' says Kate.

The fluorescent stars are fading. Marie's breathing
becomes slow and even.

'You still thinking about that bloke?' she suddenly demands.

'No,' Kate lies.

'Do you think about Jimmy?' Marie asks.

'Course I do,' Kate replies, turning onto her side, so that they're back to back. 'All the time.'

'D'you miss him?'

'Course I do.'

'But not enough to go back?'

'Shut up, Marie.'

'Night then,' says Marie.

'Night,' says Kate, knowing that she won't be able to sleep now.

Three

'The village is awash with colour. Ever since Laura, the mobile librarian, had a colour therapy consultation in the back room of the organic shop that used to be Barclays Bank, and learned that she has been both an artist and a warrior, everybody's wanting to find out about their previous lives. All you have to do is choose four colours from a rainbow of silken strips of fabric, write down your birthday, hand over £30, and the therapist will give you half an hour on where you've been and where you're going (with a tape recording of the session included in the price). I'm a bit sceptical about reincarnation – why do previous lives always have an archetypal feeling about them? Why, for instance, wasn't Laura a street cleaner or, for that matter, a horse, and would the therapist have told her if she were? Nevertheless, I too found myself the other day picking through a basket of dirty vegetables looking for the ones that would require least work to turn into something resembling a salad bag from Tesco, as I waited for my consultation. Clearly, I wasn't a kitchen maid in a previous life, or perhaps I was, and my laziness now is a reward for all that drudgery . . .'

Nell reads through what she has written and clicks the mouse on word count. Two hundred words. Five hundred to go. On a good day that would take her another hour, but she's stalled. The kitchen clock says ten o'clock. Nell saves her work, then walks wearily upstairs to the bathroom.

In the bath, she lies listening for the click and creak of the front door until the skin on her hands is pale and pruney. She would like him to find her here. Talking, like singing, comes more easily in the warm, steamy room.

Eventually, she gets out and puts on the towelling dressing gown her mother gave her at Christmas. Peach is not the colour Nell would have chosen for herself, but the cotton pile is soft and comforting. It's the sort of dressing gown to drink hot chocolate in, too warm for this evening. The weather forecast is for thunderstorms.

Downstairs, Nell reads through her evening's work again. She wonders how it is that the person on the page sounds so lighthearted when she feels so apprehensive. She stares around the living room searching for the next sentence. The predominant colours are yellow and blue. Butter yellow walls, cobalt blue sofa. Lucy's toy kitchen is red, her pots and pans yellow. The room looks like a giant nursery. She wonders if the cooler more muted sea tones of turquoise and green which the colour therapist suggested would make her feel less agitated. Ridiculous!

The kitchen clock marks out the slow drip of time.

'I'm not one of those people who believes in ologies – although I admit, the first thing I read after ripping the shrinkwrap off my glossy each month is the stars. Just for a laugh – but when the therapist told me that something happened about five years ago that completely changed my life, I began to think she might be on to something . . .'

Too specific. Nell deletes. The difficulty with writing a column is achieving a balance between honest observation which the reader recognizes, and confession. Nell usually does it by thinking of her byline Helen Hill as a character she's fond of and has a lot in common with, but who isn't herself. Now she's too tired to separate. She shuts down the computer.

In the kitchen, Nell transfers the washing up from the drainer to the cupboards and runs the tap to wash away the last swirl of Fairy Liquid bubbles from the sink. She turns off the tap, and the water sluices down the waste pipe. When it stops the house is quiet again. She has grown to hate the silence of the countryside, and the darkness outside, which is sometimes so total it feels like a wall.

She goes upstairs and listens just outside Lucy's room. She's breathing nicely. Nell's tempted to go and lie on the floor next to her, letting her daughter's peaceful sleep calm her, as hers does for Lucy when she wakes in the night.

Nell is restless and exhausted at the same time. Usually she goes to bed at eleven whether Alexander's home or not, but tonight she does not want their only contact to be the gentle draught as he gets into bed, the brief touch of his hand on her arm, a habitual kiss that falls in her hair. Tonight she cannot sleep next to him without speaking.

She tries to anticipate his reaction to the news, but cannot. She can imagine his face looking perplexed and anxious, and she can imagine it lifting with astonished happiness, but the images keep switching like the 3D picture postcard they bought in a tourist shop near the Vatican, which is the smiling Sacred Heart when you tilt it one way and Christ's anguish on the Cross the other.

Where is he?

She wishes he would use the mobile phone she bought him for his birthday, but she knows he will not. As soon as he tore off the wrapping paper, she knew he did not like the gift, and she began to stutter excuses. *I thought . . . for emergencies*. He gave her that mystified look that she used to think was intelligent, but has grown to hate because it makes her feel stupid. What emergencies? And then she did not want to give examples in case saying things out loud made them happen.

It's nearly midnight. There's a bottle of champagne in the fridge but it will be too late to drink it. Even if he caught the last train, he should be home by now.

Nell goes downstairs again, opens her computer and stares at the screen.

Where can he be?

What if he's late because something's wrong? What if he's got knocked down by a bus, or been mugged? What if he's jumped under a tube train? Why *would* he jump under a tube train? She doesn't know where the thought came from, but now it's there it won't leave. She doesn't have the same certainty about him that she used to.

There's an almost inaudible knock at the door.

'Is it you?' she whispers next to the lock.

'Yes.'

'How do I know?'

It's a long-standing joke between them.

'Oh, come on!'

The flash of relief that he's home safely transforms instantly into injustice that he's made her worry unnecessarily.

'I forgot my keys,' he says, as she lets him in.

She sticks her head out of the door and looks up into the blackness as if to encourage the imminent rain. The air is sweet with pollen.

'There weren't any taxis,' he says, as if it's the absence of taxis that's responsible for the hour.

'I don't think there are at this time of night.'

She meant it to be a neutral comment but he bristles.

'Is Lucy OK?' he asks absently picking up the local paper, glancing at the headlines.

'Yes.' She smiles at him.

'Good.'

He puts the paper down and smiles back at her.

It's a long time, she realizes, since they've looked at each other and smiled. It makes her feel exposed, almost embarrassed. A moment ago she was picturing him unconscious in a hospital bed, and now he is here smiling at her. Why does she worry so much? Perhaps if she didn't worry so much, he would smile more. Perhaps she's the one creating all the tension.

'I think these antihistamines are working better,' she says.

'Oh?'

He's clearly forgotten everything she told him about Lucy's last visit to the consultant.

Somebody has to do the worrying, she thinks, see-sawing back to irritation.

'Do you want a drink?' she asks.

'No, thanks. I've had enough. There was a bit of a leaving do for Mel and Joe,' he explains.

'Was it fun?'

'Not really. I'm sorry I'm so late. I thought you'd be in bed.'

The rare apology makes her suddenly optimistic. It wasn't unreasonable of him to assume she'd be in bed. She always is. Maybe she should wait up for him more.

'I thought I'd wait for you.'

'Oh?'

'I bought a bottle of champagne . . .' she says, unable to find a way into telling him what she has to tell him.

'Champagne?'

He glances at the calendar on its hook in the kitchen. She can almost hear his brain reading the date, repeating it, then running through birthdays and anniversaries and failing to find a match.

'I shouldn't be drinking, really,' she says, hating her coyness, but dreading his reaction.

'Why the champagne then?' he asks, and as he says the words, she sees the pieces of information she has just given him joining up in his brain.

'You're not pregnant?'

His laugh sounds as if he wants her to join in and assure him that it is a joke.

Optimism whooshes out of her like the breath from a balloon escaping before she can tie it up. She can only nod.

As she watches him attempting to keep an acceptable expression on his face, she remembers how it was the first time, and she struggles to hold back tears.

'Say something, Alex.'

'How did that happen?' he asks.

'The usual way,' she says.

'I thought the usual way was that two people talked about whether they wanted to, and took the necessary precautions if they didn't.'

His voice is cold and controlled.

'I haven't noticed you taking any precautions,' she responds.

'That's because I assumed . . .'

'You assumed that I put my cap in every night of the week and lie there waiting in case you've had a pint more than usual on a Friday night?'

God, is this what they've come to?

He looks pale and sad.

She knows he is remembering the Friday in question, and she feels terrible for describing a rare and deliciously abandoned night together as a lapse in contraception. She wishes she could take back what she's said.

'Just that once?' he says.

'Didn't they tell you that at school?'

'Don't, Nell.'

Don't be sarcastic, he's saying, because it's not you.

'I take it that's a no to the champagne, then?' Nell says. Her emotions seem to be offering her only two choices – hurt defensiveness or tears. She doesn't want to cry because she thinks it would be manipulative.

'I'm just not sure . . . can we talk about it in the morning? I'm . . . knackered.'

He chooses a word that has a history for them. When Lucy was only two, she corrected Nell. 'I'm not tired, Mummy, I'm knackered.' It's one of those phrases that become part of a family's language. It's his way of offering her a crumb of intimacy because he does not appear to be able to move across and hug her.

Nell watches him walk up the wooden staircase. She hears the creak of the board in the bathroom, the toilet flushing, water running as he cleans his teeth. Then he goes to their bedroom, walking straight past Lucy's door.

Nell sits on the bright blue sofa until she is quite sure that he will be asleep. If it were a more comfortable sofa she would spend the night there. She wonders whether something as simple as buying a sofa bed would make a difference to them. If they each had a place to withdraw to, then perhaps he would not feel the need to keep his thoughts from her.

When they first lived together, in Tokyo, their flat was so small they could hardly move without touching. He said then, in the heady days of being in love, that it made him feel free to have no secrets from her. And she remembers the thrill of receiving such a compliment tempered by a slight foreboding that he was offering her a too-extravagant present which she knew he could not afford.

Nell stares at nothing. Recently she's found that her mind keeps going back to the past, remembering how it was, and trying to work out how they got from how they were to how they are. But there's always a failure of logic, a gap she can't explain, and increasingly it's the then bit that she can't understand, not the now.

When she walked into the staffroom on her first day in Japan, he was sitting in an easy chair, smoking and reading the *International Guardian*. In a roomful of teachers preparing lessons at desks, he alone lounged. When the Assistant Director of Studies introduced her to the room, Alexander looked up from his paper and granted her a flash of smile, and she thought that his were the sort of extreme good looks that make men emotionally lazy. She said as much to Frances that evening as they consumed large quantities of Asahi Dry and became best friends. Don't be tempted, Frances told her, he's slept with half of Tokyo, and the other half leave little presents in his pigeonhole hoping he'll relieve them of their virginity in exchange for a box of heart-shaped chocolates.

They worked side by side for several months, never exchanging more than a word or two. Sometimes she would see him at a corner table in the noodle bar the teachers frequented at lunchtime, but she never took her bowl over and invited herself to share his table as she did with the crowd who became her friends. When they eventually got together, she asked him if he had fancied her before. Fancied? He gave her his mystified look, and did not answer the question. Would we have fallen in love if we hadn't bumped into each other on holiday, do you think? she persisted. I don't know. Would we?

*   *   *

Nell is so tired, she doesn't know if she has been asleep or just thinking.

'Mummy?'

The slight rise in the tiny voice indicates it's not the first time Lucy has called.

'Just coming,' Nell calls, jumping to her feet and feeling the adrenalin of fear pumping through her muscles, making her take the stairs two by two.

Lucy is sitting up with her shoulders hunched and her head bowed. Her breathing is laboured.

'I'll get your puffer.'

Nell shakes the Ventolin and fits it into the space-haler. Then Lucy puts the other end into her mouth.

'Ready?'

Lucy nods.

Four sharp squirts. The spacer rattles as Lucy breathes. Then she coughs and makes a face.

'I'll get you some apple juice in a minute to take the taste away.'

'Thanks, Mummy.'

'Are you all right?'

'Much better,' Lucy replies automatically. 'Where's Lizzy Angel?'

Nell picks up the rag doll from the floor and hands her over to Lucy reluctantly, wondering whether the doll may be the cause of the asthma attack. The consultant told her to hang soft toys in the sunshine regularly, or put them in the freezer overnight to kill the dust mites that Lucy's allergic to. But Lucy loves the doll and seems to have developed an almost telepathic attachment to her, so that whenever Nell is congratulating herself on managing to sneak Lizzy Angel out of her room and into a plastic freezer bag, Lucy will turn over and say, 'Where's Lizzy Angel? I can't go to sleep without her.'

Nell strokes Lucy's back, feeling the bones of her ribcage through her cotton pyjamas expanding then struggling to contract. She deliberates whether to give Lucy more antihistamine, while silently cursing herself for tempting fate by mentioning its apparent success to Alexander. Motherhood has made her superstitious.

Nell reads through the leaflet that came with the bottle of syrup. The effort of concentrating on the dancing words calms her down. DO NOT EXCEED STATED DOSE. The message couldn't be clearer but it doesn't say why. Nell knows that too much makes you drowsy, but now Lucy's awake and maybe it wouldn't hurt her to be drowsy? Or are there more dire consequences, like taking too much paracetamol? Maybe she should ring NHS Direct. The last time she did, they told her to take Lucy to Casualty, and she doesn't want to put her through all that again. Try to make her life as normal as possible, the consultant said.

Nell tries to observe dispassionately whether Lucy's breathing is improving, or whether she's just imagining it. She turns away from Lucy to get a sense of perspective and walks over to the window. Maybe it's just a mild attack and the reliever is working. Hold your nerve, she tells herself, drawing back the curtain. The unseasonally warm spring weather has brought the pollen bursting out early. If only the rain would come and wash it away. Try to make her life as normal as possible. What's normal about praying for rain at three in the morning, when you don't believe in God?

'I think I'm ready to go back to sleep now,' Lucy says. 'Will you hold my hand?'

Nell props up the child's pillows and switches off the bedside light. The mobile of fluorescent planets that Alexander bought her when they went to the

Science Museum recently glows feebly for a few minutes then fades.

Nell strokes Lucy's forehead. The salbutamol has worked, she notices. Her breathing is miraculously even now. Nell lies down on the floor next to the bed and takes the hand that has slipped out from under the cotton sheet.

Nell wakes up when something soft falls on her face. Its cross-stitch eyes stare silently into hers. Lizzy Angel. Nell's stiff from lying on the stripped wood floor. Her right arm, which she has been using for a pillow, has gone to sleep. The quality of the air tells her that rain has come and gone. A sudden awareness of silence alarms her. She sits up quickly. Lucy is sleeping peacefully.

Fear is a relatively new emotion to Nell and she finds it difficult to judge. Before Lucy's first admission to hospital, she had never been truly frightened. There was a ghost story they used to read at school at Christmas called 'Lost Souls' that gave her a shuddery feeling and made her look over her shoulder at night. She used to think that was what fear was. Now she knows that fear is a tiny body in the middle of the white hospital bed with a nebulizer mask over her face; fear is being totally powerless; fear is trying to maintain a calm, soothing façade while terrible, unthinkable thoughts tumble through your conscious mind. Sometimes Nell wonders if the shock of that first hospital visit actually altered her own brain chemistry, changing her personality from fundamentally easy going to fundamentally anxious. These days, she jumps at any unpredicted sound and leaps when somebody touches her if she is not expecting it.

Nell gets up, tiptoes to their bedroom. She almost trips on one of the shoes Alexander has casually dropped, as he does all his clothes, leaving a trail to the bed for her to collect up each morning like litter.

Nell drapes the peach dressing gown over a chair and slips in beside Alexander, curling her front round his warm back.

'Everything all right?' he murmurs as, still sleeping, he registers her presence.

'Fine,' she says, automatically.

Four

Alexander wonders if there comes a point in every relationship where the things you used to love about someone become the things you hate.

He watches Nell pretending to sleep. He knows that she's pretending because she's breathing heavily and deliberately. When she's really asleep, she makes no sound at all. The first few times they slept together, he used to take her pulse if he woke in the middle of the night, just to check that she was still alive.

He longs for her to sit up and shout at him, but she is not selfish enough to demand retribution for his behaviour last night. She knows that the sensible thing to do is to talk it all through over the weekend. He used to love her good sense. But now he wants to shout at her:

I don't know if I want to have another child.

I don't know what I'm doing with my life.

I don't know if I still love you.

Nell sighs and turns over like sleepers do in films. It's a silly situation, her pretending to sleep, him pretending not to know. He finds himself about to pretend to wake her to share the joke. But he does not, because if he does, they will have to have a proper conversation and he's terrified in case the bit about not knowing if he loves her comes out.

Maybe Nell doesn't know whether she loves him any

more, but he doesn't think so. Nell is able to voice problems and make it possible to continue afterwards. Come down this road with me, she says, it's dark and kind of scary, but I've got your hand, and at the end of it we may find something we really want. He's not so brave. He fears that if he says what he's thinking, there will be no future, and no way back, and he doesn't know if that's what he wants.

He doesn't plant the customary kiss on her temple in case she decides to open her eyes.

In the kitchen, he swigs from a container of orange juice, skips his usual bowl of cereal, makes a dash for the front door.

It has rained in the night and the air is colder but the washed-clean blue sky is bursting with sunshine. He finds his sunglasses in the inside pocket of his jacket and walks away from the house, plucking a dandelion clock from the hedgerow.

It is the sort of morning that makes you believe you can change.

Alexander walks into the cool entrance hall of the station as the train before his usual one pulls in. He makes an instant decision to go for it rather than stopping to buy a paper and a bar of chocolate for his breakfast.

As the train pulls out of the station, Alexander sits down in the last available seat. One or two people glance at him as if he's come to a party to which he wasn't invited. Nearly everyone is male, and dressed for the City. The man opposite him is wearing a navy pinstriped suit and though he is almost completely bald, there's dandruff on the slightly greasy collar. He looks at Alexander's khaki chinos, then back at a ringbound report he is reading.

If Alexander had been called upon yesterday to say

what colour the seats of his usual carriage were, or to describe the configuration of his fellow passengers, he knows that he would not have been able to. Now, sitting in a predominantly red compartment, he knows that his usual seat is blue, that it faces in the direction the train is going in, not backwards, like the one he's now in. His usual travelling companions are a middle-aged woman with a variety of large gilt earrings who tries occasionally to make conversation, a girl with orange streaks in her hair who touches up her make-up just before they reach Victoria, and, next to him, a younger man with a purplish birthmark on his right cheek, who has a portable CD player with headphones that rasp tinnily throughout the journey. Alexander feels their absence.

The only distinguishing mark of the man sitting beside him now is a chunky gold ring on his wedding finger; the rest of him is hidden behind the *Daily Telegraph*. Alexander takes in the headlines, then looks out of the window. Usually he sees the land-marks of the journey before the train has gone past not after, and it makes him feel a bit weird, as if he's on a slightly altered plane of reality.

A mobile phone rings. The electronic rendition of Beethoven's *Pastoral* is further down the carriage, but several people dive into their briefcases and pull out their handsets.

'I'm on the train,' says the owner loudly. 'It's on time . . .'

The words act as an automatic brake trigger. Immediately the train begins hissing and grinding to a halt. There's a collective intake of breath. The man who is speaking into the phone drops his voice guiltily. Then the train starts up again, and relief ripples through the carriage. Alexander looks at his hand and sees that he too has pulled his mobile phone from his pocket. The bald man opposite actually smiles at him, welcoming him to their club. Alexander looks from the phone to the bald man. He dials the number of the school and puts the phone to his ear.

Nobody's in yet. The answerphone clicks on. Alexander is about to cut off the call when he senses that the bald man is listening.

'It's Alexander. I'm not coming in today.'

As he cuts the call off, the phone bleeps. He looks at the screen: the message LOW BATTERY flashes. Alexander puts the phone back into his jacket pocket. It bleeps again. He takes it out again and, with a triumphant flourish, switches it off.

The train stops again on the bridge just before it reaches Victoria. The river is high and a strong breeze plucks waves from the glinting surface, making the silver water look as cool and inviting as the ocean. Alexander's fellow passengers fold their papers, close their laptops, neurotically click and unclick the locks on their briefcases. One or two stand up and make their way to the door so that they'll be first out. Eventually, the train heaves itself into the station. Alexander is the last to leave.

The station concourse smells of ground coffee. Alexander heads as usual for the entrance to the Underground, then remembers that he has given himself the day off. He doesn't know why he did that. The necessity of showing himself to be different from the other occupants of the carriage isn't so pressing now that he's not trapped with them, but since it's done, he's not inclined to change his mind. Why waste such a sunny day in the basement common room? He has no classes today, just a few reports to write, which he could stretch to fill the day, or do in half an hour on Monday morning.

If he goes home now, he will arrive back at about the

same time as Nell is returning from dropping Lucy at school. He pictures her face as she walks towards the house deep in thought, then sees him standing outside their front door. She shakes her head at him for forgetting his keys again, but pleasure shines through the mock-cross features, as she pushes the door open and lets them both in. But once they go into the house together, his imagination runs out. He doesn't know what happens inside.

Alexander's tummy rumbles and he remembers that he has not eaten breakfast. The smell of coffee and warm pastry beckons. He will treat himself to breakfast, and then go home.

He's the only person ordering coffee to drink in. He takes the cup and a plate with a pecan Danish on it to a table at the back. The top layer of fatty sugary pastry sticks to the still-tender roof of his mouth. The taste of the coffee flies him to Italy and then to the bar in Soho where he drank espresso yesterday. Quickly he drains his cup and leaves the rest of his Danish.

Outside on the concourse again, crowds of people are walking towards him looking uniformly fed up. For a moment, he feels accused, but then realizes that they're just making their way to the tube. He tries to push back through, knowing that he has less than a minute to catch the train.

A woman complains in a loud voice, 'I wouldn't mind if they kept you informed.' A man says, 'No trains until further notice, mate.' It's a second or two before Alexander understands that he's talking to him.

Near the empty platforms, a guard is writing in thick blue felt pen on a white noticeboard.

ALL TRAINS CANCELLED UNTIL FURTHER NOTICE.

'Why?' Alexander asks him.

'There's some trouble up the line,' the guard tells him.

Alexander sighs, then turns around and goes with the crowd. He is about to be washed down into the tube, when he glimpses blue triangles of sky between the scallops of the station awning. He wonders how long it would take him to walk to Charing Cross, where he'll be able to catch an alternative train.

The traffic's so loud it's a kind of torture, but as soon as he steps into St James's Park the noise level drops. He pauses for a moment, suddenly aware of his surroundings: the vibrant colours of the flowers, the random, melodious snatches of birdsong. He sits down on a bench. A couple of men in suits walk slowly past him. Civil servants, he thinks, or even MPs discussing affairs of state in low serious voices. A girl wearing running gear jogs past at the same time. Alexander pulls in his long legs to let her by and her smile is so white and orthodontic she can only be American. As he watches the small lime green knapsack between her shoulder blades bumping up and down into the distance, he wonders if the years of smiling a mouthful of metal were worth it for her. Or is the nervous eagerness to please which he caught in her eyes due to all that time lived as an unkissable teenager?

A man of about his age, maybe younger, approaches pushing a turquoise and navy Mamas and Papas pram. He sits down at the other end of the bench from Alexander, smiles, then takes a cigarette from the packet which is resting incongruously on the pale blue cotton cellular blanket and puts it to his mouth. He catches Alexander looking, picks up the packet and offers him one.

'No, thanks,' Alexander says quickly, and then, so that he doesn't appear to be disapproving, he asks, 'How old is he?'

'Four months.'

The man lights up.

'Your first?'

'Yeah. You got kids?'

'One girl. She's five.'

'S'great, isn't it?'

'When they're sleeping,' Alexander says, nodding at the baby who's lying on his back with his hands stretched up beside his head.

'Yeah, right,' says the man, blowing smoke out, and they both laugh.

Alexander feels a jolt of disloyalty to Lucy as he remembers the pure pleasure of watching her sleeping this morning, as peaceful and perfect as a baby, and the innocent smell of her skin as he bent and dropped a silent kiss just above her forehead.

Lucy is great. She's bright and she's gorgeous, and he loves the way she sticks her tongue out and over her bottom lip when she's trying to read, and he loves the paintings she does of herself, all fingers and toes, and he doesn't know why he's said he prefers her sleeping, or why he feels so beleaguered by his responsibility for her.

He glances at his bench companion who's drawing hard on his cigarette. You wouldn't be smoking if you really knew the risks, he thinks. He tries to think of a way of telling him without sounding sanctimonious, but he can't. His creeping sense of failure is like a cloud going over the sun, dulling everything.

Alexander gets up.

'See you,' he says to the new father.

'See you, mate,' the man calls cheerfully.

Instead of going out of the park at Admiralty Arch, Alexander decides to walk round again. He cannot face going home just yet.

He walks southwards past the edge of the lake, trying to make himself concentrate on the questions that are hovering around his head like persistent wasps round a picnic.

69

Question one: why was his instant reaction to the thought of another baby so hostile? Is it because he feels that he wasn't involved in the decision, or because he does not want to have another child? He thinks it is the latter, although he is still annoyed about the former because he thinks that Nell should have told him that there was a chance of conception. So, why doesn't he want another child? Is it because it would tie him closer to Nell, or because he doesn't want all the worry that goes with a child? If someone could guarantee that there would be no worry like they've had with Lucy, would he welcome the thought of the baby?

Does he still love Nell?

However logically and simply he poses the questions to himself, there are only more questions, and the same question. He tries to consider his situation from a more positive angle. What is it that he does want?

He wants to lie on a beach feeling warm sand between his toes. He wants to swim in pure underwater silence. He wants to sit in an unhurried Italian village square with benevolent sunshine on his face, and watch the world go by.

He wants what he had, and didn't imagine he would ever give up.

Alexander sits down on a bench in the shade of a tree. He puts his head in his hands. He takes a deep, deep breath, throws his head back. When he opens his eyes he is looking up through pink cherry blossom to blue, blue sky.

Five

'Daddy forgot his watch,' says Lucy, at the breakfast table. 'He was blowing the time with a dandelion clock.'

The thought of Alexander strolling down the road with a dandelion clock in his hand sends a leap of optimism through Nell's tummy.

'He forgot to wave,' says Lucy.

The image of Alexander mutates from carefree to preoccupied.

'He probably thought you were still asleep,' she says.

'I think you might be right,' says the five-year-old, thoughtfully, as she manoeuvres a spoonful of dry Cornflakes towards her mouth.

On the other side of the window, a bumble bee queen hovers just a couple of inches away from Nell's face. She remembers the day she viewed the house and rushed back to London. 'The air – it's like breathing honey!' she told Alexander as they ate dinner in the dark kitchen of the little house in Kentish Town that smelt of illness. 'It would be so good for us all!'

Nell stares at the bright lime green leaves and luminously pale blossom on the two old apple trees whose gnarled branches embrace above the drive. She knows quite a lot about the science of allergy now, but still she can't help thinking sometimes that it's a spell that turns beauty poisonous.

'Shall we do your antihistamine now?'

Nell dispenses 5 millilitres of clear fluid onto a plastic medicine spoon. Lucy takes it.

'Do you want to lick the spoon?'

Lucy laps at the clinging syrup with methodical seriousness and smiles. It's one of those moments that makes Nell feel like a proper mother. She recalls the sheer pleasure when her mother awarded her the cake spoon, the floppy floury taste of uncooked Victoria sponge, and the slightly rough softness of the damp wooden spoon against her tongue. It's one of the universal truths of childhood that licking spoons is a treat.

The father of Lucy's friend, Ben, jogs past the bottom of their drive. He smiles and waves, and then he's obscured again by the hawthorn. Nell finds herself staring at the cloudy haze of grasses in the hedgerow on the other side of the lane.

'I think I'll tell Mrs Bunting that you'd better stay inside at breaktime,' she says.

'Why?' Lucy asks, reasonably enough.

'Because I think the hay fever season is starting. I think that's why you were a bit wheezy last night. You see, there's a lot of pollen in the air from the blossom. You can't see it, but it gets up your nose and makes you sneeze a lot.'

'I see.'

Lucy is stoical, but it breaks Nell's heart to think of her sitting inside the classroom watching all her friends playing games outside without her. When they decided to move here she pictured herself and Lucy hand in hand, dancing down the country lane to school. The reality is that on summer days Lucy labours for every breath, and in the winter, the damp cold air seems to make her lungs seize up. They nearly always go by car.

All at once Nell says, 'Tell you what. It's such a

72

lovely day. Why don't we go to the seaside? We could go and see Frances.'

Frances has been back from Tokyo for nearly six months, she calculates. They've talked on the phone nearly every week, but they've yet to meet up.

'Frances, yippee! Who's Frances?' Lucy asks.

'She's an old friend.'

'How old? Is she very small, like Grandma? People get shorter when they get older, don't they, Mummy?'

'She's not really old. It just means I've known her a long time. Longer than Daddy, even.'

'What about school?' Lucy's half excited, half suspicious.

'Well, it is Friday. I'm sure Mrs Bunting wouldn't mind just one day.'

'I don't think Ben will miss me, do you?' Lucy asks.

When she asks a question in the negative, it always means the opposite.

'Not for one day. Anyway, we're going to tennis with him tomorrow morning.'

'Oh yes, that's right!' Lucy smiles with relief.

They're only five, but Ben and Lucy are a definite item. They've just got to the stage where they know it's uncool to hold hands at school. Boys now sit with boys and girls with girls in class. But they are not yet so grown up that they need to hide their love from their parents.

'Can I play on the beach?' Lucy asks.

'If it's warm enough.'

'Can Lizzy Angel come too?'

'If you remember not to lose her.'

Nell dials Frances's number. It rings and rings and Nell is cross with herself that she did not find out whether Frances was in before telling Lucy. She hates offering something and then having to withdraw it.

They'll go to the seaside anyway, she thinks. She's putting the receiver down when Frances answers.

'Bloody hell. What's the time?' says Frances groggily. 'Do people with children forget how nice sleeping is, or do they just get mean because they can't?'

'Lucy and I would like to come and see you.'

'And Lizzy Angel,' Lucy adds.

'Today?'

'Yes. Is it a problem?'

'I'm teaching this evening, but . . .'

'We'll be gone by then.'

'Fine . . . no, more than fine. Great . . . When are you setting off?'

'Now-ish,' says Nell, excitedly. 'See you then. Say, love you in the world to Frances.' Nell holds the phone in midair between herself and Lucy.

'Love you in the world!' Lucy shouts.

'Love you *in the world*?' Frances repeats.

'I used to tell her that I loved her the most in the world . . .' Nell explains, 'and her version kind of stuck.'

She's slightly embarrassed. Frances despises cuteness.

'Later!' she says, putting down the phone and smiling at Lucy.

'We're going to the seaside!' Lucy jumps up and down. 'Can I take my bucket and spade?'

'If we can find them.'

Nell steps into the garden. It doesn't get the sun until the afternoon and it's still chilly. Gingerly, she lifts the lid of the sandpit. There is a rime of green mould on last year's sand and on the handle of a spade that is peeping out of it, like a piece of modern sculpture. Alexander has not made his annual trip to the Early Learning Centre to buy fresh sand. Nell's eyes blur with tears. This is a neglected sandpit, she tells herself, not a metaphor for our relationship. Unhappiness makes you lend emotional weight to everything. Her mind revisits the blazing row she and Alexander had last week after she gave his mother's old rug to the dustmen. She shivers the memory away and puts the red plastic lid back.

The floor of Lucy's room is covered with every item of clothing she possesses, and Lucy is standing in her knickers, grey socks and school shoes.

'I don't know what to wear,' she says, shrugging like a much older person.

Nell kneels on the floor and begins to put everything back into the chest of drawers.

'How about these? I think Frances sent them to you last birthday.'

'How did she know it was my birthday?'

'I expect I told her.'

'Has Frances ever met me?'

'No.'

'Why?'

'Because she used to live on the other side of the world. But now she's home.'

Nell picks out a pair of faded jeans from Gap with flowers and butterflies embroidered on them.

I wish I was small enough to wear these, Frances's note had said.

'They're too big,' Lucy says. 'I expect she didn't know what size I was.'

'Try them. You've grown.'

Reluctantly, Lucy steps into the jeans. They're still loose but they stay up. Nell pulls a long-sleeved white T-shirt over her chest, then takes her into her arms and gives her a squeeze. Lucy's body is bony, like a bird's, but her hug surprises with the strength of her

75

affection. Suddenly Nell's excited about introducing her to Frances.

'I think you should get dressed too, Mummy.'

The almost adult concern for the propriety of things amuses Nell.

'I thought I'd go in my nightie.'

Lucy's face trembles between amazement and tears.

'Tricked you!' says Nell.

The child's gloriously disproportionate laughter gives her a belt of joy, and for one sweet moment, nothing else matters.

In the car, Nell likes to listen to Heart FM. She knows she ought to be listening to the *Today* programme, absorbing politics and literature and forming opinions about current issues, but she always chooses a bit of sentimental singing instead. On Heart FM, almost every track makes her remember some seminal moment of her life.

'I love this one!' she cries, as the DJ announces Hurricane Smith's 'Oh Babe, What Would You Say?'

She played it so repeatedly that her father actually confiscated it for a weekend and she sobbed in her room, bereft of Hurricane's blandishments, thinking she would die from missing him so much.

The DJ talks over the last few bars and says the date of the single. Nell calculates that she must have been nine, the age when you fall in love with a pop star. Now, she wonders why on earth he was called Hurricane, and as the thought surfaces, she can hear her mother's voice, the same all those years ago as it is today, saying, as if to offer proof of her vinyl lover's unsuitability, 'What sort of a name is Hurricane, anyway, darling?'

It's something she's noticed recently, that she's beginning to think and say things that have a small aftershock of déjà vu. She thinks it must be the first sign of middle age, but she feels too young to be middle-aged, much younger than she recalls her parents as being when she was young. She wonders whether they thought of themselves as young then, and whether deluding yourself that thirty-seven is still young is further proof of senescence.

'I'm Not in Love' is on the radio. It was at the top for weeks, Nell thinks, and it was always the last song at the youth club disco. Even then she found it a bit of a dirge, but now she wails along with the chorus, telling herself that she loves the words in an ironic way, until Lucy says,

'Stop that, please, Mummy.'

'When I was young, this was on *Top of the Pops*,' Nell explains.

'Where was I?' Lucy asks.

'You weren't born then.'

'Was I a baby?'

'No. Only later.'

'When I was a baby, did I cry a lot?'

'Not really,' Nell lies. She reaches her hand back and squeezes her child's knee. 'You were a good baby, and now you're a good little girl.'

'Was Lizzy Angel a baby?'

'No,' says Nell.

That seems to satisfy Lucy, who looks out of the window and says, 'I Spy fifteen horses in that field.'

She's getting ten points per horse.

'Fifteen? Did you count them?' asks Nell sceptically.

'One, two, three, four, five, six, seven, eight, nine, ten, eleven, twelve, thirteen, fourteen, fifteen!' Lucy races through the count even though they've long passed the horses' field.

'Oh well, that's a hundred and fifty points then,' says Nell, a little wearily.

When she invented the I Spy game with points, she didn't expect Lucy to cheat so unashamedly, and the target of a thousand for an ice lolly seemed an almost unimaginable score.

'Lizzy Angel saw a polar bear. How many points for a polar bear?'

'You don't get polar bears on the M23,' says Nell.

'Look!'

Sure enough there's a lorry overtaking them with a blue polar bear logo on its side.

Nell stares at Lizzy Angel in the rearview mirror, wondering how it is that a small doll with red wool for hair and a cross-stitched nose succeeds in unnerving her.

On the radio there's the unmistakable syncopated intro to Bowie's 'Let's Dance'. Nell turns the volume up, dancing from the waist up, as much as the confines of her seatbelt will allow.

When she was at university she must have danced to the song at a hundred discos, but the picture it produces in her mind is of Alexander. Alexander wearing a pair of red swimming shorts and a shirt with palm trees on, looking very brown, standing in the shadows of a bar, swigging beer from a bottle. His face is lit up every other second by the flash of gaudy Christmas lights. He raises his bottle in greeting.

Then Frances comes back from the bar with two bottles of beer, and says, 'Well, of all the bars in all the world . . .'

'Let's Dance' was one of the few discs that worked on the jukebox in the bar and it played over and over. They drank a lot of beer. She and Frances danced, drunk, prancing around exaggeratedly and laughing, with Nell half-aware of him watching them from the table, beer bottle in his hand. She stopped dancing, smiled at him, and something about the beat and

Bowie's voice and the smile Alexander gave her made it impossible to think of anything except going to bed with him.

'Why have you got a worried face?' Lucy asks.
    She's looking at Nell in the rearview mirror.
    'I haven't!'
    Nell makes her face bright.
    'I like it when you have a happy face,' Lucy says.

That was the beginning. Once she had seen Alexander's face relaxed, she couldn't remember how cool and disdainful he had looked before.
    That night, she lay awake under the palm leaf thatch of the beach hut, listening to Frances's beer-laden sleep, feeling as if she were somehow on the brink of something that might disappear if she were to close her eyes.
    The following day they had planned to go snorkelling together, but the boat was full, and two people had to stay behind. She and Alexander were the last two on and so they were the ones bumped off. Frances watched them as the little boat chugged out towards the reef, and Nell felt slightly treacherous, as if she had somehow engineered their separation.
    'What's Nell short for?' Alexander asked her.
    'Helen.'
    'Helen,' he repeated, making it sound like a special name. 'Did you know that Helen of Troy had flaxen tresses too?'
    He touched her hair.
    When the boat became a dot on the horizon, he said, 'So what shall we two do today, Helen?'
    We!
    They lay on the beach talking all morning, for lunch ate barbecued squid with their fingers, and in the

afternoon, they made love on the floor of his hut.

When the boat returned, they were waiting on the beach, holding hands.

'I thought this might happen,' Frances said.

'Did you?' Nell was astonished. 'Why didn't you say?'

And Frances laughed, drily.

Frances always knows more than other people.

'How long now?' Lucy's getting a bit restless in the back.

'Soon we'll be able to see the sea.'

When Nell thinks about that holiday, the pictures that go through her mind are of two people falling in love, talking, talking all the time. But she cannot hear what they are saying. And screwing, licking, penetrating, trying every imaginable position, laughing. But she cannot feel how it felt. It's as if she's watching a silent video of the two of them.

When she was three years old, she toppled off her tricycle into a bed of nettles and she has an image of herself sitting wailing on her mother's lap while her mother rubbed dark green dock leaves up and down her shins, but she cannot remember how the nettle stings felt, nor the sound of her howling. She knows that falling in love with Alexander was thrilling, surprising, terrifying, wonderful. She knows that she floated round in a state of amazement. She even has proof of their slightly delirious joy, recorded in the photograph that Frances took of them smiling over the top of a wedge of watermelon, but the memory has become two-dimensional. She cannot taste the cold sweetness of the watermelon, the charcoal strips of squid, the sea salt on her new lover's skin.

The car soars over the South Downs and the Pet

Shop Boys are singing 'Always on My Mind'. Nell wonders when it was that the experience of falling in love became a visual memory of it, devoid of touch and smell and sound. She switches the radio off and opens the window of the car to blow away her tears.

Six

In a white passage under Piccadilly Circus there's a notice every few yards saying: THESE PREMISES ARE UNDER CONSTANT CCTV SURVEILLANCE. But Alexander cannot see any cameras.

It feels more like a corridor in a hospital than a pedestrian tunnel. The floor is white, the walls are white and the exit is invisible from the entrance. He's the only person using it.

Alexander's walk becomes a silly strut, the soles of his shoes sticking slightly and squeaking against the shiny floor. Somewhere in the building above there must be a tiny room filled with television screens. He imagines a bored security operative alerted by the sight of a man on the monochrome monitor doing a chicken walk. He stops abruptly as a woman in a navy suit walks past him determinedly not making eye contact in case he's got violent tendencies.

Three men are playing fruit machines in the entertainment arcade inside the Trocadero mall. Alexander wonders whether they wake up in the morning intending to do half an hour's nudge 'n' collect before work, or whether they are seduced by the bright lights and the static sense of time that this place with no natural light delivers. At nine o'clock this evening, it will look no different from now.

In adjacent theatres on Shaftesbury Avenue, *Brief*

Encounter is playing alongside *The Graduate*. Were the plays created from the films, or were they plays originally? He's not sure. He tried to recall the last time he went to the theatre, but it's so long ago, he cannot remember what he saw.

He's about to go into Starbucks when he sees a small group of foreign students sitting by the window. A Japanese girl he thinks he recognizes from Mel's class is approaching her friends balancing a muffin on a plate and with a small Louis Vuitton rucksack strung halfway between her wrist and elbow. Unwilling to risk a conversation with a student, Alexander does an about-turn and crosses the road, hurrying up a side street where every doorway reeks of urine.

The girl at the front of a peep-show yawns. She's still wearing last night's make-up, a powdery coat of flesh-coloured paint that's scuffed a little. Looking in the strip of mirror that runs from the ceiling to the floor, she applies a slick of blood red lipstick, kisses a tissue, and tucks it into the sleeve of the tight fake leopard T-shirt. When her eyes meet Alexander's, she makes a what-you-gawping-at face, and he quickens his step, alarmed that he's been staring at her.

He walks into the wrong bar first. It's like a mirror of Marco's. The counter is down the wrong side and there's a plate of glazed custard tarts on top of the glass cabinet. The woman at the till has long black hair and a haunted, high-cheekboned look that he associates with Portuguese people. He says sorry, and walks out leaving her bewildered.

Marco is bent over a copy of *Corriere del Sport*. He looks up as Alexander comes in. Alexander says 'Buon giorno!' The old man repeats the greeting but does not give the impression of recognizing him.

'Per cortesia, un caffé!' says Alexander. He's pleased with the accent that comes rolling out of his mouth after so little use.

'One coffee coming up!' says the Italian, and there's a trace of something, offence possibly, or boredom, in his refusal to converse in his native tongue.

Alexander takes the small cup of espresso to a table at the back of the bar and sits down on the chair facing the door. He doesn't have a newspaper to read, and now that he's here, he doesn't want to leave for a second to pop out to a newsagent in case he misses her. Alexander's eyes travel around the bar testing if he can remember all the Italian football teams by their flags. He reads the menu that's painted on a blackboard, matching the written descriptions with the domes of sandwich filling arrayed in the glass cabinet. He wonders whether Marco washes up each oval stainless steel dish every night, and how much of the mayonnaise-bound filling is thrown away. He speculates about the sort of person who would choose a chicken escalope for their sandwich, cold and hard in its fried breadcrumb coating. After a while, he becomes aware of a clock ticking but he cannot see where it is.

A woman wearing a leather skirt comes in and orders a decaffeinated *latte* to go. A couple of builders, their overalls stiffened with cement dust, follow her in, bringing with them the smell of old bricks and recently extinguished cigarettes. One orders bacon and sausages, the other a fried egg sandwich. They sit down at the table nearest to Alexander. The woman takes her styrofoam cup of coffee and leaves. One of the men makes a joke about her bottom in a voice that's loud enough to include Alexander. He can feel them exchanging looks when he doesn't join in.

A crowd of Italian students arrives. Not from his

school. They scrape the tables together and take every available seat, including the one opposite Alexander without asking his permission. He wonders why it is that students always seem to swear more and talk louder in their native tongue when they're in a foreign country. Is it the sheer freedom of being away from home, or the collective bravura of a minority? Alexander can see that Marco, flustering up and down the counter trying to fill their orders, is irritated by their vulgarity.

The workmen wipe their plates with slices of white bread. A great fug of Marlboro Lights rises from the Italians.

Alexander doesn't know whether he's been in the café for five minutes or half an hour.

He has not experienced the agony of waiting for a girl to turn up since the humiliation of his non-date with Mandy Kominski.

Mandy was in his year and generally acknowledged as the prettiest girl in the school. It was almost an anticlimax when she immediately accepted his offer to meet for coffee after he'd spent four weeks getting up the courage to ask her. The arrangement was the Cosmo on Finchley Road at eleven o'clock on a Saturday morning. It was an unfortunate choice of venue because in those days the Cosmo had two parts: a coffee bar with its own door, and a much more expensive restaurant beside it.

Alexander arrived on time, arranged himself at a table in the coffee bar and pretended to read Stendhal. He waited, ordered a coffee, waited, drank a coffee, waited, ordered a coffee. When she hadn't turned up after three coffees, he paid and left, but as he was walking past the window of the restaurant bit, he saw her sitting inside studying the menu, determinedly not looking up. He daren't go in and explain what had happened because he'd already spent most of his money. He couldn't afford to buy lunch, certainly not in there, and he didn't think he could endure the knowing looks of the middle-aged waiters who served in both sides of the establishment. So he walked away.

On Monday morning Mandy turned her back on him by the lockers.

'I waited half an hour,' he said, 'but you didn't turn up.'

'No, I decided it was a stupid idea,' she told him, tossing her recently hennaed hair.

The sharpness with which she turned his clumsy excuse to her own advantage shocked him, and made him wary of girls who knew that they were gorgeous.

He feels a similar embarrassment now, a similar hollowness that Kate has failed to show, even though they have no arrangement.

One of the Italian girls screeches that it's time for class. They all scrape back their chairs again and pay and leave. The café's empty again.

Alexander considers his options. It's still early. If he goes home now, he can use the day he has given himself to tidy up the garden for summer. He can have lunch with Nell. He'll pick up a carton of soup and some fresh rolls from the organic shop on his way back. They will talk about the new baby. Nell will soothe away his worries.

He can see them sitting together at the kitchen table, smiling at each other. Nell takes his hand, says they've got hours till Lucy comes home. There's a hint of suggestion. He rattles through some lame protest about how he was just enjoying talking, but she asks in her quiet little hurt voice, why? What's the problem? Why did you come home early anyway? Why did you take the day off? What's going on?

He says nothing and they're back at where they were yesterday evening, in thick and oppressive silence.

Easier just to go into work late.

Marco is clearing tables. When Alexander goes up to pay he calls to a younger man who has been making toast at the back. Alexander's missed the opportunity to ask whether Kate's been in. The younger man wipes his hands on a teacloth that's tied around his middle and says in a surly voice, 'Eighty pence.'

Alexander's about to hand over a pound coin when he hears himself saying, 'Can I have a cappuccino to take away?'

The man slams the drawer back into the till and prepares the cappuccino with spoon-clattering hostility.

'One pound eighty,' he says, snapping a top onto the styrofoam cup and causing a small eruption of milk foam stained with cocoa powder through the tiny hole in the lid. Alexander picks it up and walks out into the sunshine.

It's good to be in the air, amid the smells and sounds of a city preparing for work. So much better than the stifling insulation of the tube where every morning he stands with his hands clamped to his sides trying to protect himself from any intruding sensation. Perhaps he should walk from Victoria every fine day. It wouldn't take longer than forty minutes if he took a direct route, and the exercise would do him good.

In the distance a church clock strikes nine. Counting the chimes makes Alexander feel oddly nostalgic.

The shop windows in the street he has chosen to take are full of baubles and gaudy trimmings for evening gowns. The signs say RETAIL ONLY. Mandy Kominski's uncle was in the rag trade, and her father owned a bagel factory. How weird that his mind has secretly stored a file on Mandy Kominski for twenty years which, now that he's opened it, is relentlessly downloading pages of useless information. He wonders what Mandy is doing now. Married. Probably to somebody very rich. Living in a great big detached house in Golders Green. A couple of children have thickened her and her naturally dark eyes and full lips are exaggerated with expensive make-up. She's probably wedded to the fetishistic routines that incipient middle age seems to demand. Aerobics class and facial once a week, highlights every couple of months, teeth re-enamelled. Each little imperfection patched up before the next crack appears. He wonders why he still feels hurt when he thinks of her when all she did to him was wait in the wrong part of the restaurant.

What would his life have been like now if they'd both been sitting in the café part of the Cosmo? If he'd pushed open the heavy glass door and said, 'Hey! I'm here. I've been waiting for you next door!'

Would he and Mandy still be together? Would he be any less uncertain about life today? Would they be happy?

Strange to think how one tiny action might have changed everything.

Alexander stares at the styrofoam cup in his hand.

If Kate had come into Marco's just now he would have pretended that he had bumped into her again, but it wouldn't have been chance, because he deliberately went there to try to bump into her.

What is the difference between that sort of pre-meditated chance encounter, and actually seeking her out?

Is there in fact any moral difference at all?

Seven

Kate has learned to distinguish between the noises and smells that waft in through the gap between the sill and the sash window which sticks at about three inches open however hard you push it up. She's lying awake in the near-dark room like a blind person creating pictures of the street below from sounds: the sigh of the bin lorry lifters, the cabbage whiff of rot, the clank of market stall poles, the Christmassy scent of a just-squashed orange.

The Italian shop on the corner is getting its delivery of bread. Brakes hiss, there's a snatch of news as the driver opens the door of the cab, bolts shunt and tailgate bangs down. The smell of new bread lingers on the air for a moment, so deliciously evocative it almost satisfies Kate's morning hunger.

Marie's half of the bed is empty. She left before the streets woke up, the tap of her heels echoing down the alley, the boudoir scent of Chanel's Allure trailing behind her.

Kate's been half awake since then. The tip of her nose is cold. The crispness of the air makes her feel as if she should be up and about, but there's always a time after waking when she's stranded between the pulse-accelerating recognition that she's hovering right over the heart of the city, and the paralysing thought that she should not be here.

She snuggles her shoulders down and lies in a warm cocoon of quilt, attempting to delay her return to the real world.

As soon as her eyes close, there are pictures of him: his face with the golden river behind, his expression as she says something stupid, a wince that lifts into his smile. The soft adhesion of his kiss remains on her lips like an invisible Post-It note, the uncertainty in his eyes imprinted on her mind.

Enough.

The scab on Kate's knee is tight and sore as she gets out of bed. She grabs her keys, a Dettox spray, and a roll of toilet paper from the shelf by the door. The toilet, on the next floor down, is shared by three of the bedsits. Each has a key. The girls keep it pretty clean, but Kate always uses disinfectant before she sits. The coldness of the seat against the back of her thighs makes her feel real again. Right. Now, on with life. She flushes the toilet with resolve.

Back in the flat, she pulls off her T-shirt and knickers and stands in the bath scrubbing away her fantasies. The draught from the window puckers her skin into goosebumps. She wraps herself in a towel and throws back the duvet, denying herself the temptation of a quick five minutes to get warm again. Then she crouches over the side of the bed, pulls out her suitcase and takes out her *A-Z*.

She has found that the only way to deal with London is methodically. She makes herself do something educational each day in the same way that she makes herself eat a piece of fruit. If you don't have rules then you forget, and a week can fly by without vitamin C or culture, and that's a waste. She walks her fingers along the streets from Soho to Bloomsbury wondering if there's time to make a start on the British Museum before her shift begins. She's been saving the

British Museum, and the longer she puts it off, the more daunting its huge sooty columns seem to become.

The art galleries are taking longer than she expected. She'd allocated a week for the National, but it's different when you're a paintbrush's length away from a picture, standing where Vincent Van Gogh stood, thinking about what was going on in his head. She wonders why he was so angry with everyday things, even sunflowers. Marie says it's just a bunch of flowers in a pot, but they worry Kate with their mad spikes.

She can't concentrate on more than two paintings before work, and sometimes she goes back to the same ones again. There are still vast dark rooms where she has not even set foot.

She's got the weird feeling that she might step through the forbidding portals of the British Museum and never come out.

As Kate kneels on the floor to put back the *A-Z*, a searing soreness straightens her up: the scab has split and is oozing watery blood. She grabs the toilet roll and tries to pull off a sheet with one hand, but it will not break and she ends up with a roughly torn streamer of tissue. She's annoyed with herself: her wound was healing fine and now she's going to have to get a plaster because she tore her trousers yesterday and her only alternative, since Tony doesn't like them to wear jeans to work, is a skirt, and, as Marie would say, you can't accessorize that with a wodge of pink toilet paper. A packet of plasters will cost over a pound of her budget, which means that she's going to have to swap her usual strong cappuccino at Marco's for a cup of Marie's Nescafé. That hit of caffeine is the only expensive addiction she's managed to develop since arriving in London.

Kate fills the electric kettle angrily, plugs it in

angrily, and angrily waits for it to boil. Then she thinks of Vincent Van Gogh. If he were alive today, perhaps he'd paint a furious toaster or a bad-tempered kettle. She'll have to tell Marie. And Marie will say, as she always does, 'Isn't he the one who cut off his ear? No bloody wonder he was angry.'

Kate sniffs the T-shirt she was wearing last night. The armpits are fine, but it smells like a pub. She bends down again and pulls out a clean black T-shirt, then fumbles around in the suitcase for clean underwear, but there isn't any and there's nothing she hates more than keeping on last night's knickers. She wonders if Marie would mind, just this once, if she borrowed something. They don't usually share clothes, even though they're the same height.

She approaches Marie's chest of drawers slightly apprehensively.

The top drawer contains a pair of handcuffs, a blindfold, a feather boa and a stripy school tie. Kate remembers Marie asking her to send down the tie a year or so ago, telling some lie about fancy dress. She wonders why Marie didn't buy herself a school tie in London. Did she want to make some sort of statement, the ultimate two-fingered salute to the convent? Underneath, swathed in a soft plastic dry cleaners' film, there's a very short black puff-sleeved dress with a frilly white apron attached. It's a maid's outfit, Kate realizes, imagining what Tony would think if she turned up to work in that. She pulls it out and holds it up against herself. Very short. At the bottom of the drawer is a blue and white striped dress and a flat white hat with a red cross on it. A nurse's uniform. It looks as innocent as a child's costume from the Early Learning Centre.

The other drawer is crammed with lingerie, shiny and colourful like a box of Quality Street chocolates.

The first evening Kate arrived in London, she was unpacking her things on the bed when Marie announced, 'I'd give you a drawer, but they're full of my work clothes.'

Everything of Kate's had to go back into the suitcase under the bed.

'Make sure you don't leave your stuff lying around,' Marie instructed.

No ordinary cotton knickers allowed here.

Kate pulls out bras and suspenders in purple and red and gold, all trimmed with black lace. Flamingo pink satin camiknickers with lacing up the back, a body in black rubber that smells of bin liners and talcum powder. She fingers a teddy the colour of milk chocolate with coffee lace shoulder straps, pulls it out of the drawer and holds it against herself, then, with a quick look over her shoulder, she lets the damp towel drop to the floor, and steps into the garment.

The fabric feels fragile against her skin: it's real silk, because there's the slightest catch against the pads of her fingers as she smoothes her hands down her ribcage.

Kate takes the small mirror off the wall and, holding it at arm's length, twists and bends to see sections of her body. The knicker bit is like loose shorts around her thighs. She thinks how nice it would be to walk around all the time with air blowing around down there and the light brush of silk. She holds the mirror behind her, hooking one finger under the lace edge to expose a curve of buttock.

The entryphone buzzes. Kate picks up the handset. It's impossible to hear anything over the static, but it's probably Marie who's too lazy to get out her keys, so she buzzes her in and starts to stuff the lingerie back into the open drawer. There seems to be more of it now, and the drawer won't close properly. Marie's going to be cross that she's tried stuff on. As the footsteps grow closer, Kate jumps back into bed and pulls the quilt up to her chin.

The footsteps are much heavier than Marie's.

It's a man.

One of Marie's clients?

The bloke who collects the rent and always looks as if he wants a little bit more than the notes her sister hands over?

Kate decides to keep quiet and pretend there's no-one there.

But he'll know because she buzzed him in.

She can't see from the bed whether she fastened all the locks on the door when she came back in from the toilet.

The footsteps stop outside.

Her heart's thumping in her chest.

'Kate?'

His voice!

She must be imagining it.

'Kate?'

It is him.

Kate climbs out of bed and, wrapping the bath towel around her chest like a sarong, tiptoes across the room to the door.

'I wondered if you'd like a coffee.'

His voice is louder now. He hasn't heard her cross the room. She puts her ear to the door. He's so close, she can hear his accelerated breathing after the climb.

'I'm not dressed,' she whispers.

It's not the first thing she thought she'd say if they ever met again.

There's a long silence.

A waft of scalded milk carried on an invisible wisp of steam finds a way through the keyhole to her nostrils.

'Shall I go?'

'No!' She opens the door a little, keeping her body behind it. 'No, don't go,' she says, trying to make her voice a bit calmer.

He's wearing a loose khaki shirt today, and ironed chinos. He has his jacket hooked over his shoulder by the index finger of his left hand. With his dark hair, he could be a South American revolutionary who's made a bit of an effort for Mass, or something.

'I wondered if you'd like to go for another walk . . .' he says.

His eyes don't meet hers.

'My shift starts at eleven,' she tells him.

What's wrong with her? Here he is, her fantasy materialized in front of her, cappuccino and everything, and she's doing her best to put him off.

'I thought it was Marie. You can't hear anything through this.' Kate picks up the entryphone to demonstrate. He bends his head forward slightly to listen to the crackle.

'I could have been anyone,' he says.

'Lucky you weren't.'

Then his eyes meet hers. Whatever it is between them shifts from chance encounter towards something else.

She looks down.

'You haven't got a coffee for yourself,' she says, a little suspiciously, opening the door a fraction more.

'I've already had one.'

'D'you want another?'

'Great.'

Neither of them moves.

She pulls the door open, still hiding behind it in her towel.

'Hello,' he says, stepping into the room, looking around as if he's never been here before.

'Hello.'

She closes the door behind him. He offers her a styrofoam cup with a lid on it. She takes it with the hand that's not holding onto the towel, then loops round past him keeping as far away as possible. At the other end of the room, she flicks the switch on the kettle and turns on the radio to try to make things a bit more normal.

The chirpy voice of Chris Tarrant fills the air. She wishes Marie would have it tuned to something else, like Classic FM. He's not a Capital kind of guy. He sits down on the sofa by the door, long legs stretched out in front of him.

'Why don't you get dressed?' he says. 'I won't look.'

Still holding the towel around her, she crouches by the bed and pulls out her suitcase again.

The black T-shirt, with the black skirt. They're both clinging cotton. They won't look right over the loose silk teddy, but she doesn't want to be changing her underwear with him in the room.

The kettle steams and switches itself off. She stands up, still wearing the towel, spoons Nescafé into a pink cup, then pours on hot water.

'There's no milk,' she tells him. 'No fridge, see. We used to keep one of those little half-pint cartons on the windowsill, but a pigeon knocked it off. We could hear all this shouting downstairs, and Marie's pissing herself laughing and trying to get the bloody window up to have a better look, but it won't move . . .'

She rattles the window to demonstrate.

'I like it black,' he says.

He gets up and walks across the room.

He's behind her.

'My Love Won't Cost a Thing' blares out of the radio.

His face moves closer to her neck.

Kate freezes.

He puts one arm each side of her and tries to heave the window up. It won't budge.

She's gripping the towel so hard across her chest, her knuckles hurt.

His arms drop back to his side.

She turns round.

'Here's your coffee,' she says, pointing at the steaming mug on the table.

'I don't know what I'm doing here,' he says, stepping back.

'Nor do I.'

That didn't come out like she wanted it to.

Suddenly Kate can't bear the music any more. She switches the radio off. The silence is almost more embarrassing than the song.

'I shouldn't have come,' says Alexander.

'No, it's fine.'

Her head is empty of all vocabulary.

'I'll think of something to say in a minute,' she tells him.

When he smiles it's like you can't imagine where the preoccupied person has gone.

'I'd better be off,' he says.

'No, don't go!' she says, reaching out to grab his arm as he turns to leave. The damp towel drops to her feet.

They both look at it. Then his eyes trail slowly up her body from her bare feet to the silk teddy to her shoulders, her face.

'Jesus, you're beautiful,' he says.

Did he really say that? She's so busy trying to work out whether she heard it right, and if she should say something in return, that she almost forgets to experience the moment. She's trembling so much inside, she can't believe that her limbs appear perfectly still. She can feel her flesh puckering against the caress of gossamer silk lingerie and his gaze.

She goes to pick up the towel, but he catches her hand, and stands holding it, an arm's length away from her, as if she's just curtsied and they're about to begin a formal dance.

'I don't know what I'm doing here,' he says again.

'I don't normally wear this kind of thing . . .' she blurts out. Her voice comes out sounding offended.

How ridiculous she must look to him, semi-naked in a tart's apartment protesting innocence.

'Why?' he asks, nodding at her body.

'I was just trying out what it's like being a different person,' she says.

He thinks about that for a long time, pushing his hands back through his thick dark hair, looking round the room at the pink bath, the oppressive red and gold carpet, the tented bed. Then a little laugh comes out of his mouth, even though he's not smiling.

'So, how does it feel?' he says.

She smiles at him.

'Good,' she says.

He moves a fraction closer to her.

'It's not real, this, is it?' he asks.

'Isn't it?'

He stretches out his hand, touches a coffee lace shoulder strap, snatches his hand away as if from a flame.

Her skin is so taut and goosebumpy it's like it's clinging to her bones.

'You're cold,' he says.

'Yes.'

As if it's the most natural thing in the world, he folds her in his arms.

Her face is against his chest. She breathes his smell that's fresh and unexpectedly innocent, like soap powder and steam irons.

She presses herself against him, trying to speak with

her body. There's no reaction. She looks up into his eyes, trying to ask without saying anything, what, what do you want me to do?

He pulls away, and, still holding her hand, leads her to the bed.

He unties his shoes and slips them off, then puts his arms around her and pulls the quilt up over them both. He's still fully clothed. He's breathing into her hair. She can feel the heartbeat in his chest against her cheek. In her head so many questions are jostling, she thinks he must be able to hear them. One of her arms is wedged under her. She knows it's going to get pins and needles soon and then she'll have to shift position and destroy this moment. She doesn't know what to do with the other arm. It's just there. She doesn't know whether to touch him, or to leave him alone. She's got the man of her dreams in bed with her, and she doesn't know what to do.

One floor down and two along the saxophonist from the jazz club blows his first arpeggio of the day.

Alexander sighs.

'When I was a child,' he says, shifting a little and propping up pillows behind him, 'I used to have a carpet on the floor of my bedroom. It was a Persian rug with flowers and birds on it, and intricate patterns, like mazes that you could trace with your finger but you always got lost. It had this very distinctive smell of old dust and souks, and sometimes, when my mother was downstairs working, I used to lie lulled by the rhythm of her typing, and fly away to exotic lands . . .'

He gazes up at the bright strips of shiny tenting.

'This feels a bit like that.'

Kate pulls out her arm from under her and shakes it to get the blood flowing again.

'I used to go to the library,' she says. 'Not the

children's bit, the grown-ups' bit, 'cause it was quiet up there. Like, there'd be a few smelly old blokes, but mostly it was empty except for a few kids like me who didn't have anywhere quiet at home. It's a different kind of quiet you get in a library, isn't it? Everyone's concentrating so much on being quiet, you can sort of feel the quietness like a presence around you.'

Quiet, quiet, quiet. She tries to think of another word. Why can't she just shut up?

'. . . In winter, there's the hum of the fan heaters and after a while you forget you're reading, and you're there, right in the story, you know. You're not asleep, but when they say it's closing time, it's like being woken up . . .'

She stops, mid-flow, forgetting how she got on to prattling on about her grimy local library, when he was telling her about his beautiful carpet. Her brain must have made the connection with the *Arabian Nights* or something.

'What sort of books did you like?' he asks.

'All the old ones, you know, with children who have to look after themselves because they're orphans, or something terrible's happened. My favourite was E. Nesbit. What do you think the E. stands for?'

'Don't know. Didn't she write *The Railway Children*?'

'Yes, but I liked *The Story of the Amulet* best.'

There's a long silence. Why didn't she just agree with him? Yes, *The Railway Children*, and leave it at that.

She wishes she had some idea of what he's thinking about but she can't think of a subtle way of asking him.

'Sounds like a lovely day outside,' she says, finally.

She can't believe she's resorted to talking about the weather.

He turns his head so that he's looking at her face.

'Sounds?' he repeats, smiling.

'The market men were whistling this morning. They only whistle when it's sunny,' she explains.

'And when it's raining?' he wants to know.

'Lorry tyres on wet streets sizzle like sausages dropping into really hot fat,' she says, 'and the air smells like a flower shop.'

He thinks about that for a moment.

'You're right,' he says.

'You have to close your eyes,' she says, urging him to join in, 'and empty your mind and concentrate on what you can hear and smell.'

She watches his beautiful face relax to her command. He says nothing.

She lies back with her head next to his on the pillow.

'Two pounds of bananas for a pound,' she says, repeating a distant market trader's call.

'Banana,' he corrects. 'London fruiterers always use the singular.'

'Lovely bit of grape,' she says, with her best impersonation of a cockney accent.

They lie, side by side, flat on their backs, listening to the street below.

'Charcuterie,' Alexander says finally.

'That kind of cold, smoky salami smell? It's the Italian deli at the corner.'

'Have you had breakfast?' he asks.

'I've got to go to work,' she says.

She sits up and takes the lid off her cappuccino. She knows it's gone ten o'clock because that's when the peep-show two doors up the alleyway opens and the girl on the door likes to listen to Liberty Radio. She can hear the unmistakable tinkling of 'Chiquitita' filtering up.

'Take the day off,' Alexander says.

'I can't.'

Already she's trying to think of a good excuse to tell Tony.

Does he mean it?

'I did,' Alexander says.

'You just took the day off?'

'Yes,' he says.

'Why?'

'Because it's spring. The sky is blue . . . I wanted to see you again.'

Her body is filling up with pleasure, as if pleasure's liquid.

'What if I hadn't been in?' she can't stop herself asking, trying to contain her excitement. Why can't she just keep quiet like he does? Surround herself with a bit of mystery?

'I suppose I'd have tried the restaurant,' he admits.

'Were you thinking about me all night?' she blurts out.

'No,' he says, smiling at her, putting his forefinger under her chin and tilting her disappointed face towards him, 'just this morning.'

She feels silly now.

'Where would you most like to have breakfast?' he asks.

He's used to getting what he wants, she thinks.

She doesn't know if he means now, or in an ideal world.

'Selfridges,' she says, which covers both options.

'Selfridges?'

His head drops back and he gives her this look, as if he's amazed and a bit amused.

'I could live in Selfridges,' Kate explains. 'Sometimes I think I'll just hide behind a sofa or something when the shop closes and stay there all night.'

He's clearly not keen on the idea.

'There's loads of free food in the Food Hall,' she encourages.

'Free food?'

'I go there on my days off, when I don't get a meal at work.'

'Let me take you somewhere nice,' he says, sitting up.

'What's wrong with Selfridges?'

'I haven't been there since I went to see Father Christmas,' he protests.

'You'll love it. On the fourth floor there's this—'

She stops herself.

'What?' he asks.

'Surprise!' she says.

'What?'

'You'll have to come and see.'

She can be good at getting what she wants too.

Eight

'Rough night?' Frances asks.

Nell hugs her, then stands back and they look at each other.

'I like the hair,' Nell says.

'You must be Lucy,' says Frances.

'Yes, I am.'

Lucy makes her way cautiously down the steep steps to Frances's door then clatters past them down the passageway, into the kitchen and out through the open french windows and into the little well of garden at the back.

It's like the courtyard of a Roman house glimpsed from a hot dark street, with pots and baskets of flowers and the slightly echoey drip of water. Lizzy Angel inspects each terracotta pot.

'These aren't very pretty,' she says in her doll's voice, which is curiously reprimanding and refined.

'They're herbs,' says Frances, following her outside.

'What a lovely garden,' Nell says. 'It's like having another room.'

'Small, you mean.'

'But perfectly formed,' Nell says, sitting down at the kitchen table.

The flat has the mustiness of basements. It feels and smells like a student rental. The kitchen floor is covered in battered old carpet, spotted with indeterminate spillages round the cooker. These are things that Nell notices since she has had Lucy.

'You look as if you haven't slept,' Frances says.

'I didn't, much. It was so muggy.'

'Coffee?'

'Could I have tea? Or a long drink? Perhaps a long drink.'

Frances looks at her suspiciously.

'Anything the matter?'

'No!'

It's as if they haven't seen each other for six days, not almost six years.

Nell's slightly alarmed at how well Frances knows her. She's grown used to being able to hide what she's really thinking.

For a moment, she wishes she'd stayed at home.

Frances snips open a carton of apple juice.

'It's not cold. Do you want ice?'

'Yes, please, if you've got some.'

Frances opens the fridge, pulls the handle of the freezer compartment unsuccessfully, then takes a knife from the wire draining tray and begins to stab at the bulge of ice that's growing around the freezer door.

Nell can't help noticing that the fridge contains just four items: a full bottle of Sauvignon Blanc, an almost empty bottle of salad dressing, the distinctive orange rind of a wedge of Port Salut cheese, and half an avocado whose flesh has gone dark grey.

'Don't worry about the ice,' she says.

Frances is kneeling on the floor now, chiselling with determination. 'It's no problem,' she says.

Nell points at Frances's hair.

'So, how long have you been . . . ?'

She wants to say aubergine, because that's what the colour reminds her of, but it's more red than purple.

'Scarlet and Black?' Stab, stab, stab.

'Exactly.'

'It's a great name, isn't it? It was the name that I went for.' Frances pauses, wipes the back of her hand across her forehead.

'Suits you.'

Nell's not being entirely truthful. It is a strong colour, a very Frances sort of colour, but it makes her friend's face look paler and older than she remembers.

'Jesus!'

A glacier of frost suddenly breaks away from the bottom of the freezer compartment and falls onto the scraps of food on the top shelf. Frances chucks the lump of ice into the sink, picks up the avocado, looks at it as if it's a party guest she has found on her sofa the morning after and can't quite recognize, then throws it into the bin.

She extracts the reluctant tray of ice from the freezer and plops two cubes into Nell's glass.

'Do you want some juice, Lucy?' she calls into the garden.

'Yes, please,' Lucy replies from behind a giant flowerpot of pink hydrangea.

'Apple juice OK for her?' Frances asks.

'Fine, but no ice,' Nell says quickly. She's alarmed at having to consume such ancient ice herself. It tastes of fridge. She doesn't want Lucy's stomach to have to deal with it.

Frances makes herself a cup of strong instant coffee in a mug she has cursorily rinsed under the cold tap, sits down, takes a cigarette from the packet of Silk Cut on the table, puts it in her mouth, sees Nell's face, then puts it back into the packet.

'I found grey,' Frances says mournfully. 'Have you found grey yet? God, it's a horrible moment. You're brushing away and suddenly you see it, and then you don't, so you think it's the light, but there it is again, so you pull it out and it's not just grey, it's white and it's kind of coarse too. How does that happen? I mean, one minute you've got normal brown hair, split ends, yes, so, three Hail Marys and an Alberto VO5 hot oil treatment, but now, your hair's actually mutating in front of your very eyes, I'm not kidding . . .'

Frances's voice becomes more earnest as Nell begins to laugh.

'The next day there's another one, and after a while you're stopping in front of every mirror you encounter, and I'm not just talking mirrors, I'm talking all reflective surfaces. Once you've found yourself ducking your head neurotically backwards and forwards to get a better look in your dinner cutlery' – she picks up the knife she was chiselling the freezer with and demonstrates – 'you know it's time to dye. I don't know why I'm telling you this, you bloody natural blonde . . .'

'Not quite so natural any more,' Nell says, offering her own vanity up in return for Frances's confession. 'My hair went mousy during pregnancy, and I now have a half head of highlights every three months.' She picks up a few strands of her shoulder-length fair hair.

'How refreshingly vain of you,' Frances says, 'you're normally so casually beautiful, which, I have to tell you, has made me almost hate you ever since we met.'

Nell knows she's joking and not joking. Frances is honest about things that other people keep to themselves, like envy, vanity, and the overwhelming compulsion to sing along to Tammy Wynette songs even though she's a feminist. Nell has felt Frances's hatred sometimes and the rawness of it has alarmed her, just as the rawness of Frances's love sometimes does. Frances likes or dislikes things with passion. Sometimes Nell feels a bit anaemic beside her.

'We rural housewives spend a great deal of energy trying to make the best of what nature has given us,' Nell says. 'There is a salon called the Beauty Spot. Wayne does my highlights, Lorna does a French manicure while the foil's on, and Lucy plays with Suzette.'

'Their dog?'

'Their baby.'

'Does it worry you that you're turning into your mother?' Frances asks.

'All the time! But I tell myself that it's research. It gives me something to write about.'

There's a slightly uncomfortable silence.

'I read your column,' Frances says seriously, 'and sometimes I wonder whether life isn't beginning to imitate art . . .'

'What do you mean?' Nell says, sounding much more breezy than she feels.

'Well, it started off as a parody, didn't it? The laughably parochial habits of village folk, but you can't remain an outsider for ever, can you? There's a sense of belonging creeping in.'

'It pays the bills,' Nell says uncomfortably.

'Yes, but just how much of your soul do you need to sell for that?'

Nell feels tears bubbling up. They always seem to start in her throat, making her unable to speak.

Frances looks at her, knowing she's wounded.

'Sometimes it's very funny,' she concedes.

Nell gets up and goes into the garden.

'Can you hear the sea from here?' she asks, not looking at Frances. Trying to get her composure back.

'When it's stormy,' Frances says, putting her arm round Nell. 'Sorry,' she says. 'There's nothing wrong with becoming a member of the community you live in. You've always been very good at fitting in.'

Even that sounds like a put-down.

'What are you writing about this month anyway?' Frances asks.

'My visit to a colour therapist. All for the purposes of research, you understand,' says Nell.

'Is that one of those women with lots of make-up who looks at your skin tone and tells you that your entire wardrobe's wrong because you're a winter not a spring?'

'No, much more cerebral . . . although she did think a change to peach and coral tones in the bedroom might improve my sex life . . .'

'Peach and coral tones have never improved anyone's sex life. So what is it, then?'

'Well, all you do is choose these four strips of colour and tell her your date of birth and then she tells you all about your past, present and future lives.'

'Fantastic! So . . .'

'I'm on my ninth incarnation before I move on to a higher plane. She thinks I definitely come from Atlantis. I was a teacher there,' Nell says, very seriously.

She looks at Frances totally deadpan and Frances looks at her, alarmed. And then they simultaneously start laughing. Just like they used to. It feels good to have wound Frances up even for just a second. Nell hasn't laughed hard for a long time.

'Actually,' Nell says, calming down, 'it was quite interesting.'

'Oh, you're not going to tell me that a lot of what she said was uncannily accurate?'

'She said that something happened about five years ago that changed my life,' says Nell a little more seriously.

'That must be true for just about everyone,' says Frances.

'So, what happened to you five years ago?' says Nell.

'You guys left Tokyo.'

'That was more than six years ago.'

'What's a year in a timescale that includes the lost island of Atlantis, for God's sake?' Frances points out. 'Still, I must say it's uncannily accurate about you having been a teacher, although I don't see a great deal of career development over all these incarnations . . .'

'Oh, stop!'

'What else?'

'You're very interested for someone so cynical,' Nell counters.

'Oh, please!'

Frances gets her coffee cup from inside and her cigarettes and lighter. She drags the other chair across the concrete floor of the well of garden so that she's sitting next to Nell. Then she lights up and blows the first mouthful of smoke straight up in the air.

'So what about this life? What's in store?'

Suddenly Nell doesn't know if she wants to tell Frances what the colour therapist said.

'Are you where you want to be, do you think?' Nell diverts the question back to Frances.

'What, in the here and now?' Frances thinks about it. 'Sitting in my garden with my best friend on a sunny spring day? Yes, I think so.'

'In the now, but not the here, then,' Nell says.

'Living in a rented basement flat in Brighton and teaching rows of Japanese students every day? What do you think?' Frances says, taking another long drag from her cigarette.

'So, why?' Nell asks.

'What? Here? When I could be teaching rows of Japanese students and living in a much smaller rented flat in Tokyo?'

110

'You could be doing something completely different,' Nell argues.

'Like?' Frances draws seriously on the cigarette.

'Travel?' Nell suggests.

'Oh, I've done travelling. I've met a thousand people and I've slept in a thousand different beds and I'm no different from when I started, except that my tummy's never been the same since India. Travel doesn't broaden your mind. When you're travelling your mind gets completely constipated with total mundanities like how the hell you're going to get your jeans dry in a monsoon, and how you know you're not smoking cow dung. You don't meet new people, not in any real sense, what you do is pretend to be interested in somebody's previous life as an accountant in Chislehurst while they demonstrate how their rucksack is in fact a bedroll, one-person tent, penknife and camel saddle, and portaloo all in one . . .'

Nell's laughing. 'Why don't you write?' she asks.

'What, for one of those glossy supplements? Don't think they'd get any advertising alongside my column,' Frances says. 'Oh, I know I should do lots of things, but I'm too lazy. Or perhaps I'm just not miserable enough about my life to do anything about it. What about you?'

'What?' Nell asks, pretending she doesn't know what Frances is asking.

'Are you miserable enough?'

All at once there are tears in Nell's eyes that she doesn't want, hasn't invited. She's looking straight ahead, trying to blink them away, but she knows that Frances has seen.

'You're not pregnant, are you?' Frances asks quietly.

'Why do you say that?'

'You're not drinking coffee, and you were very weepy the last time . . .'

111

'Was I?'

Curiously, the knowledge that what she is feeling may be due to hormones, rather than existential despair, makes Nell feel considerably better.

'What's pregnant?' Lucy suddenly asks. She appears to be playing a complicated game involving an invisible Bill and Ben with Lizzy Angel as Little Weed, but she's been listening to every word.

Nell had not planned to tell Lucy yet. Not for a long time yet.

'It's when a woman has a baby in her tummy,' says Frances.

'When she's fat?' Lucy says.

Her friend Emma's mother is vastly pregnant, Nell remembers. She hopes that Frances is not about to explain the facts of life.

'Mummy's not fat,' Lucy says.

'Yes, well, there we are then,' says Frances, picking up on Nell's reluctance to pursue the subject.

She mouths 'sorry' at Nell.

Nell can't quite work out how her secret has suddenly become public knowledge.

'Shall I get you a gherkin?' Frances asks.

'Oh shut up,' says Nell, laughing.

'Never say shut up, Mummy,' Lucy warns.

'You're right,' Nell says, then, seeing Frances's look of exasperation, 'Well, she's right. It's not fair to expect manners from them if you're rude yourself.'

'You *are* becoming your mother!' Frances says.

'Fuck off!' says Nell, under her breath.

Frances knows Nell's mother better than most people do because she has had the experience of living with her for two weeks.

Lavinia announced that she was coming to see Japan just after Alexander had moved into Nell's flat.

Even though her mother had the money for a hotel, she seemed quite determined to slum it, insisting that she'd just bed down on the floor, and resolutely ignoring Nell's protestations that there actually wasn't a space big enough to bed down in. She was supposed to arrive in the morning, and Nell had planned to demonstrate the impossibility of her staying, then pack her off to a decent hotel, but the plane was delayed, and they had ended up at ten o'clock that evening with everyone's nerves frayed. Nell and Alexander were at that delicate stage of their relationship where they were totally in love, but didn't really know each other. She didn't feel she could ask him to move out to make way for her mother. He did not volunteer.

To make things worse, her mother and Alexander took an instant dislike to one another at the luggage carousel after Lavinia remarked wearily that one had grown used to inefficiency from the British workforce, but it was hardly what one expected in Japan, a remark that managed to touch almost all Alexander's leftish nerves in one go. Lavinia later confided to Nell that she was suspicious of very good looking men, because they'd never had to work for women's adoration.

'And I don't just mean about putting up shelves,' she had added, with a nod and an attempt at a knowing look.

Frances had stepped in and offered Lavinia her bed, and for the duration of her visit the two of them became irritatingly close, like schoolgirls sharing a dormitory.

It was Frances, rather than Nell, who first learned the reason for her flight from England, Frances who put into words the suspicion that Nell's father might be having an affair, Frances who later persuaded Lavinia that actually she'd be happier without him, which oddly turned out to be the case.

Nell remembers asking Frances, 'Why do you like my mother?' As if she could see no reason why anyone would like Lavinia if they didn't have to.

'She's got guts,' Frances told her, 'and she's bright, and just because the entire feminist movement has passed her by for the last thirty years doesn't mean that she can't be a late learner.'

'But she supports Thatcher!'

'She won't by the time I've finished with her.'

'How is the old girl?' Frances asks.

'Very involved in the Countryside Movement,' Nell replies.

'She doesn't actually hunt?' Frances asks, aghast. She prides herself on taking the unexpected view, but there are limits.

'No. She's at the making-sure-everyone's-got-a-sustaining-packed-lunch-to-eat-on-the-march end of things. She's always turning up with baking trays covered with foil: "Darling, you couldn't just pop this ham in the oven for me, mine's full of game pies." '

'Bet Alexander likes that.'

'He's usually at work,' Nell says, noncommittally.

Frances is wonderful in many ways, but she's a terrible stirrer.

'How do they get on these days?'

'They rarely see each other. It's actually one of the benefits of living so close. We never have to have her for the weekend. She can be as much of a grandmother as she likes, but she doesn't get to be much of a mother-in-law.'

Nell's rather pleased with that construction of the situation. It sounds so good, it might almost be true.

'Isn't it a bit oppressive, living so near your parents? For you, I mean, as well as for him?'

'But in the end it's not about place, is it?' Nell

114

argues, trying to divert the particular into the general. 'Happiness is a state of mind and if you're content, then where you are doesn't really matter . . .'

It's one of the things Nell has been thinking about a lot recently. Would moving help?

'I've never been happier than I was in Tokyo, and I hated that city,' she concludes. QED.

'And I've never been more unhappy than I was there,' says Frances.

'Really?' Nell's shocked. 'I never knew that.'

'You were so busy being happy that you didn't notice,' Frances says, with a brisk smile that makes Nell feel more guilty than a moan would. Frances is such a cynic, Nell's never considered that something as banal as happiness would be important to her.

'Are you happy now?' she asks, slightly anxiously. She's never felt comfortable dishing back the intense personal probing that Frances subjects her to because she's always slightly feared that Frances might suddenly declare a passion for her. Loving someone less than they love you normally makes you powerful, but the situation with Frances seems to have the opposite effect on Nell.

'At this moment?' Frances asks, and Nell feels that she's laughing at the inanity of her question.

'I meant in general.'

'Am I happy in general?' Frances repeats the words mockingly. 'As happy as any other sad, single woman approaching forty, I suppose.'

'I will draw you a picture,' says Lucy. 'That will cheer you up.'

Nell and Frances exchange looks.

'I haven't got any crayons, love,' Frances says.

'We should have brought some,' says Nell.

'Hang on a minute,' Frances says. She goes inside and returns with a packet of coloured chalks.

115

'The school I'm at now is so behind the times, it's almost fashionably retro,' she explains. 'They still have blackboards.'

She bends down to the child's level.

'You can draw me a picture in my garden,' she says.

'Like Bert!' Lucy squeals.

'Who's Bert?'

'Dick van Dyke in *Mary Poppins*,' Nell explains.

'Cor blimey, guv!' Frances says, doing a terrible impression of Dick van Dyke's terrible impersonation of a cockney accent.

'Afterwards, we'll jump through the picture and have a jolly holiday,' says Lucy, rather formally.

'You can only do that if it's a really good picture,' Frances says.

'What shall I draw?'

'Somewhere you feel like spending a jolly holiday,' Frances says, clearly beginning to find Lucy wearying.

Nell and Frances watch as Lucy begins her task, dragging a yellow chalk across the paving stone with such determination that it breaks in her hand.

'I think I'll use a different colour,' Lucy says.

She draws a blue line across the top of the picture. Her tongue comes up over her top lip as she tries to keep the colour within the frame of the paving stone.

'She's terribly serious, isn't she?' Frances whispers.

'They all are at that age,' Nell says, immediately jumping to her child's defence, 'especially little girls.'

'So, do you want another girl, or a boy?'

It's typical of Frances to ask a question straight out of left field, which flusters Nell because she realizes she hasn't even thought about what sex the baby might be.

'It's very early days,' Nell says.

Frances says nothing. She is someone who uses

silence well. It's a natural teacher's gift. One that Nell never really mastered because silence makes her uncomfortable and she can't help rushing in to end it.

'It's a bit of a shock, actually,' Nell says, in a low voice.

'An accident?'

'No, not an accident . . .' Nell's floundering.

'What does Alexander think?'

'I really don't know,' Nell admits.

She's trying to balance the process of having a meaningful conversation with Frances with saying as little as possible that Lucy can understand. Frances doesn't recognize the sort of code that adults with children use to communicate in their presence.

'You haven't told him?'

There's an eagerness about Frances's voice that makes Nell think that she would love it if she hadn't told Alexander.

'Of course I've told him,' she says, snatching control back. 'We just haven't had a chance to discuss it properly.'

'How is Alexander?' Frances says in the slightly clipped tone she always employs to discuss him. It's as if her dislike is very near the surface and needs to be constantly kept in check.

'Fine,' Nell says. 'Working hard.'

It's the stock answer she gives her friends in the village when they enquire after Alexander. It's a commuter village. Most of the men, and some of the women, travel up to London on the train each day. Most of them have jobs in the City and some of the men arrive home late, smelling of wine bars. She thinks that Alexander drinks beer with the other teachers in the pub round the corner from the school: enough to make him too tired to speak to her, not enough to make him stagger as he walks up the lane to their house. People see him as they're locking their bolts and calling their cats in.

Alexander's late home these days, they sometimes remark, outside the school gates.

Working hard, Nell replies.

It satisfies them.

'Working hard?' Frances says. 'That doesn't sound like Alexander.'

'Can we jump through my drawing now?' Lucy asks.

'Let's have a look.' Nell gets up quickly, glad of the distraction.

It is a yellow beach with a pink person and an orange bucket almost the same size as the person.

'Is that you, sweetie?' Nell asks.

'Yes,' Lucy says proudly.

The figure is a circle on top of a triangle with four prongs sticking out, each with five more prongs attached. Nell's happy to see that the face in the circle is smiling.

'I love the way they always put blue along the top, and nothing in between,' says Frances.

'That's the sky,' says Lucy.

'But the sky comes right down to the sea,' Frances argues.

Lucy looks at her as if she's stupid. Then looks up at the sky, blue above.

'Air doesn't have a colour,' she pronounces, waving her hands around.

'No, but, if you look at the sea . . . oh, come on, I'll show you.' Frances never likes to lose an argument.

Nine

The Soho pavement's not wide enough for both of them to walk separately side by side. Kate is a couple of paces in front of him, falling back into yesterday's pattern. He catches her up and puts his arm round her, making them one unit. She looks up at him in surprise.

'What did you tell your boss?' he asks.

'That's for me to know and you to wonder,' she says.

She's got a ridiculously smug smile on her face.

On Regent Street where the pavement's wider, they hold hands. Her thumb caresses his palm. He remembers that there was a whole system of meaning involved in the position of fingers and thumbs when holding hands as a teenager. Like all the codes in the courting process, it was devised and understood solely by girls, with boys struggling to think down their pubescent erections at the same time as trying to remember which position of thumb their previous girlfriend had confided to them meant that full sex might be on the agenda.

Alexander lost his virginity to a girl called Juliet whose parents were such impeccable Hampstead liberals that they not only went out for the evening in question, but also insisted their daughter use their double bed for the event. Alexander has always slightly regretted the ease of his first full sexual encounter, the absence of all the surreptitious foreplay his less fortunate friends had to go through. The only secret about Juliet, he now remembers, was that her mother Lola informed him quietly that she was alone in the house every afternoon if he was ever passing and fancied dropping in.

'Look at that,' Kate says, stopping outside Hamleys.

The latest model of Thomas the Tank Engine is puffing around an elaborate yellow plastic railway loop with his irritatingly perpetual smile.

The Reverend Awdry's books were banned in Alexander's childhood because his mother deemed them sexist and mean-spirited. Unlike other things that were disallowed, like Action Man ('a bit perverted') and bubble gum ('common'), he never craved the adventures of Thomas and James and Gordon. He cannot understand why they are so popular with children now. It occurred to him recently that the experience of train travel for the majority of children in the South-East was probably by steam engine with a silly face tacked onto the front, at one of the many Thomas Days on bits of old track restored by enthusiasts.

'Great, isn't it?' Kate says. Her eyes follow Thomas's progress over a mountain and into a tunnel.

'You could probably buy a small car for what that lot costs,' Alexander says.

They cross the road and walk along the quieter back streets that run parallel to Oxford Street. Kate has gone silent, but the space between them feels as if it's full of her working out something she wants to say.

'What?' he says finally.

'What?' she replies.

'What are you thinking?'

She pulls in a deep lungful of air as if she's about to say something momentous, and now he regrets pressing her.

'Hey! Look!'

At the corner of Bond Street she stops abruptly and points. They're standing beside a camera and video shop. There's a television screen in the window, and Kate is on it, pointing at them. She looks different on television, larger, and her face is at a strange angle. Alexander peers around the window to see which camera is recording them, and then back at the screen. His face now looms there too.

Simultaneously, they both wave, and walk on.

He does not ask what she was about to say, and she does not volunteer.

'How old were you when you came to see Father Christmas?' Kate asks as they push the heavy revolving door into the cosmetics department of Selfridges.

He remembers being pressed against other people's carrier bags as they shoved their way in through this door, the distinctive woollen smell of damp serge overcoats and the atmosphere of bad temper.

Today, the beautifully cool air inside smells of a thousand perfumes.

'Five, or maybe six,' he says.

'How old were you when you stopped believing in Father Christmas?' Kate wants to know.

'Five or six,' he repeats. 'We stood in the queue for ages with my mother proclaiming at the top of her voice, "If it makes you understand that Santa Claus is just an out of work actor with garlic breath and a cottonwool beard, it'll have been worth the extortionate price."'

He puts on a high and haughty voice for his mother, like some old actress playing an English lady in a black and white film. Did she really sound so over-bearing? He realizes with slight shock that he can no longer exactly remember.

Kate's wondering whether he's joking.

'What a shame,' she says, neutrally.

She picks a lipstick from a rack display on a counter that's all white and pale green glass like a dispensary, and tests it on the skin between the thumb and forefinger of her left hand where women always test lipstick.

A little piece of her jigsaw falls into place.

'Is this where you do your nails?' Alexander asks.

Kate nods.

'Marie's bolder than me,' she whispers, 'she just stands there and does all of hers. She's got this look, you know, like she's daring someone to tell her to piss off. I just do one at every counter.'

She turns her nails towards her and looks at the rainbow of shades. There's something so forlorn about her little unsophisticated hands that he finds himself saying, 'I like them like that.'

'Do you?' She brightens immediately. 'Let's have a squirt of some scent, shall we? There's one that's the same for men as for women . . . ?'

She looks for his reaction.

'Bloody stupid idea, that,' she says, registering his frown.

She sprays one of her wrists with Lancôme's Miracle, which is on special promotion, then sniffs.

'A bit too sweet for me,' she decides.

He picks up a flask of Chanel No. 5, catches her other wrist in his hands, and sprays cologne on the place where the skin is so tender the veins show through. Her hand trembles on his palm.

'Mmm,' she pronounces, 'classic.'

*   *   *

122

As they walk further into the store, sharper citrus and sandalwood notes begin to overwhelm the floral scents that greeted them as they entered.

A heavily made-up woman wearing a uniform half-way between that of a nurse and an air hostess is standing beside a concession decorated in dark green and tan leather. Alexander allows her to spray the back of his hand.

'That's nice, that,' says Kate.

'I can smell saddle soap, freshly mown hay and just a hint of gooseberry,' Alexander says, deadpan.

It takes Kate at least three seconds to realize that he's joking.

'Come on,' she says, taking his hand and pulling him towards an escalator. 'Time for your surprise.'

The store has had a major makeover since he was last inside it. Unsupported escalators rise elegantly from floor to floor.

Looking over the moving rail, he can see all the way down to the basement.

'I can't look over,' Kate informs him, staring straight ahead. 'It makes me think I'm going to fall down there. On the fourth floor, there's a lift that takes you up to heaven. That's what Marie calls it. The Beauty Place,' she adds, when he doesn't laugh.

'Right,' he says, uncertainly.

'But we're not going there . . . obviously,' she says.

As they jump off the escalator on the fourth floor, she grabs his hand. 'Now, close your eyes!' she orders.

There's no-one about. He goes along with the game, allowing her to pull him along.

'There's some amazing things here,' she tells him. 'They've got these huge blocks of soap. They cut you a bit off like a tray of fudge. In fact, it looks more like you should eat it than wash with it. Brown. Hey, you'll never guess. One of them's called marmalade. Marmalade soap! I know who'd like that! Paddington Bear!'

He smells lavender and oranges in the air.

'Didn't Paddington Bear come to Selfridges?' he asks.

'Barkridge's,' Kate corrects. 'They tried to take away his hat.'

'That's right.' Alexander smiles. He loved the stories about Paddington and so did his mother, even though she disapproved of talking animals.

'Here we are,' says Kate. 'Now, take one big step.'

There's a smell that's like an echo from the past, part incense, part untreated wool. The texture of the floor beneath his feet is different.

'Sit down!'

Alexander gropes around for a chair. Then Kate drops to the floor, yanking him down beside her.

'Now you can open your eyes!'

They are in a room full of Persian carpets. There are carpets spread out on the floor, carpets on the walls, piles of rolled carpets, and carpets hung up like giant newspapers on rods. Rich reds, blues, pinks and golds dance around them. They are sitting on a carpet. The pile is short and there's a dense pattern of birds in trees with deep pink blossom. He trails his hands against the pile. The coarse dry texture beneath his fingertips brings a rush of memories.

He lies on his stomach, with the carpet smell filling his nostrils, making his eyes smart.

Kate lies on her front beside him.

'Where do you want to fly to?' she whispers.

The black brogues of a sales assistant tap across the shop floor towards them and stand, pointedly, at the edge of the carpet.

'Can I help you?'

Alexander looks up. The sales assistant is awkward and young, like a teenager going for an interview in a borrowed suit.

'We're just looking, thank you,' says Alexander.

'You're not supposed to walk on the carpets.'

'We're not walking,' Kate chimes in.

The sales assistant doesn't move.

'Oh well,' Kate says, getting up and brushing invisible dust from herself, 'we must fly!'

She takes Alexander's hand, pulls him up, and they walk away together giggling stupidly like children who've got a joke their teacher isn't aware of.

In the adjacent department are beds with squares of plastic at the foot of the mattress to protect them from shoppers' shoes, and more beds made up with designer bedlinen.

'If I were rich,' says Kate, 'I don't know whether I'd go for bright colours, like that' – she points towards a counterpane of checkered Indian cotton in vivid emerald, purple and orange – 'or pure white cotton. What do you think?'

'If you were rich, you could have both,' he points out.

'In films, they always have white, don't they? It's good taste, isn't it?'

'It's probably so that the actors' faces show up better,' he suggests.

'I never thought of that!' she says. 'How about this one?'

It's white with little flowers embroidered around the edges like a Swiss cotton handkerchief.

'Fancy sleeping on that,' she says. 'You'd feel like a princess, but I bet it'd be ruined in a machine.'

'I suppose a princess would have staff to take care of the washing,' says Alexander.

'Fantasies are funny like that, aren't they?' she says.

'I mean, you can get quite serious about them, can't you, even though you know they're never going to happen.'

'Can you?'

He watches her hand caressing the pure white cotton. She looks across the bed at him. Their eyes meet.

There are very few customers around and the only two visible staff are so busy talking about their plans for the weekend that he doesn't think they'd notice if he and Kate were to climb under the huge soft white duvet. He really wants to hold her again. So much energy is contained in her small frame, holding her feels like being recharged.

They both look away again.

'Shall we get the lift down?' she says.

'All the way back down to earth?' he says.

'All the way back down to earth,' she echoes, wistfully, unaware that he's teasing her.

The doors of the lift take a long time to close. When they finally do, he turns to Kate, and suddenly they're kissing. The sensation of touching her lips, cupping her elfin face in his hands, feeling her firm little body against his, is the most delicious relief from a craving which spirals into urgency to kiss deeper, hold tighter, push back against the lift wall.

When the lift bumps to its destination, he opens his eyes and finds his face right up against the mirror behind her.

For a moment, he does not recognize himself.

The doors open. A woman with a pushchair is waiting to get in. Kate and Alexander exit the lift on either side of her.

They're in a department full of speakers and televisions and DVDs. For a moment Kate is lost, and then her face clears.

'Oh, we've overshot. This is the basement. There's the bookshop over there.'

He watches the swing of her narrow hips, the slim legs, the improbable boots on her feet as she heads off on another mission.

Three large flat silent screens beside him show a burnt-out train with the rescue services milling around the debris. The picture cuts to close-up and a reporter's interviewing a man wearing a neon-yellow jacket over his suit, and a hard hat. Then it cuts to a Westminster studio where a minister is sitting in front of a picture of Big Ben. Alexander cannot hear what's being said but he knows it's the same sad old story about lessons having to be learned that never are. In the studio the one o'clock newsreader's sitting in front of a still from the wreckage.

'There must have been another train crash,' he says, rejoining Kate in the bookshop.

'Oh dear.'

Kate is immersed in a new hardback novel. He sees that she could happily settle down for the rest of the day here. In the far corner of the children's section, he spots a boxed set of his mother's books.

'Come on,' he says, 'where's all this food you promised me?'

They walk towards the escalator past tables laid out for dinner parties that will never happen.

'There's everything down here,' Kate tells him. 'Everything to make your life nicer. They've got little forks with corncobs on them and the only thing you can do with them is hold your corn on the cob!' she says. 'I mean, how many times a year do you have corn on the cob?'

She looks at him.

All he wants to do is kiss her again.

Ten

'Now, look,' says Frances. 'Blue, all the way down to the horizon.'

'What's the horizon?' Lucy asks.

'Where the sea and sky meet,' Frances says.

The three of them are standing facing the sea, getting the full force of the wind. If it were a fraction less sunny the temperature would be numbing.

'Did you know, Frances, that the little black bit in the middle of your eye is really a hole?' Lucy asks, apropos of nothing.

Elementary human biology is part of the curriculum for year 1. Lucy's now very exact about her body parts and knows roughly where her kidneys and heart are situated. But while she readily accepts that there's a pump with four tubes inside her chest, and little round things that help you wee, the pupil of the eye mystifies her. She asks every adult she encounters about it, as if a trick is being played on her and somebody is bound to cave in and tell her the truth.

'That's right,' says Frances.

'It's amazing, isn't it?' says Lucy, gazing at the vast expanse of choppy indigo sea and clear blue sky. 'All that seeing through one little hole.'

Frances's face softens with pleasure.

'Did you just think that?' she asks the child, bending

down and pulling the zip of her anorak right up to her chin.

'Yes.'

'Well, it's a very beautiful thought,' Frances says, patting Lucy's padded arms.

Nell has a moment of glowing parental pride. In her head she repeats what Lucy has said, pasting it into the album of Lucy stories she tries not to recount too often.

'How about a round of golf, then?' says Lucy.

Frances raises her eyebrows.

'She means putting,' Nell says.

They pay the man at the garden-shed kiosk and receive two adult putters and a child's, and three different-coloured balls. Lucy putts as if she's playing hockey, dribbling the ball up to the hole, declaring that she's won because she's first there.

They are the only people on the strip of bright green grass between promenade and seafront road.

Frances drops her ball on the ground.

'I can't believe I'm doing this,' she says. 'Tell you what, let's you and I have a bet. A pound per hole?'

'How about loser buys lunch?' says Nell.

'You're confident.'

'I've probably had more practice recently.'

Frances tees off. She hits it too hard and the ball runs way beyond the hole.

'Children really change your life, don't they?' she says watching the ball until it comes to a stop. 'I mean, it's not just that you don't sleep for a couple of years, it's that you have to be good-tempered enough to play games with them at eleven o'clock in the morning . . .'

'And let them win!' says Nell, taking her shot. The ball bounces along in a good line, but it carries just a little too much momentum and runs over the top of the hole.

'Do you like it?' says Frances, as they walk up the green.

Lucy's already on hole 4.

'What, putting?' says Nell.

'You know what I mean.'

'I love her,' Nell says, carefully, 'and I love being her mother . . . I'm not sure I particularly like *motherhood*, if that's what you mean.'

Is it possible to separate the particular from the general like that? Nell has missed this sort of conversation with Frances which makes her apply rigour to the way she thinks about her life.

'I know that I'd happily do absolutely anything to make Lucy's life a happy one,' she explains. 'I've never felt that before about any other human being, and it's a wonderful feeling, but then sometimes I find the responsibility of being in charge of another person's life until they're old enough to take responsibility themselves almost overwhelmingly frightening.'

'You just have to do your best, don't you?' says Frances.

'But you could always do better . . .'

'But you're incredibly selfless and devoted!'

Frances makes it sound almost like a character flaw.

'No,' Nell argues, 'sometimes it's boring. I don't think our generation of women learned to be bored. We're not good at it. There are days when I feel I'm just going through the motions, pretending to be interested in everything she tells me. Sometimes I find myself reading her a story and if she interrupts me I'll have forgotten where I was on the page when we go back to it. It's as if I'm on autopilot. I'm not sure I am a very good mother.'

'You are kidding! You gave up your job to look after her . . .'

'But I didn't like teaching much.'

'Nobody looks after their own kid these days,' Frances says, taking her second shot.

'They do. Most of Lucy's friends are looked after by one or other of their parents.'

'That's the country,' says Frances, dismissively.

'You can sell off bits of the boredom, to a child-minder, if you like,' says Nell, 'but there's a trade . . .'

'Yeah, you get a life,' says Frances.

'Not everyone has a child who requires such a lot of attention,' Nell says, defensively. She doesn't know whether Frances is implying criticism or whether it's just her own insecurity about not having gone back to work after having the baby that's making her feel under siege.

'It's quite a job, actually, making sure she has the right medication at the right time, cooking food that she can eat, keeping the house as free from house dust mites as possible. It's not something you can just franchise out,' she says.

'You can have too much attention,' Frances says.

'I'm talking about trying to give a child who didn't ask to be born as safe a life as possible. That's not too much attention, it's fundamental human rights,' says Nell.

She hits her putt. The ball goes in.

Frances takes two more goes.

'I hadn't thought about it like that,' she admits, picking the ball out of the hole. She gives Nell an appreciative smile which makes Nell slightly guilty for being so assertive.

'Anyway. It made me start writing,' she says. 'I never would have done that if I hadn't stopped working.'

'You're lucky you can write,' Frances says reflectively. 'Do you miss work at all?'

'I miss the conversation,' Nell says.

Frances looks at her as if she's mad.

'My name is Miguel. I hhhhave two brothers and one sister,' she says in a thick Spanish accent.

Nell laughs.

'Do you remember Mr Sato?' she asks.

'Mr Sato?'

'You know. We were doing superstitions. You must remember!' Nell puts on a very hesitant Japanese voice and says, 'Ah . . . Ah . . . in Japan, no superstitions. But . . . ah . . . not good to eat eels with plums.'

Frances looks blank.

'We nearly wet outselves laughing. It's like, oh, thanks for telling me that. Next time I'm in a restaurant I'll know not to order the eels with the plums then. As if . . .'

Frances is still looking at her as if she's crazy, and Nell suddenly remembers that it was not Frances she shared the earnest Japanese man's food-combining tips with, but Alexander.

It was one of those private jokes couples adopt at the beginning of a relationship and quote at each other the whole time, bursting into laughter at the drop of a key word, and excluding everyone around them from their new-found intimacy. She remembers perusing menus, spotting the kanji for eels, pointing it out to Alexander, who would put on a serious expression and say in an ominous voice, 'Please, no plums. I know it's tempting, but it's for your own good.'

And them both hooting with laughter.

It's so long since they've really laughed like that together, she's forgotten that it's something that they do.

'I miss the them and us-ness of the staffroom,' Nell says.

Frances pulls a face.

'The feeling that you're all thrown together in a

foreign land. You're there because you want to experience another culture, obviously, but it's just so
comforting to talk to someone who eats Weetabix for
breakfast and used to watch *Blue Peter.* The irony is
that now the only adult conversation I can get is about
Weetabix and *Blue Peter . . .'*

'It must be bad,' Frances says, 'if you miss the
conversation in the staffroom.'

'I think what I really miss is the buzz of waking up
in the morning and not knowing how the day is going
to end,' Nell says.

'I always know how my day is going to end,' Frances
says. 'Proficiency Class followed by as many pints as I
can drink before closing time.'

'The grass is always greener,' Nell suggests, trying to
lighten her friend's mood with a feeble joke as they
walk down the green together.

'Was Lucy an accident?' Frances suddenly asks.

Nell looks at Lucy. The wind is puffing up her pink
anorak and she's concentrating hard on her swing. She
feels a moment of complete love that's so strong it's
like hunger.

'No,' she says. 'She was very much planned.'

They decided very early on that they wanted to have
a baby together, although she did not fall pregnant
with Lucy for over a year. Ironically, it was an accident
of contraception which raised the subject in the first
place and it's still such an intimate moment in their
history that Nell feels a smile come to her face.

It must have been two or three months into their
relationship. Her mother had come to Tokyo and gone
home again. The weather was bright and cold. Spring.
They still made love a lot. They were both teaching in
the evenings and had fallen into the habit of sleeping
late, breakfasting in bed, having sex, drinking tea,
more sex, then going out for a walk before work. They

were using condoms, but they'd run out of English ones and were having to make do with Japanese, which were more difficult to get on.

Nell remembers the lazy weight of Alexander's chest on hers, then as he began to withdraw, the slight rigidity of panic. The condom stayed inside her, and when they pulled it out, with an agonizingly unromantic slurp, it was broken.

The relationship had been so unbelievably easy up until then. Each morning she used to watch him sleeping, half expecting him to wake up, look at her and realize that she wasn't good enough for him. When that didn't happen, she waited for an old girlfriend to reappear in his life. She imagined his dilemma and its eventual resolution with him tugged away from her by the irresistible force of complexity.

It had happened to her before. Nell was the nice girl who found damaged men, nurtured them, and when they were mended, saw them fly off to more exotic territory. Nell's least favourite word in the English language is nice.

'What are we going to do?' Alexander asked her, about the broken condom.

'I don't really want to take the morning-after pill,' she replied. 'I've taken it before and I don't think it's a good idea to take it again . . . Anyway, I should be all right. I've only just had my period.'

'And if you're not?'

'If I'm not, I'll decide what to do then,' she said with a bright smile, waiting for him to discover some previously unmentioned arrangement which meant that he had to be somewhere else fast.

Instead, he rolled over onto his side so that he was looking right into her eyes.

'Do you want to have a baby?'

She looked away.

'Eventually, yes, I suppose I do,' she said flatly, silently cursing herself for her honesty.

'Perhaps I should rephrase that,' Alexander said. 'I'm asking whether you would like to have a baby with me?'

The week before, she had told him she loved him, but only after he had said that he loved her. And she had put that down to great sex. It didn't mean anything.

'What do you think?' she asked warily.

'I think it's a lovely idea,' he said, smiling at her; then, 'I'd love to have a baby with you.'

'Really?'

'Are you surprised?'

'Yes!' she said, not daring to say more.

'So am I!' he had said.

They made love again after that, without a condom, and the sex was different, infinitely tender and beautiful, as if they had moved up from the plane of physical sensation where everything exists in the present, to a higher plane of humanity that encompasses the idea of the future too.

Afterwards, they went to Ueno Park and sat under a cherry tree in full bloom with a party of teachers from the school. And although she and Alexander sat several feet away from each other, chatting to different groups of people, just occasionally they would both look up and exchange a small, secret smile.

When Nell's period arrived as usual they were both strangely disappointed that what had felt so spontaneous had not produced a baby after all. They told each other that they would not really have wanted to have a baby in Tokyo anyway.

After that, it seemed only sensible to start using condoms again. They never discussed it. Nell thought Alexander had forgotten the conversation, or didn't want to remember it, so she tried to put it out of her mind, until one day, during the rainy season when the city felt particularly loud and dirty and busy, they both arrived home from work together drenched.

As she made tea, she could feel his eyes on her back, watching everything she did, and when she turned round, he said, 'Why don't we go somewhere lovely to live and have that baby?'

'Did you see that?' Frances shouts from the other end of the green.

'What?'

'Only a hole in one!' Frances says.

'Really? That's brilliant,' Nell says, as if she's talking to Lucy.

'Course it wasn't, you daft cow,' Frances says. 'God, your mind's gone soft. I thought you weren't meant to get nappy brain until the baby's actually born.'

'Baby?'

For a split second, Nell thinks that Frances has been able to hear everything she has been thinking, and then she remembers. Baby. The baby inside her now. She has not allowed herself to acknowledge properly that she is pregnant again. It makes her feel guilty that the tiny speck of embryo that's forming in her womb is starting its life forgotten.

Lucy is now on her second round. She's good at playing on her own. She's been an only child for five years, and Nell wonders how she will deal with having a little brother or sister. It doesn't seem fair somehow to impose it on her without her agreement, and yet it might improve her life. Being the only one can be a terrible burden. Alexander still seems to carry the weight of his mother's love on his shoulders even though she's been dead for years.

Nell thinks of her brother, and his kids who rush

around the garden with Lucy when they visit.

'I've been wondering whether to have one myself,' says Frances.

'What?'

'Jesus!' says Frances.

'A baby?' Nell asks, suddenly understanding Frances's slightly peculiar mood.

'You can talk to baby Jesus if you feel sad, can't you?' Lucy chimes in, then swipes at her ball.

'Mrs Bunting's rather happy clappy,' Nell explains.

'Who's Mrs Bunting, for God's sake?' Frances asks, clearly irritated that her big news has been hijacked.

'Lucy's teacher at school. Have we had enough of this now?' Nell asks.

'Yes, let's get some lunch,' Frances says.

'Are you pregnant?' Nell asks in a low voice as they resume their walk along the promenade with Lucy trotting along in front firing back questions that usually just require the answer 'later'.

'If I were it would be an immaculate conception,' says Frances.

Nell's never been completely sure about Frances's sexual orientation. She talked about boyfriends in the past, but Nell never actually saw her with one. She's always had the slightly uncomfortable feeling that Frances fancies her, because she's always going on about how beautiful she is, and her antipathy towards Alexander feels almost like jealousy that he stole Nell from Frances.

'Can we go on the pier?' says Lucy.

'Later,' Nell says, then asks, 'Have you got a boyfriend?'

'Are you conventional, or what?' says Frances.

'I meant, are you in a relationship?'

'You don't have to be "in a relationship" to have a baby these days. Or even before, for that matter,'

Frances says, deliberately avoiding the question. 'There's turkey basters with a handsome and intelligent friend, probably gay, or there's going down the pub and picking up a yob who's here for a weekend of sex. I haven't decided on the method of conception yet . . .'

'Can I have a lolly?' says Lucy.

'After lunch.'

Nell is trying to think of an appropriate response. She can't imagine Frances as a mother.

'How exciting,' she says lamely. 'Why do you want a baby all of a sudden?'

'I'm very selfish, and it makes me sad to think that my genes won't survive,' says Frances.

'That's the strangest reason I've ever heard,' Nell says.

'It's called the evolution of the species, I believe,' Frances says.

Nell laughs.

'I suppose you're right!'

'And I like the idea of having company in my old age. I don't mean having someone to look after me, I mean not living alone for a change.'

'You can still be lonely with a child,' Nell warns.

'I'm going to find a starfish to take back to Mrs Bunting,' Lucy announces, climbing up onto the balustrade and looking over the beach.

'I'm not sure you'll find one,' says Nell.

'They do come from the sea.'

'Yes, they do, darling, and I know a lovely shop where you can buy a lovely starfish,' says Frances to Lucy, 'with a little label on the back saying Philippines.'

'Can we go there?' Lucy asks. 'Mummy, can we go to the starfish shop?'

'I think you've missed out a word,' says Nell, gently. 'Can we go to the starfish shop . . . ?'

'Now!' says Lucy triumphantly.

'We'll go later,' Nell says.

'How will you look after it, though?' she asks Frances.

'Oh for God's sake, I'm not even pregnant yet. I'll think about that a bit nearer the time.'

Nell's about to object, when she remembers herself saying exactly the same thing. It's a universal truth that people who do not have children think that people who do exaggerate the changes they bring to your life.

'I want to go to the starfish shop!' says Lucy.

'After lunch,' Frances says to the child, then to Nell, 'There you see, I'm getting the hang of it already!'

'What?'

'Having two conversations at once.'

Eleven

Kate watches little plates of sushi chugging round the conveyor belt. Alexander is explaining how the different coloured borders on the plates correlate to the price. She's not really concentrating. It's really difficult to think about eating when you're so turned on by someone that your stomach's got a permanent sinking feeling, and the rest of you is a tightly coiled spring that'll leap if touched.

She's not that keen on fish anyway, but raw?

The things you do for love.

Love.

Sick.

Lovesick. Maybe that's where the expression comes from.

At least it doesn't smell fishy. She wishes she'd said no, but he was so excited when he saw the sushi place, and she wants him to enjoy the Food Hall, having dragged him all the way here.

'So, which one do you want to try first?' he asks.

'You choose.'

She should've refused. He's going to hate her more for gagging than he would have done for refusing to try it.

A newspaper image of an American president throwing up all over his host at a Japanese state banquet pops into her head, and then her mind won't

140

move on as she tries to remember the president's name.

Alexander selects a portion of salmon sushi and puts it down on the counter between them. She looks at the three pieces on the plate with a turquoise border.

'Am I meant to put the whole thing in my mouth?' Kate asks.

Alexander looks at her as if he doesn't understand what she's asking.

'As Monica said to Clinton,' she adds, and immediately regrets it. What's all this about American presidents?

'I can't believe you've never eaten sushi before,' Alexander says. He's pleased to be introducing her to a new treat.

He takes a piece and eats it.

She hesitates, then takes a piece between forefinger and thumb, opens her mouth wide, and puts it all in like he does.

The fish doesn't taste as fishy as she thought it would, so that's all right, but it's quite a lot to chew, and the rice is very dry.

'What do you think?' he asks.

Her mouth is so full that there's no room to start chewing. She mimes picking up a cup and drinking it. He gets the waiter to bring her a glass of water. She takes a little sip but it doesn't help. When a child does this you hold out a cupped hand under their chin and make them spit it out. She feels around her body for a hidden tissue, knowing that there isn't one.

George Bush. That's who it was. Father of George W.

Already Alexander has eaten the other two pieces of salmon and is inspecting the conveyor again. Just like a man not to notice that she's going to choke, she thinks, or maybe he's just being polite.

'You OK?' he finally asks her.

While she waves her hand around in a circle to demonstrate that she's got too much in her mouth to talk, her panic-stricken brain is trying to work out how she can lean over Alexander and grab a napkin without making it completely obvious that she's going to spit. She's about to slip down off her stool, and run for the loo, when suddenly she realizes that the food in her mouth has broken down a little and she's able to chew again. It still takes an age to reply to his question.

'It tastes like smoked salmon without the flavour.'

A grain of rice flies out of her mouth and lands on his shirt. She stares at the white spot in the little dark circle of her saliva.

It's only a grain of rice but it's a potent symbol of what she knows already. They come from different worlds. They are totally incompatible.

He looks at his shirt and starts to laugh.

So she laughs too.

Perhaps they're not incompatible after all.

'Do you like it?' he asks.

'It's a bit funny eating fish when you've not had breakfast,' she says, pleased that she's managed to avoid a blunt no.

'Try this,' he says.

Clusters of little orange globes glisten under the bright shop lights. The piece of sushi looks as if it's wrapped in black plastic.

'What is it? No, don't tell me.'

With the tip of her forefinger and thumb she takes one of the beads from the piece of sushi. It's like a capsule of seawater bursting in her mouth. Not unpleasant exactly. If she were doing a taste test on *Food and Drink* she'd use the word 'fascinating'. She takes another bead, then another, then, when she's sure that she'll be able to cope with the rest in one go, the remainder.

'It reminds me of that bubblewrap stuff, you know, where you can't stop popping the bubbles once you've started?'

'It's a type of caviare except it's from a salmon not a sturgeon,' Alexander tells her.

'What about the black plastic?'

'Seaweed.'

Seaweed? She's glad she's already swallowed.

'How come you know so much about it, then?'

'I used to live in Japan.'

'Wow!'

He smiles at her. It's his sad smile. The one that looks like he's thinking loads of things that he's never going to tell her.

Who was he with in Japan? Did he have a girlfriend? Was she Japanese like that woman in the opera? She imagines a woman with a painted face and a kimono with Japanese writing on it. She hates her.

'Do they eat stuff like this all the time?' she asks.

'Yes.'

'Don't they like hot food?'

'They have hot food too. Noodles. Miso soup.'

She leans forward and boldly takes another plate of sushi from the conveyor. Pale yellow spongy stuff, with another strip of black plastic holding it onto the rice.

'This one's like an omelette, but sweet.'

'It is omelette,' he says.

'Omelette fish?' she says, eating another piece. 'Makes sense, I suppose.'

She catches him trying not to laugh.

'What?'

'It is omelette. Not fish.'

'Well, it can't be fish if it's omelette, can it?' she says, trying to make out that she knew what he was talking about all along.

Madam Butterfly, that was it.

'What's Japan like?' she asks.

He takes a slug from his beer bottle, then looks at the sushi chef and the Japanese waitresses standing by the till.

'A lot like this.'

'That's what you said about Italy, yesterday.'

'Is it?'

He's got this way of closing down when he doesn't want to talk about something and it makes her feel loud and stupid but, at the same time, even more in love with him.

'I suppose what I mean is that everywhere's pretty much like everywhere else these days . . . there's always Gap, Starbucks, KFC . . .'

'Pokémon.'

'Exactly,' says Alexander.

'So tell me one way Japan is different from England.'

He thinks for a moment.

'The trains run on time.'

'Another.'

'People take off their shoes when they go indoors.'

'Right. Another.'

'Women cover their faces when they laugh because it's considered rude to show teeth.'

'And the Japanese?'

'They don't like to give away what they're thinking.'

'You must have fitted in well, then.'

She doesn't know why she said that, but he smiles, so that's all right.

'Raw fish, no laughing,' says Kate. 'My kind of place. Not.'

'Have you had enough?' he asks.

'Yes, thanks.'

She'd had enough before they even started.

*   *   *

'I like the idea of the conveyor,' she tells him as they walk away from the sushi bar, thinking that she'd better say something positive. 'But I'd like it better if it were chocolates or something going round.'

'So, where's all this free food you told me about?' he asks.

'There's a few scraps of raw ham, over there,' Kate says. 'They're getting a bit mean here.'

'Perhaps they've noticed that there are women who come in for a free manicure and meal,' he suggests.

The hors-d'oeuvres cabinet has an array of pale pink and cream fish terrines glossy with aspic, and half-lobsters topped with fluted blobs of mayonnaise. They look as if they should be sweet, not fishy, and they make her feel hungry.

'What's your favourite food?' Kate asks.

There are so many simple little things that she doesn't know about him, as well as all the big ones. How can she be in love with him? But it's definitely love because she's so excited inside, she almost can't stand it. It feels as if there's a part of her, really deep down, that's connected to a part of him. Marie would say that they'd met in another life.

'Pizza,' he says and smiles at her. His sweet smile. The one where you know he's a really kind person as well as being incredibly handsome.

She wonders if his answer is a subtle compliment. Is he saying pizza because that's how they met? Nobody really likes pizza that much. Not unless they're about seven years old.

'There's this little shop in Rome,' he goes on: 'nothing in it except a primitive oven, a big fat man, and these huge trays of pizza that he gets out on a kind of shovel. He cuts it into rectangles, wraps it up in waxed paper. You walk down the street eating it. The best one is potato pizza.'

'Potato pizza?'

'Yes. Just thinly sliced potato, lots of salt, olive oil and rosemary. Really simple, really delicious.'

He must have been in Rome with someone he loved, Kate thinks, because it's not the food he's remembering, it's the times they spent together wandering about in the sunshine. Nobody in their right mind would choose potatoes on pizza as their favourite food.

'Pizza is best done simple,' she says, trying hard to keep her voice from screeching with jealousy. 'We sell most of the plain ones. I mean, nobody really wants prawns on their pizza, do they? It doesn't go. What you want is a bit of tomato and a lot of cheese. It's just cheese on toast, really, isn't it? . . . Except yours was potato,' she adds, feeling a complete fool.

'What's your favourite food?' he asks.

Kate has to think about it. She likes chocolate, but she thinks it would sound a bit immature to say that.

Alexander watches her deliberations as if she's a rare exhibit. Like he's David Attenborough or someone. She quite likes being the subject of amazed curiosity. It's as if her thoughts matter.

'Perfectly ripe pears,' she decides at last. 'You know how pears are, one day too hard the next all brown in the middle. There's about two hours when they're fine. That's when I like them.'

A sudden waft of sweet pastry makes her wish that she'd said Danish pastry was her favourite food. She'd love something comforting to damp down the acidity in her stomach that's come from all the raw fish and jealousy. The pâtisserie has a display of iced birthday cakes. A red sports car, a pink castle, a big round cake that's iced to look like a pizza, with magenta slices of pepperoni and livid green strips of pepper on the yellow topping. It's so garish, it almost seems to be mocking her.

Kate takes a deep breath of the warm buttery aroma.

'You know all that stuff about molecules?' she says.

'Yes,' he replies cautiously.

'Well, if smell is just escaped molecules floating about in the air, do you think that if you breathe enough of it, you're really eating? If you absorb enough molecules . . .'

He laughs

'Are you still hungry?'

'A bit,' she admits.

'How long would it take you to breathe an oyster?' he asks.

To their left, there's a stainless steel counter she hasn't noticed before. It's got high stools, a tiled surround, a blackboard with prices chalked up.

'Don't think I'd want to,' she says, trying to take his gaze to the cakes right beside her, but he's not looking.

'Have you ever tried one?'

'No!'

'Come on!'

He takes her hand and pulls her towards the oyster bar. He perches on a high stool. Reluctantly, she does the same. Then he leans over and says in a hushed whisper, 'They're supposed to be aphrodisiac.'

His breath is warm and just slightly damp against the curly bit of her left ear. She goes all tingly down that side of her body. If he asked her to eat a live snake at this point she'd do it.

'Tell you what,' she says, trying to look nonchalant even though her heart seems to have slipped down to her crotch and started beating against the black plastic seat of the stool. 'If I dare to eat an oyster, you'll have to dare do something you've never done.'

'It's a deal.'

He asks for half a dozen oysters and two glasses of champagne.

147

'Champagne!' says Kate. 'Why champagne?'

'Do we need a reason?'

'I don't normally drink.'

'Nor do I. Not at lunchtime, anyway,' he says.

The assistant puts the plate in front of him.

He squeezes lemon over the shimmery liquid surface of the oysters. She's sure one of them shivers. They're not alive, are they? Now she's thought it, she thinks someone did once tell her that they're alive.

'After you!' Alexander says.

'What do you do with them?' she stalls.

He shows how to lever the flesh from the pearly shell.

'You can tip it all into your mouth, or you can eat it with a fork.'

He tips his head back and swallows the oyster in one.

She picks up hers with a fork. 'Looks horrible,' she says.

She puts it in her mouth. Smiles at him. Then the flavour hits her like a wave of dirty seawater. She picks up the glass of champagne and knocks it back like a can of Coke.

'Like it?' Alexander asks.

All she can taste now is the champagne. She drains her glass. The bubbles prickle pleasantly in her mouth and almost immediately the alcohol makes her feel as if she's floating.

'I like the champagne.'

She's not about to tell him she's never had that before either.

He orders her another glass.

The young male waiter, who's wearing a navy blue skullcap that looks a bit French, is trying to figure out what the relationship is between them. She doesn't like his supercilious look.

148

You can keep your dirty thoughts to yourself, she wants to tell him.

She drinks more champagne.

Alexander continues to eat the oysters. She doesn't know how anyone can stand so much cold fishy stuff in their stomach.

'I might be able to stand the flavour if they weren't so chewy and kind of animal,' Kate thinks, and then realizes that she's said it out loud.

'I'm sorry,' says Alexander, as the waiter clears the plate of empty shells. 'I'm being very selfish, aren't I? It's just that I love oysters.'

'Why?'

'We used to go to Mersea for weekends, in Essex . . .'

'Who's we?'

She can't believe she's said that.

'. . . and the whole place smelt of oysters.'

'Yuk!'

Perhaps she didn't say it. Just thought it.

'My mother had a hut, where she painted, and I used to mooch around collecting beach debris. In the evening we would eat oysters, sometimes raw, sometimes wrapped in bacon and fried. We had one of those one-ring stoves, you know, with a gas canister?'

Kate doesn't trust herself to speak. She just nods.

'Angels on horseback,' Alexander says, 'or is it devils?'

'Horses,' Kate replies.

He looks at her oddly, and she hears what she's just said; she tries to laugh as if she was making a joke. She's drunk!

She has an image of him as a little boy beachcombing. In her mind, the sea is gentle and the beach is pebbly. The sun's just gone down and very soon the only light will be his mother's little blue Calor gas stove. She doesn't know why but it makes her feel weepy.

'What about your dad?' she says.

Alexander sits up straight.

'My father left when I was five,' he says.

His body has gone all stiff and she wants to put her arms round him and feel him relax against her shoulder, but she thinks that he'd probably shove her away and put a barrier up around his sadness, and not let her back in. So she just sits there.

The champagne seems to have made the shop much more noisy.

The waiter clatters a round metal plate with the bill on it. Alexander looks for cash in his wallet, then puts down first a Switch card, changes his mind and replaces it with a Connect card.

Kate watches the swap. She knows what two bank accounts means. It means that he is married. She sees the look the waiter gives the plastic card, and knows that he's thinking the same. The till seems to take an inordinately long time to process and authorize the payment. Finally it chunters out a receipt and the noise is so loud it fills the Food Hall.

I am drunk, Kate tells herself. I am drunk and I cannot trust what I am thinking. There's loads of reasons for having two bank accounts. What's it matter if he's married, anyway? It's not as if they've *done* anything.

'So what do I have to do that I haven't done?' Alexander's asking. His voice sounds far away, as if it's in another room.

'Come on,' she says, slipping down from her barstool, taking his hand and pulling him out of the Food Hall towards the escalators, through the *chocolatier* section with its snooty-looking assistants who wear plastic-bag gloves, the pyramids of shiny dark chocolates in spotless glass cases, and the towers of red velvet boxes shaped like hearts.

Twelve

Nell and Frances are standing in a queue for fish and chips. Lucy is dropping coins into the mouth of a lifesize plaster dog which is collecting money for the RSPCA.

'I don't suppose Alexander would oblige?' says Frances.

'What?'

Nell's mind is on all the things she is going to have to ask the proprietor about the food they're about to order.

'Sperm,' says Frances, 'for my baby?'

Nell looks at her.

'You are joking?'

'Well, I suppose I must be if that's your immediate reaction.'

What Nell wants to say is: You hate Alexander and he hates you. What can you be thinking of? Instead, she says, 'Alexander wouldn't want not to be with his child.'

It comes out with more certainty than she feels.

'And you obviously wouldn't like it,' adds Frances.

'Of course I wouldn't,' says Nell, then wonders if she's being terribly mean spirited. Surely this is not a normal or reasonable request, even from a best friend? 'I'm having enough trouble getting Alexander to take an interest in his own child,' she says, and immediately regrets it. Frances has a way of being so extreme that the secrets she means not to tell her seem too trivial to hold back.

It's their turn at the counter.

'My daughter is extremely allergic to nuts and I need to ask a few questions,' Nell begins.

The homely-looking woman who is serving is wearing one of those floral wrap-around aprons that dinner ladies used to wear. Nell's glad that she got her rather than the lanky boy who's dropping pieces of fish into the sizzling oil.

'What oil do you cook your fish in?'

'Palm oil,' says the woman.

'You're absolutely sure it's not groundnut?'

Nell senses the queue behind her growing impatient. She feels like the person at the supermarket checkout who has two items in her basket and then decides to pay by credit card.

'Absolutely sure, love.'

'Do you cook anything with any nut ingredients?'

'You don't have to worry, love,' the woman says. 'My granddaughter's at school with a child who has nut allergy, and she won't let us have anything with nuts. We know how careful you have to be.'

Nell smiles with relief. Normally it's so difficult to explain and she ends up having to point at Lucy and say 'she might die' to emphasize the importance of getting accurate answers, but she trusts this woman.

'Thanks,' she says. 'Well, I'll have two cod and chips, please. Frances? Three cod and chips. To eat here.'

'Sit down and I'll bring them over,' says the woman pointing at one of the empty tables by the window.

Nell and Lucy sit down. When Frances joins them she's carrying a bottle of white wine and two glasses in her hands, and a small carton of apple juice wedged under her armpit.

'Thanks. I completely forgot about drinks,' Nell says.

'So concerned about the ingredients list, you forgot the really important things,' says Frances, pouring her a glass of wine.

She's joking, but it irritates Nell all the same. 'I have to ask,' she says.

She glances at Lucy whose face is pressed against the window watching people hurrying past outside.

'You're hardly likely to find peanuts in a fish and chip shop, though, are you?' Frances says.

'In Scotland there was a case where they fried a Snickers bar in the same oil as the fish and that was enough to set one child off,' says Nell.

'They fried a Snickers bar?' says Frances.

'Nickers bar?' Lucy says giggling. She's at the age where knickers is a very naughty word. She's writing Lucy in large letters in the circle of condensation her breath has left on the window.

'It's sort of chocolate with peanuts in,' Nell explains.

'Yuckarooney,' says Lucy. She picks up her knife and fork and holds them vertically on the table.

'Does anyone know why children get these allergies?' Frances asks Nell.

'Not really. They know the disposition to be allergic is genetic, but nobody knows why so many people have suddenly become so allergic to peanuts,' Nell says.

'Do you think that the genes came from you or from Alexander?'

'I think probably Alexander. He had asthma as a child.'

'Another reason not to use his sperm then,' says Frances.

'Do you mind if we talk about something else?' says Nell.

'What's sperm?' Lucy asks.

Nell's saved from having to answer because their meals arrive.

'Enjoy your fish and chips,' the woman says. She smells of frying and the warm, slightly sweet body odour that fat people sometimes have. She smiles sympathetically at Nell who half feels like giving her a hug. She's noticed recently that she has started to feel something almost like love for people who show kindness to Lucy.

Nell pierces the batter and steam rises from Lucy's piece of fish. 'Freshly cooked,' Nell says, encouragingly, 'delicious!'

'It's too hot,' says Lucy.

'Well, dip it in this.'

Nell peels the top off a miniature carton of ketchup. Then she pops the straw through the top of her apple juice carton.

Frances is shaking vinegar all over her meal.

'What's that?' Lucy asks.

'It's vinegar. Very sour.'

'Can I have some?'

'You can, but just have a little bit on one chip and see if you like it.'

Lucy obediently drops one drop on a chip.

'Yummaroney!' she says, taking a minuscule bite, but she doesn't eat the rest of the chip.

'Do you have fish and chips much?' Nell asks Frances.

It's a completely banal question, but she can't think of anything else to say to her because she's angry about Frances's mocking remarks about allergies. It's bad enough having to ask all the time, without people thinking that you're being silly.

154

'Not often enough. I always forget how much I like it,' Frances says with her mouth full. 'When you live by the sea, you hardly ever do the things you're meant to do at the seaside. Which is why this is so nice,' she says, leaning across the table and putting her hand over Nell's. 'I'm sorry,' she says. 'It must be very stressful living in a state of potential crisis all the time.'

Typically, Frances has come up with exactly the right words to describe what it's like to have a child with a life-threatening condition. Frances is so intelligent, it's always a reaffirming experience to talk to her.

'It is,' says Nell, feeling instantly more cheerful.

'Do you have supportive friends? I mean other parents?' Frances asks.

'One or two. Actually, nobody understands unless they've got a child like it themselves. Either they think you're exaggerating, or they look at you with hard eyes when you try to talk about it, as if you're carrying bad luck and they don't want it to rub off on them.'

'Like illness is infectious, even just talking about it?'

'Exactly! Everyone secretly wants to think that it's your fault somehow – it's to do with genetics, or it's because you're a bad mother. If it's your fault, you see, then it won't happen to them and their children.'

'I'm sorry,' says Frances, giving her hand a squeeze.

'I'm sorry too,' says Lucy, blithely, not wanting to be left out.

Nell watches the precarious journey of a flake of fish from Lucy's plate to mouth. The fork is much larger than Lucy is used to.

'Now another chip,' Nell says, trying to keep the momentum going. Lucy tends to dawdle after the first few mouthfuls and then her appetite goes before she's eaten anything like enough calories.

Nell catches her own reflection in the window,

watching Lucy, with her own mouth open in a state of suspended animation as the child brings another forkful to her mouth. She looks away, wondering whether she *is* over-protective. She must at least pretend to be more relaxed.

Nell takes a sip of wine. It's surprisingly cold and dry, and the crispness is a good contrast to the fattiness of the food. She takes another longer gulp, and feels the alcohol seeping pleasantly through her body. It is a while since she's had a drink, and the effect is immediate and rather pleasant. She turns the bottle round to read the label. Frascati. It goes well with fish. She splashes a little more into her glass.

'I'm not driving for ages, am I?' she says, permitting herself the indulgence.

'Not worried about drinking, then?' Frances says.

'Worried?' For a moment Nell doesn't know what she's talking about, and then she remembers the baby inside her.

'It's only one glass,' she says, trying to reassure herself and appear calm.

When she was pregnant with Lucy, she didn't know about the precautions you're meant to take when carrying a baby. Later, when she learned about all the foods she should have avoided, she wondered whether she could have prevented Lucy's troubles if only she'd been more vigilant at the beginning.

They had moved to Italy because they wanted to do this new thing together in a place that was new to both of them. They'd chosen a hilltop town in Umbria so as to be in the countryside after the busy sweat of years in Tokyo. The nearby university provided enough English lessons to keep them in work. They lived cheaply, ate simple fresh food and usually drank a glass of the local wine with their meals. They were incredibly happy.

Lucy was a robust baby, who smiled all the time and laughed in her sleep. When Nell tried to wean her, she developed an angry rash, and the connection seemed so obvious that Nell went back to breast-feeding. The rash, which Nell later found out was eczema, would flare up occasionally for no apparent reason, but it was only after they returned to England that her allergies became a serious problem.

When Nell thinks about their life before all the worry began, the images that come to her mind are the weekend they spent in Rome on Lucy's first birthday. It was the first time they had gone away with her and it was perfect. The hotel, near St Peter's, was better than they'd thought it would be. They had a huge elegant room on the second floor with two balconies. Lucy slept well. They made love often, the change of tempo, buzz of mopeds, and decadent smells of the city exciting them after their lazy summer slumber in the country.

In the mornings, they would stroll through streets that were half gold, half shadow, pushing Lucy in her buggy, the autumn air just crisp enough to make city walking pleasurable. There was so much to see, they ate lunch on the hoof, breaking off little bits of pizza and handing them to the baby, without even a thought about the ingredients. On the Sunday afternoon they walked in the Villa Borghese where birdsong competed with the rumble of the city. They bought paper cones of green olives from a vendor. Nell remembers chewing the olives, thinking of all the generations of Italians back to Roman times who had tasted that curiously ancient flavour. She remembers closing her eyes, taking a picture in her mind of the three of them together wandering along the gravel paths in the sun-dappled shade of big trees, and trying to commit to memory that blissed-out feeling of total happiness. She remembers buying ice-cream cones at Gioliti, the taste of peach sorbet, the cool sweet essence of peaches like heavenly balm on a warm afternoon. She remembers crouching down beside the buggy to let Lucy have a delicious lick.

It was only chance that made them choose olives, not peanuts, peach not pistachio. It's strange to think that one different split-second decision could have turned the idyll into a nightmare.

'Something happened to you about five years ago,' the colour therapist had said to Nell, 'that changed your life completely.'

'Yes,' Nell told her, 'I had a baby.'

It didn't feel right when she said it, because it wasn't having Lucy that changed things. Having Lucy made everything better. They were so happy, so complete. But were they just playing at being a happy family in some arcadian fantasy? Was their relationship so tenuous that it could not survive reality?

What changed their life was when they came back to England, and Lucy nearly died.

'Do you know what my favourite food is, Frances?' Lucy's asking.

'Sausages?' Frances guesses.

'No, silly, Chinese.'

'Really?' Frances glances at Nell.

'We went up to Soho for Chinese New Year. It was one of the most nerve-racking experiences of my life,' Nell says, 'trying to establish ingredients from a busy Chinese waiter with very little English.'

'We saw a Chinese dragon,' Lucy says, 'and do you know what it was wearing on its feet?'

She's so keen to tell this bit, she doesn't wait for a guess.

'Trainers!'

They were staying in Alexander's mother's house in Kentish Town when Lucy suffered anaphylactic shock for the first time. The duty of sorting the place out stretched endlessly before them. It was winter. It was always dark.

Ironically, Nell remembers considering a trip to the supermarket a delightful escape. The brightly lit aisles of Sainsbury's in Camden Town were an Aladdin's cave of new experience after the monotonous task of bagging up the life of a woman she had barely known. She even recalls the decision to purchase peanut butter. It was Alexander who spotted Sun Pat on the shelves and became quite animated, brandishing a jar in his hand, telling her about the peanut butter and banana sandwiches that his mother used to make them on Saturday evenings, and how he associated the taste of peanuts with the whirring music of *Dr Who*.

Nell felt happy that he was finally discovering ways to unlock memories of good times. She coaxed him to talk about other little bits of routine he and his mother had shared, offering silly little stories from her own childhood in exchange as they mooched up and down the aisles, with Lucy babbling away in the trolley seat.

Perhaps it was she who even suggested that they buy the peanut butter.

She wonders now whether the image of him holding up the jar, which seems so fundamental to their history, would have simply been erased by her memory if nothing had happened afterwards.

At teatime she smeared peanut butter onto slices of fresh white bread and dolloped wet spoonfuls of mashed banana on top. She remembers hesitating before picking up the plates to take them into the front room, fear sweeping through her that he might think she was trying to usurp his mother.

But then he called out, 'Any chance of a peanut

butter sandwich?' And she picked up the plates and carried them through, brushing aside the ominous feeling.

She heard Lucy's reaction before she saw it because it was so dark in the room with the curtains drawn against the London rain and the news flickering on the television.

The sound of a baby trying to breathe through windpipes that are fast closing up is unimaginably terrifying. First she picked Lucy up and shook her, thinking that she had something stuck in her throat, then Lucy threw up all over her. Still the horrible rasping struggle for air. She shouted at Alexander who was standing as if his feet were stuck to the carpet: 'Get an ambulance!'

And Alexander running out into the quiet side street as if to flag one down, and returning with the next-door neighbour who drove them all to the Royal Free. She remembers sitting in the back seat of a car that smelt of dog and shouting at Lucy, 'Breathe. Keep breathing!'

And Lucy's frightened wail.

If she's crying, she's breathing, if she's crying, she's breathing.

She remembers running into the Casualty area and shouting for a doctor – 'This is an emergency. My baby's going to die!'

Doctors shouting, adrenalin going in, Lucy in a nebulizer, the distorted shape of her swollen mouth and neck, the vigil that began crouched over a plastic pod that has gone on ever since.

It wasn't until several hours later that Nell noticed that her own sweater was crusted with baby sick, and that she had left the house with no shoes on.

*   *   *

160

'Eat up, Mummy,' Lucy says. 'I want to play on the beach.'

'OK,' Nell agrees.

'Have you finished?' Frances asks Nell, looking at the barely touched plate of food.

'Yes.'

'You OK?'

'Fine,' says Nell, automatically.

Thirteen

'How do I look?'

Kate is standing awkwardly in front of him, hands by her side. Her face has a delicate pink tinge, like the edge of a rose petal, and her eyes are sparkling from the unaccustomed lunchtime drink.

'Lovely!'

'No!' she blushes deeper pink. 'I meant, do I look like the sort of person who would shop here?'

He tries to see her objectively. The jeans jacket, black T-shirt and skirt make her look like a slightly less tarty Spice Girl. The scab on her knee and the big clompy boots make her look like an errant teenager from *EastEnders*.

'I want to feel what it's like to wear something that costs a thousand pounds,' she says. 'I've never dared try anything on in here before.'

He knows what she needs.

'Are there shoes here?' he asks.

'There's about an acre over there,' Kate tells him.

'Let's go there first.'

'You can always tell someone's class by their shoes,' was one of his mother's few pieces of sartorial advice. His mother eschewed sandals even during her most ethnic periods. He thinks of her shoes, neatly filed in hanging calico shelves in her cupboard. He remembers the rip of Velcro as he took them down from the rail,

162

and his misgivings about giving them to the Oxfam shop: it felt as if he were handing over a precious photograph album, to be scrabbled over by strangers.

Kate pokes her feet into slippers embroidered with sequins and jewels. She's very taken with a pair of ankle boots with an odd-shaped heel and covered buttons that look like Victorian skating boots except that they're made of purple satin. She stands like a little girl who's been at the dressing-up box, the grey nylon stocking socks the shop assistant lent her halfway up her bare shins.

Alexander takes a fine black suede mule with a kitten heel and a chisel toe from a glass shelf and asks the assistant to bring Kate's size.

'How does it feel?' he asks as her foot slides in.

'Really, really comfortable,' Kate says, surprised. 'You wouldn't think they were with this shape, but they've got this really soft leather inside.'

She walks up and down. 'They make me walk differently,' she says.

The shoes have turned her from an urchin to a lady.

He has an unwelcome vision of her as Audrey Hepburn in *My Fair Lady*, and him as Rex Harrison.

'We'll take them,' he says.

Kate's eyes widen and she shakes her head silently.

'Do you want to wear them, or shall I put them in a box?' the assistant asks.

'Wear them,' he instructs.

'OK, I'll just get you a bag for these,' the assistant says, picking up Kate's black boots, 'and if you'd like to follow me to the till . . .'

'They're ninety-nine pounds,' Kate hisses.

'I'm buying them for you,' he says.

'You can't!' Kate says.

He can see that she's caught between hating the idea of being bought something and loving it.

'Why not?'

'Because I hardly know you!' she exclaims.

The shop assistant hears, but she doesn't turn round.

'I mean, why do you want to buy them for me?' Kate says under her breath. She wants to know if the purchase of shoes is a sign of some as yet unspoken commitment.

Women always think about the subtext.

'I'm buying them for you because they look great, OK?' he says.

Kate looks at her feet.

He can almost hear her deliberations about what to do.

'You're right,' she says, eventually, 'they do!'

He uses his Connect card to pay and when the transaction's completed, the shop assistant hands Kate her boots in a bright yellow carrier bag.

As they walk together towards the designer rooms, Kate takes his arm, squeezes it and whispers, 'Thanks.' Her mouth is near enough for him to smell the slight sourness of champagne on her breath.

In the English Eccentrics concession, she chooses a dress made of pink silk velvet.

'What do you think?'

'Yes,' he says, thinking that it is the grown-up equivalent of a fairy princess's outfit, 'but try this too.' He pulls out one in pale grey with tiny glass beads that shimmer glimpses of rainbow.

Standing outside the changing rooms he feels as redundant and self-conscious as he always used to. It's ironic if Kate thinks this is something he's never done before, because he spent many Saturdays as a boy waiting just like this for his mother.

The shop was more crowded in those days and he doesn't think that there were special areas set aside for each designer. His mother would pull clothes from great circular racks, clacking the hangers together in search of her size, then queue at the side of the shop for a cubicle with a curtain that pulled across but never quite reached both sides. As he stood by the long mirrors outside he would see an occasional flash of hand pushing through a sleeve, or foot squeezing back into a shoe.

He learned to say nothing specific when asked what he thought. Comments such as 'It's too bright' would bring about uncomfortable retorts like 'And why shouldn't I be bright?' She had already made up her mind when she asked him, so as long as he said 'Quite nice', or 'All right', she could either say 'Yes, it is, isn't it?' smoothing her hands down her sides, enjoying how she looked in the mirror, or 'Actually, it's hideous', snatching back the cubicle curtain angrily.

On one occasion he remembers pleading to go home, and her snapping, 'If you can't be patient, I won't bring you with me again.'

And then her cross face broke into a smile, and she knelt on the carpeted floor in front of him, undoing the buttons of his stifling winter coat, and saying kindly, 'I don't suppose that's much of a threat, is it, my darling?'

That was the day he had his first taste of Coca-Cola with his lunch at the Golden Egg.

Memories of his mother always start with still-raw anger then slide towards guilty nostalgia.

Kate pulls open the heavy door of her changing room and emerges onto the shop floor, a vision in pink. The dress gapes a little at the top but the colour suits her surprisingly well, the boyishness of her haircut

lending the candyfloss sparkle unexpected sophisti-
cation.

'Gorgeous,' he says.

She stands up straighter, confidence filling out her
bony shoulders. She does a twirl.

'I feel like a fondant fancy,' she says. 'All I need now
is a little sugar violet on my head.'

He senses that the shop assistant who's hovering
behind him is not amused.

'Try the other one,' he says.

Kate goes back inside.

He waits again, flicking through the hangers slowly,
pausing to consider each garment like a picture in an
art gallery, as if meaning will emerge from long and
serious enough scrutiny.

After what seems like ages, the door opens a
crack.

'I think I might need a bit of help with the buttons,'
Kate says.

He hesitates, looks around. The shop assistant has
disappeared.

'There's loads of room in here,' Kate says opening
the door a bit further.

He's surprised by the vastness of the cubicle. You
could hold a small dinner party in it.

She has the grey dress on, and the fragile silk beaded
chiffon swathes her body like a dewy cobweb.

'How do I look?'

He thinks of the appropriate word. She's too human
to be a woodland nymph.

'A changeling.'

'Is that good or bad?'

'It's magical,' he says.

'A changeling in a changing room,' she says, 'I like
that.'

He loves her resoundingly human accent that brings

reality thumping back whenever he's in danger of dreaming.

'Turn round.'

She obeys.

'There are no buttons,' he points out.

'No,' she says, with a tiny throaty giggle which gives him an instant erection.

He steps towards her, looking at her face in the mirror in front of them. Then he pushes the straps of the dress off her shoulders and kisses her beautiful smooth nape. Her eyes close. Her head lolls back against him. He wants to have her like that, looking at her in the mirror. He hoists her dress up over her hips. She's not wearing knickers. He unzips and pushes himself against the peachy soft hemispheres of her bottom. Her eyes are still closed. He pushes her forward. One hand splays out on the mirror, the other is a tight fist by her side. She opens her eyes, stares into his reflected in the mirror for several long seconds. He thinks she's trying to tell him that she would let him do anything to her, which he finds simultaneously incredibly exciting and alarming.

Her closed hand opens at the same moment as his goes to his pocket.

Suddenly they're both holding up to the mirror brightly coloured condoms surreptitiously filched from Marie's sweet jar.

They exchange a wonderfully complicit smile.

He's not terrified any more.

Outside the cubicle, the assistant says, 'How are you getting on in there?'

'We're getting on really well,' Kate calls.

Her voice is muffled with arousal, like tears.

'Do you need any help?'

'I think we're fine,' Kate says, then laughter bursts out of her like a sneeze.

167

The spell is broken.

He can feel the sharp edges of the glass beads pressing against the most sensitive bits of his flesh. He drops another kiss on her shoulder, puts his hands on her waist, gently turns her round. Her palm print remains like a ghostly flower on the mirror, and then vanishes. She turns into his chest, embarrassed now to show her face, having made herself so wanton.

He leaves her in the cubicle to get dressed.

They hand the shimmery dresses back to the assistant.

Neither of them says a word.

He tries to enter into the spirit of shopping with her, stopping to suggest a short silver dress made of fabric that looks like tinfoil but feels soft to the touch.

'It's the sort of thing you'd wear at Christmas,' Kate says, as he holds it up for her to look at: '. . . if you were a turkey.'

She marches on through the shop, barely glancing at the clothes. Clearly, she has a destination in mind.

The Armani section is situated at the far end of the shop. It's all plain dark suits, impeccably tailored, the working clothes of the successful career woman, as uniform as Marks and Spencer but three times the price.

'How many am I allowed to try?' Kate asks the assistant, taking a black jacket in one hand and a short skirt in the other.

The assistant gives Kate's footwear an almost imperceptible glance. 'As many as you want,' she says.

'Could you carry some?' Kate asks Alexander as if he's a tame bodyguard she's known for a long time.

He collects up size 8 jackets in every style and muted shade and follows her. These cubicles are at the edge of the shop and natural light floods into them from tall windows. All the doors are open.

The strangely prosaic thought occurs to him that he has yet to see any other shoppers on this floor. How on earth does it make a profit?

Inside the cubicle, Kate is already stripped down to her chocolate silk lingerie.

He hands her a black skirt and a short black jacket.

'Put these on,' he says.

She steps into the skirt and he holds up the jacket for her to slip her arms into. When she turns round, she looks like a French film star at a funeral, all buttoned up and serious, with sex smouldering just below the charcoal surface.

She takes a step back to show him the outfit. Her lips are pouting into the look she thinks is sophisticated, one hip thrust forward.

He drops to his knees in front of her, pushes up her skirt, and with his nose in the damp crotch of her underwear, he begins to lick. Her spine arches back, and she lets out the tiniest sigh, not as loud as a breath.

He enters her soft tight vagina from behind, one hand clamped over the soft tight bush of pubic hair, his index finger on her clitoris that's slippery as satin.

In the mirror, he watches her sinuous neck stretch as her head tips back.

He turns his face away, closing his eyes as he climaxes, unable to bear to witness himself so powerless.

He finds a tissue in his pocket and wraps the condom in it. She hangs the skirt back up on the hanger, inspecting it for stains, then puts her boots back on, pulling hard on the laces and tying them in a double bow.

'I didn't know what it meant,' she says, slipping the velvety soft mules lovingly back in the bright yellow carrier bag.

'What?' Alexander says.

'Fuck me shoes,' she says, with a little smile.

Her accent swings between wonder and dour bluntness and makes every sentence finish differently from the way he expects it to.

They hand the clothes back to the assistant, and walk away with their arms around each other.

Kate says, 'I've never done anything like this before, you know.'

'Nor have I, you know.' He mimicks the long vowels that make *know* sound like *nor*.

'It must be the oysters,' she says, with a giggle.

'Definitely the oysters.'

He knows nothing about her except that her name is Kate. She is a waitress. Her back arches like a gymnast when she comes, and her energy has got into his bloodstream. She makes him feel as if he's standing tantalizingly on the edge of happiness and one leap will get him there.

Beside the escalator, next to the Nicole Farhi section, there's a mannequin wearing an ice blue cotton jumper he recognizes.

Nell has that jumper.

Nell.

He has been unfaithful to Nell.

It's such an old-fashioned word, it doesn't seem to appropriately describe what he has done. He repeats it in his head, bracing himself for the flood of guilt. Instead, there's a curious feeling of elation, as if he's been waiting for this to happen, dreading it like an exam, and now it's done, it's not nearly as bad as he thought it would be.

He understands for the first time how little effort it takes to betray someone you love, how curiously unintentional it is.

He steps onto the escalator, feeling oddly relaxed.

Fourteen

The promenade is almost deserted.

A couple of truanting teenage boys weave slaloms around an old age pensioner out for an afternoon walk.

'Hardly *Quadrophenia*, is it?' says Frances, disparagingly.

'You can't look very mean on a micro-scooter,' says Nell.

Lucy's playing a kind of hopscotch on the paving stones a little way ahead. An elderly couple walk slowly past her, amused by the innocent concentration she's putting into the game.

'Why do old men at the seaside always wear beige caps and shoes?' Frances asks when they've passed. 'Do you think they automatically collect them at a certain age?'

'Like bus passes?'

'Exactly. Do you think we'll ever get to the age where we think a headscarf is a good idea?'

'Or a Tricel dress with a pleated skirt and waistband?' Nell adds.

'Do you ever try something on in a shop and think, no, I'm too old for this now?' Frances asks.

Nell laughs.

'There are things I think I'm too young for,' she says.

'Like?'

'Leggings. Leggings and big jumpers.'

'Oh, God, yes,' says Frances. 'Especially worn by people who think that the jumper is so huge, they'll be mistaken for slim inside it.'

'I do find some chain store stuff a bit skimpy though,' says Nell.

'So do I!' says Frances, 'but I think it's a sign. As soon as you start to think that manufacturers are using less fabric than they used to, it's the onset of middle age.'

'What's strange is that I don't weigh any more than I used to,' says Nell, 'but I feel sort of lumpy.'

'Well you don't look it. You're the only person I know who could wear that sweater under that jacket and still look thin.'

She glances enviously at Nell's chunky blue jumper and suede jacket and her slim jeans.

'It's horrible, growing old, isn't it? The only thing I take comfort from,' says Frances, 'is seeing someone of my age who looks older than me.'

'Like?'

'Jerry Hall,' says Frances.

'Jerry Hall? But she's a supermodel. She's the example against which we're all held!' says Nell, loving Frances's perversity.

'But have you had a really good look at her?' Frances insists. 'I mean, you wouldn't mistake her for thirty, would you? She looks every day of forty. Actually she looks more than forty, because you'd expect her to look so much better with all that money and make-up. She's got lines round her mouth. Now, look at me, do I have lines round my mouth?'

She smiles a big false smile.

'But she's suffered,' says Nell, thinking that Frances is being a little unfair on Jerry.

'I would suffer for all those riches,' says Frances.

'Would you?' Nell says. 'I don't think money makes up for a broken marriage.'

'Hey, he is Mick Jagger, you know,' says Frances.

On the lower level of the promenade, the cafés and fortune tellers' kiosks are still closed up for the winter. A single metal café chair scrapes along the ground, blown about by whirlwinds of sand.

Nell and Frances sit down side by side on a small wall, hugging their coats around them while Lucy runs along, with her hood up and her eyes down, scouring the beach for unusual stones.

The coldness of the concrete seeps into Nell's thighs and lower back.

'Have you noticed,' Frances says, 'that on a beach, girls always look for pretty things to collect and boys always throw stones into the sea? They're still hunter-gatherers even though they generally gather in Gap Kids and hunt in McDonald's.'

'That's rather good,' says Nell. 'Do you mind if I use it in my next column?'

'Be my guest! Course, women have to hunt too these days . . .' Frances says.

'But men haven't really learned to gather, have they?' Nell finishes her sentence for her.

Frances laughs.

'I wouldn't mind if men could really do the hunting stuff properly. But women have to do that too,' says Frances. 'Does Alexander mind appearing in your column as a useless git who spends all his time reading the paper?'

'God, that's not how it comes across, is it?'

'That's why the column's so popular,' Frances says. 'Because it reflects most women's experience of men.'

'Maybe I'd better skip the hunter-gatherers, then.'

'I thought you were writing about your colour lady?'

'Actually, I'm finding that a bit close to home too.'

'Why?'

'Just something she said.'

'What?'

'You'll only mock.'

'Promise I won't.'

'She said that there was going to be an opportunity for change soon.'

Nell realizes as soon as she's said it how idiotic it sounds. 'Something momentous,' she adds, to convince herself as much as Frances.

The woman had guessed that Nell was unhappy. Whether she saw it in her aura, or in her eyes, Nell does not know, but she was impressed that someone who had no previous knowledge of her wasn't fooled by the smiling façade.

'Something will happen soon,' she said, 'that will make you feel fulfilled again. It might involve pain or a difficult choice, but it is there for you.'

'This was before, or after, you told her you were pregnant?' asks Frances.

'I didn't tell her I was pregnant,' Nell says.

'Well, she should get a kiosk,' Frances says, gesturing at the boarded-up arches behind them. 'I shall be her first customer.'

Nell stares out to sea. She had not connected the pregnancy with the woman's prediction. She feels really stupid now.

'Have you and Alexander had a row?' Frances asks.

'Not exactly,' Nell says. 'Why do you ask?'

'Because you seem awfully subdued.'

'Sorry.'

'So, what's the problem?'

The wind is so cold that the water in Nell's eyes feels as if it will freeze. 'I don't want to say it, in case it makes it true,' she says.

175

She slots each of her hands into the opposite sleeve in an attempt to keep her fingers warm.

'Say what?'

The silence stretches between them.

'I don't think Alexander loves us any more.' Nell enunciates the words slowly one by one. It's the only way she can say them without crying.

She thinks of Alexander's face when they went up to Chinatown recently for Chinese New Year. Amid all the whirring, noisy vibrancy, he simply stared, disconnected from experience, and when she caught his eye and made a face, trying to prise a smile from him, he looked at her as if he didn't know who she was.

'Don't be ridiculous. Alexander adores you. You're having another baby.'

'It wasn't exactly planned. Sex is so rare, I wasn't prepared,' Nell confesses.

'Rare?'

'Well, at midnight after you've spent the whole day doing housework and school runs and writing, you don't tend to feel much like sex. I don't anyway.'

'Jesus! So when Freud said "what do women want?" . . .'

'The answer was sleep.'

'I can't imagine living with Alexander, and not having sex with him,' Frances says. 'Or any man,' she adds.

'It's different when you have children,' Nell says.

Is it? Or is it just them?

'I think Alexander feels trapped,' she tries to explain. 'I know he does. I do too sometimes. But I accept it. It's part of being with someone, part of being a parent. I don't think Alexander can accept it.'

'Didn't Alexander's father do a bunk when he was little?' Frances remembers.

'Yes, he did.'

'Perhaps Alexander finds it difficult being a father because of that?'

It's remarkably astute of Frances to make a connection that now seems so obvious, but hasn't occurred to her before. Nell is a little unnerved.

'Perhaps he doesn't know how to be a father?' Frances says.

'Perhaps.'

'Do you still love Alexander?' Frances wants to know.

The trouble with talking to Frances is that she always seems able to voice Nell's worst fears. Sometimes it's helpful. Sometimes it's very frightening.

'I'm not sure any more what love is,' she wavers.

'How very Prince Charles.'

'No.' Nell tries to rise to the challenge of defending herself. 'I'm really not sure what love means. I know what it feels like to fall in love. It feels like you can't believe it's happening, but at the same time it feels like it's going to go on for ever. It's more fundamental and powerful than anything else. It has a kind of imperative about it.'

Frances is nodding.

'But one day, it's not like that any more. You're just used to someone. You've got into a habit of being with them, and you know them quite well, and there's no particular reason for doing anything different. Yes, there are moments of complete brilliance when you have a kind of flashback to what it was like in the beginning, but that's about five per cent of the time. Maybe five per cent is what you call loving someone. It's what makes your relationship different from friendship, or companionship, or even indifference. But then, if it starts to become four per cent, or three, or so infrequent that you can't trust it will ever happen again . . .'

177

'What's happened to you?' Frances butts in. 'You're so cynical. I'm meant to be the cynical one!'

'No, you've always been the romantic.'

'How d'you work that out?'

'Because you believe in having one great love, and every time you go out with a man you think you've found him, and when you fall out, you blame him, and not your romantic view of human nature.'

'You're not indifferent to Alexander,' Frances says, refusing, as usual, to analyse her own behaviour. 'Alexander's not someone you could be indifferent to.'

'No. Not indifferent. If I were indifferent, then there really wouldn't be any point. It's more like weariness . . . I'm weary of his moods, his silences. What I used to find so thrilling about him was the way he kind of simmered. You just knew there was so much lying beneath and it was a challenge whether you could unlock it, you know?'

Frances is nodding again.

'That's what made him so attractive. Lucy put it really well the other day. We were reading a story which had a volcano in it, and she wanted to know what a volcano was. So I told her that it's a mountain that has fire inside and sometimes it just can't keep it in, so it explodes. Lucy turned to me and said, "Daddy is a volcano." '

'Bless!'

'I think she meant his temper, but it didn't used to be just his anger. It used to be his wit, his laughter . . . his passion . . .' Nell's voice trails away. 'But now that's all locked up, and I can't seem to release it . . .'

'Why do you think he's so buttoned up?' Frances asks.

'His mother,' Nell says immediately. 'I mean, I know my mother has her moments and everything, but his mother was truly awful.' She giggles nervously. It feels

178

disrespectful to speak ill of the dead, but it's still horribly good to say it.

'I know I only met her when she was ill, but she hung around Alexander like a leech, and the more he was with her, the more he closed down. Then she died, and I think he was in such pain, he decided not to love anyone again. And then Lucy nearly dying too. He just switched off his capacity to love.'

'People don't do that,' Frances protests.

'They do. Subconsciously, maybe even consciously . . .'

Tears begin to slide down Nell's cheeks. She turns her face inland so that Lucy won't see her crying.

'I know, because I could have done it. In the hospital, when Lucy had come through but they were still observing her. They kept telling us how careful we were going to have to be. They were all so serious about it. I remember thinking, they've got grave faces, and then trying to erase the thought because of that word, grave. You get superstitious when you're stressed out with anxiety.'

She pauses, watching Frances's face.

'. . . Later that evening, when I was on my own with her, I was looking at her, and I thought, I don't know if I am strong enough to get through every day being frightened that I'm going to lose you. I knew at that point I could just decide not to love her so much . . .'

Frances is still silent, as if she's waiting for the punchline to a long anecdote.

'That's it?' she says finally.

'Yes.'

Nell's never told anyone before, and now she has, she's not sure why it seems such a big deal.

'But you didn't make that decision,' says Frances.

'She smiled at me. She gave me this really big smile, as if she'd read my mind and wanted to say,

179

we'll get through this, and I knew that I couldn't let her down.'

Frances doesn't say anything for a few moments. Then she puts her arm round Nell's shoulders. 'I never knew it was like that,' she says simply.

For a second, Nell lets her body relax into Frances, who sits very straight, supporting her weight. Nell thinks, my friend is supporting me. It's the first time she's truly understood the expression.

'What's the matter?' Abruptly, Lucy turns round and sees her leaning on Frances, sobbing.

They spring apart like teenage lovers caught in a clandestine embrace.

'Nothing, darling,' calls Nell.

'Well, have a happy face,' Lucy urges.

'Are you angry with Alexander?' Frances asks.

'No,' Nell says.

'I would be,' says Frances.

'I feel sorry for him. It must be horrible to feel so isolated. Sometimes I think that he's still in a state of post-traumatic shock.'

'He has you.'

'Yes, but I'm part of the problem.'

'Problem? I think you're a saint!' Frances says.

'Oh, I'm not at all saintly, actually,' Nell says.

'You're too nice,' says Frances.

'God, I hate it when people tell me that,' Nell says, crossly.

'Alexander was always a loner,' Frances muses. 'It was so weird when you got off with him. Nobody had ever seen him have a relationship with anyone before.'

Something about this recollection jars in Nell's mind.

'You said he had loads of girlfriends . . .' she says.

'Did I?'

180

'On my first day!'

She remembers the conversation distinctly because she's always slightly resented the way that Alexander looks mystified when she refers to his old girlfriends, as if he's forgotten he ever had any.

'I probably said lots of people wanted to . . .' Frances says quickly.

'Who thought it was weird when I got off with him?' Nell asks.

'Everyone!'

Nell's a little unsettled by the thought of all the other teachers in Tokyo being amazed behind her back. Stiff with the cold, she stands up and beckons to Lucy.

Frances stubs out her cigarette with the sole of her boot.

They both watch Lucy's stumbling progress up the beach.

'Look!' she says. Her little hands are cupping three big pebbles. 'This one is for Frances. This one is for you, Mummy, and this one is for Ben.'

'Who's Ben?' asks Frances.

'Boyfriend,' says Nell.

'He'll probably just chuck it back out to sea,' Frances remarks.

'Do you like them?' Lucy asks.

'Lovely,' Nell and Frances say together.

'What about one for Mrs Bunting?'

'No, she's going to have a starfish,' Lucy says. 'Can we please go to the starfish shop now?'

'All right then,' says Nell, pleased to get moving again after the long cold wait.

Wooden wind chimes on the door of the shell shop rattle as they push it open. Out of the wind, the inside of the shop seems cosy. There's a dry, slightly fishy smell exactly like somewhere else Nell has been, but she cannot immediately place it.

Sea urchin lamps and mobiles made of translucent slices of shell hang so low from the ceiling that Frances catches her hair. On the floor are baskets filled with graded sizes of cowries, scallops and spiky white conches.

Lucy picks up a handful of the tiniest cowries. 'They're speckled like ladybirds,' she says.

Nell crouches down beside her. Of all the gifts of parenthood, she most loves being shown the world again through a child's eyes.

'And look at this!' She picks up a half-abalone with a silvery rainbow inside.

'Is it made of metal?' Lucy asks.

They've been doing materials in school.

'No. It's shell.'

Nell knows that's not quite an adequate answer. She's trying to think what shell actually is. Calcium of some sort? Is calcium a metal?

'Where are the starfish?' Lucy suddenly remembers her quest, letting Nell off the hook.

'Over here!' Frances calls.

Lucy chooses the biggest starfish she can find.

'Look at that!'

Frances points to a kitsch tableau of three rabbits made of shells.

'It's so lovely!' says Lucy. 'Can I have it?'

'No, darling, we're just buying a starfish for Mrs Bunting,' Nell intervenes.

'But I do want it so much, please, please, please!' Lucy jumps up and down.

'No darling, it's hideous,' says Nell.

'Frances likes it.'

Nell looks despairingly at Frances, who shrugs her shoulders.

'I want to buy it as a present for Daddy,' says Lucy, trying another tactic. 'Because,' she tries to think of a persuasive reason, 'because he's not having a lovely day at the seaside.'

'I don't think Daddy would like it,' says Nell.

'He would! Daddy loves rabbits. Do you remember when Daddy and me went for a walk and we saw the field with the rabbits in?'

'I take Lucy for a walk every day. We see cows in fields and magpies. Alex takes her once and they see rabbits!' Nell explains to Frances.

'I know,' says Frances, 'I read about it in your column.'

'God!' says Nell. 'I can't believe I'm so unimaginative!'

'I freeze my tits off playing golf, I buy her lunch. I get a stone. Alexander does bugger all, and gets this charming little *objet d'art*,' Frances whispers.

Nell laughs.

'Bloody men!' says Frances.

'Bloody men,' Nell agrees.

They smile at each other. They haven't had a bloody men conversation since the long drunken evenings they used to spend together in Tokyo before she and Alexander got together.

'This shop smells terrible,' Lucy announces.

And suddenly Nell knows what the smell reminds her of.

Alexander's mother's hut in Mersea where they went because Joan wanted to see the sea before she died.

The day started inauspiciously when Joan refused to acknowledge that Lucy needed to be strapped into a car seat for the journey and accused Nell of wasting her precious time by going to Mothercare to buy one.

It was the first occasion that Nell caught a glimpse of

183

why Alexander had spent his adult life living as far away as possible from his mother. She felt sorry for her, and guilty for using up one of the few hours left to her, but she was appalled by the sheer selfishness and immediate emotional blackmail Joan was prepared to employ. It was a battle Nell knew she had to win, not just for Lucy's safety, but for her own integrity. She also saw that, left to his own devices, Alexander would have backed down and taken the risk with Lucy's life to pacify his mother. And that realization had shocked her.

On the way to Mersea, the atmosphere in the car was thick with Joan's bad temper, and Lucy, normally such a happy baby, cried almost non-stop. Whenever Nell thinks about Joan, which she tries not to do often, she sees her expression as she craned her neck round from the front seat, her eyes sliding from Lucy's wailing face to Nell's, making her feel like a totally incompetent human being.

Once they had managed to open the great rusty padlock on the hut, the inside was like a time warp, with nets and lines left for twenty years, and the stale smell of shells and old creosote. The striped fabric of two deckchairs had rotted through, so they stood just inside the hut watching the tide come in. The faint mist of drizzle became rain so heavy and fast that the sky merged into the sea. Alexander draped a perished yellow waterproof cape over his head and ran to buy oysters. His mother wanted to fry them with bacon in a blackened pan, but they couldn't get the one-ring Calor gas stove to work, and so ate them raw.

A few days later, when Joan died, the taste of oysters was still in Nell's mouth.

Perhaps Lucy thinks that the shell shop smells horrible because of some forgotten memory of that ghastly day.

Nell wonders what has happened to the hut at Mersea. Has Alexander sold it? Alexander's immensely disorganized about his mother's estate. Letters about her books pile up on his desk; he can't seem to bring himself to open them. It was only when Nell took a desperate phone call from a publisher on the point of printing new editions of Joan's Sasha books without signed contracts that Nell realized that Alexander's inability to sort out her affairs was actually losing them money. She made him promise to deal with everything, or at least put it in the hands of a lawyer. She offered to do it herself, but he wouldn't let her. She knows that he hasn't done anything since then.

The shop assistant wraps the horrible ornament Lucy has insisted on buying her father in tissue paper and puts it in a plastic bag.

Serves him right, Nell thinks, wondering whether she was being completely truthful when she told Frances that she was not angry with Alexander.

'Let's get some air,' she says, needing to blow the stench of shells from her hair and clothes.

Fifteen

There's a camera attached high up to one of the lampposts of Portman Square and it's pointing in their direction. They say that if you've got nothing to hide you shouldn't mind being filmed, but Kate looks down at the pavement guiltily the moment she spots her hidden observer.

If they were to play the film back later on television, she wonders if the viewers would be able to tell anything from the blurry sequence of still frames. She and Alexander are obviously together, because they're walking along the broad pavement at the same pace, but they're not touching or talking. They could be colleagues, or cousins. There's no visible sign that half an hour ago they were having sex.

Were there security cameras in Selfridges watching the changing rooms?

Kate feels her face going bright pink.

A sharp breeze is blowing down Baker Street, cutting through her clothing, making her skin feel bare, cooling the dampness at the top of her legs. She feels as if she looks different, like when she first lost her virginity, guilty and at the same time glowing with the aftermath of pleasure.

She glances at Alexander at the same moment as he turns his eyes to her. They smile as if they're sharing a private joke, then, equally quickly, look away.

Did the camera's shutter open for that exhilarating second of intimacy or will the record simply show fuzzy figures taking giant jerky steps up the street, their heads bent against the wind?

Out in the open air, she can't find a way of starting a conversation with him. They've just skipped all the getting to know each other part of the relationship and they're too far on now to ask the usual questions.

Kate saw a programme on telly recently about social etiquette. It said that if you're nervous, it's best to start a conversation with family, work, education and recreation. The initials spell a word that's easy to remember. FWER. That can't be right. Trouble is, she doesn't really want to ask him about his family because it's a bit sad. She knows what his work is. She can't start asking how many GCSEs he got now. So she's left with recreation.

'If we were in a film now, what would the film be?' she ventures finally.

You're not meant to ask questions that can be answered with a yes or a no, but that sounds stupid, like one of those silly games Marie's always getting her to play, where they have to be a meal or a character from history.

He doesn't say anything and now she's torn between enquiring whether he heard, and wanting to take the question back in case he says something that she doesn't like.

If he replies *Pretty Woman*, she's going to feel like a tart. If he says *Sleepless in Seattle*, then she'll have to ask him if he's got a child, and she doesn't really want to know. She does. But she doesn't.

What would Marie do?

Marie would say, 'It's just sex. Why do you have to dress it up?'

God, it's weird making love with your clothes on.

Kind of like being a teenager again, with hands going everywhere under the cover of fabric.

A giggle blurts out of Kate's mouth.

'What?' Alexander asks.

'Nothing,' says Kate.

He laughs. She's right on the edge of feeling special and feeling patronized, but he puts his arm around her, and it settles her.

Perhaps he's got a girlfriend, but he's bored.

A taxi stops beside them at traffic lights. The smiling voice of Sophie Ellis-Bextor floats out of the driver's open window. 'If This Ain't Love . . .'

Kate knows that whenever she hears this song in the future she will think of him.

'*Last Tango in Paris*, perhaps?' Alexander says. 'Last Tango in Selfridges.'

'What?'

For a second, Kate doesn't know what he's talking about.

'The film,' he says, looking a bit embarrassed.

It's one of those movies she's seen bits of, flicking over from something on another channel, or turning off when her brothers come spilling in from the pub on a Saturday night. She has an impression of arty graininess, and a camera that whirls in and out of focus. And sex.

'D'you think it's just sex, then?' she says. Why *last* tango? Is he saying that they're not going to do it again?

'I don't know. Is it?' he says.

She knows that the answer she gives now is so important that if they were in a movie, there would be a freeze frame.

'I don't know,' she says eventually.

They walk a little further.

'To be honest,' she says, feeling the need to

elaborate, 'I can't really remember a lot about it, except that Marlon Brando was wearing a sort of long overcoat.'

Then it's Alexander's turn: his laughter comes blurting out. 'You're unbelievable!' he says.

She loves the way he says that.

Unbelievable. It's not a word she's thought a lot about before, but when he says it it's full of wonder and fun and it makes her quiver with pleasure.

'What's your favourite word?' she asks him.

The homeward bound traffic is beginning to build on the Marylebone Road. There's a queue of red brake lights as far as the eye can see westward.

'Spontaneity!' Alexander shouts. 'What's yours?'

The revving of engines and beeping of horns is so loud it does something to Kate's brain, making her unable to think. Alexander takes her hand as they cross.

When the noise level drops enough to allow speech, she says, 'Serendipity's a good one. I think it was voted top in one of those polls.'

He smiles at her. 'What film were you thinking of?' he asks.

'I don't know,' she says.

Stupid! Having answers ready is part of the art of conversation.

'There was that one with Meryl Streep and Robert de Niro, where they meet on a train . . .' She grabs at the first film she can think of but her voice trails away as she remembers the title.

'*Falling in Love*?' says Alexander.

'It was meant to be kind of a modern version of *Brief Encounter*,' she says, trying to gloss over the L word.

Why does saying the word love matter so much? He's fucked her wearing borrowed Giorgio Armani in a cubicle observed by the entire security team at

Selfridges, so what's so outrageous about telling him that she loves him?

'You're nothing like Meryl Streep,' he says.

There's an amused look on his face that makes her feel slightly defensive. She wasn't claiming to be like Meryl Streep.

'You're nothing like Robert de Niro,' she retaliates. 'As a matter of fact,' it occurs to her, 'in that film, Robert de Niro wasn't much like Robert de Niro either.'

'So, not at all like today, then?' he says with a smile that bursts over his face like a firework.

It's beautiful enough to change things, his smile, like a spell, or a charm.

Is that where the idea of people having charm comes from?

'It wasn't much of a movie,' he says, after a moment's thought, 'because it hadn't updated the moral dilemma in *Brief Encounter*, so you didn't care about the characters. It was like, well, if you're unhappy, why don't you just leave?'

It's the most she's heard him say in one breath.

Perhaps he's divorced.

They cross the road into Regent's Park. They've gone quiet again, so she might as well not have asked about films.

'Is this your favourite park?' she asks.

Yes/no answer, but what the hell? She's got to say something.

'I suppose it's the one I know best,' he replies.

'I've not seen this one yet. I've been to Hyde Park,' she tells him.

'Regent's Park is a bit more formal,' he says, pointing up at the grand white terraces which edge the Outer Circle. 'I've always wondered who lives in these buildings. I remember coming past in a taxi one night when I was a child. It must have been early evening in winter because the curtains weren't yet drawn and from a distance the windows were all lit up like orange lanterns. When we were closer, I could see chandeliers inside, and people at a party. It was like getting a glimpse into a secret world . . .'

Kate pictures his face pressed up against a dark window of the taxi. She can imagine him easily as a five-year-old boy still curious about everything.

'Did you want to be the sort of person who lived there and had the park for a garden?' she asks.

His expression changes, like a shutter going down.

'I don't think so,' he says.

There are one or two people in boats on the lake. Sunlight glints across the surface of the water making it look dense, like mercury.

A bundle of toddler on reins, so well wrapped up in fleecy hat and jacket it's impossible to tell whether it's a boy or a girl, is throwing pieces of bread delightedly at an audience of ducks and geese. A pair of swans glide regally up to the bank and the squabbling mass of birds parts before them. The toddler is frightened and trots away.

'Did you know that swans belong to the Queen?' Kate asks, breaking the intense silence that has fallen on them as they watch the water.

'Yes,' says Alexander. He stares over the lake. 'Funny, isn't it, that there are certain facts that everyone knows, like about swans. It's trivia that gives you your identity. A Japanese person might be able to speak English really well, but he wouldn't know about the swans . . .'

'He would if he'd taken the riverboat to Richmond,' Kate tells him. 'They told us on the commentary.'

Alexander looks at her with his surprised expression.

'It's ever so nice down there,' Kate says, quickly, 'like countryside.'

Now he's laughing.

Now what's she said that's so funny?

'Would you like an ice-cream?' he asks.

'Yes. All right,' Kate says.

He runs off towards a little café at the edge of the lake. Kate sits down on a bench, feeling slightly self-conscious, as if someone's looking at her, but no-one is.

On the next bench along, a couple of women are gossiping about the progress of a relationship. Kate's always surprised by how loudly women in London talk about their love lives in cafés, or walking down the street shouting updates into their mobile phones. It must be because London's so big, the chances of being overheard by someone you know are a lot less. She stares at the island in the middle of the lake, trying to look as if she's not listening to what they're saying.

'. . . I mean, if he really didn't like me at all he wouldn't have said it, would he?' says Number 1.

She's got long dark hair that she keeps throwing back over her shoulder and she's smoking.

'Depends. I mean it's an easy way to get a fuck, isn't it?'

Number 2 has a bleached blond crop and a diamond in the side of her nose. She's eating sandwiches out of a triangular plastic Pret à Manger box.

'He would have got that anyway!'

Dirty cackles from both.

'How was it?' asks Number 2, through a mouthful of food.

'Fantastic!'

'Well then . . .'

Kate thinks that Number 2 is jealous. She wants to say to Number 1, I really wouldn't tell her anything that you wouldn't want spread around. But then Number 1 isn't a very nice person either because Number 2's got a blob of mayonnaise on her nose and she's not telling her.

'Trouble is there's you know who . . .' says Number 1, putting one cigarette out and lighting another, drawing in the smoke as if it's her first of the day.

'Is she still around, then?'

Is this an ex-girlfriend who's trying to make a come-back, a wife, or a confidante who doesn't approve of his liaison with Number 1? Kate wants to know.

'He says that they haven't been getting on . . .'

'They always say that. So, are you going to see him again?'

'Well, he said—'

Alexander plonks himself down beside Kate and hands her a white chocolate Magnum. Kate's a little disappointed not to hear the rest of the story.

'How did you know it was my favourite?' she asks him, peeling off the wrapper.

'It was all they had,' he says.

He's got an orange Calippo himself.

'You seem more like a white chocolate kind of person,' he says, retracting his original reason as he catches her glance at his lolly.

He's used to buying white chocolate Magnums, Kate thinks. That doesn't mean anything, except that he's used to being with a woman. Men aren't as crazy for white chocolate as women are. What did she expect? He's hardly likely to have no past. Everyone's got some baggage. You can't assume a wife from a white chocolate Magnum. Can you?

'How much do I owe you?' she asks, getting her purse out of her jacket pocket.

'Don't be silly.'

'I haven't paid for anything today.'

'Well, when you're in Bali, you can have a fresh pineapple juice on me.'

Kate takes a very tentative bite, but an enormous crack opens up down the side of the chocolate coating, and she knows that a big piece is going to fall off onto her lap as soon as she takes her mouth away.

Bali. She had forgotten all about Bali.

The chocolate falls, she kicks it away with her heel. A lone pigeon pecks at it and tries to carry the whole piece off to some less public place where he can eat it all by himself, but he's not quick enough and a whole flock of pigeons descends squabbling; some of the geese look up from the lake to see what the matter is.

Alexander, who appears unaware that he's sitting on the edge of a major bird incident, suddenly notices. His eyes fall on the piece of chocolate and on Kate's boot trying surreptitiously to shoo the birds away. He looks from the ground to her face and smiles. And then he puts his free arm around her shoulder. She lets her head rest on his shoulder, and he squeezes her arm, gently, just above the elbow, and there's more intimacy in that small squeeze than in anything they have yet done together.

She sits perfectly still, not wanting to move a cell in case it makes him take his arm away as casually as he draped it there.

How sad he is.

She would love more than anything in the world to make him happy.

She watches the passers-by.

A woman with a toddler in a buggy is smoking, flicking her cigarette ash far too casually near the child's head. She's wearing a cheap-looking waisted leather jacket and her ears are pierced in about twenty places.

Next there's a couple with a pram and it looks like their first time out with the baby. The guy keeps bending over the pram to tuck in the baby's blanket, and the woman's tummy hasn't yet gone back in after birth.

An old bloke hobbles past. He has a shock of white hair and a stick, and looks a bit like the one who used to lead the Labour Party, the one who wore a duffle-coat to the Cenotaph, and that's all anyone can ever remember about him. Kate can't think of his name.

There's an elderly woman with a fitted greenish tweed suit and two miniature dogs on leads who are straining to get away. Her hair is exactly the same colour as the dogs' coats, white with a sort of yellow tinge, like a nicotine stain. The woman stares back as Kate's eyes fall on her. Slightly changing her orientation, she walks towards the bench they're sitting on.

'It is Alexander, isn't it?'

Alexander's hand drops instantly, tellingly, from Kate's shoulder.

'Hello!' he says, jumping up, his face all huge, false delight.

'You're back in your old stamping ground, are you?' says Tweed, in a loud, posh voice.

'Just for today,' he says.

The dogs yap around Kate's ankles as if they can tell she's an impostor. She doesn't know whether to stand up or remain seated.

'Lovely day!' Tweed says.

'Lovely!' Alexander repeats. He looks up at the sky.

'Well . . .' says the woman.

'We'd better be getting along,' Alexander says to Kate.

'Yes,' she says, standing up, and even though it's

only one word, she knows that Tweed has picked up her accent and slotted it into the profile she is creating that already has her clothes and age recorded.

At the same moment as Alexander turns to walk away from the woman, Kate takes a step towards her as if to pass her.

'Better decide which way you're going,' says Tweed.

It's probably just a casual remark, but it sounds as if she's chosen the words for maximum innuendo.

Alexander does an about-turn and hurries after Kate.

'Sorry about that,' he says, as he catches her up.

'About what?'

She's walking very fast and determined not to look at him.

'About not introducing you. I couldn't remember her name.'

'Really?' she says sarcastically. 'Can you remember mine?'

'Kate . . .'

He looks so mortified that she wants to snatch back her sarcasm, but she doesn't believe he has forgotten the woman's name.

'She was a friend of my mother's. Except they hated each other. You know how it is sometimes?'

'No, I don't know how it is sometimes,' Kate says.

He stops walking. She stops too. Glares at him.

'What's up?' he asks.

'You were embarrassed by me,' she says.

'No.'

'She looked at me like I was something the dog dragged in,' Kate says.

It sounds absurd given the insect-sized dogs the woman was with.

'What do you think those dogs are capable of bringing in?' Alexander asks, tuning into her thought. 'A letter?'

'A leaf?' Kate joins in.

'She looked at you like you were a leaf. That's terrible!'

'An ice-lolly wrapper?'

'Oh dear!'

'You know what I mean!' Kate protests. But her anger's gone now.

'I think she was a magistrate,' Alexander says, as they start walking again. 'She looks at everyone as if they're a young offender.'

'Look, there's a black swan!' says Kate, pointing across the lake.

They've just had their first argument!

'Would you like to go rowing?' he asks, as if he's offering her a treat as a kind of apology.

'I don't know how to row,' she says, eyeing the lake warily.

'The point is that I row. You just sit looking picturesque,' says Alexander.

The unexpected compliment gives her the confidence to say, echoing his nice pronunciation, 'The point is that I can't swim.'

'I expect they have life jackets,' Alexander says. 'And if you fall in, I'll save you.'

He puts his arm around her again.

'That sounds like the lyric to a song,' she says, brightly; then, before she can stop herself, 'If we were a song, what song do you think we would be?'

Sixteen

Alexander wonders whether Kate's desire to define their relationship is a girls' thing, or simply a human impulse he's trying to deny. He wants only to experience being with her in the present. Maybe it's just that she's more honest than he is. He finds it easier to let things go along, not lying, but not telling the truth either, but he knows that they're close to the limit of behaving as if they have no past and no future. They already have half a day's history together.

How strange it is that she asked whether this is just sex, because the sex felt like it was so many things. Amazing, uplifting, profound, stripped-bare, dangerous, tender.

He looks at Kate. Curious Kate. Kate who wants to know what he's thinking. He wants to reassure her that it isn't just the surface of her that he likes, although he does like the surface very much, and the way her emotions seem so close to it, as if she's lacking a layer of protection. He likes her walk which expresses her mood, and her vitality even when she's quiet. She brings to mind distant science lessons about electricity – the potential that is always there, ready to be switched on, and she's got so much energy stored that some of it can't help spilling out, filling the space around her with shimmering possibility.

He knows that if he says all this, she will only ask for more.

Women always want more.

The wooden scrape of oars twisting in rowlocks and the slop of the blade pulling through water is soothing for him, but he's aware that her small body seated stiffly on the plank opposite him is getting more and more rigid the further they glide away from land. He's half tempted to rock the boat a little, to scare her in a boyish prank, but she's proud and she would find it humiliating to have her fear exposed.

Close up, the water looks dirty and has a faintly stagnant smell.

'Is it difficult, rowing?' she asks.

'Not when you get the hang of it. D'you want to have a go?'

'No!'

The word comes out with several syllables and much shaking of head.

'You should learn to swim.'

'I know.' She stares at the water as if she can see something very interesting about four feet under it. Then she looks straight at him.

'My dad drowned.' She says it so matter-of-factly that for a moment he thinks she's joking.

'I'm sorry,' he says, ashamed now for making her come onto the water. 'You should've said.'

'He didn't drown in a lake,' she says, staring at the water. 'He was drunk. He fell over, knocked himself unconscious and drowned in a puddle on his way back from the pub. Can you believe that? A puddle! Silly sod!'

Alexander's shocked, not just by the revelation, but by the flat, unemotional manner in which she delivers it, which he recognizes as a front for hidden pain.

199

'How old were you?'

'Fourteen.'

He pulls the oars up so they're just drifting in the middle of the lake. His imagination had given her two healthy smiling parents, but it had no reason to.

'Do you still miss him?' he asks.

She looks at him with large clear eyes.

'You know when you think about someone you always have one picture that comes up first?' she says.

He nods.

'Well, I have this image of us all walking to Mass on Sunday. We're dressed up in our best clothes. Marie's wearing this lemon yellow dress which sort of rustled. It was really her party dress, but Mum said she was growing up so fast she might as well get some use out of it . . .'

She looks up to see whether he's still with her.

He nods.

'. . . She's about ten or eleven, just at the point where she's turning into a woman, but she's still a little girl, you know, with her hair in bunches, and she's laughing and skipping along. Suddenly my dad raises his arm and clouts her round the head. Marie just stands there, then she puts her hand up to her ear, and this drop of thick red blood drips onto the puff sleeve of her dress. And it kind of stays there as a blob for ever such a long time and we're all staring at it, and then suddenly it's not a blob any more, it's kind of splatted into the material, spreading out into the fibres, showing up the weave, you know? Then I'm crying and my brothers are terrified thinking they'll be next. And Marie says to him, really cool like, "What did you do that for?" And my dad replies, "Nothing. And if that's what you get for doing nothing, think what you'll get for doing something!" '

Alexander's been sitting so still, he shivers all over when he shifts position.

'I don't miss him,' says Kate. 'It took a while to get used to him not being there. Not being frightened all the time. No wonder Marie's like she is. What's the point in being good if you're punished for it?'

Alexander's thinking about the party dress. He doesn't know what to say to her.

'Oh, sometimes he was great, you know, but he always spoilt it with violence,' Kate says.

Alexander takes up the oars again. His instinct is to start rowing, to make some sound to fill the confessional silence.

'Do you have one image of your mother that you always think of?' Kate asks.

Her words seem to come from further away than the end of the boat.

She's standing in the kitchen wearing a big purple sweater which hasn't been washed for a while and the undersides of the sleeves are slightly shiny . . .

'Yes I do,' Alexander says, stopping the image going any further.

'Do you miss your mum?' Kate asks.

It's only what he asked her, but the silence in which he should reciprocate a few details yawns between them.

He can't think of his mother as Mum because she despised the word, but he can't explain that because it will make him sound like a snob. It's such a simple question, but it panics him because his mother seems to be with him more now she's dead than when she lived, and his emotions are all tangled up in a mesh he's trying to clamber through that's barbed with anger.

'Yes, I do,' he says, gazing across the lake to the

sloping lawn of the American ambassador's residence, refusing to engage in further probing.

'Did you miss your dad when he left?' Kate wants to know.

Alexander brings his focus back to her. This is much easier territory. He has his answers all worked out because he's had more practice.

'When he left, he told me he was going away for a while, so I assumed that meant he was coming back,' he says, with a short wry laugh.

'. . . He took me out for treats every so often, and every time I saw him I got a present, so, no, I didn't miss him. Then I was about ten and I happened to see him one day on Parliament Hill Fields. He was with his new family and they were flying a kite. He didn't see me. He looked so happy and free with them, not anxious like he was with me, and I suddenly realized that he wasn't ever going to come back. Then I missed him a lot, and I told him that I didn't want to see him any more. It was meant to hurt him, but I think he was probably relieved.'

A large tear has formed in the lower lid of Kate's right eye like a glass bead, then the surface tension breaks and it travels in a thin wet line down her face.

He feels a fraud for adding that last sentence. He has no way of knowing whether his father was relieved or not, but it sounds good and it has always elicited sympathy from women. It occurs to him that this exchange of parental details is like a courtship ritual, a kind of verbal genetic test perhaps, to reveal your background. It normally happens before you mate.

'Hey,' he leans forward, touches her knee, 'it was a long time ago.'

'Didn't you see him again?'

She's like a child, wanting a happy ending to a story.

'Yes. I did. Once. When I was at university. I invited

him up for Sunday lunch. He came, with a lot of swagger and flashing of credit cards and cringe-making talk about how he used to smoke reefers when he was a student . . .'

'What's reefers?'

'Dope.'

'Cannabis?'

Kate's clearly shocked that a parent would do such a thing.

'He took me out to lunch at a very expensive restaurant. We pretended we were having a good time, enjoying each other's company, saying absolutely nothing to each other of any significance. We argued a bit about politics. He's a Tory, of course. Then I asked him why he had left my mother, and I suppose he was a bit carried away by the cigars and brandy and general bonhomie. He said, "She's a marvellous but impossible woman!" and he sort of winked at me, as if I was simply going to agree, now that we had become friends, men together. So I hit him.'

This is the part of the story where the woman normally gasps or claps, but there's a sharp intake of breath and he realizes how inappropriate it was to tell Kate that after her description of her father. And it's not even true. He did feel like hitting him, and somehow the impulse has become an action in the telling.

'I've never hit anyone in my life,' he stammers.

'Sounds like he deserved it,' Kate says, uncertainly.

'The shameful thing was,' Alexander's desperate to inflict some sort of punishment on himself for such a lie, 'I wasn't cross with him for sullying my mother's reputation, or anything noble like that. I was furious with him because it was true, and I was so angry that he left me to cope with her on my own.'

He's never admitted that to anyone before. It makes him feel better about defrauding Kate of her sympathy.

If either of them had the choice, he thinks they would go back to how they were before they got into the boat, both deliberately not asking about each other's past. Now they have each offered up a little of their suffering, they have allowed reality to slide into the boat with them, bringing all its attendant hypotheses and doubts, irrevocably muddying the clarity of passion.

The boating attendant grabs hold of the prow and pulls them in. There's the soft thud of wood on wood, and Kate exhales, as if she's been holding her breath all the time they've been on the water. Alexander steps out of the boat first then stretches out his hand to her. She takes it. He pulls her up and out of the boat and she stands on the jetty again, slightly wobbly. She looks at their hands locked together, then up at him. They walk away from the lake, still holding hands.

It's warmer away from the water, almost summery.

On one of the open playing fields, there's a group of men playing softball. A heap of sports bags on the sidelines has a row of computer cases beside it. The paths are deserted apart from one or two lone figures. It's that transition time of day when mothers are waiting for their children outside school. In half an hour, the park will be full of little boys and girls tearing around running off the energy they've cooped up all afternoon in a sunny classroom.

'What's that?'

Kate's pointing at a group of buildings in the distance surrounded by a fence.

'London Zoo,' he says.

'You can see into it without paying!'

'Yes.'

'Well, I never knew that,' she says.

They stop and watch, right opposite the elephants'

enclosure. One keeper is brushing the dust off an elephant's back with a broom; the other orders a second elephant to lie down, which it does, slowly, almost gracefully, offering up its foot for the keeper to clean with a stick.

'She's having a manicure,' Kate observes.

There's something incredibly calming about watching the unhurried preparations for the elephants' afternoon bath. When the beasts eventually lope into the water, Kate and Alexander start walking again.

'So, you used to live round here, did you?' Kate asks.

He knew that he was not going to get away without further questioning after the meeting with Helge, who looked much the same today as she did – what? – thirty years ago. Like a tweed-covered barrel, Joan used to say.

They're on the Broad Walk, beside the wolves' enclosure.

'Sometimes, as I lay in bed, if it was a very clear night, or about to rain, I could hear the wolves howling,' Alexander says.

He can't work out whether it's chance, or whether he has chosen to court danger by coming back to an area of London he's familiar with.

He and Joan lived on the wrong side of the Chalk Farm Road in a street that was virtually under a railway line, but in distance it wasn't far away. Some of his friends lived in Primrose Hill. Before they all went to university, they used to hang out in the pubs round here. Then, they were traditional boozers with sweaty-faced landlords, red wallpaper and old men coughing in the corners. Now, he knows from reading the Sunday supplements, they're stripped-out spaces that serve char-grilled vegetables and pasta adorned with a few shavings of parmesan or white truffle.

Pop stars live here now.

Then, the only famous person was Kingsley Amis. His mother had met him once at a party in the Sixties and she used to get uncharacteristically fluttery when they passed him walking up Regent's Park Road to the pub. She would say hello, and he would return the greeting with a polite, but slightly mystified smile. And later, Alexander would hear her recounting to her friends: 'We ran into Kingsley, looking tired and emotional, as per usual, the old lech . . .'

In those days his mother's friend Helge lived in a tiny top floor flat in a converted Victorian house on Ainger Road. Perhaps she still does. Then, the dogs she owned were a couple of heavy bull terriers with short bristly white coats like pigs. They used to bound around the flat, playing madly enthusiastic doggy games. He and Joan would sit side by side on the only sofa, like defendants facing Helge who sat on a hard kitchen chair. Slowly the room would fill with smoke from Joan's cigarettes that muffled the pervasive doggy smell. While his mother and Helge gossiped unkindly about the other members of the local Labour Party, Alexander would pass the time imagining what the people who lived downstairs felt about the constant pounding of their ceiling by the pig-dogs.

In his mind he created a mild-mannered couple called the Dismals who were driven to feats of uncharacteristic wickedness by the constant aggravation. He had them devising increasingly desperate plans to rid the house of the dogs, which always failed.

As he and his mother walked home together, across the railway bridge and down the Chalk Farm Road, Alexander would amuse her with the Dismals' latest exploit. First, it was poisoned bones left on the communal staircase, and mistakenly eaten by a visiting poodle. Over the years, the plots became more and more bizarre.

His mother's favourite was when Mr Dismal suspended a giant rumpsteak out of his window on a fishing line in the hope that the dogs would take a flying jump from the third floor window to claim it and land with a suicidal squelch in the basement courtyard below. Unfortunately, on the day in question, Miss Lo, the pretty Chinese woman Alexander imagined living in the garden flat, dragged her mattress out onto the paving to sunbathe, and was just inside mixing herself a cocktail when the beasts took their giant leap. When she returned she found them bouncing up and down, barking wildly at the empty well above.

His mother had laughed so much she started coughing.

They always used to stop at the window of Marine Ices to buy him a double cornet. Melon and chocolate was his favourite combination at the time, the delicate fragrance of frozen cantaloupe swirling in his mouth with the deep thick taste of chocolate. It would last him all the way home.

'We've been to Helge and back,' Joan would say, as she put her key in the door.

The pavement outside the school on Princess Road is blocked with parents. As the doors of the school burst open, the air is suddenly full of the random joyous shrieking of children let out at the end of the day.

Alexander and Kate cross the road and walk up the broad incline of Chalcot Road and up to the square.

'What's this area called?' Kate wants to know. 'It's so pretty.'

'Primrose Hill,' he tells her.

'Where Cruella De Vil lived?' Kate says.

'I don't know. Did she?'

'Pongo and Missis called all the other dogs from the

top of Primrose Hill,' Kate remembers. 'The Twilight Barking.'

He's startled by the odd way that her mind seems to be synching with his, but he assures himself it's not surprising that they've both been thinking about dogs. Every other person who passes has one on a lead and is hurrying towards the park.

He's not sure why he lied to Kate about forgetting Helge's name. Perhaps testing how much she's prepared to forgive him. Perhaps pushing her to condemn him and bring this whole crazy thing between them to a halt.

Men find it impossible to make moral decisions, so they manipulate women into doing it for them. It was one of his mother and Helge's constant themes.

'Do you fancy a coffee?' he asks, as they turn into Regent's Park Road. Next to the bookshop whose owner his mother knew, there's a Polish café which was one of the first places in London you could get a reliable cappuccino. Now every other shop in the street has turned into a coffee bar with tables and chairs outside.

'Ooh, yes please.'

'Outside or inside?'

'Outside,' Kate says, sitting down at the last table left.

'In Italy they would think it completely crazy to sit outside in winter.'

'It's pretty crazy to have spaghetti as your staple food, though, isn't it?' says Kate. 'All that winding!'

'What would you like?' Alexander asks. 'I can recommend the apple crumble.'

'Yes, please. And a cappuccino. But I want to pay this time,' Kate says.

'No, let me.'

'Why?'

'Because you're on a budget.'

'I haven't used any of it today,' she protests.

He watches her through the window. She's a bit cold and she pulls her jacket around her, but she's too proud to change her mind and come inside the steamy warm café. Aware now that she's being observed, she waves at him. She's only three feet away but it seems further separated by plate glass, a passion cake, and a basket full of croissants.

What is he doing?

Alexander puts a mug down in front of Kate and draws up a chair. She skims the dappled froth from the top of her coffee, and puts the teaspoon in her mouth as if it's a most delicious dessert.

'Cappuccino's still a rarity where I come from,' she tells him.

'It's almost unavoidable here,' he says.

'The trouble with the middle classes is that they're bored by nice things like Costa Coffee and Pizza Express because it's all the same, but if you're poor it's a treat.'

'So what are you saying? That poverty's more interesting?'

'No, poverty's much more boring because you can't go out and be bored by a cappuccino, you have to stay in and be bored by the mould on your kitchen wall, but at least if you do have a cappuccino you enjoy it,' she says tersely, 'so that's something.'

Then she digs at the slab of apple crumble he has bought her. The cold slices of cooked apple have a crumbly coating of thick white icing sugar.

'I think I've been rather selfish, haven't I?' he says.

'Why?'

'You didn't like sushi, or oysters . . .'

'You bought me a cappuccino this morning,' she says.

'Did I? Oh yes.'

It seems a lifetime ago that he was standing in the alleyway outside her flat wondering whether to press the bell marked Joy.

It started with him buying her a cappuccino, and this is where it should end, he thinks. If he were sensible, this is where it would end. He takes a deep breath.

'That woman we saw in the park . . .' he says.

'Tweed?'

He smiles.

'Yes, Tweed . . . Her real name is Helge.'

He waits for Kate's reaction.

'Why did you say you couldn't remember?' she asks.

'Because I didn't know how to introduce you,' he says, 'I didn't know what to say you were.'

'A friend?' Kate suggests.

'Is this what this is, then, just friendship?' he asks.

She smiles, acknowledging the echo of her earlier question.

'I'm sorry,' he says.

'What for?'

'About Helge.'

'It's OK. I knew,' she says.

This isn't what was supposed to happen. He told her about Helge to make her cross with him, but if anything she seems more contented.

'What's the time?' she asks.

He looks at his wrist. No watch.

There's a clock inside above the counter. He peers through the glass window. 'Nearly four o'clock,' he says.

'We'd better be getting back,' Kate says. 'My shift starts at six.'

210

Now he doesn't want this to end, even though he was just making an effort to put a stop to it.

The air between them is buzzing with questions he daren't ask and cannot answer.

What happens now?

What happens when we get back to the flat?

What happens when you go to work?

'Would you like to go up to the top of Primrose Hill and look at the view?' he asks, trying to postpone the moment for all these decisions.

'Yes!'

'Come on then.'

'Wait here a minute!'

Alexander stands on the pavement outside the bookshop while Kate's inside chatting to the owner. He sees the old man's face lift with pleasure at something she says. She's holding a book, but he can't see what it is.

Then she's out again with a broad smile on her face and a plastic carrier bag in her hand. 'I've bought you a present,' she says, holding it out to him.

'But . . .'

'It's only a day's budget, which you haven't let me spend,' she insists, pressing it into his hands.

There's something about the size and weight of the book inside the bag that he recognizes immediately. His heart starts to thud against his ribcage. It's like a scary moment in a film he's seen before. He knows what's going to happen, but he still doesn't want to look.

Kate's so eager to have his reaction to the present, she won't let him put it off any longer.

'Come on!'

She jiggles up and down.

It's a children's book, a shiny new paperback edition that smells slightly of chemicals.

'Look,' she says, pointing to the picture on the front of a little boy lying on a brightly coloured carpet. 'It's you!'

Alexander's past rushes into his present.

'*Sasha's Magic Carpet*,' he reads.

'It's about this little boy who has this magic carpet – see,' Kate enthuses.

'I know.'

She takes the book back and flips through, showing him, stopping at favourite pictures and glancing at him for his reaction. She's smiling really hard as if the sheer smiliness of her smile will force the corners of his mouth to turn upwards.

He lifts the book from her hands and opens it at the first page.

The book's dedication reads:

'For Alexander, of course.'

He points to each word, like teaching a child to read.

Kate looks at it. At him. Still not understanding.

'My mother wrote this,' he says.

'You're Sasha?'

Seventeen

'Fifty people feared dead in this morning's train crash,' the DJ on the tannoy announces as Nell and Frances step onto the pier. 'And enjoy the sunshine, because it's not going to last. That's the news headlines. More on the hour. Now, if this ain't love . . .'

The dance rhythm of Spiller's summer hit pounds out of the speakers on the pier. Nell watches as the music filters from Lucy's ears to her legs making her walk in step to the beat. The single was popular with Lucy's class at the school Christmas party, where she and her friend Ben were the last two left in the game of musical statues. Ben eventually won the prize of a packet of stamper pens, but being a nice well-brought-up child, he offered Lucy the pink one as a consolation. Nell recognized the shining look of gratitude on Lucy's face as love.

'Do you notice how he said "this morning's train crash", as if there's one every morning?' says Frances.

'It's beginning to feel like that,' says Nell.

'Since I've been back there's about one a week. What's the country coming to, that's what I want to know?' says Frances, self-mockingly. 'That's another sign of middle age, by the way, when you start saying things like that.'

'Do you find it very different from when you left?'

'Lots more coffee shops,' says Frances. 'Which is

weird because everyone seems to be on caffeine-free detox. Better sandwiches, but everyone's on a diet. No banks, because they're all restaurants. It's like the country is defined by consumption and denial.'

'How was it defined before?' Nell asks.

'Just denial,' says Frances.

Lucy turns round.

'Ben has a sun denial in his garden,' she says. 'How far is the funfair, do you think?'

'Tell you what, why don't you count how many steps it takes to get there?' Nell answers, trying to contain her laughter.

'How many do you think it is?' Lucy asks.

'Oh, about a thousand,' Nell guesses.

'How many do you think, Frances?'

'About two thousand,' Frances obliges.

'I think about a million!' says Lucy. 'OK, I'm starting! You count too, Mummy.'

'I'm counting in my head,' says Nell.

'One, two, three . . .'

They let her get a little way ahead, then Frances says, 'You don't think Alexander's having an affair, do you?'

Nell knew that she would ask. Frances always thinks men are having affairs. Often she's right.

'I think Alexander's probably too lazy to have an affair,' she replies.

'Perhaps he's using up all his energy having one, and there's none left for you?'

'Jesus, Frances!'

'Sixteen, seventeen, eighteen!' Lucy shouts.

'Sorry,' says Frances.

'I don't think he's having an affair because I think he would be nicer to me if he were,' says Nell, carefully.

'How do you figure that?'

214

'Well.' Nell hesitates, making sure Lucy's out of earshot. 'Well, at Christmas he came home really late from the school party and he'd definitely been snogging. He had lipstick round his mouth, and those kind of hollow eyes that you get when you've been drinking too much, you know?'

'Snogging?' Frances repeats, disbelievingly.

'I'm sure that it wasn't more than snogging because he caught the last train, and, actually, if it had been more, he would have taken at least one glance in a mirror before coming home, don't you think?'

'Not that you spend hours coming up with this rational explanation, or anything,' says Frances.

'I was completely paranoid for a while,' Nell says. 'I even went through his jacket pockets. I really hated myself for doing that.'

'But you failed to unearth any evidence of wrong-doing?'

'Just a joint bank account with his mother which he should have closed. He's so hopeless at dealing with things like that. Anyway. The next day, he had a terrible hangover, but he wasn't grumpy or moody. He was trying really hard to be nice. He helped me with the tree. He played with Lucy . . .'

'So?' Frances says.

'It was like he'd had a glimpse of what it was like out there, and he'd decided not to go there.'

'I don't get your logic.'

'What I'm saying is if he were having an affair now, I think he'd be nicer because he would be feeling guilty.'

'That's a bit tortuous.'

'Oh well, maybe he is having an affair,' Nell says, bowing to Frances's greater tenacity in argument.

'You don't seem bothered about it.'

'I was at Christmas.'

'Did you ask him?'

'No.'

'Why not?'

'I didn't want to nag him. Everyone's allowed a Christmas snog, aren't they? You know, mistletoe, and all that.'

'Very understanding of you.'

Nell sighs.

'Sometimes I think it would be easier if he was having an affair,' she says.

Frances raises her eyebrows, but Lucy comes running back to them.

'How many steps?' Nell asks.

'Two hundred million,' Lucy says.

Most of the funfair rides are too old for Lucy, but there's a shallow water tank with rubber dinghies floating in it, a child's version of bumper cars. It's the sort of attraction that Nell likes because Lucy is visible and safe, but it gives her a little bit of independence.

'Would you like a go on that?' Nell asks.

There are several younger children in the boats.

'Yes, OK then,' Lucy says uncertainly.

She gets in. A little boy in an orange boat bumps her. There's a moment when she could either laugh or cry. She laughs.

'She likes boys, doesn't she?' Frances observes.

'Boys like her,' Nell says. 'Her friend Ben is completely smitten.'

'Bless,' says Frances.

They watch Lucy motoring around the tank, growing in confidence.

'I read an article about the chemistry of love the other day,' Frances says. 'Apparently you display measurable physical changes when you fall in love. All these hormones are released. They wired these people up and showed them a picture of someone they loved and their brainwaves went crazy.'

'Really?'

'Someone could make a lot of money out of it,' Frances continues, pointing at a kiosk that's advertising computerized astrology charts.

'You could call it the Love Test. You pay to have your man wired up and presented with a photo of you, and if the screen lights up, then you're all right.'

'The screen might light up when he looks at all sorts of different pictures,' Nell points out.

'I suppose you're right. Like pornography, you mean? How come you're so practical?'

Nell feels almost guilty for ruining Frances's wacky business venture. 'So, how long does this chemical reaction go on for?' she asks.

'About eighteen months, apparently,' Frances says. 'And then you either split up or continue without the chemicals, which is not nearly so much fun.'

Nell laughs.

'Another alternative is to have a baby. Apparently giving birth produces more or less the same hormones as falling in love. That's why I'm thinking of skipping out the man bit altogether and going straight for the child . . .'

Nell's not really listening. She's thinking that the scientific explanation fits in more or less exactly with the history of her relationship with Alexander. Can love really be reduced to the flow of hormones? And if it can, where does that leave them now? Are those increasingly infrequent moments of sheer bliss just blips of oxytocin? She can't get her head round it.

'Any chance of a lolly?' Lucy says, when her turn runs out.

*　　　*　　　*

Nell's relieved to see a Wall's logo on the kiosk. Calippo is one of the few lollies that doesn't carry a nut warning. She buys one for Lucy and white chocolate Magnums for herself and Frances.

'So, tell me about this boyfriend of yours,' Frances says as they sit down on a line of abandoned deck-chairs on the east side of the pier which is sheltered from the wind.

'Mummy, do I have to?'

It's one of those phrases that Lucy's heard older children saying but has not quite understood. She uses it brightly, at the beginning of explanations or stories as an alternative to 'Well . . .'

'He's not really a boyfriend . . .' Lucy continues.

'No?'

'A boyfriend is someone you marry, isn't it, Mummy?'

'Sometimes.'

'So, who are you going to marry?' Frances wants to know.

'I want to marry Daddy.'

Frances laughs.

'He's not married, you know,' Lucy tells her earnestly.

'But you can't marry your child,' Frances explains.

'I don't mean when I'm a child,' Lucy tells her, in a voice that's at the very limit of patience, as if Frances is deliberately failing to grasp the simplest point. 'I mean when I'm an adult.'

'But you'll still be Daddy's child, and my child,' Nell tells her.

They've had this conversation before, and she knows that Lucy's convinced that there's some trick involved.

'Mummy is a mummy and a child,' Lucy announces to Frances. 'But Daddy is only a daddy.'

'Not how I think of Alexander, somehow,' Frances says to Nell across the back of Lucy's deckchair.

'Ben is just a friend,' says Lucy, loudly, anxious not to lose command of the conversation. Adults have a way of getting sidetracked.

'Ben has a beautiful house just for him, with a garden, and everything.'

'Sounds like a good prospect.'

'Ben's daddy is a cabinetmaker,' Nell explains to Frances. 'He's made him a sort of Wendy house in the garden with a little picket fence and a flowerbed where they plant seeds and dig them up again to check what's wrong when they don't start growing immediately.'

'Chris is going to build me a castle this summer,' Lucy announces.

This is news to Nell.

'Where?'

'In our garden,' Lucy says.

'Is he indeed?' Nell feels herself flushing with irritation. 'Well, we'll have to see about that.'

It's peculiar how readily phrases emerge from her lips that used to sound so unreasonable when her parents said them.

'A castle in the garden!' Frances says.

'So I can be a real princess.'

Lucy is talking directly to Frances now, intuitively sensing that she is the more sympathetic audience for this particular story.

'It's going to have battlements and a tower and a moat . . .'

'Not a moat!' Nell says.

'And will Chris be your handsome prince?' Frances asks, getting into the excitement of the project.

'Not Chris!' Lucy explains. 'Chris is Ben's daddy!'

'Sorry. I meant, will Ben be your handsome prince?'

Lucy gives this question some thought.

'Ben likes being Batman best. Or Buzz Lightyear . . . Chris made Ben a real Buzz Lightyear outfit! With wings, and everything!'

'And can he fly?'

'No,' Lucy corrects her, 'but he can fall with style, can't he, Mummy?'

She takes a very serious lick of her lolly.

The noise in the amusement arcade is so loud it's like an electronic torture chamber. Most of the machines are for teenage boys. One boy, who cannot be more than twelve, is summarily executing real-looking terrorists who leap out menacingly on a video screen, felling them with shots from the pump-action machine gun. Another youth is standing on a hydraulic surf-board, a lit cigarette in his mouth, riding imaginary waves. There is nothing suitable for a small child except a glass case which houses a claw that grabs ineffectively at the mound of soft toys inside.

'Can I have a go?' Lucy says, her eyes gleaming acquisitively at the toys.

'Come on,' Frances says, putting in a twenty pence coin. 'Now look, you just get two goes. This moves the crane away and this moves it along.'

She crouches down beside Lucy.

Carefully, Lucy does as she's told. Nell watches the series of emotions on her face as the claw drops, opens, closes round the head of an imitation Tele-tubby, then fails to pick it up.

'You never win anything from these things,' Nell says, 'they're just a waste of money, darling.'

'But I almost got it,' Lucy says.

'You're a bit old for Teletubbies anyway,' Nell says, trying to move away.

'I do like Tweenies though,' Lucy says, looking long-ingly at the next cabinet.

'All right, one pound. You can have five goes. And that's it.'

Nell hands over the money. Lucy puts it in.

'Did these places used to be so awful?' Nell says to Frances. 'I seem to remember betting on little horses that jerked along a racetrack. At least you had some chance of winning.'

She sees Frances's face.

'OK, don't say it. Middle-aged.'

They both watch Lucy concentrate on her futile task. The claw goes down again. Fizz Tweeny slips away.

'Last go,' says Frances. 'Do you want a bit of help?'

'No.'

Lucy is determined to beat the machine on her own.

The claw goes down again. Miraculously it holds Fizz Tweeny's head. The brightly coloured little doll is lifted precariously into the air.

Nell is transfixed. It's such an unexpected bit of luck that she suddenly feels as if their fate is hanging in mid-air.

Don't drop, please don't drop, she pleads silently.

The claw hovers shakily for what seems like a long time, then opens and Fizz Tweeny falls. There's a satisfying clunk as she's discharged down the prize chute.

'You've won! My God, you've won!' she says, hugging Lucy. 'That's so lucky, we should make a wish together . . .'

She closes her eyes tightly.

'It's only a toy, Mummy,' says Lucy, giving Fizz a quick kiss.

Eighteen

Sasha watched the worker ant struggling along with a woodlouse on his back towards the lichen-spattered stone where the ants lived. All the ants had jobs to do and places to go. Sasha wondered if they talked to each other in ant language, and whether some of them were friends and others didn't like each other much. He looked down at the city which stretched as far as the eye could see and much further. The vastness of it was as amazing as the smallness of the world beside his foot which he stepped over carefully as he climbed back onto his magic carpet . . .

London stretches out before them like a huge model village.

'I always thought Sasha was a bit of a fraud,' Alexander says.

'Why?' Kate asks.

'He never really goes anywhere on his bloody carpet.'

Kate turns her head sharply away from the view and looks at him.

'He *does*,' she protests. 'He goes into his imagination. Sasha finds magic in everyday things.'

Alexander's eyes trail along the horizon. 'Sasha!' he repeats with contempt.

'I always wondered why he had a girl's name,' Kate agrees.

'It's not a girl's name. It's the Russian diminutive of Alexander.'

'Was your mother Russian?'

'No, just pretentious.'

He watches a plane drift slowly across the sky towards Heathrow.

'I think my mother would have loved to call me Sasha, but I wouldn't have it. From the earliest age, apparently, I would always correct people who tried to shorten my name. You know. In that very precise way that children do?'

'Were you like Sasha?' Kate wants to know.

'Probably. I don't really know any more where Sasha ends and I begin. Look,' he says pointing, 'can you see Big Ben? It's just to the right of the Wheel.'

Kate squints.

'Oh yes! And look, over there, St Paul's! It's a bit of a well kept secret, this, isn't it?' she says.

'What?'

'The view. I never knew there was somewhere you could see all of London,' she says. 'Should have done, I suppose.'

'Why?'

'The Twilight Barking, of course.'

She links his arm excitedly. His instinct is to wriggle away from this little act of possession, but he likes the sensation of her arm squeezing his each time she spots another familiar landmark.

'Canary Wharf! It's so far away it looks like a shadow,' she says.

'Is it your favourite big view?' Alexander asks.

Kate considers the teasing question seriously.

'I think it probably is now. Not because it's more beautiful, but because it's, like, infinite. You stand here and you know that London's so big, you couldn't possibly ever come to the end of finding out different things about it . . .'

He remembers watching her hurrying along in front of him down by the Thames yesterday, and the strange sense that their meeting had been foretold. Now he thinks that perhaps it was simply that her ideas about big and little views echoed across the years from his childhood. Perhaps the way Kate sees things was even formed by reading his mother's books.

'Why didn't you tell me about your mother being a writer?' Kate asks.

Again, her thoughts seem to be running alongside his. 'You didn't ask,' he says.

'Oh I hate it when people do that,' Kate says, impatiently. 'Making something that's their fault into your responsibility!'

Her eyes flash with annoyance. To see her as a product of his mother's writing would be a perverse denial of her identity. A hundred thousand children read his mother's books, but no-one is like Kate.

'Sorry,' he says.

'It's not the sort of thing that just crops up, is it?' Kate argues.

'I'm sorry.'

'You let me bang on about being a writer and now I feel a right idiot.'

'Why shouldn't you write?'

'It's easy enough for you to say . . .'

Another plane floats slowly, silently westward.

'My mother used to get cross with people who said that they thought they had a book in them. "The point is not whether you've got a book in you," she said, "but whether you can get it out!" You're only a writer if you can write.'

Kate thinks about that for a few minutes.

'Where did she get her ideas?' she asks.

It's one of the questions the brighter children would

ask when Joan came in to give a talk to his primary school. He hated the days she visited when his teacher would be uncharacteristically nice to him and speak in a slightly louder voice than usual. However much he asked Joan not to mention his name, she always did, and he would feel the eyes of the school turn to him. The other children enjoyed her visits because it meant an afternoon with no work, but the whole day was ruined for Alexander, even the morning before she arrived, when his every thought anticipated the outfit she would choose for her appearance. The clothes she wore 'as an author' were always her most embarrassing – long skirts made out of Indian cloth that smelt of incense, a floor-length knitted cardigan, bright silk scarves, bangles that clinked, and once, to his horror, a bindi mark on her forehead because it was Diwali.

'But we're not Hindu,' he remembers pleading over his Sugar Puffs.

'But it's lovely to celebrate all our cultures, darling,' she told him, licking the tip of her kohl pencil.

He can see now that she enjoyed the visits because it gave her people to talk to during the day. It is only since he's been a parent that he has been able to imagine the loneliness of her life then, and it makes him sad that she died without knowing that he understood. But even though he can acknowledge that she didn't set out to humiliate him, the recollection still makes him simmer with anger.

'Where do you think she got her ideas?'

He throws the question back at Kate, then pulls the book out of the bag and flicks through, stopping at certain pages: a little boy lying on a Persian carpet, a little boy beachcombing in drizzling rain; a little boy with his nose pressed up against the window of a taxi looking at the lighted windows of an elegant Georgian terrace.

'Every single thing I ever did or said went into a book.'

Kate takes the book from his hands, sits down on a bench and starts to read it. She's sitting right back and her legs are crossed from the knees, swinging. The slow rhythm of her concentration eases the tension that is stretched across his shoulders. He walks backwards and forwards in front of her.

'She must have been really proud of you,' Kate says at last, closing the book.

'It's not as simple as that,' Alexander says, suddenly irritated by Kate's straightforward take on everything. 'She stole my childhood.'

He remembers the time when Disney expressed interest in the film rights to the Sasha books. For a week or two, the excitement in the dark little house was almost tangible as Joan made mental lists of what they would do with the money, and all the time Alexander was secretly hoping that some miracle would prevent his life from becoming a two-dimensional cartoon with an American accent, like Christopher Robin had. When Disney pulled out of the deal, the guilty feeling that he had somehow caused his mother's disappointment was tempered by the balm of his relief.

'It's part of being a family, isn't it?' Kate says breezily. 'I mean you have all these stories and memories, but there's like this official version that one member of the family tells best, so they're the one that always has to tell it at weddings or family get-togethers.'

Alexander's immediate reaction is to disagree. His family was not like other families. He has always thought that his childhood was uniquely dis-advantaged. He wants her to feel sorry for him, he realizes. Women have always felt sorry for him when

226

he's told them about his mother's books. It's another stage of the mating ritual. If he allows Kate's version to be correct, then several of the pillars on which he has built his life come crashing down.

Kate picks up the book again.

'It's better than a photo album, this,' she says, patting it. 'Most parents record their children with a camera, don't they? Or a video, if they can afford it.'

'It's not the same thing,' he protests.

But he's asking himself, why? Why isn't it the same?

'Not everyone has to put up with kids at school taking the piss out of their photo album,' he says. But it sounds rather lame, and he knows what she's going to say next.

'Oh, I expect they were just jealous.'

'It didn't feel like that.'

He's horrified by the childish petulance that still has him in its grip.

'No, not then, maybe, but now that you're grown up,' Kate says encouragingly. 'I mean, if she'd been a photographer and taken pictures of you all the time, you wouldn't feel robbed, would you?'

'I don't know,' he admits.

'Or a painter who'd painted you?'

'I don't know . . .'

'It's just what she did.'

Half of him thinks Kate's reasoning is simplistic, half of him wonders why he has never constructed his past in this attractively uncomplicated way. He loves the clarity of her thought and the refreshing absence of amateur psychology.

Why not? he begins to ask himself. Why not see it like this?

A future free from angst and recrimination beckons and he realizes that it is an option he can choose if he wishes to.

'It's not just that,' he says, trying, but unable yet to forgive. 'She stole my imagination. Even the things I made up, she would just take for herself . . .'

He can still feel the sensation of raw disbelief as his mother handed him a proof of her novel for older children entitled *A Way with Dogs*, with illustrations by Bertie Rush. It was a story about a couple called the Dismals who lived in a flat beneath a woman who owned two heavy dogs who used to bounce around bringing down chunks of plaster from the Dismals' ceiling.

When he demanded that his mother stop turning everything he said into copy, he heard her on the phone only hours later relaying even that to her friends: '. . . and guess what he said, darling? Joan, do you have to make your living out of my life? . . . Yes! It's such an intelligent thing to say, don't you think? He's eight. Only just eight as well . . .'

'It must have been hard for her,' Kate says.
'What?'
'Well, she was a single mum, wasn't she, after your dad left? It's difficult for single mothers 'cause there's no-one to share all the stories with, is there? No-one's really interested in other people's children, are they?'

Can this be right? Is he capable of seeing his mother in this way? Has he the rigour and the strength? It's so much easier to let the mess that his life is be her fault.

'. . . everything's always their fault. If they don't love their child enough, their child's going to hate them, if they love them too much, the same,' Kate is saying.

What would Joan have made of Kate?

If she had been a next-door neighbour, or a baby-sitter, someone who didn't threaten closeness, he thinks she would have liked her. But Joan never managed to be objective about his friends. She was always horrible to anyone who attempted to like him, particularly girls. Mandy Kominski ('she was only the pastry chef's daughter, but she looked like a bit of a tart'); Juliet? ('hardly the stuff of Shakespeare, is she?').

He sees his mother standing in the kitchen of the house in Kentish Town, wearing a huge purple Aran sweater over an old, brushed-cotton nightie. The sweater hasn't been washed for a while and the undersides of the sleeves are slightly greasy. She's grinding fresh basil with a pestle and her chest is concave with the effort of it . . .

He switches the memory off. There's a great rush of relief that she's not there to judge Kate.

'What happened to the magic carpet?' Kate wants to know.

'It got thrown out,' he says.

Kate winks at him, and then she's off, running straight down the steepest part of the hill through grass that has grown long with the onset of the fine spring weather and has not yet been mown this year. He watches her skip and leap over the bumps and clumps, then stumble and roll over and over and over. He starts to run after her, falling and rolling, and they both end up at the bottom panting and laughing, lying on their backs just a few feet apart, looking up at the sky. His laughter stops abruptly. He turns his face towards her, tries to laugh some more and cannot. Her face is so close he can taste her warm, apply breath.

He wants very much to make love to her again.

'We'd better be off, then,' Kate says, getting up, brushing grass from her front, then turning, not waiting for him.

Bits of grass cling to her back. He brushes it with the flat of his hand in swift strokes. She makes him turn around and does the same to him.

He steps towards her and takes her in his arms, holding her against him so tightly that her warmth seems to cross the boundary of clothes and skin and seeps into him.

He kisses her lips, a quick, firm kiss, then another, softer, drawing away after each, searching the beautiful face that's uptilted to his.

He smoothes the hair from her face, kisses her again, drinking the sweetness of apples and chocolate, closes his eyes, wraps his arms tighter around her, keeps kissing.

Their lips and bodies are having a silent conversation.

Do you feel this way?

Yes.

Do you want to make love?

I do.

Are we falling in love?

Alexander pulls away. Her navy blue eyes stare at him through long wisps of fringe, determined not to close before his do.

'It keeps feeling a bit like you're still inside me,' she says, matter-of-factly.

The core of him shifts from his head to his groin. Her body is like a force field pulling him towards her, absorbing him, taking his breath and making it hers. In his head, he tests the words, I love you, and instead of curdling like a lie, the silent phrase excites him like a secret gift he has for her.

They start walking again. People pass by. Nobody pays any particular attention to them. Couples kiss in parks. It only feels special to him because it's their first public kiss. He feels as if they have a halo around them, an arc of lights.

He stops and kisses her again. He can't get enough of the taste of her.

'I've got to go to work,' Kate says.

Alexander calculates that it must be five o'clock. Her shift starts at six. He wants to make love to her. He wants to feel her surface against his, to bury his face in the coconut fragrance of her skin.

It's taken them five minutes to walk a hundred yards.

'I'm sorry,' he says.

'I should have told my boss I was sick,' she says.

'So, what did you tell him?'

She looks at him, weighing up whether she'll divulge this information which is precious to her.

'That's for me to know, and you to wonder,' she says.

They cross the road to Regent's Park, veering away from the spot where they watched the elephants' bathtime, hurrying along the diagonal path that crosses the vast open expanse of park.

Alexander stretches out his hand and catches hers.

A bright yellow plastic carrier bag swings between them with a pair of kitten-heel mules and his mother's book inside.

Nineteen

Kate glances back at the elephants. Other people are now standing where they stood on the park side of the fence watching the great grey beasts lope around their concrete garden. An elderly man wearing a beige cap; a woman with three small boys each a head taller than the other, standing in a row like a bar graph plotting age against height; a couple of oriental students in silver puffa jackets. If she and Alexander were standing there now, she thinks, an observer would see them differently from the way they were an hour or so ago.

She cannot pinpoint when it changed. Was it when she gave him the book, was it looking down from Primrose Hill at the panorama of London, or tumbling, or kissing? Perhaps there was no one moment, only a chain of circumstances that gathered momentum and whirled together, turning the attraction of strangers into something else. Closeness? Affection? Love? She imagines a tornado pulling them inexorably into a twisting vortex, and it's so scary she wants to break free and run across the great green carpet of grass so fast she can't think.

A hundred questions buzz around her brain.

Is the feeling that she knows him real, or is it a distant memory of a child in a story? What happened to the curious little boy to make him grow up into a man who's so ill at ease with his past? Does he really have no idea how lucky he was to have a mother who could write, a house full of antique carpets, a childhood spent hopping in and out of London taxis? Get real, she wants to tell him. Which is strange because he almost seems less real now than before, when she didn't know anything about him.

When she looks at him, she gets a hit of desire, as if he's so beautiful she can't believe she's with him. Her body sparks when they touch, even if it's just his jacket against hers, and when they kiss she finds it almost impossible to stop herself saying 'I love you' to him, as if something's compelling her to express the deliriously wonderful sensation, and they're the only words that come close to describing it.

Is it possible to love someone and know so little about them? Perhaps it's only possible to love someone *when* you know so little about them? Or do you only truly love someone when you know and are prepared to accept the things about them that you don't like?

Clasped in his hand, her palm starts to sweat.

Is this the beginning or the end?

If it were the beginning, they would be eagerly talking to each other, wouldn't they? Divulging secrets, telling little stories about themselves.

'You're unusually quiet,' he says, as they reach the edge of the park.

She's not going to be the one to go first.

She can't.

They cross the road into a formal garden that's laid out like a pen and ink illustration from an old book. There are fountains and low clipped holly hedges and stone urns bursting with spring flowers. The air smells of hyacinths and orange blossom. In the flowerbed beside her, the faces of blue pansies and nodding white and orange narcissus seem to be smiling at her.

A box hedge at the end of the path separates the idyllic peace of the garden from traffic and buildings and reality. This is her chance, she must say what she has to say in this magical garden, before they are swallowed again by the city.

Kate takes a deep breath.

She wants to tell him the truth, but different words come out of her mouth. 'I told Tony that there was this chap I was madly in love with, and I had to spend the day with him,' she offers, into the sweet-smelling air.

'Who's Tony?'

'My boss.'

Alexander's face is smiling, but he says nothing.

There's only the splash of babbling water.

'He's Italian. I thought he'd fall for the romance of it,' Kate continues, trying to make her voice light. 'He said I could swap shifts. He must be only half-Italian!'

'I see.'

She's flattened, angry with herself that she was crazy enough to tell him that she loves him.

Now the vivid faces of the flowers are laughing at her.

'Are you still madly in love with this chap?' Alexander finally asks.

Her heart's beating in her mouth.

They're almost at the box hedge.

'Yes,' she says.

If she was expecting him to pick her up and swing her round, her legs flying out in a deliriously romantic twirl, she's disappointed.

Well, that's that, then, she thinks. Blown it completely, left without a shred of dignity, as if there was any left after the changing-room incident anyway.

Beyond the hedge is a patch of meadow that's been left unmown. Pale cream daffodils shine out of the lush green grass and there's a cherry tree in full bloom at the very edge of the garden, breathtakingly pink, so spectacularly pink it almost looks artificial.

Alexander grabs Kate's hand and pulls her through the grass, ducking beneath branches laden with extravagant clusters of blossom.

He drops to the ground and pulls her down beside him.

It's quiet under the branches and if they lie low nobody will see them in the long grass and flowers, under the canopy of blossom. Kate feels as if she's in a child's playhouse, all secure and secret. She rests her weight back on her elbows and looks up.

'This is what it must be like to be a bee inside a flower . . .' she says.

The blossom is so abundant she can hardly see the sky above it, just flashes of intense clear blue as the branches sway. It's really bright inside, as if the flowers themselves are giving out pink light.

'. . . or in Heaven.'

'A bee in Heaven?' he teases.

'No!'

She joshes him with her arm.

'Heaven. You know!'

'Do you believe in Heaven?' he asks.

'Of course.'

'Why?'

'Because I believe in possibility,' she tells him. 'Otherwise, life is too sad.'

He thinks about that for a while. Props himself back on his elbows next to her.

'We ought to have a feast,' he says. 'In Japan, every-one takes a feast and sits under the cherry blossom.'

'Really?'

'They take it very seriously. They even have a cherry blossom forecast on television.'

'Go on!'

'No, really. It shows when the cherry blossom's going to be out in every region. The blossom comes earlier in the south you see, and moves up the country.'

He gestures with his hands like a weather forecaster. She can't tell whether he's still teasing. It's such a lovely thought.

'So what do they do sitting under their tree?'

Alexander picks up a twig, and inspects it as if it's a precious artefact, looks up at the blossom, sighs, throws the twig down.

'Get pissed out of their heads on saki and beer.'

'Because it's so beautiful?'

'It's a tradition. Japan many tradition country,' he adds in a Japanese accent. 'I think it's from the Samurai. The cherry blossom is a symbol of bravery. It blooms and dies on the branch. Something like that.'

A slight breeze rustles the flowers around them. He lies flat on his back, looking up at her.

It's terrifying to have him look at her like that as if he'll find something deep if he stares long enough. She doesn't want to say anything to spoil it, so she leans over and kisses him.

His hands come to her face, palms flat and dry against her cheeks, trembling with tenderness, and his eyes close.

Floating in their pink cloud, she knows that at this precise moment he loves her. She wishes she could freeze time here, now, in cherry blossom heaven with him.

His hands move from her face, smoothing over her shoulders, down her arms, taking her hands, inviting her gently to lie down beside him. She feels the bite of twigs against her back. He's looking at her and she wants to tell him that he can do anything he wants to her.

He sits up again abruptly, as if he's suddenly remembered where they are.

'Let's go home,' she whispers, her voice throaty with emotion.

She sits up.

He brushes twigs from the back of her hair, then pauses to smooth her fringe across her forehead, out of her eyes. It's become his special gesture of affection towards her.

He takes her hand and, crouching like crabs, they scuttle away from their cherry blossom hideout.

The sun has dropped in the sky and the air feels a few degrees colder. Kate pulls the edges of her jacket together.

The Friday night traffic is stationary on the Euston Road. After the stillness in the meadow, the traffic noise is disorientatingly relentless.

Outside the Great Portland Street station, an *Evening Standard* billboard proclaims in bold black handwriting:

TRAIN: 50 DEAD

Alexander is pulling at her hand and running, shouting as if his life depends on the taxi he's spotted. It stops. They jump in, tumbling against each other into the corner of the back seat, laughing.

Her head is on his chest right where his heart is thudding. His outer thigh is pressed up against hers. As the taxi sprints down to the next red light and brakes, they're thumped closer together. She recalls their chaste taxi ride the evening before, both of them as far apart as possible against the side windows with seatbelts sensibly fastened against any unpredicted movement. She stares out of the window. It feels like the height of decadence to be travelling by taxi when the sun's still shining and the pavements are littered with people drinking after work.

Her gaze fixes on a blonde young woman with a small child who is standing outside the doors of an office building. The child asks something. The woman bends forward and sticks a dummy in its mouth. The automatic doors of the building open, and four people spill out. Three men, one red-haired woman. Two of the men have mobile phones clamped under their chins. They hurry away. Something about the configuration of the redhead and the remaining man makes it clear that there's an attraction between them. They stop at the bottom of the steps and have a conversation. Red says something that makes him laugh. Then the woman with the child spots them and starts walking towards them. The laughing couple haven't seen her. They step towards each other for a kiss. The woman with a child is right behind them, and they're about to kiss. Then the woman with the child taps the red-haired woman on the shoulder . . .

The taxi lurches off, and Kate's kneeling on the seat, like at the back of the school bus, to watch the denouement.

'Phew!' she says, turning round, and slumping back in the seat. 'She's her sister.'

'What?'

Alexander has not been aware of the unfolding drama. Men never seem to see things like that.

'Maybe they meet up once a month or so, so that the one who's working can see her nephew and the mother can get out of the house for an afternoon,' she elaborates. 'What?'

'You're unbelievable,' Alexander says, kissing her nose.

*   *   *

She's never really noticed how hideous the carpet in the hall is and how horrible the lingering scent of air freshener which doesn't quite mask the cooking smell underneath. When the timer on the light runs out halfway up the second flight of stairs, she's almost inclined not to push it in again so that Alexander doesn't have to look at the dirt in the corners and the scuffed skirting board. The landing reeks of pine toilet cleaner and cigarettes. There are burn marks in a semicircle on the floor around the payphone.

In the room, she holds up the jar of Nescafé like a character in an advert.

'Coffee?'

'Yes. Yes, please.'

Now, it's as if they're rerunning the awkwardness of the day before, both determined to create distractions from the palpable desire that shoots between them. Yesterday they held back from making love because it would have meant too little. Twenty-four hours later it means too much.

She spoons coffee into a mug, fills it with steaming water and hands it to him. 'I'm going to have to go soon,' she says.

There's so many things she wants to ask him but he walks towards her and stops her with a kiss that feels like it's answering all her questions.

He takes off her T-shirt, pushes the lace strap of her underwear down over her upper arm.

Instinctively, she inclines her head, trapping his hand for a moment with her cheek.

He guides the other strap down. The top half of the teddy falls to her waist.

She takes a step back so that he can look at her.

They fall back onto the bed together, kissing. She's on him, he's on her, rolling one way and back.

He draws away, looks at her. She wriggles out of her

skirt, flops back on the bed, stretching her arms back behind her head, offering him every inch of her body, her ribcage taut, belly hollow, pelvic bones thrusting towards him.

He kneels astride her, unbuttons his thick cotton shirt. She pulls the edges apart, kissing his chest as she spreads the fabric away, licking his fresh-smelling skin, unzipping his chinos, pulling the waistband down over his hips.

'Put your hands on my back,' he murmurs.

She touches the sensitive bit at the back of his waist, feels him tense with pleasure.

'Pull me inside you.'

She feels the soft nudge of his penis pressing against her closed flesh, and the give as he pushes into her. She feels as if he's inside the core of her self, as close as any human being could be to any other. They stare at each other, daring themselves to continue.

He's the first to blink. He withdraws, leans over to the sweet jar and takes the first condom that his hand touches, holds the packet in his teeth, rips it open, puts it on. It smells of Parma violets and plastic bags.

She wants to say, just fuck me, please, please, but now he's fingering her and her clitoris becomes liquid. She tries to pull him back on top of her, but he resists, and she feels his strength beneath the tenderness and abandons herself. Deep inside her an acuteness of sensation begins to build. A voice that sounds as if it's outside her whispers, yes, yes! Her body feels as if it's filling up with hot liquid from her clitoris to the top of her head.

'Yes, yes, yes. Oh God!'

He slips back into her like a pole. The inside of her leaps as he pushes in hard, harder. Her bottom rises off the bed.

'I love you! I love you! I love you!'

Her head's going to go through the headboard if he thrusts any harder and just as she's going to break, he spasms and pours into her.

He pulls his head up from the pillow beside hers. His face is frightened now, as if he's only just heard himself shouting.

They lie side by side, taking turns to sip coffee that has gone cold.

'That's never happened to me before,' she says after a while.

'What?'

'I've never . . . you know.'

After all they've done, she's still embarrassed to talk about it.

'You've never made love?'

She laughs, partly because he's teasing her, and partly because she's relieved that he said love and not something crude.

'I've never had an orgasm,' she says, looking the other way. 'I have in dreams, because sometimes I wake up thinking, Mmmm, and I'm all twitchy down there, you know?'

He laughs.

'But never with a man.'

He draws her closer. She senses that making her come has made him feel good. She never thought men cared about that one way or the other. She smiles into his chest.

' "Perfect Day".'

She opens her eyes, thinking for a moment that she has dreamt the whole thing and she's back to where she started, in bed, talking to Marie.

Except Marie's not here.

He's here.

'What?'

' "Perfect Day",' he says again, louder. 'If you were a song, that's what you'd be.'

The piano intro, Lou Reed's voice, almost a whisper. Lyrics she didn't even know she knew. Park, zoo, home.

Alexander puts his hand on hers. It's a beautiful hand for a man, with long fingers. It doesn't look right on top of her glittery nails.

'It's about heroin, that song,' she says. 'That's what Marie says.'

'That's one of those facts that everyone knows, but nobody knows why they know,' he says.

'Like the swans?'

'A bit like the swans,' he says with a sigh.

She wants to ask if they can just start that bit of conversation again.

'Perfect Day.' It's the song you would most want to have as your song and he's chosen it for her, and she's just ruined the most romantic moment in her life with heroin and swans.

'You made me feel like a different person today,' he says.

'What do you mean?'

'Happy,' he says.

Excitement zips through her. She wants to punch the air and shout, 'Yes!'

It's so much of a compliment she almost feels it will bring her harm to acknowledge it.

'I'm sure the weather helped,' she says, idiotically.

Twenty

The sky has clouded over and there's a bitterly cold wind blowing against them as they walk back along the seafront. The sea is dark like pewter and a mist further out on the water makes it impossible to see where sea ends and cloud begins.

Lucy dances along in front of them holding both Fizz Tweeny's hands in hers, singing snatches from the theme tune to Disney's *Sleeping Beauty*. It's her video of the moment. Lucy watches videos with complete concentration as many times as it takes to know them off by heart, and then amuses herself for days acting out all the female parts. *Sleeping Beauty* is a good one because it has not only the princess, but the three old fairies, whose antics Lucy finds vastly amusing. She never takes the role of Maleficent, the evil fairy. She's frightened by the thought of anything bad and makes an excuse to leave the room during the scary bits. Sometimes, just as she is drifting off to sleep, she confides to Nell,

'You know what will happen to that wicked witch? Ben will kill her with his laser!'

And Nell wants to say, you kill her! You don't have to be beautiful and helpless, you don't have to buy into Disney's whole philosophy! But instead, she normally just says, 'Good for Ben. Now, you go to sleep.'

Nell wonders whether Chris has really promised to

build Lucy a castle in the garden, or whether there's an element of wishful thinking. She imagines a wooden castle with turrets, painted pink. They could make banners with invented coats of arms, and in the summer they could hold a theme party for Lucy's class, with jousting on hobby-horses, paper crowns, Ribena in plastic goblets to look like wine, and coloured lights strung from the apple trees.

'Mummy, come and dance with me?'

Nell takes Lucy's hands and they begin to waltz to 'Once Upon a Dream'. It's one of those moments that Nell feels she's been put on earth to experience, twirling along an empty promenade with her child, hearing the thin little singing voice that manages to be high and flat at the same time, and watching Lucy's face beaming at her in a bubble of salt-spray happiness.

When Lucy reaches the end of the song, Nell observes that her puffed-out breathing returns to normal before her own does even though her cheeks are raspberry red from the wind.

'We should live by the sea,' Nell says, falling back into step with Frances. 'Lucy's healthier here after just one day.'

'Move down. It would be so great to have you around. Although you'll forgive me if I don't encourage you to join my salsa class.'

'Salsa class?'

They turn off the promenade into the street which leads up to the square where Frances lives. There are a couple of FOR SALE notices nailed to a post outside a dilapidated terraced house.

Nell wonders what Alexander's reaction would be if she were to go home and say, 'Let's move to the seaside.'

She imagines his face lighting up and everything

being all right again, then she remembers his expression late last night when she told him about the baby.

The baby!

She's not sure whether she could go through all the business of moving while she's pregnant.

Maybe after.

Lucy's so happy at school, it would be a risk to move her now.

All the pressing reasons for moving quickly give way to pressing reasons for staying put.

'Maybe next year,' she says to Frances, as she pushes open the door to her basement flat.

'Can I watch *Blue Peter*, Mummy, before we go? Please, please?' Lucy pleads.

'I didn't know *Blue Peter* was still on,' says Frances.

The front half of the knocked-through room, that stretches from the window below street level to the back garden, has a hard sofa covered in brown and cream bobbly material, the sort you'd never buy yourself, and an ancient television with a brown mock-teak casing. When Frances switches it on, Nell half expects to see the picture in monochrome, but it's colour, and clear enough. The title music is just finishing and the presenters are sitting on the *Blue Peter* sofa, smiling at the camera, exuding personality and enthusiasm.

'It's quite good, actually,' Nell remarks, perching on the back of the sofa.

'Mummy, please be quiet!'

The two adults retreat to the kitchen bit and close the double doors so that they can talk without disturbing her.

'There's this presenter called Simon . . .' Nell says.

Frances pulls a face.

'I always thought that the presenters were supposed

to appeal to the children, but now I realize they choose one of the guys specifically to appeal to the mothers,' Nell tells her.

'Please! They're half your age!' says Frances.

'Says the woman who goes to salsa classes. For the dancing, of course. Not the lithe young Latino male bodies . . .'

Frances sticks her tongue out at Nell.

'Lithe, young, gay Latino bodies, unfortunately,' she corrects. She can't resist a peek through the crack in the double doors. 'The blond one?' she asks.

'Tasty or what?'

'Jesus! You're beginning to sound like a frustrated housewife.'

The words hang in the air, uncontradicted, as Frances fills a kettle. 'Maybe you're the one who should be having an affair,' she adds mischievously.

Nell says nothing.

'It's a pity I've got to work,' Frances says. 'What I'd really like to do is open a bottle of wine and get totally plastered.'

'Me too,' Nell agrees.

Frances bends down, takes a bottle out of the fridge and holds it up by the neck.

'Just one glass?'

'No, I'm driving,' says Nell.

'Depressing, isn't it?'

'What?'

'Being grown up.'

'Do you find that a glass makes you as pissed as a bottle used to?'

'One glass and I'm anybody's,' says Frances, dismally, '. . . if there was anybody's to be.'

She puts the bottle back into the fridge.

'What time are you teaching?' Nell asks her. She feels slightly panicky now. They're going to have to go

246

home soon and it will be just the same as when they left. Why did she think one day away would change anything?

'First lesson's at eight, but I've got to go in a bit earlier,' Frances replies. 'Photocopying to do.'

'Photocopying is something I don't miss,' says Nell.

'So what's going to happen with you and Alexander?' Frances asks, impatient with small talk. 'You going to split up?'

'Jesus, Frances!' Nell shoots a glance at the double doors. 'We can't. We've got Lucy . . .'

'And the new baby,' Frances adds.

'And the new baby,' Nell echoes.

Frances puts her arm around Nell's shoulder.

For a moment Nell wallows in the welcome clutch of her friend's sympathy, but almost instantly she sits up straight, shrugging away Frances's embrace. 'It's not all Alexander's fault,' she says.

'Oh, don't do that female thing of blaming yourself,' says Frances, irritably.

'Some of it is my fault,' says Nell.

'How do you figure that?' Frances wants to know.

Which came first? Alexander abandoning her, or her starting to withdraw from him? And does the order of it really matter? And will telling Frances do any good?

Nell looks at her friend's eyes and she cannot bear deceiving her any longer.

She takes a deep breath.

'Because,' she says, 'I think I'm in love with someone else.'

Twenty-one

'How do I look?'

Alexander opens his eyes. He's been pretending to doze. They've tasted and touched each other's bodies but it's almost too intimate for him to watch her getting dressed.

She's found more underwear in Marie's drawer. A red satin bra with black lace and matching panties. The panties are loose. She hoiks them up round her waist.

A thin blade of jealousy slices through his stomach at the thought of anyone else seeing her like that, her small high breasts encased in scarlet satin.

'You'll get good tips,' he says.

'I understand Liz Hurley now,' she says, taking the mirror off the wall and twisting one way then the other to look at herself.

'. . . I used to think she was a right old tart, but when you wear this stuff, it kind of makes you feel nice.'

She pulls on her black T-shirt and skirt, and takes some little butterfly clips from inside a cup beside the kettle and pins her hair back with them.

'All right?'

'Lovely.'

They're running out of time. He knows she's about to ask him what happens next. He doesn't know what he's going to say.

'Will you be here when I get back?' she asks as casually as she can.

'I don't see why not,' he says, avoiding a direct lie.

Now her eyes are sparkling, excited. She was not expecting him to say that, and it makes him feel even more of a coward.

'You might meet Marie,' she says. 'Don't worry about her.'

'Why don't I wait for you in Marco's?'

'OK, then.'

She's at the door.

It's all happening too quickly.

She waves, her face all smiles, then just as the door's about to close behind her, she pokes her head back round.

'Did you mean what you said back there?'

'Which particular thing?'

'You know . . .'

'I meant it.'

'Really?' She does a little skip.

'Later!'

'Later.'

He hears her running down the stairs, the front door slamming, and the squeak of her boots as she walks down the alley. Then a burst of police siren so near he feels it's coming for him. When it screams away, her footsteps have been absorbed into the chaos of urban sound.

Images of her running towards the cherry tree play behind his eyes like a home movie, as his mind begins to archive snapshots of her, storing them under sight, taste, sound, ready to call them up when he sees pink blossom, or eats oysters, or hears Lou Reed singing 'Perfect Day'.

He lies with his hands propped behind his head, staring at nothing.

In this room he is a different person. The rest of the world is happening outside but it seems to have no relevance here in this half-harem, half-bedsit.

The sudden terrifying thought that this is the reason Kate's sister painted the windows slips through his mind. Do her clients rationalize their behaviour just as he is doing? Has he become the same as them? Is the transformation into being a man who visits a prostitute so rapid and imperceptible?

Kate is not a prostitute.

Kate shivering in her borrowed underwear, too-large panties tugged halfway up her narrow chest. Her face astonished at her own audacity. There's something quintessentially innocent about her.

Sasha sees magic in everyday things!

The voice that swings between dourness and wonder and makes every word finish differently from the way he expects it to.

He sees her standing on the top of Primrose Hill with London stretched out below, asking, 'What happened to the magic carpet?'

Nell got the dustmen to take the moth-eaten old relic away one day last week when he was at work.

'It wasn't doing anyone any harm!' he shouted at Nell, when he noticed its absence that evening.

'Oh for God's sake, it was a carpet, not some incontinent old family dog, even if it smelt like one! As a matter of fact, I think it was giving Lucy asthma. It probably gave you asthma when you were small.'

'Didn't,' he said, like a child.

But Nell was probably right, he thought. She usually is. Nell is admirably practical. Nell has read all the available literature about allergy. Nell doesn't let things frighten her irrationally, she controls them by becoming an expert. Nell knows that carpets harbour dust mites and so they must all pad about the house on stripped wood or unforgiving flagstone.

Nell.

He had been unfaithful to Nell.

He wonders if the sin is multiplied by repetition. Was he more unfaithful the second time they fucked than the first, or is it the same quantity of wrongdoing each time?

The second time felt like more of a betrayal, making love naked, skin upon skin.

Can he and Nell ever go back to how they were, or has what he has done changed their relationship so irrevocably that nothing will make up for it?

Will he tell her?

Perhaps he should come straight out with it: look, I've done a terrible thing, but it's made me think about my life and I feel better now. Will you forgive me?

No, best not to tell her.

Will she know?

She did not notice when he came back from the Christmas party reeking of Mel's scent. When he looked guiltily in the mirror that night, his lips were a different colour, but Nell did not see.

She will know.

Will she shout at him and throw him out, or will she retreat into martyrish silence, determined not to let their child suffer? Which punishment would he prefer? To be disgraced, cast out, or to continue much as they do now, like the rainbow soap bubbles Lucy blows that float around the kitchen never making contact, because if they do they might both become nothing.

He closes his eyes, trying to conjure Kate for one last time shivering in her chocolate silk lingerie. He hears her saying, 'You know how you have one image of someone that always comes first when you're thinking about them?'

But now, he can only see Nell. Nell's uncomprehending frown, Nell's despair, Nell's disappointment in him.

He must go.

He must wash the smell of sex away and go home.

Alexander draws a bath and lies in it. He lathers himself all over, then sniffs the soap bar. It smells of coconuts. Kate's smell. In the warm water, his penis begins to harden, he slides further down.

Keys jangle in the door. Alexander sits up and a wave of bathwater sploshes over the edge of the tub.

The door opens and the draught turns his wet skin cold. The light's switched on.

'Don't you ever knock?' he jokes, nervous about still being there, but gladdened she's returned to delay his departure just a little longer.

'You'd better be out of here before I count to ten, or you'll be out the window. One, two . . .'

The voice is like Kate's, but harder. Much harder.

Alexander turns round very slowly, half expecting to see a gun pointing at him.

Kate's sister is standing in the door, her small figure straight and determined. For a second, he wonders how she plans to throw him out of a window that she can't even open. The thought makes him smile.

'Hang on,' she says, focusing on his face, 'I've seen you before.'

She looks around the room, taking in the open lingerie drawer, the scattering of underwear.

'I'm a friend of Kate's,' Alexander explains, stretching his fingers towards the bath towel on the bed, but unable to reach it without standing up.

'Friend?'

'I met her yesterday.'

'The little slut,' says Marie. Her voice contains both shock and admiration. Then: 'Oh hang on, you're not the stoopy one?' Stoop-eh.

'I'm sorry?'

'The teacher.'

'Yes.'

'Oh, I see.'

He's oddly pleased to know that Kate talked about him, but alarmed by Marie's description and the obviousness of her disappointment. Stoopy?

Her eyes slip from dishevelled bed to the surface of the bathwater.

'Well, make yourself at home . . . ?'

'Alexander.'

It's hard to muster any dignity with a stranger when you're naked and lying without permission in their pink tub.

'Alexander.' She repeats it in exactly the same way that Kate did yesterday, as if the four syllables are almost unbelievably pretentious.

'And you're?' he asks, trying to grab back a little respect.

'Bloody hell!' she says. 'I'm Marie. And that's my bath you're in. Sir!' she adds with insolent mock-deference.

One little word tells the entire history of her teenage years at school.

'I'm not that sort of teacher,' he says.

'You're still in my bath.'

'Well, if you'll give me a minute, I'll get out,' he reasons.

'Go on, then. I don't suppose it's anything I haven't seen before.'

In the bathwater his penis shrinks to its minimum size, the soft shrunken thing it becomes when he's got flu. He doesn't move.

With an impatient sigh, she turns her back to him.

He hears the rasp of a cigarette lighter and a long intake of breath. He grabs the towel and is about to step out onto the carpet.

'Dry yourself in the bath, will you?' she says, then exhales. 'I don't want the carpet going mouldy.'

Alexander rubs the damp towel over himself as quickly as he can and pulls on his shirt. The circle of back beneath his shoulder blades is still wet and he feels the cotton fabric sticking to it. He rubs his legs down and steps out of the bath. He suspects his underpants are hidden somewhere in a fold of rumpled duvet, so he pulls his chinos on without them.

'Peter Stringfellow doesn't wear underpants,' Marie says.

And he realizes that she's been peeking at him.

'How do you know?' he asks, as if they're making polite small talk. He feels his whole body flushing, his penis smaller than ever but with a flashing red light on it.

'Everyone knows that,' Marie says, blowing a smoke ring at him. 'I've always wondered how he stops his pubes getting caught in the zip.'

It takes a moment or two for Alexander to realize that she's really asking a question, but he feels that he'll be in more trouble if he tries to explain that he really isn't an authority on the subject.

Marie struts across the room and switches on the radio. 'Terrible about this train crash, isn't it?' she says.

'Yes,' Alexander agrees.

'You wouldn't believe they could let it happen again, would you?'

'No.'

The disc jockey is just finishing the weather.

'Shit,' says Marie and switches the radio off.

Her fidgetiness is rubbing off on Alexander. His damp back itches. 'I'll be off, then,' he says.

'Not on my account,' Marie says, glancing at the bedside drawers. 'I've just come back to pick something up.'

Alexander pulls out the bath plug and makes a performance of folding the towel so that he doesn't have to look at what Marie's up to. From the way she's shielding what she's doing, he thinks there must be an esoteric sex toy in the drawer, or perhaps it's a drug stash. For the first time in this weird room, he experiences a *frisson* of fear.

'Well, then,' Marie says, turning round with a big satisfied smile that shows she's found what she's looking for. 'Have a nice evening!'

She sashays to the door.

'Oh, and Alexander,' she says, ridiculing his name with a ludicrous posh accent, 'don't muck my sister around or you'll have me after you.'

It's halfway between intimidation and invitation.

He listens to her heels tapping down the stairs. He's sweating, and his heart is beating fast.

He must go.

Reality blew back into the room with Marie and it's lingered with the smell of her perfume and the artificial light from the single bulb that dangles from the ceiling. The sisters look so alike that now if he tries to think about Kate he can only see Marie's knowing smile.

He rushes to the door, grabs at the Yale. Stops. When the door closes, he will not be able to come back in.

He puts his feet into his shoes, picks up his heavy jacket, shoves his socks into the outer pockets, gives the room a final once-over: the painted window, the improbable tented bed.

This is it. This is the impetus he needed to say goodbye.

His eyes fall on the plastic carrier bag containing a pair of kitten-heel mules, and *Sasha's Magic Carpet*. He takes the book out, hunts in his inside pocket for a biro, opens the book at the front page where there's a rectangular box with a fringe drawn round like the tassels of a carpet.

Printed in the box is the message, 'This book belongs to . . .' And there are two empty lines beneath.

Alexander scrawls 'Kate' on the first, and below it, after a second's thought, he writes, 'Thanks for giving me back my life! Love, Alexander.'

He imagines her reading it, crying a little, flinging it across the room in anger, then retrieving it, reading it again, trying to work out the meaning of what he has written. He kind of likes the idea of her face frowning as she grapples with a message she will never properly understand.

Twenty-two

'Who?' Frances wants to know.

In the next room, Nell can hear the theme music for *Neighbours*. She doesn't usually let Lucy watch it, but it probably won't do any harm just this once.

'We haven't done anything about it, yet . . . well, not really . . .' she says, finally.

'But who is it?'

'I'm surprised you haven't guessed.'

'Guessed?'

Nell thinks about his face, smiling. She thinks how much he would love it that she was telling someone, how he would see it as a step forward. She hesitates. Is it an irreversible step once she takes it? Or is it inevitable anyway, whatever she does or says?

'It's Chris,' she says quietly.

'Chris?' Frances echoes, bewildered.

'Ben's father,' Nell whispers.

'Do I know Ben?'

Nell's impatient. Did Frances really expect it to be someone she knew?

'Ben. Lucy's beau.'

'Oh my God! I can't believe it! Like daughter, like mother!'

Frances squeals so loudly Nell's fearful Lucy will hear and want to join in with the excitement. She's momentarily stunned by the gleefulness of the expression on her friend's face, which seems somehow inappropriate.

'And what does Chris do?' Frances asks, more seriously.

'He's a cabinetmaker.'

'Oh yes, you said. Is that really a carpenter?'

'He wasn't always a carpenter,' Nell feels obliged to explain. 'He was a foreign exchange dealer, but he'd had enough. So, when they had Ben, he decided to look after him and set up his own business. His wife still works in the City.'

'Ah, his wife . . .'

'Ah, indeed,' says Nell.

She kind of hates the way that Frances is assimilating the details as if it's a tabloid soap shock.

'Useful to have someone around who's good with his hands,' says Frances.

Nell feels colour rising to her face.

She loves his hands, his broad hands that are hard and rough from his work. She loves the dirt that runs along the grain of his fingernails and the faint smell of new timber that blows through the door with him.

'. . . I mean, putting up shelves, building castles in the garden, that kind of thing,' Frances adds.

'Yes.'

'It's such a cliché to want a man to be able to do manly things, but you kind of do, don't you?' says Frances. 'I don't know what happened to our generation of men. My father was always planing bits off doors, and plunging blocked drains. It's what he was for. I don't know what men think they're for now, do you?'

Nell laughs.

'Can he do decking? Decking's the thing, isn't it? All these gardening programmes are about wood, and a bit of gravel. There's no lawns any more, or plants. I was thinking about getting my patio decked . . .'

'He's very good at decking,' Nell interrupts.

'I'm delighted to hear it,' says Frances.

They catch each other's eye, and then Nell can't help giggling. 'He restores antiques,' she says.

Suddenly every simple sentence seems full of innuendo.

'Useful,' says Frances, 'especially at our age.'

'There's a big demand for it.'

'I bet there is!'

'Stop!'

'So how did you meet?' Frances asks.

'Ben and Lucy went to the same playgroup. And before you ask, I don't know which came first. I suppose you try to encourage your children to be friends with the children of adults that you like, but Ben and Lucy always got on well together. Then, they started to come round to our house, and we went to theirs, and after a while you begin to notice that you're spending quite a lot of time together.'

'And what does Alexander think of this cosy foursome?'

'Alexander's never been the slightest bit interested in our boring domestic details.'

'Have you told him?'

'That I spend a lot of time with Chris? I don't *not* tell him . . .'

Sounds a bit feeble. Should have known that it's no good trying to sell Frances half a story.

'He might be a lot more interested in your boring domestic details if you say, "Do you know that I'm flirting away my mornings with the local cabinet-maker?" mightn't he?' Frances observes.

'I'm not flirting . . . all right, I'm flirting. Whose side are you on, anyway?'

'Hang on . . .' Frances is frowning as her brain busies through the logistics. 'Lucy, and presumably Ben too, go to school all day now.'

'Yes.'

'But you and Chris . . .'

'We don't see each other as much now, obviously.'

'But you do meet?'

Nell nods.

'Alone?'

'Oh, for heaven's sake. Why shouldn't I have a friend? If it was a woman, you wouldn't think anything of it.'

'Hang on. Hang on!' Frances holds up her hands like a traffic cop. 'You're the one claiming to be in love.'

Nell shrugs her shoulders.

'I don't know.'

'So, how come I've never read about a cabinetmaker in your column?' Frances asks.

'What's to write about? We have coffee. We chat.'

'Very innocent.'

'It *is* innocent,' Nell protests.

'So far,' Frances adds.

'So far,' she concedes.

'What's he look like?'

Nell hesitates. Talking about Chris gives her relationship with him the wonderful kick of possibility. But after keeping the secret like treasure hidden away inside her for so long, it is strange to let it go. As the precious details slip from her protection into the public domain, they no longer belong to her. She's not sure she wants Frances to own any more of them.

'He's very good looking,' she says, neutrally.

'Natch.'

'Conventionally good looking,' Nell says. 'When you see him you think "What a good-looking man", but you don't think "Wow! I'd like a piece of that . . ."'

'Hair?'

'Fair.'

'Eyes?'

'Blue. They call him Stefan at the tennis club.'

'Why?'

'He looks a lot like Stefan Edberg.'

'Who's Stefan Edberg? Not the England football manager?'

Frances prides herself on knowing nothing about sport.

'Didn't you ever watch Wimbledon?'

'Please,' says Frances, toying with her packet of Silk Cut. The mere mention of sport has triggered a desire to smoke. 'You don't play tennis, do you?'

'I used to at school,' says Nell, blushing.

'And you've taken it up again recently?'

'How did you guess?'

'God, Nell,' says Frances.

The tennis seems to have depressed her more than the illicit attraction.

'I didn't mean it to happen,' Nell says, trying to deflect the criticism she senses is about to come.

'No?'

Frances suddenly seems to have lost interest, and now Nell has an urge to tell her everything, to explain how unintended it was, to defend herself against the impending moral charges.

'It was never a conscious thing,' she says. 'We were just friends.'

'So . . .'

'When Lucy and Ben were going to playgroup, we used to pick them up from the village hall each lunchtime. One day last summer, one of those beautiful balmy summer days we had in June, Chris wasn't there, and my heart kind of flipped over with disappointment. I was struggling to do the normal chit-chat with the other mothers, wondering where he was, wondering whether I should offer to take Ben home myself . . . then, just as Lucy and I were walking home, he comes running up the road. I felt my face break into this huge smile. His did too, and suddenly we were looking at each other like we hadn't done before, and then we both looked away. That's when I realized. It wasn't the looking at each other, it was the looking away . . . like we were both acknowledging, hey, there's something going on here . . .'

Frances smiles encouragingly, but her eyes are not really engaged. A shutter has come down. Nell reminds herself that it is boring to hear about other people's love lives, especially when you aren't involved with anyone yourself.

'. . . and after that, I literally could not stop thinking about him,' says Nell, winding up. 'It was like having a schoolgirl crush.'

'Hormone rush,' says Frances.

'I suppose so,' says Nell, reluctantly. There's something inhuman about the notion of all those wonderful giddy feelings being simply a chemical reaction. 'Do you think if we'd known the scientific explanation for love right from the beginning of time we would still have a word for romance – or destiny?' she asks.

Is Chris her destiny? Once, they allowed themselves to talk about what would have happened if they had met before. It's a question that they have tried to leave unspoken because it's so laden with frustration and regret. Strangely, their lives have almost collided on two previous occasions. Chris was present at a ball she went to in New College, Oxford with her cousin when she was just seventeen, which has always felt like a key moment in her life, even before she discovered that he was there too. It was the first time that she became aware that she was pretty, and the first occasion that she smoked grass. The combination made her float around the ancient quads feeling as if she had a spotlight trained on her. Now the significance of the evening seems more potent, knowing that somewhere under the same marquee, Chris was dancing to 'Tiger Feet'. Did they smile at each other? Chris doesn't think so. He says that if he had seen her, he wouldn't have been able to let her go. All that he can remember about the ball is being one of the five people who managed to eat cooked breakfast the morning after. He sees it as a badge of honour, like being one of the elite gathering at the bar of a cruise ship in a stormy sea.

The other place they might have met was Japan. Chris went to Tokyo on a business trip during her time there. Being a man, he cannot remember where he stayed, or when it was exactly, and so she does not know whether it was before or after she hooked up with Alexander. In her heart, she knows it would not have made any difference. She would not have wanted Chris then. In Tokyo, she was still at the stage in her life when she found difficulty attractive. She wasn't ready to settle for safety.

'Oh dear, you have got it bad,' says Frances. 'Destiny!'

'Do you think we'd have still invented poetry?' Nell asks, embarrassed by her romanticism and trying to pretend she's after a more academic conversation about love.

'A world without poetry?' says Frances. 'Now there's a nice thought!'

'Oh come on! Imagine a world without Keats or Shakespeare!'

'Or Roger McGough?'

'I suppose you have a point!'

They both laugh.

'So, we're still at the poetry stage, are we?' Frances asks.

No point in trying to divert her.

'We're still at the stomach's-in-an-elevator-when-ever-I-think-about-him stage. I went through this period when every time I closed my eyes I would see him. It was incredibly difficult to write my column, because he was all I could think about. Then the children started school, and we didn't see so much of each other, and I started getting all these doubts about whether he felt the same way, or whether I had just imagined it, and then, at Christmas, there was the school party. We were helping lay the tables together, and I was so nervous being near him. I was pouring the drinks with one of those huge metal jugs they have at school, you know? I kept splashing squash all over the place. Then we were standing at the kitchen hatch watching the disco. Lucy and Ben were dancing together. We were exchanging proud parental glances. We were standing about a foot apart but there was this magnetic field between us which felt like it would literally hurt if we got any closer. And then he said, "She's beautiful. Just like her mother." '

'Jesus! He's not always so corny, is he?' Frances interrupts.

It's irritating of Frances to point it out, but she's right. It is corny. It didn't feel like that then. It felt like she was Meg Ryan and he was Tom Hanks and they were meant to be together. Which is also appallingly corny, and just shows how out of her mind she is because she's never been able to stand Meg Ryan's pert cookiness, and Tom Hanks's sanctimonious sexlessness. Thank God for Frances!

'No,' she says, 'he's not corny. He does tell me that I'm beautiful a lot.'

'Nothing wrong with that,' says Frances.

'No . . .'

She's become ridiculously dependent on him telling her, though, so that now, if he doesn't tell her that she's beautiful at least once every time they see each other, she thinks he's gone off her. She does not tell Frances that.

'Christmas!' Frances remembers. 'No bloody wonder you were so saintly about Alexander's peccadillo . . .'

Her honesty can sometimes feel like cruelty.

Nell looks at her feet.

'So, since then?' Frances asks.

'Since then, we've talked a lot, and he says that he loves me, and wants to be with me, and . . .'

'What about his wife?'

'She's tough and ambitious . . .'

'Not sins,' Frances reminds her.

'No.'

'She doesn't seem to care about Ben.'

'Oh come on, Nell. This is about you and him. Let's not pretend that it would be better for the children . . .'

'No . . .'

It's right to discuss it with Frances, Nell tells herself, even though it's painful. Frances never lets you get away with anything. With Frances's cool analysis, she's going to be able to make a proper decision. She hasn't trusted herself to do that before. You can go mad thinking about the possibilities on your own, and sometimes you can miss out the most obvious facts in your pursuit of logic for your fantasies.

'His wife . . .' she continues, hesitantly.

'Name?' Frances demands.

'Sarah. Sarah doesn't want to have any more children. Chris does. I do. I think I do . . . with someone who wants one . . .'

'How very symmetrical!'

265

'Yes!' Nell agrees happily, and then realizes Frances is being ironic.

'Sarah and Alexander don't fancy one another, by any chance?'

'I don't think so.'

'How inconvenient. Jesus, it's not his, is it?'

Frances points at the waistband of Nell's jeans.

'No.'

'Sure?'

'Quite sure,' says Nell.

The fact that she was thinking about Chris, imagining it was him inside her, imagining that she was lying on the kitchen table in the middle of the morning with Chris thrusting into her, pouring his semen into her – that doesn't make it Chris's baby.

It's Alexander's baby, even though she knows he doesn't want it.

'Jesus. You have fucked up, haven't you?' says Frances.

Nell feels her soul plummet.

'He's really kind,' she offers feebly. 'He's got a kind of feminine quality about him. I don't mean effeminate. He's thoughtful. He notices things like flowers and clouds . . .'

'Jesus, he's not vegetarian, is he?'

'No!'

'Does he own a pair of sandals?'

'Oh, for heaven's sake!' Nell can't help laughing. 'I think he does, but they're those trendy ones that walkers wear. You know, Teevers or Beavers or something.'

'Walkers? Hang on . . .'

Nell knows what's coming next.

'No, he hasn't got a beard,' she says. After sport and exercise, facial hair is what Frances most dislikes.

'He's not like you're thinking at all. He's a cool guy,

you know. He looks good in clothes. He's kind of sussed. You feel confident in him. You could tell him anything.'

'Have you told him about the baby?'

'Er . . . no.'

'But he's really into children, right?'

'Yes, but not in a boring way. In a sexy way.'

'You're weird.'

'He's the only person in the world I feel entirely comfortable leaving Lucy with,' says Nell, trying to explain. 'Sometimes, if I'm struggling with a deadline, he'll take her home from school and give her tea. He's made his house nut free so that she's safe there. I know that if she falls over, he'll know what to do. If she starts wheezing, he'll notice and give her her inhaler. He's been trained to use the EpiPen . . .'

'And that's the sort of thing you find sexy???'

'I'm bored with everything always having to be so difficult. I know that the difficulty is what I really loved about Alexander initially, but after a while it's just boring.'

'You want a nice, predictable existence . . .'

'I want reason. I know it sounds impossibly middle-aged . . .'

'Reason?'

'You don't feel like sex unless you're relaxed, do you? I've found it hard to relax since I've had Lucy.'

'Doesn't Alexander ever look after Lucy?'

'Alexander thinks that looking after her is sitting on a bench on the village green reading the Sunday newspapers while she plays on the climbing frame. She fell off once, and had to have stitches in her ear.'

'Poor Alexander,' says Frances.

'Poor Alexander?'

'He must have felt terrible.'

'He should have been watching,' Nell snaps back.

The words hang in the air, making Nell feel as if she's the one who's been unreasonable.

'They go for walks, find rabbits . . .' Frances remembers.

'Once.'

'Oh come on, Nell, he's Lucy's father and she loves him. Lots of fathers don't quite know how they're supposed to be with small children. Mine didn't, but it didn't mean I didn't love him, or him me.'

Frances stands up, busies herself collecting all the dirty cups from the kitchen surfaces. She turns on the hot tap, squirts Fairy Liquid into the sink and plops the mugs in. The atmosphere in the room feels as if she's angry with Nell. Nell's confused. She thought Frances was just being devil's advocate, but it seems that she really is defending Alexander. She doesn't understand why Frances of all people should sympathize with Alexander of all people. And yet what she's saying is undeniable. It's not what Nell expected from her, but she should have known better than to predict what Frances would say. Nell feels an enormous well of fondness for her friend. She watches Frances throwing mugs into the sink and scrubbing them with a long-handled brush. She notices that her shoulders are heaving.

'Frances, what's the matter?'

She stands, stretches a comforting arm towards her back. It is shrugged away before it even touches.

'Nothing,' Frances says curtly.

'Tell me.'

Frances turns round, drags her sleeve across her eyes.

'I'm just jealous,' she says.

'Jealous?'

'Yes, jealous, you daft bitch!'

The words are said affectionately, but alongside the

crying, they're a shock. In all the years of knowing her, Nell cannot remember seeing Frances cry.

'Jealous?' Nell reiterates, remembering what it felt like to be an English language teacher trying really hard to understand what a student was struggling to say, but unable to get through the mispronunciation. There was that terrible time when she mistook 'homeless' for 'omelettes'.

'You don't see it, do you, Nell? You've never seen how lucky you are, have you?' Frances says.

There's a mountain of foam building behind her in the sink. Nell wants to say, 'Turn the tap off,' but she doesn't dare. All at once Frances laughs, and turns round again and swishes through the foam with her washing-up brush muttering to the wall in front of her.

'You look like Meryl Streep, or a Botticelli angel or something; you get the dream relationship with a bloke everyone else wants to fuck; you get the baby, the house in the country. You have to give up your job but, surprise, surprise, you get a new career instead that you enjoy and pays you more money. And now there's a strapping great Swede trying to get into your knickers for daytime sex. And you're like,' Frances puts on a whiney voice, ' "How did I get into this mess?" '

Nell's stunned, not just by the words, but by their fluency. It sounds almost as if Frances has rehearsed the outburst many times.

Frances continues washing up increasingly vigorously. Little clouds of suds dance around her weightlessly, like snow.

'He's not Swedish.'

It's the only thing Nell can offer in her defence.

Frances turns round again, brandishing the washing-up brush as if she's going to hit her with it, and suddenly they both burst into almost hysterical laughter.

'So, how do I get out of my mess?' Nell asks when the laughing has become gasping, and died down as instantly as it started.

'Don't ask me.'

'What would you do?'

Frances gives it serious consideration.

'I'd have fucked the Swede by now,' she says, eventually. 'I mean, first things first. I think you owe it to yourself to do that before even thinking about anything else.'

'Owe it to myself?'

'You have to see whether he's as fantastic a fuck as you dream he is.'

'It's not just about sex . . .'

'What, you'd feel the same way about him if he had a willy the size of a walnut whip?'

'Oh, yuk!'

'Oh, sorry, I forgot he keeps a nut-free house.'

Nell tries to look disapproving. 'Kindness is very important,' she says firmly.

'Oh please. Kindness doesn't do you much good when you want to be tied to the bedposts and fucked raw.'

'True,' Nell admits.

All her sexual fantasies about Chris are to do with him taking her, possessing her, giving her no choice, taking away her responsibility for it. But they're never going to happen. If she wants to have sex with him, she is going to have to say so, and she can't imagine herself doing that. She can't imagine getting the tone of it right. She wonders whether she would find sex with him as sexy as the possibility of it, and she suddenly feels rather panicky, as if she's set something in motion that should have been left dormant, and it's taken on an inevitability she's not sure she's ready for.

'What's the point, in the end?' she asks dismally.

'What do you mean?' Frances asks, sitting down at the table again. The brief flurry of washing up appears to have restored her composure.

'The weird thing about falling in love is that it makes you think that you're unique,' Nell tries to explain. 'It makes you think that this special sensation is more important than anything else. It makes you disregard sense, it makes you disregard experience. It makes you really arrogant, like, yes, I know he's married, I know I'm effectively married, I know that these things never work. *But this is different.* Falling in love is like childbirth. You forget about the pain of splitting apart the next time you do it . . .'

'Can I feel a column coming on?' asks Frances.

'I suppose it is *really* like giving birth,' Nell muses, 'given all that stuff about hormones. I hate that. Once you know it's just a hormone rush and it's going to wear off in a year, you wonder if it's worth all the bother . . .'

'Of course it is!' Frances exclaims. 'A comet might collide with earth and finish us all off in a year. We might all have new-variant CJD . . .'

'But we might not,' says Nell.

She finds herself actively wanting to be persuaded, but thinking that Frances is going to have to do better than that. Which is ridiculous. She has to make up her mind. She has to decide. Nothing is going to make it easier for her.

In the next room, the thumping heartbeat of the BBC News titles is playing. 'Hang on,' says Nell, 'I always watch this with Lucy, in case it's horrible.'

She slides open the double doors, smiles at Lucy and perches on the arm of the sofa.

'Another train crash kills dozens of people . . .' the newsreader begins.

Usually, at this point Nell would reach for the

remote control in an effort to protect Lucy from the grisly evidence of a major disaster, but Frances has no remote, and if she walks across the room and switches the television off, it's such a deliberate act of denial that Lucy will feel as if something's being hidden from her, which will probably make her more interested in it. Parenthood is full of these fine judgements. Nell makes the split-second decision to remain seated. She puts a hand lightly on Lucy's shoulder, and together they watch the aerial pictures of the train, followed by a reporter standing in front of the wreckage. Back in the studio, the newsreader is interviewing the Minister for Transport. Then there's another report, from a station car park where the reporter is saying with grave melodrama,

'. . . and only time will tell whether the owners of these cars will return tonight to drive them home . . .'

As the camera pans out, Nell's clutch tightens on Lucy's shoulder.

The car park in which the reporter is standing is unmistakably the next stop down their line. Some of the fast trains stop there and not at their station. Nell sits forward listening intently for a repeat of the details of the train they're talking about.

'Mummy . . .'

'Shush!'

'. . . our main story tonight is the train crash on the . . .'

'Mummy!'

'Yes, what?'

The news moves on from national disaster to foreign famine.

'Mummy, is that Daddy's train?'

Twenty-three

'. . . *And now back to our top story today. Another packed commuter train has crashed just outside London,*' says the DJ. '*Our reporter's at the scene. Andy, do we know anything further about why this happened?*'

'*We have a few more details, mostly just confirming what we had been unofficially told,*' the reporter replies and then, as if he's reading from a press release, lists the time of the train, its starting point and its destination.

Alexander's standing in the newsagent's on Old Compton Street. The words from the radio echo in his head like a premonition, because he has heard them before.

He hears the same words every morning crackle over the loudspeaker at his station.

The information takes a moment or two to sink in.

It is his train that has crashed.

In a flash of extraordinary clarity, he suddenly understands why this day has been so unreal.

He is dead.

The unnatural light under the cherry tree was Heaven.

For a moment, relief floods pleasantly, warmly, through his veins. He's perfectly happy, like the moment just after waking in a palpitating sweat from a bad dream.

He is dead.

He is not responsible for anything that has happened today.

He finds himself staring at the cover girl on this month's issue of *FHM*.

This morning, he remembers, he caught the earlier train.

'. . . *fire in the front two carriages was so hot, about 1,000 degrees we understand, and the emergency services are saying that it may be impossible to tell how many people have perished in there for some time. Recovering the bodies is going to be a long and gruelling process. I understand they're going to have to identify people by jewellery, and frankly, they're saying that they may never know the exact number of people who travelled on the . . .'*

Alexander's thinking of the gilt earrings of the woman who sits opposite him, the Walkman earphones clamped round the brush head of the man in the seat beside. It occurs to him that if he'd been in his usual seat, there would be nothing to identify him. If he had waited for his usual train, he might now be a pile of gravelly ash, the products of cremation.

Instinctively, he touches his arm, taking a pinch of shirt sleeve between thumb and middle finger and rubbing it together as if testing the quality of the fabric.

'Anything else?' the man at the till asks him.

Alexander roots about in his jacket pocket for change.

He takes an *Evening Standard* off the top of the pile and pushes past the queue that has built up behind him.

Outside, he scans through the first few pages for details.

*   *   *

Nell!

Nell will have heard about the crash and will have tried to ring him.

His school will have told her that he hasn't been in.

He switched off the mobile she gave him and he doesn't know whether when she rings it, there will be a message to tell her that it's off, or whether it will simply ring and ring and ring.

He remembers the Paddington crash, the terrible poignant ringing of mobile phones all round the burnt-out carriage as people desperately tried to speak to relatives who would never answer.

He retrieves the mobile from the depths of one of his pockets and switches it on. It beeps twice, then the screen says 'Low Battery' before cutting out.

Nell.

Nell will be beside herself with anxiety.

The magnitude of his betrayal suddenly seems infinitely greater.

He needs a payphone, but he can't find one. Every other person who passes him is chatting into a mobile. He's tempted to grab one and run off.

Nell.

There's a payphone in one of the streets that leads down to Shaftesbury Avenue. A couple of tramps are sitting by the door, but the booth is miraculously empty. When he steps inside, he realizes why. The stench of urine is so strong he nearly gags. Someone has tried to smash out one of the panes of glass. Probably to get rid of the smell.

The connection is made.

Alexander breathes again.

The phone rings.

Nell has a phone right by her desk. Usually she picks it up straight away.

He pictures the phone ringing in an empty living room.

Nell's in the bath and doesn't hear it at first, then she's out, dripping all the way down the wooden stairs.

Ring ring.

Nell's in the garden picking a bunch of narcissus. She drops her secateurs and runs to the house pulling off her gardening gloves as she goes.

Ring ring.

If Nell knows about the train crash, it's very unlikely that she's gone out, especially without putting on the answerphone. Nell listens to the radio all the time. There's no way that she hasn't heard about the crash.

Alexander puts the phone back down. He sucks in breath, trying to slow down his heartbeat, clasps his hands tightly together. The touch of palm on palm is strangely reassuring.

In front of his face are several dozen prostitutes' cards advertising sex with and without violence. What sort of a man rings one of these numbers? He thinks about Marie's room, the tented bed, the painted window. He switches off the memory.

Alexander picks up the receiver again and redials home very carefully in case he stabbed out the wrong number the first time. He listens to the familiar ring of the telephone at home, silently rehearsing: Hi, it's me. Look I've just heard about this crash . . . Yeah, I went for a bit of a walk in Regent's Park . . .

If he says no more, Nell will believe it.

It will even be true.

Ring ring.

After the initial relief of knowing that he's alive, she may even be pleased to imagine him wandering round the park.

Ring ring.

She'll assume that he was thinking about them. About the new baby.

Ring ring.

He'll have to say that he's happy about it now.

Ring ring.

Maybe it's not so bad.

Ring ring.

It'll be a new life!

Ring ring.

Not as bad as being dead, anyway.

Alexander replaces the receiver again, and stares at it as if there's a chance that Nell might at any moment ring him back.

He tries to picture the calendar that hangs in the kitchen. Was there an appointment that he has forgotten, a parents' evening, a meeting of Nell's book group?

Perhaps she has gone to her mother's.

He tries to remember Nell's mother's number, but his mind is blank.

He rings Directory Enquiries, but Lavinia is unlisted. 'Oh. Really?'

He sounds more disappointed than he actually feels. Speaking to Nell is going to be difficult enough. He doesn't think he could cope with Lavinia right now.

He can't believe that Nell's just gone out.

He rings home again.

Ring ring.

Where is she?

Ring ring.

Why would she go out?

Perhaps Lucy's been taken ill.

Surely the chance of two disasters befalling them in one day is too great?

Except that disaster has not befallen him, not a real disaster.

He drops the receiver back onto its rest.

There must be a perfectly simple explanation that's eluding him in panic.

Make a plan.

Ring from the station.

And if she still doesn't answer, he'll call in at her mother's on the way home.

He opens the newspaper.

All railway services on his line have been suspended.

In the bar, a television is showing aerial pictures of the crash sight. The camera zooms in.

Half of the train is burnt-out like scrap in a breaker's yard, half of it still looks as it usually does, but it's lying on its side, zigzagging across the line like a child's toy that's been played with and discarded.

He's standing on the footrest of his barstool trying to get a better look when the bartender asks what he wants, and he sits down quickly, afraid to appear inappropriately ghoulish.

'An espresso, please . . . That's my train,' he adds, quietly, wanting to tell someone. Sharing information will make it sink in.

'One espresso coming up!'

On the screen, the reporter is standing a few yards away from the train. Behind him, a couple of emergency workers at either end of a stretcher with a covered body on it walk from the left to the right of the screen and then out of view.

That could be my body.

The bartender puts a tiny china cup in front of him. Alexander sips it even though the coffee's too hot. It's reassuring to feel it burning his tongue and throat and oesophagus as it trickles towards his stomach. The pain is proof that he exists.

Alexander thinks about all the minute decisions

he made this morning that have put him here sitting at the zinc counter of a bar in Soho watching his alternative fate on the television screen.

If I had slept for five more minutes, I would be dead.

If I had kissed Nell goodbye, I would be dead.

If I had eaten breakfast, I would be dead.

Alexander tips the last bit of coffee sludge into his mouth and puts the cup back down on its saucer.

He feels like doing something really rash, like cadging a cigarette and smoking again. Something to mark the passing of a momentous event that didn't happen to him.

He's alive, but he shouldn't be. He could be a pile of ash.

It occurs to him that at this moment, no-one knows that he is alive.

It's a peculiar feeling. Sort of powerful. He's a ghost who can view the world without taking part in it, like one of those high-concept Hollywood movies. He imagines the portentous voice of the man who does the voice-overs for feature film trailers.

'Everyone who knows him thinks he's dead . . .

If you could disappear, would you . . . ?'

Alexander goes to the phone in the corner at the back of the bar and rings home again.

No answer.

He drops the phone back into the rest, walks slowly back to the bar, orders another espresso.

He can no longer taste the coffee, but the double hit of caffeine makes him lightheaded. And somewhere at the very edge of his consciousness, there's the glimmering of an idea that is so wrong it feels wicked to even think it.

*   *   *

'*If you could disappear, would you?*' the trailer man asks insistently in Alexander's head.

'*Second Chance . . .*'

The film even has a title now.

'*. . . coming to a screen near you . . .*'

Alexander tries to shake the voice away.

He asks for a glass of water.

The cool clear fluid washes icily over the soreness of his tongue and throat.

Better.

'*It only takes one decision to change your life . . .*'

Alexander sees Bruce Willis sitting at the counter of a diner.

The backstory is that he's had a row with his wife this morning. She's played by Meryl Streep and she's got that Meryl Streep victim look as she goes about her day, putting on a brave face for their child.

Back in the bar, Bruce Willis puts up the collar on his camel overcoat, leaves a $5 bill on the counter and slips out of the bar into the dark street.

Why Bruce Willis? Several people have told Alexander that he looks like that actor with the wet shirt. Not Bruce Willis, for God's sake.

'*Bruce Willis is Alexander . . . Second Chance . . .*'

Alexander rests his elbows on the counter and puts his face in his hands. It's not exactly a headache, more a whirlwind of images that he can't control.

Simply, inexorably, unintentionally, the idea has begun to take form, and the logic of it is undeniable.

If he had been on the train in his usual carriage, he would now be dead.

It is entirely likely that he would have been on the train.

Therefore, he should be dead . . .

Enough.

But it doesn't stop there.

Nell would be without her partner, Lucy without a father.

An image of them standing beside a grave leaps unbidden into Alexander's mind. Two female figures, one big, one small, holding hands.

Enough.

Alexander takes another slug of water.

Nell would hate it that their last moments together had been so unsatisfactory, but Nell's too sensible to make a few fraught hours eclipse everything that was good between them. He thinks of the effort she made to dredge memories of lovely times out of him after his mother died. He remembers her sweet face trying to maintain an optimistic smile on all the long walks they took over Hampstead Heath and how she would occasionally give him a sideways glance to check whether there'd been a surprise thaw in his frozen stare. He feels a great welling of fondness for her now, which he could not feel then.

If he were dead, Nell would cope, just as she's coped with everything life has thrown at her: with Lucy's allergies, with Lucy's asthma, with earning a living as well as being a full-time mother. Nell is resourceful. She's coped with his moods, with his total uselessness about almost everything.

In fact, he has become virtually redundant.

She'd be better off without him.

'*And tonight, at all stations down the line, cars are parked, which will not be driven home, and relatives wait, hoping for miracles . . .*'

The reporter hands back to the main newsreader, who continues with the rest of the day's news in the low and reverent voice they're trained to use in tragic circumstances.

*   *   *

281

Will Nell be hoping for a miracle, or will she be secretly relieved?

Alexander is not certain of the answer.

He knows that five years ago she would have wanted him to be alive more than anything else in the world.

Then they had Lucy. People say that the love for a child is different from adult love, but he has come to believe that human beings have a finite capacity for love, especially when they're tired and worried, and all of Nell's went to Lucy. Suddenly it was unreasonable to ask for what they had had together. It was as if his love was no longer important to her. He didn't resent it. Or is that dishonest? They never talked about it. It's second nature to him to retreat into silence, but he never thought that Nell could.

In the beginning, he knows that she thought herself unworthy of him. She mistook his moods for depth, his emptiness for mystery, and his temper for intelligence, and he didn't let on because he is weak and a coward.

Nell is strong. Strong enough to survive on her own.

Would Lucy miss him?

He doesn't think she'd really notice. It's only recently that he's started to feel some of the emotions of fatherhood that people talk about. He enjoys taking her out for walks, and swimming once a week, but he thinks that the pleasure is mostly his. Only last Saturday, as they were setting off for the pool, Lucy turned to Nell and said,

'Oh, Mummy, do I have to . . . ?'

Two female figures silhouetted by a grave, holding hands.

They will be happier without him. The undeniable truth of it brings a lump to his throat.

He has to remind himself that he is not dead.

He has been presented with a Faustian opportunity

to abandon his previous life and the sheer possibility of it fascinates him, and fills him with self-disgust.

Alexander puts a £2 coin on the counter, turns up the collar of his jacket.

'The headlines again. A train has crashed outside London. Up to fifty people are feared dead, many more have been taken to hospital with severe injuries. That's the news tonight.'

Alexander does not say goodbye to the bartender. He mustn't draw attention to himself. A quick surreptitious glance around the bar tells him that no-one has taken any particular interest in him. There is a flashily dressed man reading the *Daily Mail*, and three Eastern Europeans wearing waisted leather jackets still zipped up and smoking.

He sets off northwards, his eyes on the pavement, dodging in and out of groups of loud women on their way for an after-work drink, and shaven-headed couriers on micro-scooters. He feels he is being watched, as if he's the moving target in a computer game and any moment someone he knows is going to pop up, with a greeting instead of a gun – 'Hello, Alexander!' in a bleeping electronic voice – and that will be the end of it.

Game over.

There's a camera sticking out of a building above a sign that says REAL NUDITY. Who's watching? The police? A security firm? MI5? Are they near, or far away in some other city, the task of spying contracted out to somewhere where the price of spying is cheaper?

How many security cameras have caught him in their sights? How many miles of videotape would have to be examined to create a jumpily edited film of his day?

'Here's a number to ring if anything in this recon-struction jogs your memory . . .'

Alexander imagines the presenter of *Crimewatch* gloating over the moments of salacious footage. Corrr, did you see that? Unspoken, but there in his smug smile. A ratings winner!

Alexander tries to list the people whose memories might be jogged as they recognize him: the unfamiliar City commuters on the train he took; the man with the pram in the park; the cocky little waiter at the oyster counter in Selfridges . . .

But he won't be on *Crimewatch*.

It's not a crime to disappear.

Is it?

No-one's going to be looking for him, because he's dead.

There's nothing suspicious about it.

Nothing to trace him.

He even has his passport.

In his pocket, his hand finds the envelope with his passport in it. Why didn't he take out the passport last night and put it in a drawer?

It's like that game show. *Don't Forget Your Tooth-brush*. The contestants came prepared to fly off to the Bahamas at a moment's notice if they won the show.

Money?

Nell would spot an unauthorized withdrawal from their own joint account the moment the statement arrives, but he has not used the account today. He has paid for everything today with his mother's debit card. Nell doesn't even know the joint bank account he has never put into his sole name exists. He hasn't told her, because she would be so annoyed with him for not sorting it out. Nell likes ends to be tied.

The logistics are all in place.

'Just one final question and tonight you will be on a plane . . .'

As he approaches the neighbourhood of the school, the streets begin to feel more dangerous.

This is crazy!

He wishes that someone he knows would come out of the pub and see him. He slows down, almost dawdling.

He'll go in. Malcolm will be inside, drowning his sorrows with Vivienne.

Amid the fog of cigarette smoke he sees a group of men who have been drinking all afternoon. His eyes scan each table for familiar faces. The men – football fans? A rugby club at the start of a weekend break in London? – launch into a chorus of 'Daydream Believer' by the Monkees. The singing's so loud it blasts Alexander from the pub like a beery explosion.

The pizzeria where Kate works is just fifty yards further up on the other side of the street. A man in a white chef's apron comes out and picks up a swinging sign that has blown over. He sets it down, then goes back inside. A taxi roars past. The sign flaps in its wake. It says OPEN.

There is a single red tulip in a slim white vase on each of the tables inside. A man and a woman are sitting at a table in the middle of the restaurant with pizzas in front of them, not eating.

Alexander pretends to be studying the menu that's taped up at shoulder height inside the window.

At the back of the restaurant, Kate pops up from behind the metal shelves, with a triumphant smile on her face. She's been searching for something in a low cupboard and found it. In her left hand there's a flask of chilli oil with a long neck and a metal spout. Her head bobs along as she walks to the table, throwing back laughter to the man in the chef's apron who's whirling a pizza behind the metal shelves. She has a white tea towel tied round her hips.

Alexander watches the profile of her face, lit by the light above the table, making her look, just for a moment, two dimensional, then the slight frown as she listens to a request from the man. Her mouth moves silently in reply, probably saying something as simple as 'Anything to go with that?' but Alexander's jealous of the man. Kate smiles, tucks a pencil behind her ear. For a second she looks in Alexander's direction, but doesn't see him. She bobs away out of sight behind the cappuccino machine.

Alexander ducks his face behind the menu, feeling guilty to be watching her.

He loves the way she occupies the space she's in, the way she moves, the energy that's contained in her neat outline.

He knows he must go.

He crosses the road and walks into a pub.

There's a payphone at the back beside a fruit machine that's alive with flashing lights even though nobody's playing it. Alexander picks up the receiver. The fruit machine suddenly plays a rushed electronic scale, which makes him jump.

He puts the receiver back.

Twenty-four

'No answer from the school,' Nell says. 'They must have all gone home . . .'

Palpitations of fear race across her chest down her arm to her fingers each time she dials a number and melt into numb paralysis when it isn't answered.

Each call, she's stranded between the relief of a little more time to hope, and the frustration of uncertainty.

'Hang on . . . oh,' she puts her hand over the mouthpiece, 'it's an answerphone . . . oh yes, hello. It's just Nell, calling to see if Alexander's there. Can you ring me at Frances's flat if you are. The number's . . . ?'

She repeats the numbers after Frances, then puts the phone down, and looks up at her for more ideas. She doesn't know what to do next.

'Try home again,' Frances instructs.

Nell dials.

'Engaged,' she says, over the top of the phone, feeling her face break into a smile. 'It's engaged.'

He's there! He's home! It's going to be OK!

The adrenalin of excitement flows through her body like the first sip of champagne.

'Try again,' Frances says.

Nell presses out the number carefully.

'Press redial,' Frances says, impatiently.

'I never quite trust redial,' Nell says. 'It's giving me a

message. The number knows I'm waiting! Come on, Alex, put down the phone!'

'Press five. Now put the phone down,' Frances instructs.

Almost instantly, Frances's phone rings. Three short bleeps.

Nell looks at it.

'Pick it up!'

She does as she's told.

'Now, it should be ringing.'

'It is.'

'It's ringing your number back.'

Nell waits and listens. The phone at home is ringing, and ringing, and ringing.

'Come on!'

The ringing sounds hollow, as if it is happening in an empty room.

'It's still ringing,' she says.

After a few minutes Frances takes the receiver from her and replaces it.

'There's nobody there,' Nell says, disbelievingly.

'Your phone must have been engaged because someone was ringing you at the same time.'

'Alexander?' Nell says, hopefully.

'Could be.'

'Well, who else could it have been?' she demands.

Frances doesn't say anything but shrugs.

What's the point in asking her for reassurance she hasn't the power to give?

It could have been anyone. It could have been a friend who's worried, or even a friend who doesn't know calling for a chat, or her mother. It could have been the police.

It occurs to Nell that she experienced exactly this panic of dread when she was waiting for Alexander to come home last night. But then he arrived. The anxiety was just as strong, but it didn't mean anything. This pressing sense of dread doesn't mean anything. Unless last night was a sort of presentiment. She doesn't believe in things like that.

'You wouldn't expect him to be home though yet, would you?' Frances asks.

'It would be unusual, on a Friday,' Nell agrees. 'If he's OK, I'm sure he would call if he heard the news. The answerphone's not even on. I must have switched it over when I was sending a fax yesterday. So if he's called he won't have been able to leave a message, and he'll be wondering where we are. Oh God! If only I'd left the answerphone on, I think there's a way you can call it and pick up your messages . . .'

'There's no point in feeling guilty about things you didn't do,' Frances says. The words have an unpleasant edge to them, as if she's implying something else.

'I don't suppose you know how to retrieve your messages anyway, do you?' she asks.

'No,' Nell admits, cursing her own technophobia.

'What did the emergency number say?' Frances asks.

'They took my details. They said they'd be in touch if there was anything. It might have been them calling just now.'

'Who else might know where he is? Come on, think. How about one of the teachers?' Frances chivvies her.

'I know one or two of them a bit. I don't have their numbers in my head.'

'Names?'

'Vivienne . . . only first names . . . wait a minute.'

Nell puts her head in her hands, trying to think of any occasion when Alexander might have used a colleague's surname. There's Mel, she remembers, and Malcolm, but that's as far as she gets.

'Mummy, what's the matter?'

Lucy's face is peeking through the double doors, anxiously.

'Nothing, darling.' Nell sits up, as if she's been caught doing something she shouldn't. 'Why don't you play with Lizzy Angel for a little while? I've just got to make a couple more calls, and then we'll go home.'

'Lizzy Angel!' says Lucy delighted. 'Where is she?'

After a thorough search of both rooms, Frances remembers that they were playing in the garden. Lizzy Angel is retrieved, slightly damp, and is introduced to Fizz Tweeny.

'Now, it is extremely silly of you to go out on a cold night without a coat on,' Lucy scolds.

'Sorry,' says the doll in Lucy's doll voice.

'Come on, let's do some dancing to warm you up.'

Lucy disappears into the front room.

'Come on, think logically,' says Frances. 'If he's rung and you're not there, who would he ring? Your mother?'

'Maybe,' says Nell uncertainly.

'What's her number?' Frances has the phone in her hands. She dials the digits as Nell says them.

'Lavinia? Frances. Yes. Fine, thanks. You? Good. Look I've got Nell here and she's wondering if you've heard from Alexander. No?'

Frances gives a thumbs down.

'. . . Shall I hand her over?'

'Mummy!' says Nell. Unable to hold back the flood of tears as she hears her mother saying her name. So weird how a parent's voice can make you a child all over again.

'This train crash? It's Alexander's train! I'm down at Frances's place with Lucy . . .'

'Isn't it a schoolday?' her mother asks.

'Yes, but it was such a lovely day, I thought Lucy and I could do with a blast of sea air,' Nell explains.

'You don't want her to keep missing school . . .'

'She doesn't keep missing school . . .'

'You don't want to give them the idea that school is optional if it's a nice day . . .'

'Oh, shut up about school, will you? It's not important right now . . .'

Nell's never told her mother to shut up. At least she's not crying any more.

'Just listen a second . . .'

There's a hurt silence at the end of the phone. She doesn't know how her mother manages to get so much feeling into a silence.

'I'm going to drive home now,' Nell says, slowly. 'If Alexander rings you, tell him I'm on my way home. Find out where he is . . . Find out everything you can . . .'

'All right, my darling . . . now don't start getting worried before you know anything. It won't help . . .'

'I am worried. I can't help it!'

Before the wailing child can return, Nell puts down the phone. 'God!' she says. 'You'd think I'd made it up.'

'She never cared for Alexander,' Frances says.

'She wouldn't want him dead,' Nell says, sharply.

Lavinia's her mother. She can say what she wants about her, but Frances can't. Frances has never been very good at respecting that fundamental familial truth.

'No. She wouldn't,' Frances concedes.

There's something about the way she emphasizes the word *she* that bothers Nell, but she determines to ignore it.

'We'd better get going,' Frances says.

'You're not coming with us?' Nell says.

'Of course I am.'

'No, look, I really appreciate it, but we'll be fine.

291

Lucy?' she calls. 'Lucy, love, why don't you go for a wee before we go? It's a long journey home.'

'Do we have to go home?' Lucy calls back.

'Yes, we do. Come on. Let's get ready.'

'Ohhhh.'

Great prima donna-ish sighs of disappointment emerge from the front of the flat. Nell smiles a don't-you-remember-being-like-that smile at Frances, and when Frances doesn't return it, she feel slightly unnerved.

'I'm not sure you're fit to drive,' Frances persists.

'Well you don't drive anyway, do you?' Nell points out.

She doesn't want to have an argument about it, but she's absolutely determined that Frances will not accompany them, although she doesn't really know why she feels so strongly.

'Moral support,' Frances says.

Why does the prospect of taking Frances home just not work?

'It's really nice of you, but I'd prefer to be alone,' Nell says.

'But you won't be alone, you'll be with Lucy. I'll look after her.'

'No, Frances. Thanks, but no.'

It's ironic because Frances is always the one who tells her to stick up for herself, be assertive, and now she's doing just that, and Frances doesn't like it.

'Why not?'

'You're teaching, aren't you?' Nell says. She wishes she was the sort of person who could just say 'I don't want you to.'

'I'll call in. It's a good enough excuse.'

'Look, I just want to be on my own,' Nell says.

She doesn't want Frances with her because she is always so quick to decide what stance she's going to take. Sometimes Nell feels she's being corralled by the force of Frances's opinions into a place she doesn't want to be. She can't have that right now.

'Oh yeah, sure you do,' Frances says, with a nasty bite of the sarcasm that's been nibbling at the edge of the conversation.

'What's that supposed to mean?' Nell says, rather glad now that Lucy has taken not the slightest notice of her instructions to get ready. She's alarmed by the look on Frances's face.

'It'll be very convenient for you if Alexander has died in this crash, won't it?' Frances says icily.

'*No!*'

'Oh, come on. You can do what you've been planning to do, *and* have everyone feeling sorry for you.'

Nell shrinks away from Frances.

'I haven't been planning to do anything,' she says.

'You even look good in black.'

'Stop it!' Nell shouts.

'. . . You won't even have to look like a bitch.'

'Stop it,' Nell whispers.

She feels as if she's being battered.

Is this what Frances really thinks, or is it some horrible, inappropriate joke? Nell stares at the person she thought loved her just a little bit too much, and sees how wrong she was. Frances hates her.

Suddenly all the tiny oddities and signals that didn't seem to fit Frances very well, which she always privately put down to a slight inclination towards lesbianism, fall into a different shape.

'Why do you pretend to hate him?' Nell asks.

'It's easier,' Frances says simply.

'Lucy!' Nell calls, her focus suddenly sharpening.

'Oh, Mum-my!'

'Get ready. Now!'

Surprised by the hard edge of Nell's voice, Lucy puts on her anorak and picks up her dolls immediately.

'I am ready,' she says.

Nell hurries her along the dark passageway to the front door, opens it and hustles Lucy up the slippery stone steps to the car. She does not look back. Her hands are shaking as she does up Lucy's seatbelt and closes the car door. As she walks round to her side of the car, she can hear Frances inside the flat howling Alexander's name. And still half of her wants to go in and tell her that everything will be all right, and the other half just wants to get the terrible anguished sound out of her head.

Nell's on the road out of Brighton before it occurs to her that other cars keep flashing her. She looks at her dashboard display and sees that she has forgotten to turn her headlights on. She twists the left-hand indicator wand. The lights come on. She breathes as if for the first time since getting away from Frances.

'We had a lovely day, didn't we, Mummy?' Lucy says.

'Yes, we did,' Nell says.

'It doesn't matter that we didn't say goodbye to Frances, does it?' Lucy asks.

Their hurried exit has obviously disturbed her.

'No, it doesn't matter,' Nell reassures her.

'It doesn't matter that we didn't say goodbye to Daddy this morning, does it?' Lucy asks.

Nell hesitates.

'No, we'll give him a big hug when he comes home, won't we?'

'Yes we will.'

In the rearview mirror, Nell watches her child settle back happily.

If he comes home. Should she prepare the child for

the possibility that he might not return, or that he's injured? No. Not yet.

A car passes her. She had not been aware of its approach. She grips the steering wheel very hard. She has no confidence about where her car is on the road. She sees red lights in front of her and takes her foot off the accelerator. The red lights recede and she realizes that they were not the brake lights of the car in front but the tail-lights. It's as if the part of the brain that holds the memory of driving has been shut down. She looks at her speedometer. She's only doing 30 miles an hour on a dual carriageway. At this speed, it'll take over two hours to get home. In the opposite lane the traffic returning from London looks like one entity – a string of chaser lights – moving towards her. Nell wonders if shock actually alters perception.

Mirror, signal, manoeuvre, she tells herself, recalling the basics of driving from long ago.

'Shall we have the radio on?' she asks Lucy.

'All right, but no news,' Lucy says. 'I'm completely sick of news.'

Where does Alexander sit on the train? It's the front two carriages that are affected. Does he always sit in the same place? Does he get himself a cup of coffee from the buffet and read the paper? Is there a buffet? Or one of those trolleys? Is there enough room for him to sit down and prepare his lessons? Does he sit at a table, or in one of those seats with a pull-down tray like on a plane? Or does he stand up, trying to affect indifference as he's pressed against other people's bodies as the train goes round bends? She doesn't know. She has never asked him. She knows nothing of the details of his day.

She pictures him standing there, his first inkling that something has gone wrong, the train skidding to a halt, making himself rigid for impact. There's a burning smell, and Alexander's shouting that they must get out. Quick.

'Mummy?'

They're coming up over the South Downs. They've gone at least five miles and she can't remember anything about the road. Nell wriggles her back straighter in her seat. Concentrate.

'Yes, darling.'

'I'm dying for a wee,' Lucy announces.

'We'll stop at the next place we see,' she says.

Is Alexander a hero? Does he help other people or push them out of the way?

She remembers crossing the road with him in Rome, somewhere near the Colosseum, dodging in and out of traffic with the buggy and being really frightened of getting run down. Then, when they finally reached the pavement, Alexander turning round and braving the mad erratic charge of traffic twice again. He'd spotted an old lady in black, bent almost horizontal from the waist, whom Nell hadn't even noticed. She remembers him holding up his hand like a traffic policeman challenging a lorry to stop, and half of her feeling tremendous fondness for him, and half of her being exasperated that he should risk his life in this kind of chicken run just to help an ancient crone whom he did not even know.

'Mummy!'

'Yes?'

'Aren't you going to stop?'

The green and yellow sign of a BP garage is fast approaching on the left. Nell swerves the car onto the slip road without indicating, and slams hard on the brake pedal. There's a scream of horn behind her.

'Sorry about that,' she says.

'That's OK,' says Lucy, unaware of her dangerous driving.

There's a cold, dirty reality about the toilets. Nell takes a wodge of tissues from her pocket and drapes them all round the seat for her daughter to sit on. It occurs to her that it's crazy to be so concerned about a few germs touching Lucy's skin when she's almost killed them both with her lack of concentration. They wash their hands under a dribble of warm water, taking care not to touch the bowl and then Nell takes her into the shop and buys crisps, fruit pastilles and drinks.

Lucy sits in the back happily sucking apple juice from a box with a straw and crunching crisps. From time to time her hand slips to the side where Lizzy Angel is guarding her packet of fruit pastilles. Salt and sugar. It doesn't matter, Nell tells herself, just this once. This is a special occasion. She knows that the crisps and fruit pastilles are what Lucy will remember most about the day. She imagines her telling her mother: 'Grandma, do you know what I had for my tea? Crisps and sweets!' And Lavinia's face, smiling indulgently at Lucy, then shooting a frown at Nell.

Perhaps in the future Lucy will have a Proustian memory of sitting in the unnatural light of a petrol station eating noisily. Maybe the smell of petrol, or feel of the hard sugary surface of the pastille against her tongue and the flow of sweet fruity flavour will bring back a memory of this night and she will say to her friends, 'This reminds me of the night my father . . .'

No!

Nell sips from a can of Coke.

She eats a crisp. It tastes of holidays in Cornwall when she was a child. Standing on the beach with her own packet of Smith's. Her hand searching for the little blue twist of salt at the bottom. Sometimes finding two, or even more. Then pouring it in and shaking the packet. And then the first wonderful greasy salty crunch.

'Mummy?'

'Yes?'

'Mummy, I've got a pain.'

'Oh darling, where does it hurt?'

Lucy's hand is on her chest.

'Right in my heart,' she says.

'Oh darling,' Nell says, fighting back the urge to dissolve into emotion, 'it's probably just indigestion, in your tummy,' she explains. 'Let's get you home.'

Twenty-five

'The man on table twelve's complaining there's not enough anchovies,' Kate tells her boss, Tony.

'I gave him extra.'

'He says there's only five and a little bit.'

'How many anchovies can anyone eat?'

'I can't stand anchovies,' says Kate, 'but he's the world's biggest anchovy fan and he's getting stroppy.'

'There's something fishy about this,' says Tony.

He tells the world's worst jokes.

'What shall I tell him?'

'Ah, tell him to fuck off.'

'You tell him to fuck off,' says Kate.

She hates this sort of thing. She wouldn't mind so much if it were a real complaint, like a snail in the side salad, like she had on her very first day. (Don't shout about it, sir, or everyone will want one, Tony said, and then wrote 'Escargots' above Today's Specials on the blackboard.) But she half thinks the bloke on table twelve is complaining just to wind her up. He's been fussy right from the start, sending back his knife for having a water mark on it, demanding chilli oil. She wonders if he wants to impress his girlfriend, or whether he's deliberately trying to make her hate him because he's bored with her but can't be arsed to pack her up. Men do that. Kate glances at the couple from over the top of the cash register. He's certainly succeeded in annoying his companion. She's put down her knife and fork as if she's finished, and she's only eaten one wedge out of her Quattro Stagioni.

'Oh give him this,' Tony says, handing her the big glass bowl with the evening's supply of anchovies in it. There are at least enough slimy brown fillets in the bottom to fill a cereal bowl. Kate picks it up and carries it over to the table.

'Here's your extra anchovies,' she says sweetly, depositing the bowl beside the man. 'With the compliments of the chef.'

She retreats behind the till again and watches. The woman's having a good snigger. The man doesn't know whether to leave them, or to eat them. He'll never put away that lot. Nobody could eat that many anchovies.

She thinks of Alexander tipping oysters down his throat and smiles at nothing.

'So, how was lover boy?' Tony asks.

Is it that obvious?

Kate feels colour rush to her face.

'Good,' she says, noncommittally, picking up a cloth, wiping down a spotlessly clean surface.

'Did you mean what you said?'

'I meant it.'

Her bits feel raw and hot as if Alexander's still touching her.

'So, are you seeing him again?'

'Will you be here when I get back?'

'I don't see why not.'

She notices that Tony's also wiping surfaces that don't need cleaning. He doesn't fancy her, does he?

'Hope so,' she replies.

She'll go to Marco's first. He said he might wait there. Or maybe she'll go back to Marie's first, just to check. Then Marco's. If he's not there, at least she'll be with people. She wonders why it is that she doesn't really believe he's going to be there. He said he would, didn't he?

'*I don't see why not.*'

Why didn't he just say yes?

'What's he do?' Tony asks.

'He's a teacher.'

'Right.'

Even Tony can't think of anything funny to say about that.

If he's there, what will they do? Where will they sleep? Perhaps Marie'll go and stay at Des's, if she's in a good mood. And tomorrow morning?

Kate watches the man with the anchovies. He puts his fork into the bowl, prongs a single fillet, puts it in his mouth, then puts his fork back into the bowl. Then he sticks up his hand, and writes in the air.

Kate rings his bill up on the till, and takes it over on a saucer.

'Have you finished with these?' she asks, looking at the virtually untouched pile of oily fish.

'Yes, thank you,' he says, with a smug little smile.

His companion rolls her eyes.

Men! she seems to be saying, assuming Kate understands.

They're not all like that, Kate wants to tell her.

The couple don't leave a tip.

Kate clears the table, takes the bowl back to Tony.

'Sorry about that,' she says.

'No worries,' Tony says. 'I gobbed on them, anyway.'

'Ugh, gross!' says Kate, but she's laughing. 'You're not putting them back?'

'Course not.'

Tony's large hand stops midway to the shelf, and puts the bowl to one side, but Kate knows that he'll replace it as soon as her back is turned.

'So was it love at first sight?' Tony wants to know.

'Something like that,' Kate says. She's not inclined to share the experience with Tony, who'll only make dirty jokes. For a moment, she's tempted to pre-empt him – guess what? We fucked in Selfridges – just to shock him, but knowing Tony, he'll only come up with a list of unusual locations where he's made love, or friends of his have.

'Where'd you meet him, then?'

The hesitation and the glance around the room give her away.

'He's a customer?' Tony's triumphant in his powers of detection. 'Doesn't like anchovies, does he? Cos I've got a whole bowlful going to waste . . .'

'He likes oysters,' says Kate.

'I see.'

'Have you ever tried one?' she asks Tony.

'I've had one too many,' Tony says, grimacing.

'Disgusting, right?' Kate says, thinking that it's quite nice to talk to someone about it after all.

'Meant to be, you know . . .' Tony shakes his hips.

'Really?' says Kate, disingenuously, but she knows that her colour's given her away again.

'Quiet tonight,' she observes.

'Always is at this time on Friday. The sane ones have gone home for the weekend, the mad ones are getting rat-arsed. They'll be in later, stuffing garlic bread down their throats to sober up. You do not want to think about the toilets after a Friday night. Don't worry. Greta's coming in later to help. I gave her a couple of hours.'

Kate pulls a face. She doesn't believe that Greta puts all her tips in the communal jar.

'She did your shift today,' Tony says, with a note of warning in his voice. 'At very short notice.'

He likes his girls to get on.

Kate looks at the clock. The hours until midnight stretch agonizingly ahead of her.

Did she tell him how long the evening shift is? Will he wait? Is he there now, lying naked, thinking about her? Or is he in Marco's, drinking coffee, reading a paper? Watching football? She doesn't even know what team he supports. Or has he got fed up and gone home? Where is home? Where's Kent?

'What's Kent like?' she asks Tony.

'The orchard of England,' says Tony. 'Apple trees, oasthouses with pointed roofs for drying something . . . Oats, I suppose.'

'Why would anyone live in Kent?' Kate asks.

'Why would you live anywhere in England, when you could live in Spain?' says Tony.

It's one of his themes. He's heard you can buy a goat shed in the Sierra above Malaga for a few grand. He dreams of opening a pizza restaurant up there.

Kate doesn't think it will ever happen.

'You can't get a decent pizza in Spain,' Tony tells her for the hundredth time, as if it's a charming eccentricity in an otherwise perfect nation.

She wants to say, bit like here, then, or ask him if he knows whether Spanish people actually like pizza. But this evening she's in no mood to challenge anyone's dreams.

The door to the restaurant opens. Two women, a mother and daughter, struggle in with carrier bags and plonk themselves down with exaggerated, exhausted sighs at table four. You'd think they'd been shovelling coal instead of shopping in Oxford Street. The younger woman has a big box with a cord handle and Pronuptia written across it. A wedding dress. She orders a ham and mushroom pizza, then at the last minute changes her mind and asks for a salade Niçoise.

Slimming for the big day, Kate thinks.

'I'll hold the anchovies, shall I?' Kate offers. 'Very oily.'

'Oh, OK, then.'

As she hurries off to get their drinks, Kate hears the mother say, 'What a nerve!'

The door opens again, and a man wearing a suit comes in with a boy in school uniform. They sit at a window table, staring out of the window, saying nothing. One big man, one little, as awkward as each other in their uncomfortable clothes.

He's divorced, Kate thinks, and this is his once a month weekend with his son. She wants to take him on one side and say: Look, save the pizza till Sunday. It'll give him something to look forward to.

The boy wants a Coke float.

'My mouth's really dry,' he explains to Kate, sticking out his tongue. Five she thinks, or six at the most, the age just before boys realize that it's not cool to tell the world every little thing they're thinking.

'Mmm. Looks it,' she says, giving the outstretched tongue a quick check. 'Coke float all right with you, Dad?'

The man stares at her. It's not just a normal hostile London stare. His eyes are full of fear.

'A cup of tea,' he says.

'Anything to eat?'

'James?' the man asks across the table.

'James!' Kate repeats.

The man stares at her again.

'I like the name James,' she explains, flustered by his look of bleak terror. 'Are you a Jamie or a Jimmy?' she asks the boy.

'Just James,' he says.

'*James and the Giant Peach*,' Kate says. 'Right. What would you like to eat? How about a nice pizza, with

304

some cheese and tomato, and . . . let me guess . . . ham?'

'No ham, thank you,' says the boy. 'I'm vegetarian. Mummy's vegetarian, but she still got ill.'

He says it like a question. He's been told that vegetables are good for you, so what's going on?

The father doesn't know what to say.

'Oh, I'm sorry about that,' Kate says busily. 'How about if I get the chef to put some extra cheese on?'

She picks up the wine glasses that are on the table, and shakes one of the paper napkins onto the boy's lap. Anything to move the man on from his catatonic state. Get a grip, she wants to tell him. You're frightening your son. You're frightening me, and I don't even know you.

In her head, their story's changed. Father and son have come to visit the boy's mother in hospital. There are lots of hospitals round here. She's desperately ill, and the man's terrified of being left alone. The boy's mouth is dry because they've been waiting for news all afternoon in one of those hot hospital corridors where staff are always rushing past, but nothing ever seems to happen.

The woman on table four has her hand in the air like a schoolchild.

'How long does it take to make two salads?' she asks when Kate gets to her.

'I don't know, how long does it take to make two salads?' Kate asks, as if she's listening to a light bulb joke.

The daughter giggles nervously.

Kate glances at the counter. The salads are there waiting for her to collect. She brings them to the table.

'The only big decision now apart from the flowers, is up or down,' the mother is saying, deliberately ignoring Kate as she places the bowls in front of them. 'Are we thinking tiara or floral garland . . . ?'

There are so many rules and regulations about correct procedure at weddings these days, Kate doesn't know who they're meant to be for any more except for the dozens of caterers and hoteliers and florists and beauticians and hairdressers, and cakemakers and dressmakers, and disco owners and printers who all make a living out of it.

Kate scoops an extra large spoonful of vanilla ice-cream into a tall sundae glass, and pushes the Coke button on the fizzy drink dispenser. The mixture froths alarmingly. She puts it on a tray, with a teapot, milk jug and cup, and carries it carefully to the window table. A peak of creamy foam floats on top of the glass defying gravity. It looks like the scum on the water at Blackpool that never goes away. Is that what happens when seawater meets dropped ice-cream cones, she wonders, or is it pollution?

'Sounds like a job for International Rescue,' the little boy is saying. He has a plastic model Thunderbird 1 in his hand which is dropping little pink sachets of Sweet 'n' Low on some invisible enemy.

'Sorry,' his father says, collecting up the packets, as Kate approaches.

'No problem,' Kate says.

As she picks up the tray, she says from behind it, in as good a *Thunderbirds* voice as she can remember,

'FAB, Virgil!'

The little boy's face lights up, then falls.

'Virgil is in Thunderbird 2,' he corrects her.

'Ooops! So who's this, then?'

'Scott.'

'Course it is.'

She winks at the father, and for the first time, he tries to smile at her.

'Kate!'

Tony's calling across the restaurant.

'Kate!'

'What?'

'Phone.'

Tony's face is anxious.

Who could be calling her here? No-one has her number, except Marie. Marie wouldn't phone unless there was a good reason. What's so urgent that it can't wait?

Jimmy! Please God, don't let anything have happened to Jimmy!

Suddenly, she's running across the room.

'He says it's an emergency,' Tony says, with his hand over the receiver. He remains standing next to her for support.

He?

Her heart is thumping in her head as she takes the receiver from Tony. He leaves his fingerprints in flour on it.

'Hello?'

'Kate?'

The voice is so familiar but she's not sure who it is. She's thinking doctor, policeman . . .

'Speaking.' She makes her voice as old and responsible as she can.

'It's Alexander.'

The adrenalin that apprehension has created inside her escapes in a surprised, relieved giggle.

'All right?' Tony mouths at her.

Kate nods and shifts her body round so that Tony can't see her face. 'How did you get my number?' she whispers.

'It's on the menu in the window.'

Kate glances over at the window, half expecting to see him standing outside with a mobile phone, but the street outside is empty. A slight frisson of discomfort shivers through her.

'Hey, you're not a stalker, are you?' she jokes.

'I have to talk to you.'

'Where are you?'

'In the pub across the road.'

The urgency in his voice is kind of flattering. Her shoulders relax. She can see the first window of the pub on the corner. It's novel, talking to each other on the phone when they're only a few yards apart. It turns her on.

'So, talk away. We're not very busy.'

'Come here.'

'I'm working.'

'But you're not very busy . . .'

She doesn't like the quickness with which he throws her words back at her.

'I'm the only one on.'

'There's something I want to ask you,' he says.

'Can't it wait till later?'

The phrase sounds odd. Like they're in a proper relationship.

'Say it's an emergency?' He's used to getting his own way.

She presses the receiver against her ear. Her body's starting to want his like she can sense his wanting her.

'I've got a break in an hour.'

'Come now . . . please . . .'

Kate sneaks a glance at Tony, who's pretending not to be listening. He starts to whistle, which is something he never does. The door of the restaurant opens. Kate glares at it. With only two tables, and both of them eating, she might just be allowed to take five minutes, but with a third, even that slim chance is gone. Then a smile breaks uncontrollably over her face. Greta has arrived early. 'I'll be there as soon as I can,' she says, and puts down the phone.

'You making yourself too easy,' Tony says, shaking his head. 'Men like a woman to say no . . .'

'I'm always saying no,' Kate banters, 'but this one's . . .'

'Different? Yeah, yeah. Nothing's ever different.'

Tony splats a spoonful of tomato sauce onto a circle of raw pizza dough. 'He won't respect you if you come running whenever he calls,' he tells her.

'OK, OK,' Kate says.

She wants to tell him, look, he really is different. He's not like you. He's not so crude as to want me to pretend that I don't like him when I do.

'I promised double cheese,' she says, pointing at the meagre scattering of mozzarella gratings.

'More anchovies, more cheese,' Tony mutters, 'you'll drive me out of business.'

Greta is tying a tea towel round her waist, surveying the virtually empty room.

'Where are we with table one?' she asks.

'We're waiting for a Neapolitan with double cheese, and we're letting him play with the sugar bowl because his mum's in hospital,' Kate tells her.

'Got it.'

As Kate goes to pull open the door, a smartly dressed woman pushes it from the street side. Kate stands back to let her in. The woman's shoulder-length hair looks as if she's just brushed it, and her lipstick is exactly the same red as her jacket. Her heels tap straight to the window table and she bends to hug the boy. The man stands up and clasps her to his chest, then holds her at arm's length and looks at her as if words cannot express how good she looks.

What's that all about then?

*　　　*　　　*

Alexander's sitting at a corner table. His leather jacket is saving the seat next to him for her.

He stands up when he sees her peeping over people's shoulders on tiptoe. When she smiles at him, he smiles. Then she's standing in front of him and neither of them seems to know how to greet the other. He touches her arm, quickly, like a child in a museum who has to see if an exhibit's real.

'Don't ever do that again,' she says to him.

'What?'

'Say it's an emergency when it's not.'

'I'm sorry.'

She picks up his jacket to hang it over the back of the chair. It's very heavy.

'You're like a snail with your house on your back,' she says, jerking her arm, pretending that the weight of the jacket has dislocated it.

He buys her a glass of orange juice, and puts it down in front of her. For someone who wanted to say something urgently, he's very quiet.

'This better be good,' Kate says, 'because I'm going to have to work four hours without a break now.'

He looks perplexed, as if he doesn't know why she's there, or what she's just said to him. Suddenly she thinks that what he has to tell her isn't good news, and she wishes she'd taken a moment to compose herself for rejection, instead of rushing to him like someone in soft focus commercial for body spray.

Alexander sips from his tall glass of beer. She wonders if it's still his first pint, or if it's his second or third. The Friday night drinking noise all around them makes the silence feel even longer.

'Don't you get bored working there?' he asks finally, jerking his head in the direction of the restaurant.

What's this leading to? Is he saying that he despises her job, that she'll have to change it to have any chance with him? Kate's body stiffens with pride.

'Not really,' she says. 'The customers are interesting . . .'

He looks at her sceptically.

'I don't just mean you,' she says. 'It's like each table has its story. There's this couple sitting by the window now with a child, and I'm trying to work out whether she's his new girlfriend, or his sister, and why they're meeting in some crappy pizza restaurant on a Friday evening. They arrived separately, and they're quite smart, you know, and he looks really sad . . .'

'Perhaps they're divorced.'

'If they are divorced, I think he really regrets it,' Kate says.

'Perhaps it wasn't his fault,' Alexander says.

'Perhaps she's the doctor who looked after his wife. She's very smart. Maybe she's developed a good relationship with James . . . maybe she's the only person he trusts . . .'

She stops, aware that she's creating an episode of *Casualty* out of one glimpsed greeting.

'James?'

'The little boy's called James.'

'You really are unbelievable,' Alexander says, smiling at her, and she feels the colour rush to her cheeks because he looks like he's really fond of her.

'So how long's it going to take you to save the money?' he asks.

'What money?'

'For going round the world.'

She laughs because he says it as if it's really going to happen. She wants to tell him: Nobody really believes I'm going to do it.

He beckons. He's going to tell her a secret. She leans across the table and puts her ear close to his lips.

He says, 'Why don't we go right now?'

311

He plants the briefest kiss on the tender skin beneath her ear. Such a soft, secret, sensual kiss, it's almost unbearably pleasurable. Her shoulders hunch up to protect her neck from further touching, as if she's being tickled.

'Stop!' she whispers, unconvincingly.

'Come,' he says, standing up, stretching out his hand.

'Where?' She remains sitting.

He sits down again, leans across the table, con-spiratorially. He doesn't want anyone else to hear.

'If we hurry, we'll get a flight tonight,' he says quietly.

'A flight?' Her voice comes out unexpectedly loud. She laughs to try to cover it.

'Where to?' She too leans forward, whispering, joining in the game.

It is a game, isn't it?

'Does it matter?'

He's not really asking her to just get on an aeroplane with him? Can you do that? Can you just go to an airport and step onto a plane like it's a bus or some-thing?

'We'll get the first one and go wherever it takes us . . .' he suggests.

Is he crazy? Mad? Has she fallen madly in love, literally?

'Why?' she asks incredulously.

'I want to wake up tomorrow morning with you beside me. I really don't care where . . .'

'You are crazy!' she says.

'Am I? I thought you believed in possibility,' he says.

It's weird when he quotes her own words back at her, like that. Most of her really likes it, but there's a tiny part of her that doesn't. Like a warning. Her brain repeats everything he's said over and over, searching for misunderstanding.

'You're joking, right?'

'I'm not joking.'

He is Sasha. He is asking her to ride on his magic carpet.

'OK, then, let's go!' she says, as if it's a dare.

He stands up.

So she stands up.

They look at each other as if each is challenging the other to sit down again.

Then he smiles, the brilliant smile that makes you think that it's enough just to look at him and do nothing else for the rest of your life.

He offers his hand. She takes it. He pulls her through the crowded pub. Outside, they're both running and laughing, like teenagers who've eaten in a restaurant and left without paying the bill.

Twenty-six

The sound of tyres on gravel wakes Lucy up as the car turns into the drive.

'Is it snowing, Mummy?' she asks.

'No, it's just the blossom from the trees,' Nell says, watching the bright white petals dance in the head-lights. She switches off the ignition. For a moment, it's so dark she can't see the house, then her eyes adjust. As she gets out of the car she sees that there's a dart of sky that's still palely gold, like a glimpse of yellow sugar paper that's escaped the determined black strokes of a child's painting of night.

'Is Daddy home?' Lucy asks as she scrambles out of her seat.

'I don't think so,' Nell says. 'Not yet.'

Inside, the house is just as they left it. Nell picks up the phone, listens to the dialling tone, then puts it down again. Then she dials 1471. The number is familiar to her. The call was at 19:10. Ten past seven, Nell thinks. She realizes, disappointed, that it was her own call from Frances's. So there have been no calls since then. Nell checks her watch. No calls in almost two hours. She can't decide whether that is good news or bad.

'Can I go to bed without a bath, Mummy?'

'Of course you can, my darling. Go and brush your teeth. I'm just going to look at my e-mail and then I'll come up.'

She feels as if she's acting her role as a mother over the top of the turmoil inside her, going through the routine of bedtime on automatic pilot, but so far, Lucy does not seem to have noticed the difference.

There's a brief surge of optimism when she sees that there are three e-mails in her in box. The first two are from the editor of her magazine sent twice by mistake. The third is from Frances. It's several Ks long and the subject is *Sorry, sorry, sorry*.

Nell shuts the computer down without reading any of them.

'What time is Daddy getting home?' Lucy calls through a mouthful of toothpaste.

'He's usually late on Fridays.'

Nell goes upstairs.

'Why?'

'He goes out for a drink with his friends,' Nell explains.

'Or lots of drinks?' says Lucy, and spits out into the sink.

Enough time has passed since Daddy's day ended for him to consume a whole barrel of beer.

'Bed,' Nell orders.

She helps Lucy undress and tucks her into bed, then just as she's creeping out of the room, Lucy's little voice says,

'Mummy? I think Lizzy Angel is still in the car.'

The sky is now a great dome of stars. Something about the myriad twinkles makes Nell feel as if there's benevolence at work. She picks Lizzy Angel and Fizz Tweeny off the back seat and gives them each a cuddle.

'What do you think, Lizzy Angel?' she whispers, making the doll's face look up at the heavens too. 'Is Alexander OK?'

She nods Lizzy Angel's flat knitted head. The cross-stitch eyes seem full of optimism. But she's never trusted Lizzy Angel.

Alexander asked quite recently, 'Why did Lucy call her Lizzy Angel?'

'It's what your mother used to say. Never just Lucy. Lucy, angel . . . Alexander, angel . . . Don't you remember? Lucy was just beginning to talk. She thought you added "angel" to everything.'

'Do you think she can remember my mother?'

'We've talked about her. What she was like. She knows she gave her Lizzy,' Nell told him gently, surprised at his eagerness to find a link between the generations. 'You should read Lucy some of the books.'

But she doesn't think that he has.

She has the fleeting thought that the books will be a comfort to Lucy, a way of fleshing out a memory of Alexander. She stamps on it, hating her imagination for being so morbid. No news is good news.

Nell tucks the doll in next to Lucy. The cross-stitch eyes stare up at her, keeping a waking vigil.

As she tiptoes out of the room, Lucy turns over.

'Mummy?'

'Yes?'

'I love you in the world.'

'I love you in the world, too.'

Downstairs, Nell switches the television on. A bespectacled man will win £125,000 if he knows how many miles the Moon is from Earth. With one hand she flips through the listings guide. There's no news until ten o'clock.

What now?

She picks up the phone, hesitates before dialling, then presses out her mother's number.

'Mummy, we're home.'

316

'Alexander too?'

'No.'

'Have you heard from him?'

'No.'

'I'm sure he'll turn up.'

Well, that's all right then.

'Mummy, I don't know what to do!'

'No news is good news.'

'You won't say that if there's no news by midnight, or tomorrow, or . . .' Nell's voice peters out.

'Shall I come over, darling?'

'No. No, I don't think so, thanks.'

'Do you want me to have Lucy?'

'No, she's asleep now.'

Her mother has recently adopted an injured hound with three legs whose basket in the kitchen makes Lucy sneeze. Nell doesn't want to take Lucy there unless it's absolutely necessary.

'*Morse* is on, darling.'

'Oh, sorry.'

Nell puts down the phone. It's strangely reassuring to know that her mother's unruffled enough to be watching *Morse*.

Nell picks up the address book by the phone, and flicks through it. She's not really expecting to see Alexander's handwriting, but under S for School he has scrawled the word Vivienne, and a number, and under that Mel, and a number.

Nell tries Mel's number first. She knows that Mel is his friend at work. He sometimes mentions lunch with her, and if he comes home with a joke, it is usually Mel who has told him it. Recently, he hasn't mentioned her, and Nell wonders whether that means they have fallen out, or whether they are getting closer.

The woman who answers says, 'No, they left this morning.'

317

'Left?'

'Left the country. They've gone to Indonesia.'

For a second, Nell imagines two people on a white beach, holding hands. A woman and a man, and then the man turns round and it's Alexander.

'Oh.'

'I've got an e-mail address for Joe . . .' the woman offers.

'No. No, it's fine,' Nell says, remembering now that Alexander said something last night about a party for Mel and Joe.

She rings the number next to Vivienne. A bright voice answers, 'Hello?' as if she's been practising saying it in a sexy way.

'Oh, hello, sorry to disturb you,' Nell begins. 'It's just Nell. I live with Alexander, and he's not home, and I was just wondering if you knew . . .'

She hates herself for not rehearsing something better, as she hears herself sounding like a wronged wife.

'I thought he was sick,' Vivienne interrupts.

'Sick?'

'He wasn't in today. He left a message, didn't he?'

'A message?'

'I didn't take it. It must have been Malcolm. Hasn't he been at home?'

'No. Well, I don't think so. I've been out.'

Nell looks around the room. The newspaper is still on the table folded in its pristine state, just as it was delivered this morning. Proof, if she needed proof, that Alexander has not been here. Of course he hasn't been home.

'I hope I haven't said something I shouldn't,' Vivienne says.

'What time was the message?' Nell asks.

'I don't know exactly. There's usually someone in by

318

nine. Have you got Malcolm's number – but I'm not sure he'll know any more than me.'

There's relish in her voice at the possibility of intrigue.

'Early morning, this message . . .'

'Early morning,' Vivienne confirms. 'Very early,' she says, as if that somehow makes it worse.

'The reason I'm asking is that the train Alexander usually catches crashed today,' Nell tells her. Impatience makes her speech fast and cold.

'Oh my God! That wasn't Alexander's train, was it?' Vivienne says.

'I think so.'

'Oh God, I'm so sorry . . . God, he was on the train and he wasn't in work . . . I don't know why nobody thought . . . maybe because he called. We just assumed . . . Look, ring Malcolm. Do you want me to ring Malcolm?'

'No. I'll ring,' Nell says, guessing that this is the woman who turns everything into a drama. She knows instinctively that Alexander will be furious with her for explaining the situation to her if . . .

'You will ring me and let me know?' Vivienne pleads. 'I'm so sorry . . .'

Nell puts down the phone and stares at the receiver until the outline of it blurs, but no tears come. Logic tells her that he must be dead or injured. There's no other possible explanation for his not appearing at work, not being at home, not ringing. Dead, dead, dead. Nell tries to make it more real by concentrating on the word, but she can't. She's suspended in a state which is devoid of emotion except hollow fear. She stares at the phone almost wanting it to ring and for someone to confirm the worst. Then she might be able to feel what she's supposed to feel.

*   *   *

There's a camp message on Malcolm's answerphone saying that he's out celebrating being single again. She listens to it, then puts the phone down

Why did Alexander make a phone call to school to say that he wasn't coming in? When? Alexander never uses the phone if he can help it. Far more likely that Vivienne is mistaken and Alexander didn't call at all.

Nell goes into the kitchen and clears away the breakfast things from this morning. She tips the half-eaten bowl of Cornflakes into the swing-top bin and rinses the cups. Tomorrow there will be another bowl of Cornflakes set out optimistically, and Lucy will take another few spoonfuls and Nell will tip the rest in the bin again. A child's life is all about ritual and routine. How will she ever be able to explain to her that Daddy went out as usual but did not come back? How will Lucy ever be able to rely on anything again?

'It doesn't matter that I didn't say goodbye to Daddy . . .'

Nell didn't say goodbye to him either. Deliberately. She was awake when he left, listening to him shower, get dressed; pretending to sleep. She could not bear to open her eyes and see him looking at her again as if he no longer knew who she was. Is it worse to have had no last goodbye than to have had an argument?

Alexander! Nell screams his name silently, searching for him inside, trying to connect with him again.

Please, Alex, please be alive. Please don't do this to us!

Nell goes upstairs and creeps into Lucy's room. She leans over the bed and sniffs the soft warm sweet smell of her child, the smell of innocence. She sits down on the wooden floor, comforted by the tiny, even sighs of peaceful breathing.

Nell makes silent promises, like prayers.

If you're alive, Alexander, we'll move.

If you're alive, we'll go back to Italy, or wherever you want.

If you're alive, we'll have so much to be grateful for, we'll never have a reason to be unhappy.

If you're alive, we'll talk like we used to, and tell each other everything we're feeling.

If you're alive, we'll make love.

Downstairs the phone rings.

Nell runs down the stairs.

'Alexander?'

'Nell, it's Chris. Are you OK?'

She was so sure it was going to be Alexander.

'Look, if it's a bad time . . .'

'Alexander's not come home. It was his train . . .' Nell starts to cry.

'Oh, God, Nell . . .'

The sorrow in his voice alerts her for the first time to the fact that she is not the only person who's affected by the crash.

'Is Sarah OK?' she asks.

'Yes, she drove in today. Miraculously.'

'I've rung Alexander's work. He wasn't in today. He can't be dead, can he?'

There's a long silence in which she can only hear her own racing heartbeat.

'Nell, I don't know.'

Chris is too honest to lie to her.

Nell's suddenly crying uncontrollably because he's allowed her to let go of hope. Of course Alexander's dead. She knew it in her heart as soon as she saw the reporter standing in the station car park on the news. It was like a message, just for her, and for Lucy.

'Is that Daddy's train?'

The voice in her ear is saying, 'Nell? I'm coming over. Nell. Hang up, Nell!'

She does as it tells her to, then sits down on the sofa.

The tears have stopped now and a thick, bleak emptiness has descended. She sits with her arms crossed, as if she's physically holding herself together. After a while her fingertips tell her brain that she's still wearing her jacket. She has not taken it off since they arrived back. Her room has become a waiting room.

There's a knock at the door and a whispered shout – 'It's Chris!' – giving her no chance of a split second's joy.

She walks wearily to the door, wondering why he's come.

He is just the same height as the doorframe, she notices, as he stands there. She had thought him a little taller than that.

'Sarah says that she drove past Alexander this morning. She's sure he must have caught the earlier train.'

'Is that what you came to tell me?'

'No, I came to be with you. She told me as I was going out the door.'

His eyes crinkle with concern.

Behind him, the apple trees are briefly lit by the headlights of an approaching car. The blossom glows luminously white for a moment, then slips back into the darkness.

She realizes that he is waiting for her to invite him over the threshold. 'You'd better come in,' she says, taking a step back to allow him.

Automatically she leads him into the kitchen where they usually sit. She doesn't want to sink into the sofa beside him. In the kitchen they do not have to whisper for fear of waking Lucy.

'Coffee?' she asks.

'Whatever you're having.'

'You decide.'

There's something irksome about his solicitousness, and yet it gives her something to focus on. It was too frightening just to sit by herself preparing for the unthinkable.

'Tea, then.'

'Herbal?'

'No.'

She's immensely relieved that he's said no. She thinks she would have hit him if he'd said anything about the soothing properties of camomile or peppermint.

'Where were you today?' he asks.

'We went to the seaside.'

'Oh.'

'Did Ben miss Lucy?' she asks.

'He missed her terribly.'

It's horribly coy to use their children to express their own feelings and she hates herself for falling into it, especially tonight, but she cannot help smiling at him. She turns her back on him to fill the kettle.

'They did counting in twos. Ben counted to a hundred in twos on the way home. He was delighted with himself.'

'Lucy's brought him a present. Only a rather dull pebble, I'm afraid. And she won a Tweeny! You know those machines with claws that never ever pick up? Hers picked up.'

Nell remembers the brief moment of triumph holding Fizz Tweeny to her chest like a talisman. How long ago it seems. And what was it that she wished for then, with her eyes closed, like a child catching a leaf?

That everything would be OK.

But what was she really wishing for?

She pours boiling water into the teapot and puts it on the table between them.

'Nell?'

Chris is looking at her anxiously.

'Yes?'

'You didn't put any tea in.'

'Oh God!'

She laughs, fills the kettle again, then sits down while she waits for it to boil.

They look at each other.

'Ben's looking forward to tennis tomorrow.'

'Lucy too.'

She wonders what they would be talking about if it was a normal Friday evening and she knew that Alexander was coming home. She would probably be telling him more about her day, she decides, about her conversation with Frances. About how she had almost decided to sleep with him. That seems long ago now too, and strangely irrelevant.

The kettle clicks off.

Nell empties the teapot and puts two teabags in, one, two, smiling at him. Then pours in water.

'Biscuit?'

'Thanks. Have you eaten?'

'Not really. We had snacks at a service station.'

He pulls a face.

'Lucy enjoyed it.'

'I bet she did.'

Nell opens a packet of biscuits and puts them on a plate. A tiny heart-shaped window of red jelly beams through each moulded shortcake surface. She wishes she'd chosen to open the digestives.

'Do you think you know when someone's dead?' Nell asks. 'I mean, can you feel it in your soul?'

'I don't know. Do you?'

'Now? No.'

'How do you feel?'

'I just want to *know*. I can't bear not knowing. I feel like I'm bracing myself for impact. It's rushing up on me, getting closer and closer, but never hitting. I keep forgetting to breathe.'

He goes to touch her hand that's resting on the table top, but she shrinks away.

'When did you hear about the crash?' she asks, in a clipped tone that makes it sound as if it's a little piece of local news.

'Lunchtime news. I was in my workshop . . .'

'Was there a moment when you thought "Sarah!"?'

'I knew that she'd driven.'

There's a long pause.

'I know what you're feeling,' he says tentatively.

'How?' Her tone's dismissive.

'There *was* a moment when I thought "Nell!" When you weren't at school, and you didn't answer your phone. I even came round. The car was gone . . .'

'But you saw me this morning. You waved.'

'I always wave. I couldn't remember whether I'd seen you today.'

'You wave at the house?' Nell asks. 'Even if you don't see me?'

'I wave in case you're looking and I can't see you.'

She laughs, unable to decide whether she likes him more because of that, or less.

He smiles because he's made her cheerful for a second, but her face immediately returns to seriousness.

'God, Chris. What am I going to do?'

'Pour the tea.'

She pours tea into two mugs, pushes one across the table to him. They cradle the mugs in their hands, blowing steam away from the hot surface, as if it's a very cold night, which it is not.

'Have you rung the emergency number?' he asks.

'Yes. Do you think I should ring again?'

He looks at his watch.

'It's only 9.15.'

'I'll ring at ten, shall I, if . . . ?'

'Yes.'

Cradle, blow, sip.

Nell suddenly notices that he's wearing a track suit.

'Where does Sarah think you are?'

'Out for a run . . . I said I might call in to check you were OK. That's when she said about seeing Alexan—'

'She must think you're training for the marathon,' Nell interrupts. 'All this running.'

She doesn't want him to say Alexander's name, yet whenever Sarah's is mentioned, she finds herself feeling all brittle and saying pathetically sarcastic things, like a jealous teenager.

Nell stands up and tips the remains of her tea in the sink.

'I'm going to check Lucy,' she says. As she passes him, he catches her hand.

'Nell . . . if . . .'

There's the slightest flicker of emotion in his pale blue eyes which seems to disappear as she observes it. She wonders why it is that blue eyes are so much less expressive than brown ones. Alexander's eyes are like unfathomable pools, and Chris's are like the surface of the sea at sunset, pale and opaque as steel.

'What?'

He lets go of her hand.

'Do you want me to stay? For a while,' he adds quickly.

'I'll be down in a minute.'

She walks upstairs, stands just outside Lucy's room. Lucy senses her there and turns over, muttering something in her sleep, then she settles again. Nell breathes slowly in and out. Once. Twice. Three times, then she goes back downstairs.

Chris is standing in the kitchen now, arms folded over his chest. 'I'd better go,' he says.

'Yes, perhaps you had,' she says, still standing in the kitchen door.

Neither moves. She's blocking his exit through the living room to the door. Simultaneously, they dodge one way to allow the other to pass, then the other, then smile embarrassed at their impromptu little jig. Nell takes a step backwards, Chris forwards. She turns to say goodbye at the same moment that he goes to kiss her cheek. His lips catch the side of her mouth. Her hand comes up to her face as if she's been slapped.

She's staring at him.

'Chris, I'm frightened.'

'I know.'

He holds out his arms. She steps forwards, he enfolds her. She lets her head loll on his shoulder for a moment. He's stroking her back.

'Nell, if . . .'

'No,' she stops him speaking.

'No.'

'I didn't make this happen, did I?' she whispers into his neck.

He draws back to look at her face, to make sure he's understood what she's saying.

'No, Nell, you didn't. Of course you didn't.'

And now his mouth is seeking hers, finding it, and his lips are much softer than she imagined them.

Twenty-seven

'Wait a minute!'

Kate grabs his hand to make him slow down. He stops and she tugs him towards her, backing into a shadowy doorway next to a shop that sells cut-price stationery.

'Do you really love me?' she says.

'Yes!' he says impatiently, and plants a quick kiss on her nose. He's eager to move on, keep up the momentum. She puts her arms round his neck and pulls his mouth onto hers, kissing him hard, thrusting her hips against his. Here, now, kiss me, touch me, fuck me.

'Let's go!' he says, pulling away from her.

Her eyes widen, stung by rejection, so he steps towards her again, kisses her lingeringly. In the window behind he sees that Post-It notes are 10 for £5; 3 rolls of Sellotape for £1. He wonders if there's something wrong with the glue.

'But will you still love me tomorrow?' she asks.

'You know, that sounds just like the lyric of a song,' he mocks, tugging gently at her hand.

'Will you, though?'

'Yes,' he insists.

'I mean if we don't go.'

He pretends to bang his head against the shopfront in exasperation. 'Why do women always want more?'

'Why do men never answer questions?' Kate counters. 'Why are you in such a hurry anyway?'

'Spontaneity,' he suggests, desperately, feeling it all slipping away from him.

'There's things I have to sort,' Kate says.

'What things?'

'Just things.'

'I thought you wanted to escape,' he says.

'I want to escape. I don't want to run away.'

Her wonderfully fresh way of expressing the obvious suddenly sounds as if she's reading from the script of some awful film.

'What's the difference?' he asks her.

She looks as if she's searching for the answer then admits, winningly, 'I don't know.'

'Is it money?' he asks. 'I've got enough money.'

She shakes her head. Something is bothering her, that's not going to go away. Something she has not told him. He watches her face twisting with indecision, he wonders why he told her he loved her, and what made him think that taking a plane with her was going to solve anything.

'Shall we go back to Marie's?' she asks.

'Let's get a coffee,' he says.

He wants the clarity that caffeine will bring, not the confusion of sex.

'Marco's?' she suggests.

The remains of his espresso have dried to a stain in the little white cup. They're both waiting for the other to start the conversation that will inevitably separate them.

Kate is clearly grappling with some secret she's failed to share with him. He wants to say, look, why don't we just leave it here, where we started? Let's not get into recrimination and explanation. Let's call it a day.

Marco puts a bowl of *spaghetti alla carbonara* in front of Kate. A plume of steam rises between them.

'I'm starving,' Kate says, half apologetically.

Gas in the green San Pellegrino bottle escapes with a prolonged sigh as Alexander twists the metal top off.

Kate picks up her fork and spoon and begins to tackle the bowl of pasta. 'You haven't guessed, have you?' she says, as if the mechanical distraction of eating food has finally allowed her to speak.

'About what?' he asks. He's no longer very interested.

'About my boy.'

'Boy?'

'Son. My son.'

He laughs.

There's a little bit of eggy sauce clinging to each side of her mouth. She looks about twelve. He can imagine many guilty secrets she might have omitted to reveal to him, but not a child.

'Jimmy,' Kate says.

Now she's smiling. She looks down, digs enthusiastically into the spaghetti. 'He's seven,' she says, through the pasta.

A child who is older than Lucy. He can't believe it, but why would she lie?

'It's better if you use the side of the plate,' Alexander tells her. 'Look!' He takes the fork from her hand, pulls a couple of strands out of the pile and winds.

'That's how they do it in Italy,' he says. 'It's so much easier.'

She looks sceptical, but tries it.

'You're right!' she says, surprised.

'The secret is not to take too many strands at once,' Alexander says.

'And then you don't have to open your mouth so

wide,' she says, happily depositing another forkload in.

'Where's he now?' he asks, because he feels he ought to.

'Home,' she says. 'With my mum and my brothers.'

Another forkload of spaghetti goes in.

Alexander tries to enjoy the fact that she's such an incompetent pasta eater, but can't. It turns him off.

Kate takes a gulp of his mineral water to wash the food down. Her lips leave a cloudy imprint on the rim of his glass.

'Did it not cross your mind?' she asks, swallowing.

'Why should it?'

'Not even when I gave you the book? How did you think I knew about *Sasha's Magic Carpet* if I hadn't been reading it to a child?'

He'd pictured her poring over a worn-out copy in her local library. He hadn't calculated that by the time she was old enough to go to the library, she would have long outgrown Sasha. *Sasha's Magic Carpet* wasn't even in print when she was a child. The *Sasha* books' politically correct quality went out of fashion during the Thatcher years when children's minds were fed on a diet of *Teenage Mutant Ninja Turtles*.

He's certain that it has not for one second crossed his mind that she might have a child. Is that because he's insensitive, stupid, or just selfish?

He imagined her free and thought he loved her.

Now, he feels nothing at all.

'Why did you tell me you were going round the world?' he asks.

She thinks for a moment.

'I was testing out how it sounded. You can be a different person with someone you've never met, can't you?'

He nods.

'Anyway, I still want to,' she says.

More pasta.

'You've got a child, haven't you?' Kate asks.

He nods again. No point in dissembling now.

'D'you know how I knew?' she asks, brightly, almost triumphant in her powers of detection.

'No.'

But he's sure that she's going to tell him.

'When I cut my knee yesterday. You crouched down to look at it, and your voice was different. Just a bit kinder than it usually is. I knew that you'd dealt with some grazed knees before.'

'You knew yesterday?'

'I didn't know consciously,' she says, backtracking. 'Well, if I did, I pretended to myself that I didn't.'

Women are better at the subconscious. They absorb theories about it from articles in glossy magazines, just as they effortlessly absorb biological facts about the elasticity of the skin and the structure of hair. They blame men for failing to recognize their hidden motives and desires. But isn't that the whole point of the subconscious? Is it technically even possible to be conscious of your subconscious?

Kate is scooping up the creamy leftovers in the bottom of her bowl. She puts the spoon in her mouth and holds it there thoughtfully for a long time.

'And you're married,' she says so definitely that he thinks she might be trying to tempt a negative.

It's something that he can confidently answer no to, but if he does, he won't be telling her the truth. He's got no reason to lie to her any more, and if he had, his hesitation has already given him away.

'I'm not married, but . . .'

'You're with someone?'

'Yes, I'm with someone.'

'Oh.'

332

'What?'

'I hoped that you might be divorced,' she says. 'Shit, I didn't mean it to come out like that.'

She's looking at the table. He doesn't want to feel guilty. He says, 'And the father of your child?'

'He's back home.'

Her eyes are glassy with tears.

They stare at each other. Both with other people, both miserable, both unable now to reach out to the other and take away the pain.

'What were you on about going to Heathrow, then?' she asks, as her brain works through everything he told her.

'I wanted to run away,' he says.

'But I stopped you?'

'I think I might have gone,' he says, choosing his words very carefully, 'if you'd come.'

'And now?'

Now, he feels as distant from her as from the female students at his school who come to London looking for romance, and always seem to pick him to fall in love with.

'We're not the same people,' he says.

'We are the same people,' she says, with a short laugh. 'We're just not the people we thought we were.'

She pushes the plate away from her.

Marco is there to collect it so rapidly that Alexander thinks he must have been listening. He hopes that she's going to ask for the bill, wrap this thing up, but she orders a cappuccino. It comes with a heart swirled on top.

'What's your man like?' he asks, trying to push some of the discomfort he's feeling back onto her.

Kate thinks for a moment. She doesn't smile fondly or frown, but she's clearly searching for a fair description.

'When I was fifteen I fell in love with him because he was eighteen, and he seemed, like, sophisticated. We used to head out to Blackpool on his bike, really fast, and it was like it didn't matter if we died, because we were really living, we were going places, you know? We'd go on the rollercoaster . . .'

She looks up.

He nods.

'Then I fell pregnant. And we weren't going any-where any more. He wanted to get married and have a family. People thought I was really lucky. He didn't think it mattered if I did my GCSEs or not . . .'

'But you got them?'

'Yeah!'

She smiles at him.

'Not that they've done me much good.'

'But you didn't marry him,' he encourages her to go on.

'No,' Kate says. 'We're meant to be saving for it, but it's a lot of money to waste on a white dress you'll never wear again. He's like part of the family now, anyway. My mum does his tea twice a week . . . she doesn't understand what I'm doing.'

All those lives, all that complexity, when he had thought her unencumbered.

'What *are* you doing?' Alexander asks.

Kate looks down, sighs.

'I worked out that I spend twenty-five minutes a day with Jimmy on average. He's at school, I'm at work. He likes playing football. He's good at it too. He's been seen by Premier League scouts already. They've got their eye on him . . .'

She stops, realizing that she's diverted herself.

'The time we do get together is a duty for him, we do his homework and I'm giving him nothing, you know? Parents are supposed to know about things, aren't they? I don't know about anything. I work all day and I come back and I'm lying in bed at night panicking, really sweating, you know?'

She looks up as if to ask whether he understands. He nods.

'And I don't want to spend the rest of my life with someone who thinks William Blake's the leader of the Conservative Party, and D.H. Lawrence is that bloke with the camels,' she announces, with an autodidact's seriousness that makes him burst out laughing.

Now she's laughing too, not quite sure what she's said that's so funny, and for a moment it's as if they're back to where they were, enjoying each other. Then she's serious again and looking at him as if she's weighing up whether she'll let him into another secret.

'They said I was suffering from depression,' she says, quietly, 'but I wasn't depressed, I just felt the world was racing on and I couldn't catch up with it. There's all sorts of things I want to do, you see, like visit Cuba before Castro dies, and find an island where there's just white sand and palm trees and no McDonald's . . . I want to feel whether the Taj Mahal is rough or smooth to touch. Do you think that means I'm mentally ill?'

'No!'

'I can't pretend it's all for Jimmy. I want it for me.'

'There's nothing wrong with that.'

He hates the way he sounds so much older than her.

'. . . the doctor gave me Prozac. He said it'd put a smile back on my face. But I didn't want to be drugged into liking my life. It's the wrong way round. I wrote to Marie and she says, no way are you taking drugs, which was funny coming from her. You're not mad for hating your life, she says, you'd be mad if you liked it. So I came down to London . . .'

Hearing about Kate's problems makes him feel

affectionate towards her, but also uncomfortable. He doesn't want to know all these things because he doesn't want to be responsible for her.

'I met Marie,' he says.

'Oh?' says Kate.

'You're like twins in a fairy tale. You look the same, but one's good and one's bad.'

'She's not all bad,' Kate leaps to her sister's defence. 'And I'm not good,' she adds. 'Marie hasn't got a fiancé and child back home . . .'

'What's he think of you being here? Your fiancé.'

The very word sounds as out of date as an avocado bathroom suite.

'. . . I mean, coming to London like this.'

'He said that if you love someone, you have to let them be free,' Kate tells him.

'That's good, isn't it?' Alexander can't help feeling a grudging admiration for the poor bloke.

'I think he got it from *Little Voice*,' Kate explains.

'And your son?'

'All he wants to do is play football with his mates. He doesn't really notice that I'm not there,' Kate tells him.

'I bet he does,' Alexander says quietly. She's someone with such presence, her absence must feel like a bereavement.

'I miss him. I miss him more than I thought I would,' she says, wistfully. 'I made a promise, last night, if I could have a day with you, I'd go back.'

'You knew I'd come?'

'No. I thought it was impossible.' She laughs. 'That's why I promised!'

'That's why you slept with me?'

'Sleeping's about the only thing we didn't do,' she says, suddenly a prude.

To his left, he can sense the old man Marco rapt by

the unfolding drama, stranded mid-wipe with a tea towel in one hand, a saucer in the other. When Kate looks up, he goes back to his drying up.

'I thought you were gorgeous,' she says, shyly looking down again.

'I thought you were gorgeous too.'

Just for the moment, the attraction's there again, like a secret only the two of them know. They smile at each other and look away.

She pretends to be interested in the coloured sticks of sugar.

He looks at the television. *Série A* is on.

'Which football team does your boy support?' Alexander asks, trying to move them on.

'Which do you think?'

'Bolton Wanderers?' he guesses.

'No. His dad does. Jimmy's for. Man United. What about yours?'

'She's a girl.'

'Doesn't like football then?'

'She's only five.'

'Oh, she doesn't have to like it yet, then,' Kate says. 'Girls only get interested in football when they're going out with lads.'

'Is that right?'

It's kind of odd chatting about their children, but it feels safer.

'What's her name?' she asks.

'Lucy.'

'Lucy,' she repeats. Loo seh.

'It's really Lucia,' he says. 'She was born in Italy. It means light.'

'I knew you were in Italy with someone.'

'How?'

'Because I could tell that you had really great memories, and you never have really great memories

337

of being on your own, do you? Not ones that make you smile.'

It's a casual observation, as if it's self-evident. It's something he's never even considered. He doesn't understand how Kate knows so much about the world, when she's so unworldly. Except she isn't unworldly, he reminds himself. That's only what he wanted her to be.

'Is she Italian?' Kate asks. 'Your partner?'

She puts heavy emphasis on the word partner as if she thinks it's pretentious.

'No.'

He doesn't want to talk to her about Nell.

'So now you live in Kent.'

'Yes.'

'Why?' Kate's asking.

'Why Kent?'

'Why do you live in England, when you could live anywhere you wanted?'

'We had a few problems with Lucy,' he finds himself saying. 'We never got round to going back.'

'What sort of problems?'

'She has asthma and really bad allergies. She nearly died when she was just one. When something like that happens, you want an ambulance to arrive when you dial 999. You want to be not too far from a hospital. That wasn't going to happen where we were in Italy.'

Is that really the reason they have stayed in England, in a village that neither of them likes much but is close enough to London, close enough to a hospital, close enough to Nell's parents? Is it simply fear? He's never explained it to anyone before, not even himself.

'Peanuts?' Kate asks.

'All nuts.'

'There's a lad in Jimmy's class like that. We're not allowed to put peanuts in his packed lunch, not even cereal bars. You have to read the labels really carefully, don't you? There's so many things with nuts in.'

'Yes,' he says. 'It is difficult.'

She's a mum who makes sandwiches for her child and shops for cereal bars.

'Are there a lot of peanuts in Italy, then?'

Alexander laughs at her logic.

'No! But you know how you kind of get stuck?'

Kate nods vehemently.

It's what they have in common. The responsibility of being a grown-up, being a parent. The great leveller.

'I was the one who bought the peanut butter,' he suddenly confesses. 'I'd been abroad so long . . . it was going to be a treat . . . and, then . . .'

The thought of it still makes his hands tremble so much that he has to sit on them to stop anyone noticing.

Nell's yelling at him to do something. He's thumping Lucy on the back, trying to dislodge what's stuck in her throat. Nell's snatching her from him, screaming at him as if he can't see it himself and it's all his fault. 'She's getting worse!' He runs out into the street, shouting 'HELP!'

'Well, she would have come across it sooner or later,' Kate says matter-of-factly.

'What?'

'Nuts. There's almonds in Bakewell tart . . .'

Kate starts to list all the foods she's come across which contain unexpected nuts: 'Most chocolate bars have a nut warning now, and Easter eggs . . .'

It's as if he's hearing for the first time that Lucy would have had anaphylaxis whether he had bought the peanut butter or not.

It's a leap from guilt that he has not been able to make before.

Kate has stopped talking. She's frowning with

concentration, working through something in her mind, and when she speaks again, her voice slices him apart.

'What were you going to tell Lucy . . .'

He wishes now he hadn't told Kate her name.

'. . . about us going to Heathrow?'

They keep referring to Heathrow as if it's a destination in itself: neither of their imaginations can now stretch to getting onto a plane and away.

'What were you going to tell Jimmy?' he parries.

'At least I *was* going to tell Jimmy,' she says.

Is she guessing wildly?

His silence incriminates him again. He looks at her curiously beautiful face, the uncomprehending frown.

'She's the age you were when your father left you,' she says quietly.

He doesn't know whether she's offering him an explanation for his behaviour, or further condemnation. He wonders how something so simple and obvious has eluded him.

'I didn't do it, though,' he offers. 'I didn't go.'

But that's not good enough for Kate and he's relieved because now there's no possibility of the attraction that crackles between them like static overcoming their circumstances.

Would it have been possible to go on knowing nothing about each other for a while? If they'd got as far as a white sandy beach, would they then have needed a past? How soon would she have discovered that he was not good enough for her, not a good enough person? She's found out in one day what most women take years to discover. That he's a coward. And her clear disgust is like a punishment. But one that he accepts.

In twenty-four hours this love story has run its course. Attraction, sex, love, a moment that changes it all to disillusion . . . an attempt at friendship that was bound to fail.

Kate's waving for the bill.

A white china saucer is deposited between them. She reaches for it, but he snatches it up.

'What are you going to do now?' he asks.

'I don't know,' she says, not looking at him. 'I can't face going back to work.'

He's relieved that she has taken the question to mean only the immediate future. The rest of her life is none of his business.

'What are you going to do?' she asks, her eyes flicking round the room. Anything but eye contact with him.

'I'm going to try to get home,' he says. 'That train crash was on my line – but by now, they may have laid on a bus.'

He says it without really thinking.

Now she is staring at him. Her mouth is open, eyebrows slightly raised, as if she's about to ask a question. Then her mouth closes. And he knows that her intelligence has processed all the little pieces of information and created a hypothesis too dreadful to speak.

Attraction, sex, love, disillusion, an attempt at friendship that was bound to fail . . . hatred.

The noise of her chair scraping back is like a blast of drill as she stands up hurriedly.

He stands too.

'Goodbye,' she says, holding out her hand.

He looks at it.

Her pale serious face breaks into an embarrassed smile remembering all the nice things they did. Her fringe flops over her eyes and she pushes it back quickly, before he has a chance to lean forward and touch her.

There is to be no embrace, no final kiss.

'I think you'll be a great writer,' he says, wanting to make her look at him just once more. Inwardly he winces at how arrogant he sounds.

Her face lights up like the beam of a lighthouse.

'Why?' she can't resist asking.

Women always want more.

'Because you see magic in everyday things.'

It was a kind of love, he thinks. They have even started their own little language of phrases special just to them.

She smiles again, nods, turns. Her steps become springier as she walks away.

And then she's gone, vanished into the thousands of people celebrating the end of another week.

Staring at the open door of the café, he feels suddenly, self-consciously tall. At the till, he hands over the saucer and a £10 note, not bothering to wait for change.

A taxi just misses him as he distractedly steps off the pavement. The scream of brakes and the proximity of the cab, so close it's as physical as a punch, makes him shiver with an acute awareness of his existence.

He is not dead.

Today he has survived.

He approaches Cambridge Circus, about to cross the road at the same place where yesterday evening Kate led the way.

He stops in his tracks and turns right instead.

It's a tiny choice but it feels bigger with each step.

He begins to feel the ground beneath his feet, the grey clog of exhaust in his lungs, and, as he approaches Leicester Square, sweet aromatic wafts of Chinese spices. The smell conjures dragons dancing among the crowds in Gerrard Street; the crushing squeeze of Lucy's tiny hand in his, her little face stranded between delight and terror, the vast steamy interior of a Chinese eating hall where Nell's tenaciously quizzing the mystified waiter about ingredients; Lucy's bewilderment as she tastes her first char sui pork; the happy jingle of Nell's laughter as she pronounces the food 'Yummaroney!'

Alexander quickens his pace towards Charing Cross station. His thoughts become resolutions, one for every five steps. They must come to London more often. They must do more things together as a family. Lucy loved the Science Museum when he took her the other day. He recalls her amazement as the hot air balloon went up at the push of a gas flame button, and the demonstration of giant rainbow bubbles.

Carnival, museums, ballet, galleries, perhaps even a Prom.

He imagines how her face will look watching the spectacle of the *Nutcracker* or listening to Rachmaninov thumped out on a grand piano, or the soft evocative notes of a saxophone at twilight on the South Bank.

On summer evenings, when opera is broadcast live outside the House on a screen in the Covent Garden piazza, perhaps he will take Lucy along, and whisper to her stories of mistaken identity, treachery and love. And when she grows bored, they will buy ice-creams and sneak away down to the sparkling river.

Twenty-eight

Why does kissing stop when you grow up?

Nell cannot remember the last time she really kissed standing up, only that it feels odd to have her feet flat on the floor because she associates kissing with standing on tiptoe.

His mouth is exquisitely gentle. His palms are flat against her cheeks, holding her face as if it is very precious to him. He keeps pausing to look at her.

'You're so beautiful . . .'

'No, I'm not . . .'

He silences her protests with a kiss.

Their mouths, but not their bodies, are touching. Her arms are held straight against her sides. She daren't touch him because that would be crossing some invisible moral boundary, but the more rigid she makes herself, the more she's melting inside, pouring more and more of herself into the kissing.

Kissing is allowed. Kissing is only a little bit worse than flirting. Kissing is what you do with a guy you've always fancied in the kitchen at a party when you've had two glasses of wine too much, and your partner's dancing to 'Hi-Ho Silver Lining' in the other room.

She's never kissed nor been kissed like this before. They are not teenagers simulating sex, not yet lovers initiating foreplay. They are grown-ups and this is a silent exploratory conversation at the beginning of a

344

long journey they will make together, the kissing more powerfully communicative than sex because it allows no words. Everything they have to say to one another is in the kissing. Fear, regret, excitement, trust.

She moves slightly closer to him. His hands drop away from her face. She freezes. Gently, he pulls her hips against his, holding her belly against his hard, straight erection. She closes her eyes, quivering as he kisses her again, knowing that she could come like this. His hands move back to her face. Their hips rest together. Skin against fabric against fabric against skin.

The phone rings.

They jump apart. Stare at it. It rings again. She leaps across the room, breathes, swallows, braces herself for bad news, or good news, snatches up the receiver.

'Hello?'

'It's me.'

'Alexander?'

Nell looks across the room at Chris, who smiles at her, making a big effort to force enthusiasm into his face.

'Are you all right? Where are you?' she asks.

'I'm at Charing Cross. There aren't any trains. I've been trying to ring you all evening.'

'No, you haven't,' she says.

'Where *were* you?' he demands.

This is the wrong way round.

'Where were *you*?' she asks.

'I've been wandering around.'

'Wandering around?' she repeats.

An hour before, she promised to change everything if he was alive. Now that he is, she's almost instantly annoyed with him.

'Thinking. Nell, I've had lots of thoughts . . .' He sounds excited.

345

'Thoughts? We thought you were dead,' she shouts and bursts into tears.

'Nell?'

'Where the hell have you been?' she spits through her tears.

'I tried to ring,' he falters.

She feels him slipping away again. He sounded so enthusiastic a moment ago, and now she's chased that away with her impatience. Is this what she does?

Chris is pretending to look at the spines of books on the shelves by the door. Is he shocked by her behaviour?

'We've been with Frances,' she says in a more conciliatory way.

'Really? How's Frances?'

'It was such a lovely morning, we took the day off.'

'I didn't feel like going to work, either,' Alexander says, sympathetically.

He sounds astonishingly breezy.

'You do know about the crash?' she asks him.

'Yes.'

'When did you know?'

'About six-ish, I suppose. I rang. I even tried to ring your mother. She's ex-directory.'

That's true.

Is she being completely unfair?

Nell looks at her watch. 'It's nearly ten o'clock,' she says.

'Is it? I left my watch at school yesterday. I've had no sense of time all day.'

'Four hours, Alex.'

Is that so very long to be wandering around in London?

He says nothing.

'You're alive. That's what matters,' she says quietly.

On the other side of the room, Chris lifts the latch on

346

the front door. She waves at him not to go. Carefully he pulls the door to again, not making a sound. He picks a gardening book from an eye-level shelf and flips through it.

'Thing is, Nell, I don't know how I'm going to get home,' Alexander is saying into her ear.

'Shall I come and pick you up?'

'Would you?'

He has the same sheepish tone as the time he drank far too much and fell asleep on the last train home, ending up in Ramsgate. Then, she had to put Lucy in the car and drive through the middle of the night to the coast with huge goods lorries thundering past her towards the Channel Tunnel.

'I'm not coming all the way to Charing Cross,' she warns.

'Where could I get to?' Alexander asks. 'How about Greenwich?'

'Greenwich?'

'By the *Cutty Sark*? Should be easy enough to park at this time of night.'

'All right, then,' she agrees. 'But it'll be over an hour by the time I've dropped Lucy.'

'Midnight at the *Cutty Sark*,' he says.

He makes it sound like a romantic rendezvous, the title of a song from the 1930s.

'OK.'

She's about to put down the phone.

'Nell?'

'Yes?'

'Love you in the world!' Alexander says brightly.

'Are you sure you're all right to drive?' Chris says.

'I'm fine,' she says.

How different he is from the man she's just spoken to. It wouldn't occur to Alexander to think about the stress the day has put on her, the fact that she's already driven over a hundred miles today.

'Why don't I take Lucy back with me? We're going to tennis in the morning anyway. You probably need some time on your own together.'

'Are you sure?'

She wasn't looking forward to the thought of imposing on her mother, who sloshes a double measure of whisky into a cup of hot milk at this time of night and goes to bed with the three-legged dog and a copy of *Country Life*.

'Sure.'

Is Chris giving her this time with Alex so that she can tell Alex about them? Is that what he's offering?

'I don't know . . .' she begins to say.

'It's OK, Nell.'

Does he mean that there's no rush, or that he knows she's going to go back to Alexander, or what?

Does the lack of pressure mean that he's gone off her?

Perhaps there's no subtext. Perhaps he, like she, just doesn't know.

Upstairs, Lucy is sleeping so peacefully Nell hates to wake her.

'Come on, darling,' she whispers soothingly.

The child's body is so much heavier asleep than awake. She relaxes automatically against Nell's chest, turning her head so that it fits snugly against Nell's shoulder, entrusting her unconscious self entirely to familiar maternal curves.

On the stairs, she lifts her head suddenly and asks, with her eyes wide open, 'Is Daddy home yet?'

'He's stuck in London and I'm going to get him. You're going round to sleep at Ben's.'

Lucy's eyes close again, and she sighs. Nell doesn't

348

think she was really awake when she asked the question. She's surprised by how close to the surface Lucy's love for Alexander is.

She carries her out to the car. Chris sits beside Lucy in the back, and when they get to his house, Nell carries Lucy indoors and up to Ben's room, where there's a bed already made. She thinks how excited Lucy's going to be to wake up in the morning beside her love.

Downstairs, she hands over the waistbelt that contains Lucy's emergency medication.

'I'll look after her,' Chris says.

'Thanks. Where's Sarah?'

'Talking to the States.'

'Tell her I said thank you, won't you?'

'I will.'

It would be normal for two people who were as good friends as they are to kiss at this moment, but they're both very deliberately keeping a distance of about a yard between them.

'Good luck,' he says.

His steel blue eyes give no further meaning to the words.

'Yes,' she says.

It's disco hour on Heart FM.

'Next up,' says the DJ, ' "You're The One That I Want".'

Nell switches the radio off; her head's too full of possible scenarios to crowd it with memories of trying to look like Olivia Newton John, curling her hair with Carmen rollers and wearing skinny black cap-sleeve T-shirts.

How different the motorway is at night. During the day the land around is so flat it makes the sky seem huge and light, and it's possible to see for miles. But at night the road is unlit, and when there's a break in the traffic the black motorway is so dark it feels like she's hurtling through a tunnel towards an uncertain future.

Love you in the world.

Alexander sounded so unlike Alexander on the phone that she can't quite suppress the odd feeling that she's not going to recognize him, that this is all a hallucination, or a strange joke that she doesn't understand.

Midnight at the *Cutty Sark*.

Is it a thriller, not a love song?

In her mind, she repeats what he said:

Should be easy enough to park at this time of night.

Was that a none-too-oblique reference to the last time they were in Greenwich together?

New Year's Eve before the millennium.

They'd both woken up with the feeling that they should be doing something to mark the last day of the century. It was Alexander who thought of Greenwich. She hadn't realized how near this part of London was by car, having always travelled up from home by train.

They stood Lucy's legs on each side of the time line, Nell holding her east hand and Alexander her west. She remembers him kneeling next to Lucy to explain how it all worked, how at midnight it would be the beginning of a new 1,000 years, and Lucy beaming at him, saying, 'I'm standing on both sides of the world, Daddy.'

'I came on a school trip here,' he told Nell, happily, as they walked away from the Maritime Museum.

It would have been a wonderful day, if it hadn't been for the car getting clamped. It was Nell's fault for parking it illegally, never dreaming that traffic wardens would be working.

Alexander's mood turned so foul as they waited by

350

the immobilized car that eventually she took Lucy off down to the quay, where there were clowns and musicians and children running around with sparkly headbands with 2000 spelt out in glitter.

Nell remembers the effort it took to keep a happy face for Lucy, when she felt utterly desolate inside, not just because she had ruined the day with her foolishness, but because to be so miserable on the last day of the millennium seemed to bode so badly for the future.

The sound of her tyres bumping over cat's eyes at the side of the road makes Nell grip the steering wheel so hard she's in danger of cutting off the circulation to her fingers.

Alexander has chosen to meet her at Greenwich because it's the furthest the tube goes south of the river, Nell reassures herself, not because it has a particular history for them.

Men don't understand symbols or invest their faith in omens and signs like women do.

From the junction with the M25 onwards, the road has more light. Nell relaxes, only aware when she sits back that she has been hunched over the steering wheel all the way up the motorway. She rolls her head from side to side, the conscious relaxation recreating some of the sensation that Chris's neck massages give her.

Alexander has no idea about everything that has gone on today, she tells herself.

What has gone on?

Nothing.

Nothing for her to feel guilty about.

So why does she?

Because of what Frances said?

Because it might have been true?

Has Frances always loved Alexander?

Nell shakes her head, trying to make the tangle of thoughts in her brain settle. She imagines a mass of connections like the wires inside a telephone junction box that are exposed when the engineers are mending a line. So many strands . . .

Red traffic lights.

She sees them late, brakes hard, only just manages to stop before a major crossroads. Her heartbeat races. There was no danger, she tells herself, no car in front, not even any traffic crossing on green. As she pulls away again, the pumping adrenalin subsides, leaving a simple clarity. The important thing tonight is to get them both home safely for Lucy.

It is all that matters.

For now.

Twenty-nine

If it's an even number, then everything's going to be all right.

Alexander takes the steps up to the Charing Cross footbridge two by two, counting silently behind his quickened breath. Fifty. A scruffy youth on a skateboard swishes to a stop beside him and looks at him oddly. Alexander realizes he's smiling.

He looks along the length of the bridge. How wide? It's more difficult to estimate distance in the darkness. He decides that if the bridge is less than 500 paces across, everything's going to be all right.

His strides are determined, but not so stretched that they might be construed as cheating by the unseen judge of such challenges.

When he was a boy he measured out his existence in unspoken Herculean trials.

Nineteen, twenty . . .

He wonders whether every child interprets life with primitive chaos theory, giving each action a false connection to every other, trying to exert a reductive control on the complexity of the world.

Sixty-seven, sixty-eight, sixty-nine . . .

Alexander stops counting and leans against the iron barrier. A police launch passes beneath him, trailing an incomprehensible snatch of two-way radio. The tide's lower than it was yesterday. The wash of the launch sloshes peaceably against the bridge's supports. The inky water is almost invitingly silky.

Along the Embankment, a slight mist gives the lights smudgy haloes. The lights of cars going over Waterloo Bridge are visible, but it's just too far to see if there is anyone looking back towards him at the view.

The memory of standing there with Kate hovers like an angel.

Alexander senses someone approaching his back and turns round quickly. It's a middle-aged woman in a camel overcoat with a patterned silk scarf at her neck. She looks as if she has just been to a concert at the South Bank. Her lipstick is freshly applied, and she smells like his mother did when she was out for the evening – a quick top-up squirt of Chanel No. 5 in the Ladies giving her confidence to face the world, over the ever-present acridity of tobacco.

The woman's face is concerned, curious, tentative, but when his eyes meet hers she pretends not to have been looking at him at all. She clutches her small leather bag more closely against the buttons of her coat. The heels of her expensive shoes tap hurriedly on towards the north side of the river.

Did she think he was going to jump?

He looks again at the water. Liquid so dark it looks solid.

The woman's footsteps grow fainter.

He has a sudden irrational desire to run after her and tell her that he wasn't going to jump. He wants to tell her how he almost died this morning through no fault of his own, and how, through no merit, he survived; how he was tempted to do a most wicked thing, and how he resisted. He wants to tell her that it is more frightening to live and more difficult to be good. He wants her to wish him courage.

He listens to the metallic tapping of her shoes until

he's not sure whether he can hear it any longer or not. Her perfume lingers in his nose.

He stares at the space she just occupied, at the crisscross of iron girders which separates the pedestrian bit from the railway line, at the old puddle on the uneven surface of the walkway.

He sees his mother standing in the kitchen of the house in Kentish Town, wearing a huge purple Aran sweater over an old, brushed-cotton nightie. The sweater hasn't been washed for a while and the undersides of the sleeves are slightly greasy. She's grinding fresh basil with a pestle and her chest is concave with the effort of it, and even though she's dying, she's determined to demonstrate that she's still capable of producing fresh pasta sauce more delicious than anyone else's.

It's the first time Alexander's been alone with her since they arrived from Italy the day before. Nell has just taken Lucy to buy a car seat. He watches them walking up the street. Nell's long fair curtain of hair falls forward as she bends over the buggy, chatting to Lucy, putting every dirty dustbin and bumpy paving stone into words for her. A natural teacher. A natural mother.

It's the first opportunity he's had to ask his mother, 'Well, what do you think?'

He's spilling over with pride in his beautiful partner and their beautiful child, and the only possible response is that they are beautiful, that he is a lucky man. But he suddenly knows that his mother is not going to say anything like that.

First there's the horrible effort of a false smile and then she says, with sneering contempt, 'I'm surprised you've chosen someone so *good*.'

The word in her mouth contains all the things she despises: piety, blandness, boredom. For a moment he's stunned, and then he laughs bitterly, and says, 'How perverse of you to take a dislike to someone on the grounds that they are good. And how typical.'

But she does not attempt to take her remark back, nor to contradict him. She does not even see that he's hurt; instead she smiles, enjoying the trade of banter with her clever son, like old times. He knows that this is the point where he should become a grown-up and defend Nell. But he is a coward. He does not want to quarrel with his mother when she is dying.

She goes to hug him, but he steps back from her embrace, leaving her stranded in her ugly jumper with the slimy green pestle held aloft.

After that, they only went through the motions of conversation, saying nothing of any significance to each other. A few days later, she died.

He's never been able to forgive her, nor himself, and perhaps he's never forgiven Nell for unknowingly separating them at death.

Good.

Such a benign little word.

Why did it annoy him so much? Why has he never been able to talk to Nell about it? Was there something about his mother's description that rang true?

When Nell arrived in Tokyo his impression was of an infuriatingly capable girl. A nice girl. The kind of nice middle-class girl who played tennis. The only feeling he had for her was a vague desire to put her down, especially when she became friends with the poisonous Frances.

It was only when he bumped into her by chance in the Philippines that he saw something different. Standing in the dim red light of a dodgy bar, she was a person he recognized but did not know, her long-limbed body in vest and cutoff jeans so unsophisticated compared to the smart trousers and ironed shirt she always wore to work, her hair loose around her face, not scraped back in a sleek ponytail. When she saw him, her face lit up like a lottery winner unable to believe her good fortune, and he was touched by the transparency of her pleasure.

He didn't see Frances at first. If he had, he would probably have tried to get away. And they would have returned separately to Tokyo and continued as before, existing in the same space, never making contact. And his life would have been so much less rich.

He remembers walking on the beach with Nell that first day they spent alone together, the sensation of sand between his toes, a warm damp wind blowing in his face, and Nell saying, 'It's so like you expect a paradise island to be, you can't believe it's real, can you?'

The pure guilelessness of her smile and her golden hair in the sunshine made her breathtakingly beautiful.

He let his hand reach for hers and connect with her for the first time, and it felt like a watershed in his life, as if he was choosing goodness over cynicism.

It's hard to be good.

Far easier to rail against unfairness, be ground down by routine, live every day under the shadow of non-specific anger.

Alexander is halfway down the steps to the South Bank when he realizes that he has lost count of the number of paces it has taken to cross the bridge.

He gazes back over the water that sparkles like jet, and says, out loud, 'Sorry!'

The word floats out over the river, carrying his anger

with it, expanding in the air, like smoke, until it's so finely dispersed, it's no longer there.

There's a cartoon picture of a panicking traveller in the advert above the head of the passenger sitting opposite Alexander.

Flight in four hours. Plane tickets. Passport. Wallet. Suitcase. Travel insurance???? Instant Quote.

Alexander imagines calling the company and the operator saying, 'Tis better to have loved and lost than never to have loved at all.' Or, 'When a man is tired of London, he is tired of life.'

The shoutline of the ad next to it asks:

Feel like a total change of job?

It pictures a quartet of men in lounge suits. Three of them are playing cellos, one is shearing a sheep. It's an arresting image, but Alexander's not sure whether it's the sheep shearer who's always wanted to be a cellist, or the other way round. He tries to imagine how the designer of the ad would make a wacky image of an EFL teacher who wanted a change of career. An image of rows of Japanese students set out like the pins in a bowling alley comes into his mind.

Further down the carriage another ad announces:

A message that may change your life . . .

The print's too small for Alexander to read the rest from where he's sitting. He's never recognized before how all the adverts on the tube taunt their captive audience with dreams of escape.

The sound of the train accelerating out of the station is like an aircraft's engine going down the runway. The carriage is nearly empty apart from the black man opposite who's wearing a navy wool overcoat over a smart suit. A pale curly line has been shaved out of the close-cut hair on his head, just above the hairline, like an engraving. The frivolousness of such an adornment against the sobriety of the overcoat gives Alexander a little flip of enjoyment.

Almost every station on the Jubilee line extension offers a promise of future adventure.

Waterloo for connections to Eurostar. Paris for a weekend, the view from the Sacré Coeur, *cassoulet* in La Coupole, maybe even EuroDisney.

Southwark for Tate Modern.

Alexander imagines Lucy's serious critical appraisal of Matisse's *Snail*.

'Do you know something, Daddy? I did one just like that at school.'

The view towards St Paul's. The wobbly bridge. Shakespeare at the Globe.

Canary Wharf will be a future history lesson in Thatcher and the follies of capitalism.

He's never been aware of the adverts as messages before, nor the stops as destinations. Normally, he stands braced against the invasion of other people's bodies and breath, trying to let his surroundings intrude as little as possible. Now he lolls in his seat, legs splayed, amazed at his sudden willingness to engage.

He wonders if this is what people mean when they talk of being born again: a moment of epiphany after which everything that was dull becomes vibrant.

At North Greenwich he gets off the train. The walls of the station are covered with tiny deep blue tiles like the lining of a Hollywood swimming pool. The vast hall of station that stands as a monument to the failed ambition of the Dome is empty like an airport terminal that has closed for the night.

Outside, it is eerily quiet. Alexander looks at a map of the area and then at the bus information. The tube station is much further from the centre of Greenwich than he imagined. There are still buses due, but it's difficult to believe that they will be making the journey to this deserted place on the chance that there's a passenger.

There's nothing lonelier than standing at a bus stop late at night when you don't quite trust that a bus will come. Alexander fidgets from foot to foot, then sets off walking away from the great white hump of the Dome.

A sense of foreboding settles on him as he crosses the wasteland of the Greenwich peninsula, his footsteps echoing metallically around him. He walks past the looming skeleton of a gas cylinder, a vast empty car park. The new, well-signposted, well-lit roads are sinister without traffic.

Underground he was shrouded in the cosy security of optimism, but the real world above feels boundless and unwelcoming. Doubt rippled with fear races through his mind as he quickens his step across the tarmac and concrete no man's land.

Perhaps he was naïve to think that everything can be all right after what he has done today.

In the distance, a brightly lit double decker bus rises out of nowhere on its uneconomic route to a place where nobody goes any more. Alexander sprints towards a bus stop.

The driver opens the doors to let on his sole passenger but does not return his huge, relieved smile.

Inside the bus is full of colour. Bright yellow poles to grip, jauntily patterned seat coverings. The doors hiss and clunk shut behind Alexander like a protective valve. He feels safe again.

Signs of life begin to appear beside the road. A car wash. A warehouse of tiles. A council estate. A hospital. Now the bus is back in familiar territory, trundling through the mix of drab poverty and gleaming wealth that characterizes the streets of inner London. There's a tattoo shop, a tatty fish and chip bar and next to it a brand new Internet café; a Chinese supermarket, a side street of bijou terraced Georgian houses with Saabs and Japanese 4x4s parked outside; an old-fashioned barber's shop with a red and white twirly pole, a cut price furniture store. The grimy thoroughfare becomes a boulevard running beside the elegant white palaces and colonnades of Greenwich College and Maritime Museum.

Alexander remembers walking in an unruly crocodile down this very street with his school class. He can't recall much about the observatory, or the museum, except standing astride the time line being slightly disappointed that it felt exactly the same as standing anywhere else.

In the afternoon, they were allowed to run loose in Greenwich Park. His mother had forgotten to pack him a lunch. He sat slightly apart from the other boys in his class, and Mandy Kominski sashayed over and offered him half of her bagel. He remembers the softness of the cream cheese and lox, the hard shine of the crust, and Mandy smiling at him as he took his first bite and his attempt to smile back as best he could with his mouth full.

'She fancies you!' the boys chorused.

And later, Mandy's friend, whose mouth was full of braces and whose name he cannot remember, came over to deliver the whispered message that yes, Mandy did fancy him. But he had no idea what to do or say, and the smoked salmon repeated on him all afternoon.

The bus stops outside the museum to pick up a middle-aged woman with dyed blond hair, painted dark eyebrows and a fake fur coat. She glances at him, then sits down, tossing her head a little haughtily. The bus starts again.

Mandy's declaration by proxy was his first experience of relationships with girls. He remembers her confidence, how attractive it made her, and how devastated he was to be dismissed a few weeks later for his failure to turn up to their first date. She never gave him a second chance. It made him wary of confident women for many years.

At university, and beyond, the women he chose to go out with were usually beautiful and neurotic, with long dark hair and suicidal tendencies.

And then there was Nell.

Nell has an inner confidence that makes him feel safe. He used to think it was the glimpse of her vulnerability that attracted him, but perhaps it was not. Perhaps that was merely what allowed him to admit that he liked her. Or maybe she was the first woman who let him see both sides of herself, and asked to see both sides of him.

Images of Nell flood through his mind: Nell breastfeeding Lucy in Italy, a serene madonna with a backdrop of soft Umbrian hills; Nell standing slightly awkwardly in a bar in Borocay, her face lighting up in the dingy smoke, like a Botticelli angel emerging from a cloud; Nell sitting under a white cherry tree in Ueno Park, smiling and smiling like a bride.

His love for her did not die, he realizes, it just withered like blossom on a branch, and was waiting to burst into flower again when it was the right time.

And then there was Kate. Kate the guardian angel who saved him from denying his existence.

Alexander suddenly understands how adulterous husbands can tell their wives, 'It didn't mean anything.'

Because it didn't. Not as far as his relationship with Nell was concerned. It was nothing to do with Nell.

But he doesn't think that he will try to explain it to her.

His hand reaches for the passport that's still in his jacket pocket. He was free to leave, but he chose to stay. He chose to be responsible, not to run away.

It feels good.

Nell is standing in the place where a three-piece Irish band was playing the last time they were here.

She and Lucy had left him to deal with getting the car unclamped. Bastard traffic wardens!

When he came looking, he spotted them here, dancing a little jig together, holding hands. There was a crowd of people sitting like an audience on the bank of steps that leads up to the pier, watching.

Nell bent and scooped Lucy up and danced with her in her arms; they were laughing delightedly into each other's faces, their joy making the air around them sparkle. He watched them for a little while, a spy in the crowd of millennium revellers, feeling so proud, and so very lonely.

Now the pier is deserted. An empty crisp packet blows around in circles at the top of the tier of steps.

'Have you been waiting long?' he asks her.

'Not too long,' she says, her face lighting with a smile that disappears almost instantly as he approaches, as if she hasn't seen him for a while and isn't sure what their relationship is.

He goes to kiss her. The kiss falls on her cheek as she turns quickly, tossing the car keys up and catching them in one hand.

'You look very happy,' she observes.

They start to walk away from the river.

'It's quiet, isn't it?' she says.

She never feels comfortable with silence.

He reaches out and catches her empty hand in his. It's such an unexpected gesture, she flinches, stops, looks at him anxiously.

'Nell, I've been thinking,' he says. 'Why don't we go somewhere lovely to live and have this baby?'

Thirty

Kate's applying a coat of shiny scarlet polish to the nails of her left hand. Her fingertips feel cold as the varnish dries. She shakes her hand to make the process quicker and glances quickly around the perfumery department. No-one's seen her. There is no-one there, she suddenly realizes. No staff, no customers. She has the whole department to herself. Emboldened, she squirts her neck with Calvin Klein's Eternity, but she can't smell it. She picks up the bottle again, squirts it on her left wrist, feels the coldness, waits a few seconds, as Marie has told her to, so that the alcohol evaporates, but still there's no smell. Nothing. She picks up the bottle, sniffs the stopper. Nothing. They've filled it with water. Or maybe they're tricking her.

She's not alone.

At the Clinique counter, Jimmy's sitting on a high stool, drawing a picture on the white counter. As she comes closer, she sees that he's not using crayons for his work of art, but lipsticks. The tops are strewn all around the picture, like so many felt tip pens. He's holding the stopper of a nail varnish pot, a full brush of pearly blue about to drip.

'Jimmy!'

'I need some blue for the sky, Mum.'

'It's stealing!'

He looks at her left hand, insolently, as if to say: Well, what are you doing, then?

'Come on,' she says, holding out her hands to jump him down from the stool. 'Let's go home.'

'This is home, Mum,' he says.

Together they walk through the store, and he's showing her everything.

'This is where I get my tea,' he says, at the cake counter, pointing at a birthday cake that's iced to look like a pizza.

'You don't just eat pizza, do you, Jimmy?'

Then he's off, running away from her, dodging through the racks of ties and cufflinks in menswear, and she's trying to chase him, up the escalator, but she chooses the wrong one and she's running against steps that are travelling down and she's puffed out but she's not going anywhere, and somebody is shouting, 'Kate? Kate?'

Kate wakes up. Marie's perched on the bed next to her, dressed in jeans which have had the waistband ripped off and a tight black T-shirt with a heart motif in silver studs.

'Didn't know whether I should wake you up or not,' she says.

'Thanks,' says Kate, glad that she's not on her own.

There's a draught coming in through the open window. Her left hand is cold.

'You were thrashing around.'

'I was having a dream and it turned into a nightmare.'

Marie looks round the room.

'Where did he go?'

'Jimmy?'

'Alexander!'

For a second, Alexander is so distant, she thinks

366

maybe he was part of the dream. How does Marie know about him? He met her. She remembers now. He thought her the bad twin in a fairy tale.

'Home,' Kate says. 'He went home.'

'And?' Marie's face lights up in anticipation of the details.

'And, nothing.'

'Nothing as in, that's it, or nothing as in, you're not going to tell me?'

'Both.'

'Oh.'

Marie gets up and lights a cigarette, offended that she's not going to be trusted, and Kate's filled with remorse.

'He went home to his girlfriend and kid,' she admits.

'Oh. Sorry.'

Marie sits down again. Puts her hand over Kate's. Sighs.

'It's OK,' Kate says.

How weird that she asked God to give her a day, and Marie said it wouldn't be enough, but it was.

'He left his pants,' Marie remarks, picking them off the top of the chair. She sniffs them like a wine buff. 'Persil,' she pronounces, 'with a background note of latex, and . . .'

'Stop!' Kate shouts.

Marie chucks the black cotton briefs at her, and they're both laughing.

'He was very good-looking,' Marie concedes, with a certain surprised admiration.

'He was so good-looking I thought I knew him,' says Kate. 'D'you know what I mean?'

'How many good-looking chaps do you know, then?'

'I don't mean like that. I mean that I thought I knew his character from his looks. I thought he was deep, but I'm not sure he was, really. I thought he was the love of my life, because that's how I'd like the love of my life to look, but he wasn't.'

Kate bunches up his pants in one hand and sniffs. They smell of his skin. The fresh smell that evokes a rush of indefinably pleasant memories she suddenly recognizes as baby soap.

They probably use baby soap at home because it's mild for the child. Lucy. Lucy's probably allergic to too much perfume.

Kate gets up, goes over to the window, opens it as far as it will go, squeezes her hand through, then opens her fingers to let go of the pants.

'Hey! What are you doing?' Marie is mid-drag on her cigarette. She puts it down, leaps to the window, trying fruitlessly to grab the pants back, but it's way too late.

'What will people think if there's men's knickers raining down from our window?' she shouts and the words come out with little clouds of smoke, like signals.

It sounds as if she's genuinely outraged by the impropriety, and when she hears herself, she blows out the remaining smoke with her laughter.

'Hey! What'd you get in Selfridges?' she asks, distracted by the bright yellow plastic carrier bag that's lying on the sofa on the other side of the room.

Kate nods, giving her permission to look, even though she's sure she has already.

'Nice,' Marie says, taking the velvety soft suede mules out of the bag.

'He bought them for me,' Kate tells her. 'So that I looked like the sort of person who could wear expensive clothes.'

'Ninety-nine pounds,' Marie frowns at the price label that's stuck to the smooth leather sole of the left shoe.

'You should have asked for the money, then got a pair in Dolcis.'

'It wasn't like that,' says Kate. 'It was like, I knew that it couldn't last, but at least I'd have the shoes to remind me.'

'Cinder-bloody-rella!' says Marie.

'You can borrow them if you like,' Kate offers. She can see Marie's itching to try them on.

Marie squeezes her foot in.

'Too small for me. I must be the Ugly Sister.'

It was like a fairy tale. For a moment, Kate wonders whether it could have had a happy ending if only she hadn't stopped the story with her incessant questions. If they'd reached the white beach fringed with palm trees, would they have lived happily ever after?

How strange it is that human beings talk about life as a sort of continuum, trying to do everything as a smooth preparation for the next bit. They learn and work and save and marry and reproduce as if they're on a sort of gently rising curve on a graph. But it's not like that. Life pivots on single moments. Sometimes they're so tiny and fast you don't even see them happening, and sometimes they're so unexpected you don't allow yourself to believe.

It would only be an illusion of happiness, she tells herself, because if he'd gone with her, he would have been a bad person, wouldn't he? And she wouldn't want to be with a bad person, would she? But he didn't go. So he was a good person after all.

She can't get her head round that.

'Do you think you can have a future if you don't have a past?' she asks out loud.

'Christ, I bloody hope so,' says Marie, delving into the bag again.

'What's this, then?'

She's holding up *Sasha's Magic Carpet*.

'A book.'

'You're kidding,' Marie says with deep sarcasm. She flips open the first page. 'Hey, look what it says here!'

'Kate. Thanks for giving me back my life. Love, Alexander. What's that all about then?' Marie asks.

Kate takes the book from Marie and hugs it to her chest. She will keep the book for ever, and as the memories grow weaker with time, it will remind her that she met someone who thought she was special.

He was not a dream, not a fairy tale, but a real person that she chanced upon.

And the world is full of possibility.

'What's the time?' Kate asks Marie.

'Coming up to midnight?'

'Shall we go out and have some champagne?'

'Champagne? What are we celebrating?'

'Do we need a reason?'

For a moment, Marie looks shocked.

Then she says, 'I know just the place.'

'So you saw, you conquered, you came!' Marie shrieks.

Kate's sure that everyone in the room has heard, but nobody looks at them. They're sitting at the bar of a very exclusive club. She doesn't like to think why Marie's allowed in when she's not a member. In the corner by the door, there's an actor Kate recognizes from a television cop series. When he gets up to go to the toilet she sees he's much smaller than she thought.

'Yeah,' she says, nonchalantly.

'Jesus!'

'Haven't you ever?' Kate guesses.

'Not really,' Marie says, taking out a cigarette.

Either you have or you haven't, Kate wants to tell her, but she doesn't. It's funny to have experienced something about sex that Marie hasn't. She feels a little bit superior, and a little bit sad for Marie.

'So did you fuck all day?' Marie asks bluntly.

'No. We talked a lot.'

'Tell me about it,' Marie says wearily.

'What?'

'Most of the punters want to talk. They want to tell you about their marriages and why it's not their fault that they've failed, and I'm lying there thinking, oh just shut the fuck up and get on with it. I don't want to know . . .'

Which is why it was different with Alexander, Kate thinks, because she did want to know about him. He is not a punter and she is not a whore.

'He'll be back,' Marie surmises.

'I won't be here. I'm going home. I said I'd go home if I had a day with him, didn't I?'

'You crazy?'

'It's not him . . . not like that . . .' Kate tries to explain. 'Last night I thought if I could have him for one day I wouldn't want anything more. I'd be happy with what I've got for the rest of my life—'

'Oh please!' Marie interrupts, exasperated.

'Wait! I know that's not true now. I do want more. And I'm going to get it.'

'What?'

'I want to write.'

'You've always wanted to be a writer,' Marie says, bored with something she's heard a thousand times before.

'Well, if you're going to be a writer, you have to write. That's what he says. So that's what I'm going to do. Write.'

'What'll you call it? *Love with a Stranger?*' Marie says mockingly.

'Not an adult novel. Not yet. I'm going to write stories for children. I've had this idea—'

'You'd be really good at children's stories,' Marie interrupts.

'Why?'

Kate waits for the inevitable sarcastic one-liner, but Marie takes a long drag of her cigarette and smiles at her.

'D'you remember, when I had nightmares and you'd make up stories to get me off to sleep again? I used to love lying in the dark, listening to your voice. It made me feel safe.'

'Really?'

Of all the feelings Kate has experienced on this most extraordinary day, this is the nicest.

'Do you want to know the story I'm thinking of?' she asks.

'Yeah, go on then.' Marie sits forward, waiting eagerly for her to begin.

'Well, once upon a time there was this boy whose parents were very forgetful and they kept leaving him behind in places—'

'Places?' Marie interrupts again.

She was always impatient for clarification, Kate remembers.

'Places they went, like art galleries, or a department store,' Kate adds quickly, seeing that she's losing Marie. 'And these places become his home for the night, you see. He finds out all about them . . . so it's a bit educational as well . . .'

As she talks, the ideas begin to form. She has a very clear picture of what the boy will look like. He's small and thin and his mouth is always the colour of what he's been eating, and his clothes are a little bit big. He's got freckles on his nose, and an impish smile. He's just like the pictures she used to draw of Jimmy when she was teaching him adverbs, she realizes.

'Home for the Night,' Marie says, as if it's a title. 'I like that. If it were a department store, he could sit at one of those tables laid out with candlesticks and pleated napkins and everything . . . and lounge on a stripy sunlounger . . . and try out the DVD . . .'

'And play with all the toys . . . and eat all the chocolates,' says Kate.

'What's he called?' Marie wants to know.

'I might call him Alexander,' Kate says.

Would he hate that very much? She imagines him a few years from now in Waterstone's with Lucy, seeing a display of books. He walks over, drawn by the title, then sees her name on the cover and smiles. She doesn't think he would mind having his name in a book now that he's grown up.

'Alexander,' says Marie. 'It's a bit long. Why not Jimmy?'

'Not Jimmy. Wouldn't be fair.'

Marie clinks her champagne flute against Kate's, and drains it.

'Here's to *The Adventures of Alexander*. To fame and fortune!' she says.

'Don't know about that,' says Kate.

'That Harry Potter woman's a single mum,' says Marie, as if it's the only qualification needed.

Kate takes another small sip from her glass. The bubbles prickle her tongue. 'I'm going to have a go, anyway,' she says.

'Why do you have to go home?' Marie asks.

There's a wobble in her voice that makes Kate look up. A single tear is slipping melodramatically down Marie's cheek.

'I miss Jimmy,' she says. 'And he probably misses me a bit, even though he'd rather die than say so.'

'But there's nothing to do there,' Marie says desperately.

'So I'll have no excuse not to write. No distractions . . .'

'You're not going to get married?'

'No. I'm not going to get married.'

'If I got a proper flat, you know, just you and me, here in London, would you stay?' Marie asks.

'I don't think so.'

'Not even if I got a proper job?'

'You like your job,' Kate says.

'Do I?' Marie looks as if she's never thought about it before. 'I suppose I do. Champagne can make you a bit weepy, can't it?' she says brightly. She wipes her forearm across her face just like she used to at school when she'd forgotten her hanky.

'You won't forget me when you're rich and famous, will you?'

'We'll go round the world together,' Kate promises. 'Where would you like to go?'

'Las Vegas! What about you?'

'Bali. Or somewhere unspoilt like the Philippines.'

'Don't you want to go anywhere in America?' Marie asks, disappointed.

'New York, New Orleans, Hollywood.'

'We could drive across in a Cadillac!'

'Neither of us can drive,' says Kate.

'We'll learn. Des can teach us.'

'Is Des coming too?' Kate asks.

'No. I want to meet new people.'

'Who would you most like to meet?' Kate asks.

'Brad Pitt.'

'He's married.'

'For heaven's sake, you've got to write the books,

get the money, learn to drive, buy the car and everything . . . he might be divorced by then.'

They both giggle.

'It's possible,' says Marie.

'It's possible,' Kate echoes.

Thirty-one

'We could always go back to Italy . . .' Alexander suggests.

'Things are never as good when you go back.'

'No, you're right,' Alexander agrees. He thinks for a moment. 'How about Spain?'

'I don't know,' says Nell, braking as the red tail-lights of a lorry appear on the distant incline in front, her brain refusing to make the leap of faith that the vehicle is moving.

'I don't know Spain at all,' she says, putting her foot on the accelerator again when they're close enough to see the lorry itself, indicating to overtake, even though there's nothing behind her.

'Neither do I,' says Alexander, brightly. 'We could discover it together. The three of us . . . The four of us?'

She knows he's looking at the side of her face, smiling, trying to elicit a positive response. She can't look at him, because she's so tired that the road is taking all her attention.

The headlights of the car light up a white sign that says 'Tiredness can kill. Take a break.'

She should stop, but she wants to get home. The road is so dark it feels like uncharted territory, and Alexander is being so uncharacteristically chatty and charming, she's lost confidence in her judgement.

Has she been too hard on him? Has she merely imagined all the moods and silences of the last few months? Has she even created them to fit in with some subconscious plot of her own? There's no possible reason to leave him if he's like this. He's like the man she fell in love with. She wishes that she could react more positively to his suggestions.

It's been a long day, she reminds herself, as their turning off the motorway approaches. She's tired and tense from driving. Everything will be clearer after sleep.

The tick-tock of the indicator as they turn into the drive and the crunch of gravel, like the drag of a wave on a shingle beach, are comforting sounds for Nell. They remind her of waking up after the long journey back from childhood holidays in Cornwall and the poignant but complete feeling that another summer was over.

She switches off the engine with a sigh, turns off the headlights.

'Where's Lucy?' Alexander asks, as if it's only just occurred to him that she will not be at home on her own in a dark house.

'Chris took her for the night,' Nell says, opening her door and getting out.

Alexander gets out too.

'Chris?' he says. 'Who's Chris?'

'Chris and Sarah, you know. Parents of Lucy's friend Ben?'

'The waving jogger,' Alexander says, with a hint of contempt in his voice.

'Have you ever slept with Frances?' she suddenly hears herself demanding, looking straight at him across the car roof as if it's a negotiating table.

Alexander hesitates long enough for her to know that whatever he replies, he has.

'Yes,' he admits.

She's much more shocked than she thought she would be, even though it now seems so obvious she can't imagine how she missed the signs.

'Why didn't you ever tell me?' she says, crisply, unable to look at him now. She stoops down and snatches an empty sweet packet off the floor beneath the driver's seat.

'You never asked,' says Alexander.

She looks at him despairingly.

'Sorry,' he says. 'I do that, don't I?'

'What?'

'Make things your responsibility when I'm trying to avoid answering questions.'

'Yes. You do.'

She's amazed that he's prepared to acknowledge it. It makes her feel really bad for underestimating him.

'It was only once,' Alexander explains. 'I don't know why I did it. Drink, I suppose.'

Nell slams the car door. Locks it. She doesn't know whether she wants to hear the details or not.

They walk towards the front door side by side.

'We'd been to see this peep-show in Shinjuku . . .' Alexander says. 'No, not like that,' he adds, as she looks sharply at him. 'A whole crowd of us. We were drunk. It seemed like a bit of a laugh, but it wasn't. It was just sad, tawdry . . . Afterwards we drank a lot of beer. And then it was just me and Frances . . .'

'And?'

'It was long before I met you. I was ashamed to tell you, I suppose.'

He finally answers her question.

'And what happened after?' she says, more softly.

'I made it clear that it was a one-off. She did quite a good impersonation of the woman in *Fatal Attraction* . . .'

A giggle that's both nervousness and relief bubbles out of Nell's mouth.

'So it wasn't just fate that made us bump into you in the Philippines? It wasn't destiny.'

'No, I think it was probably Frances,' Alexander says. 'Does that make a difference?'

'I don't know.'

It somehow seems significant, but she can't think why.

'I love you,' Alexander says.

'Do you?'

'I'm sorry,' he says.

'For what?' Nell says.

'For lots of things,' he says.

'Did you have other girlfriends?' she asks.

It's weird talking in the dark on their own doorstep, but it feels easier than going inside, somehow.

'In Tokyo?'

'In Tokyo, yes, well, anywhere . . . before you met me?'

'I never really had a proper relationship until I met you,' he says.

How strange to find this out now, after seven years of knowing him. She has always assumed that there are great unresolved passions in Alexander's past, but she never dared to ask before. It's odd to learn that the person you thought you knew is different. Rather nice.

She puts the key in the door of their home.

She thinks of the moment she saw him this evening at Greenwich, his smile so incandescent it made her remember how thrilling it had been to love him.

As they walk through the door together, she takes his hand, just for a moment, as he did hers, and she looks at him, and she wants to say: I know you're trying. I am too.

He squeezes her hand back tight, as if he knows that he's nearly lost her and wants to hang on to her now.

She does not turn away from his kiss, but the kiss she returns is as brief as the ones she gives to Lucy when she drops her at school when the bell has already rung and her class is lined up and about to go in.

'I'd better ring Frances,' she says, taking her hand from his grip.

Alexander takes off his leather jacket and chucks it onto the sofa. His keys, a handful of coins, his passport and a sock all cascade out of one of the pockets onto the floor. She sometimes thinks that Alexander looks as if he's carrying the whole world on his shoulders because he actually is.

He looks at the mess, then at her. There's real anxiety in his eyes. She's horrified to think that she is usually so strict and fastidious.

She picks up the phone and dials Frances's number.

Alexander wanders into the kitchen, opens the fridge. He pulls out the bottle of champagne, looks at the label, turns around and holds it up to her like a question.

She shakes her head in reply.

He replaces it.

'Hello?'

Frances sounds as if she's drunk.

'Frances, it's Nell. I'm just ringing to tell you that Alexander is OK.'

As she replaces the receiver, she hears Frances crying, 'Nell? Nell?'

'We thought you were in the train crash.'

Nell walks into the kitchen where Alexander's drinking milk straight from a two-litre bottle. He swallows.

'I caught the earlier train,' he says.

'You said.'

'I was lucky.'

'It's weird to think . . . horrible . . .'

'Yes.'

He has reverted to monosyllables. Nell wonders if his earlier garrulousness was a kind of survivor euphoria that will now be followed by sombre guilt.

'So you went to the park?' she says brightly.

'Yes.'

'Which one?'

'Regent's.'

'It was a perfect day, wasn't it?' she says, remembering the seafront, the biting wind, the sky so blue and the sun so bright it made rainbows on the watery surface of her eyes.

Alexander's face freezes as if she's said something so shocking he's not sure that he's understood her.

'I meant the weather,' she says, quickly. How could she talk about perfection on a day when so many people have perished?

Alexander turns his back on her to fill the kettle.

'Shall I make some tea?' he asks.

She can see his reflection in the kitchen window. His hands are trembling.

She feels terrible.

'I think I'd just like some water. I'm so exhausted, I can't think,' she says, trying to explain how it came out like that. She didn't mean to sound so callous.

'Why don't you go to bed? I'll bring you a glass up,' he offers.

It's a small gesture of kindness, but it fills her with a disproportionate sense of gratitude.

'Thank you!' she says.

Nell looks at her body in the mirror on the back of the bedroom door. Her breasts are already swelling from the hormones of pregnancy. The line between her tummy button and pubic hair is darker. She recognizes exactly the same overwhelming, inarguable pressing tiredness that she had when first pregnant with Lucy.

She wonders if the child inside her is another girl.

'*Something momentous is going to happen . . .*'

She can hear Alexander downstairs in the kitchen washing up the cups. He is showing that he wants to try. If they both try, maybe there's enough love to get by, and to make a happy life for their children. Maybe that is what grown-up love is – an unspoken decision to stick together, because it would be worse to be apart.

She pulls a long nightie over her head. It's tartan winceyette, dark green and red, very practical for getting up in the night.

Tonight, she remembers, she does not have to get up.

She takes it off.

Alexander is coming up the stairs.

'It's funny without Lucy here, isn't it?' she calls.

'Very peculiar,' he says.

Nell gets into bed, pulling the duvet up to cover her body, suddenly shy at the prospect of him discovering her naked.

She hears him brushing his teeth and flushing the toilet. He's taking an inordinately long time, and when he emerges, he has taken off his clothes and folded them in a neat pile. He's holding a bath sheet around his bare body.

Is Alexander so determined to change his ways that he's now resolved to fold his clothes as well? This is a day she thought would never come.

'*Something momentous is going to happen . . .*'

She's about to say: Look, you don't have to go to such lengths!

But she stops herself. Like most resolutions, this is bound not to last, so why not enjoy it while it does?

'Did you bring my water?' she says, as he comes over to the bed, still in his towel.

'Oh, I'm sorry . . .'

'Doesn't matter.'

He hesitates, weighing up whether she means it against the bother of going downstairs again, then he switches off the light, drops the towel to the floor and gets into bed beside her.

He rolls onto his left side with his back to her, the way they always sleep.

'Are you tired?' Nell asks him.

She feels wide awake all of a sudden, and strangely happy.

She can't tell whether he's even noticed that she's naked.

'Very,' he murmurs.

'Me too,' she says.

She turns over so that they're lying like spoons and when he doesn't stir at the touch of her skin on his, she tells herself that it's wiser not to attempt to make love now when they're both exhausted.

In the morning, she'll bring them tea and toast in bed, and maybe, without the threat of interruption, they will have a blissful time together among the crumbs, as they always used to.

And then they will collect Lucy, and she will present Alexander with his hideous shell rabbit, and maybe they will all go out for the day as a family.

She moves her head across the pillow and plants an affectionate kiss on Alexander's back, nuzzling her face in the soft warm hollow between his shoulder blades.

She wonders why his skin smells of coconuts.

THE END

Imogen Parker is the outstanding author of compelling novels about modern women and their lives.

WHAT BECAME OF US

'THIS SUPERB NOVEL IS A CELEBRATION OF WOMEN'S EXPECTATIONS'
Good Book Guide

'FINE OBSERVATION AND VASTLY ENTERTAINING'
Image

0552 99994 6

MORE INNOCENT TIMES

'ENTHRALLING READING'
Cosmopolitan

'A WONDERFULLY WOVEN TALE OF TANGLED RELATIONSHIPS. I LOVED IT'
Penny Vincenzi

0 552 99992 X

THESE FOOLISH THINGS

'PARKER WRITES WITH SYMPATHY AND WRY HUMOUR'
The Times

'AN UNFORGETTABLE NOVEL OF PARENTAL LOVE, PASSION AND FRIENDSHIP'
Woman's Weekly

0 552 99993 8

THE MEN IN HER LIFE

'A SPARKLING NOVEL OF WIT, SADNESS, AND WOMEN'S RESILIENCE'
Sunday Mirror

'MISS THIS BOOK AT YOUR PERIL – IT'S SIMPLY TERRIFIC'
Woman's Own

0 552 99991 1

BLACK SWAN